AN IMBECILE PALES TO MATTE GREEN.

a poem by
TIGER MOODY

a United Crud book
NEW YORK, NEW YORK

Dopey, dear, this is for you!

"__Bring me a bulletproof vest.__"
—- James W. Rodgers

Snowing again. Also I am 25 now. Big f'n deal.
Day off bc of b-day. I didnt want the day off
and said I would prefer just to work but the
boss said that is what people are supposed to
do and that I should learn to live a little.
Wonder how many panthers I missed. Tried
reading that wierd western some more but its
so hard to understand. What is a meridian anyway? Went to the meteropolitan museum (sp?)
by myself to celebrate old age and looked at
the american wing. Empty except for me and a
little retarded black girl that I think was lost bc
she kept following me. I hope the world is nice
to that poor kid. Bought some billy holliday cds
at tower. Went to see "dont be a menace to
south central while drinking your juice in the
hood" on 3rd ave. Sucked. I swear the dude
spit in my popcorn to. Then I got drunk at the
beauty bar. The ring was burning and made me
keep thinking about her jumping over a fence
naked every time I closed my eyes. I told avery
and he said holden wouldnt be crying over a
stupid bich and something else about rising
above. Then he got tossed for pouring
beer on a fat girl.

"I am not a prisoner of the past."

DESPITE A CRIPPLING HANGOVER,
I somehow phoned Adolfo.
  'Terminado' was sadly rasped through
moans depressed and woeful.
  A lemon glob of hacked phlegm quivered on a
thumb. The dollop brimmed micro-gems,
pulsing red and black aplomb.
  Morning beams slicing bedroom blinds lumed
a constellation. Slowly shifting clouds
of smut defied evacuation.

THE DUST AND I SHARED A RAILROAD
in the Guineatown of Williamsburg. The BQE.
Bamonte's bounds. Withers Street. Sicilian turf.
  Save Luigi on the second-floor, I was the bricks' sole
Native Son — all the others greying boors from a
nation overrun. Though I'd been a fixture on the
stairs for a span of two-plus years, no passage ever
lacked hinge-whines/hexes/one-inch slams/rude leers.

EXTENDING SPINDLY ARMS, I watched a curl
glide past, drifting smooth across the room, halting at
silvered glass. The heavy mirror proudly crowned a
pine Art-Deco vanity. Aside from one small pistol,
its drawers confined mundanity.
  Rising to inspect the strand, I grew lost in wan

refract. Receding hairs and swollen glands aided
God's ransack. I scanned a Scotch-Taped halo
of Sharpied index-cards; a plan sniped from
harpy dykes whilst stalking Tompkins Park.
  I may be one in near 4 billion, but I am also one
in near 4 billion. Life applauds my every act
like Peoria-cheered vaudevillians.
  Hacking up more phlegm, roars
aped a witness-shoved attorney.
  "I'm trailed three ways to Bethlehem
by Forgiveness-Love-and-Mercy!"

A DOOR SLAMMING AGAINST THE DUST

quashed all escape/pursuit. Within a hallway's shabby
truss, dross screamed scraped/unglued. A totality
of tragedy wreaked by transom-borne sauce steam.
  Tarnished fixtures stabbed tin ceilings.
  (Cloth-wired/pushbutton schemes.)
  A squat troll combed a thin mullet beside
a rubbed and chipped balustrade.
  "Yo! My man! Youse fuckin' pull it? Lemme see!
Ain't got no time to waste!"
  To Luigi, I was just *'My man'*.
  He'd never sought my name.
  Reaching within a rear waistband,
I withdrew the snubbed magnum-frame.
  I'd acquired the gun several weeks prior by abusing
a friend's kind assistance; misleading Avery,
a murder-dick; musing stiff slime-resistance.
  My true pine — suicide, after shattering El's
kneecaps. Alas, a West Coast huff to conjoin a
khaki-buff had dashed designs to crap.

As the Troll appraised the pistol, my hand swiped gabardine. I hoped his dew would not imbue any white salts sad/unclean. Hailing from the 1940s, the slacks hadn't come cheap. My whole wardrobe was likewise sporty. I smacked of self-pampered creep.

"My man, nice *balance* on this thing!"

"Careful now...it's loaded!"

Phantom prey was targeted.

Combustion was lip/throated.

"Not bad! Youse fire it yet? Do it fuckin' shoot true?"

"Don't think it matters much...strictly belly-use."

Fat hands accented vents. I pondered great mime-potential. His pathos mooted costly grease-paints lessers dawned essential. "Fuckin' Giuliani! Prick's in office two years an' away with all the good stuff! No fuckin' guns! No Ching-chong boom-booms! Fuckin' *feast* gets the bishop rebuffed!"

Palms harked surrender.

"I voted Grandpa Munster!"

Five steps into a slog re-entered, barks tore new strides asunder. "Yo! My lady wants some neat stuff fitted! Some kinda parrot on her leg!"

An acid-washed cuff fleetly flitted.

A slap thwacked a varicose frog's peg.

"You'll have to come to Jersey. Landlord says no kitchen-tattoos anymore."

"Yeah, but will youse do the right fuckin' thing?"

"C'mon, dude...can the bitching... what're you even asking for?"

"Youse the fuckin' *man*, my man!

4

Knew I could count on youse!"
 A black mustache was trisected
by mounds of fawnish menthol goo.

August, 1993

The brass ring was thrust beneath the Moon's brimming
bulge. Heavy. Satin-finished. Cold.
 Verdigris peppered dented/Death's Head depressions.
 Sockets were sloppily daubed with
violent/blood-red impressions.
 "This means that you now belong to me alone.
That I can do with you what and when I see fit."
 "Um...okay. Yeah, sure. I get it."
 "Do you understand me, Daddy?
Have I made myself clear?"
 "Yeah. I, like, totally get it. So...um...
wanna go grab some beer?"
 "You must enter freely and of your own will.
Mark my words, this won't always be cherries. But play
your cards perfectly right and we'll fuck atop a pink cake.
On that day, things become mutually proprietary."
 Palms sliding like spatulas caressed
a denim sheathed derrière.
 Cicadae clattered feverishly distant.
 Sirens histrionically blared.
 A Puerto Rican bellowed 'Puta!' to his wife.
 Amorous Pit Bulls bayed betwixt quakes.
 "Listen to them, Daddy! The children of the night!
What rockin' music they make!"

"I deserve a partner who loves and accepts me."

DRIFTING SOUTH TOWARDS ADOLFO'S,
the Sun stalled Februus balms — scorching flesh,
foisting shadows, blocking pursuits of all calms. While
my pane's low price was a nice surprise, its tint dulled
the coup's edge. The glazier had avowed to source
a true amber, but unveiled Bud's red bole instead.

Within a Grand Street pet-shop's window,
I spied a lifeless hermit crab. An electronic jingle
heralded wafts of Lysol/dried fish/vermin-scabs.
Scoping aisles beneath faint Salsa, no clerks clogged
any scans. Loping onwards, I surveyed glass-tiers,
focusing upon a frogman. Bobbing atop a jeweled
chest, he was doomed to observe but not fondle.
Another tank housed a sleek corn snake coiled
atop a woodchip's plush/blond hill.

"She ain't for sale, yo! Nigga's my goddamn baby! Got
some mad nice pythons down the stairs though!
Youse wanna go see 'em maybe?"

The words belonged to a goateed Puerto Rican,
hair shorn in Caesarean-fashion. Cross Colours
were clipped with three Day Glo beacons.

Dead eyes were devoid of all passion.

**A PIECEMEAL STAIRWELL SLATS SHY OF
COMPLETION** led to a basement's raw/earthen
floor. Fungal brick-walls were beam-intersected.

Bulbs hung from cloth-covered cords.
A container was rife with tiny red frogs.
Another was choked with small toads.
A large glass box housed a King Cobra.
The monarch's head banged in hello.
"Oh shit, Papi! He don't like you!"
"Apparently not."
"Just kiddin', man! Nigga don't like nobody!"
An immense wire coop overflowed rollers —
Birmingham and Galatz conferees. Beside the pigeons
stood several crate-towers, each housing an
individual gamecock. Myriad bantam strains were
present; some clean, some almost punk-rock.
A carpeted treadmill was crusty with dung. The
windows were foil-obscured. Verily, these animals saw
neither daylight nor fun. This hellish broil was pure!
(The Puerto Rican grinned as a tank writhing
with scorpions echoed frenetic waves.)
"*Look*, Papi! They hungry!"
"I see. What kind of food do they crave?"
"Mostly just crickets...mealworms sometimes.
But I like to keep 'em starved to stay mean."
"Why would you want to ever do that?"
"Shit...so's when I *pit* 'em, they's killin' machines!"
"Against each other? Really? But they all look
like they're getting along okay."
"Nah, Papi! I mean 'gainst *them!*"
A thin finger jabbed wildly astray.
A stack of small tanks, capped with blue lids,
contained spiders of various species.
Some were plump. Some were sticklike.
(All were vandalized by feces.)

"What are those sponges?"

"That's how they drink'! If they's thirsty, they's lappin'. Even soaked one in *Courvoisier* once, just to see what fuckin' happen!"

"And...?"

Cringing, the Puerto Rican slapped at my shoulder until guffaws mellowed to heaves.

A full thirty seconds duly elapsed before the fond memory's expiry.

Milky joy-tears gluishly dangled, like rain reticent in the sky.

"Shit, Papi...figger he at least get *drunk* first or some shit! Nigga just curled-up and died!"

So last night I dreamt I was sailing around the city like a horse fly or a bat or a moth or something. Landed near the meteropolitan and dragged that little retard into a tunnel to give her a hicky. This bothers me. Not bc she was black or even bc she was retarded but bc she was just a little kid. Some people were yelling at me to stop but I just kept on hickying like she was a root beer float. Very very wierd. On a brighter note cliff said that lisa marie presley is now divorced from michael jackson. Maybe I have a shot? Fat chance. What could I have to offer besides some old comic books and the ocassional so so foot rub? Also cliff sneezed on 3 customers today.

Panther $75

Panther $75
Cock diesel weasel $65
Skull w/blunt $85
Colby loves booboo $50
Chinese letters for "dry ice" $55
Panther $75
Cancer crab $60
Beauty mark $50
Nubian princess $75

Fuck lisa marie. Shes not so hot anyway. I hope nobody ever reads this. Even ghosts. Ok good night. If you are reading this elvis I was just kidding. I would totally bang your fat daughter.

"I am conscious of the needs of others."

TOTING THE SACK, I GLIMPSED WITHIN, examining my myriad passengers — carefully avoiding pedestrians to ensure no serious impasse occurred.

Anchored inside a hinged carrying case, the spider jounced with each tread; an eight-legged bumpkin running beers with peers, straddling a pickup-truck's bed. While the existence of arachnidian emotion was still indeed a great mystery, I made a point of keeping things level — placating latent anxiety.

Cricketville's mood was a different story — a mosh-pit within tied polyethene.

Fearing the dancing Asphyxia's throes,
I amped an already naiant speed.
　(I'd habitually rushed since an ancient hobo
had declared *'Laggardness'* worse than *'Acedia'*;
applying this credo to everything,
be it sex/food/blow/print-media.)
　Suddenly, Brutal Truth struck — flattening fine cheer
to pulp. By getting a pet I'd shorn a safety-net!
　Can't off yourself now, Herr Dope!
　What fog had inspired such blunder?
　Some form of cowardly/unconscious intent?
　What did my id dread so goddamned much?
　(Tedious purgatorial laments?)
　Brick walled, I glanced to the sack, tarantula
gaze-affixed...hearkening back so many years...to the
tender young age of six...to the Bubblegum
Graveyard of my windowsill...glue-dousing a vagabond
wayfarer...freezing the creep within a paste halo...
a readily willing pain-bearer.
　I'd left the atrocity on the aperture's ledge,
a menhir of petrified nobility.
　A martyr, yes, but what was its cause?
　Did nullifidian shahids not match Imbecility?

September, 1993

On Seventh and B I was hailed by Renfield,
a wilting ape of my old salad days.
　Amidst grips shaken, he surveyed the ring, requesting
a closer appraise. Donning it, he smacked a paw,
impressed by the skull's brassy heft.
　"Word! HELLS YEAH! Shit is da bomb!
Fuck a nigga up if ya crack him with a crucial right/left!"

Pleased to receive a true thug's raised thumb, I greenlit a
proposed convoy towards work. Despite the touch's prelude
being artlessly dumb, I was tolerant
of a broke chum's odd quirk.
  At the Southwest wedge of A and Saint Mark's,
I noted Sinéad O'Connor lodged in a dubious pack —
kneeling upon a saloon's cement stoop,
a stalwart spare-changer's bivouac.
  (I'd oft observed her curbside punk-mingles, buying liquor
and feeding typhoidal pet rats — doling out cash
in egregious lumps unstrung by all caveats.)
  Rarely did the Ape-Man pass crusties sans spit, this stroll
being no such exception. Alas, sneering back was all they
dared snip, fearful of dull switchblade dissections.
  Rounding the corner onto Saint Mark's,
I mentioned the big wheel in our midst.
  "What? That ugly bald cunt? The fuck's her deal?
Keen cancer enthusiast?"
  Apprised of her papal brouhaha, Renfield's eyes gleamed
jubilation; gait increasing as fingers wagged,
spurred on by Loki's dictations.
  Entering a bodega, susurrating, 'Order some joe!', he
pilfered eggs 'til pockets sagged; steering me back to the
congregation; my coffee sloshed as I eschewed lag. Halting
before a dreadlocked blonde (forecasting the crooner's
spread palm) several tense moments passed beneath
shadows before hoarfrost invoked the embalmed.
  "Dost thou take some umbrage, friend? Speaketh thy
mind, if thou hast one! If not, please begone!
The day is young and thou art blocking the Sun!"
  The Ape-Man's reply was succinct and emphatic;
engendering terrific surprise.

Hand thrust above head, posture pneumatic,
the missile rained betwixt unsmiling eyes.
 The Crooner gaped, taciturnly appalled. Albumen
pendulously dangled from a proboscis' cleft ball.
 ## "THAT'S FOR THE POPE, BITCH!"
 Bolting like shells Howitzer-purged, the Crooner
commenced hot pursuit. A tangerine yolk, launching off
from her scalp, ruptured against the vamps of my shoes.
 The squatters paused, marmoreal,
'til one trembled with jittery quakes.
 The palm-reader slapped the sinner's epoxied mohawk.
 Inches severed with a sickening/potato-chip break.
 "Yeah! Real funny, you stupid dirtbag! Now who
the fuck's gonna buy us the day's skag?"
 I dogged the Gaelic obloquy at a diminished clip,
unctuous soles precluding gestalt; my jog finishing alongst
the First Avenue strip as patrolmen oozed to a halt.
 Tears mixing with froth, Hibernian claws
jabbed towards a market's glass door.
 "In there he lays, gents! The blackguard who defiles!
Seize him ere he wreaks havoc more!"
 Several thuds later, the Ape-Man emerged, chuckling
despite blood and cuffs; the cops grinning reciprocally
jocund as they skippered his Fred Perried scruff.
 For one brief moment, Renfield broke free —
swiveling with an unhesitant twitch: "DON'T YOU
DARE FUCK WITH THE POPE NO MORE!
YOU BALDHEADED/LESBIAN BITCH!"
 The Crooner's lambasting shifted my way
as if I'd just passed a bad cheque.
 I granted the cruiser long-lasting survey.
 Renfield wasn't Catholic.

"Mi casa es su casa."

PAUSING BY A ROWHOUSE WHERE A MACAQUE LIVED, orbs strained through congestions of smut. I spied the primate squatting atop a vinyl-sheathed couch next to an elderly Hessian slut.

The semi-nude pair were intaking *'Love Connection'* on a safe-sized/rabbit-eared TV, the goblets of wine coffee-tabled before each separated by a cask of wicker-wrapped Chianti.

LUIGI WAS RIGHT, RUDY'S FIST HAD SWUNG HARD, forcing changes mercilessly rapid.

Across the river, the East Side had been hammered into something insipid, vanilla, and vapid. All the heroin-bakeries and cocaine-bodegas were now thoroughly boarded and shuttered. Mom-and-Pop stores had been churlishly demoted to heed Midwestern/Cowtown chain-clutter. Even CBGBs had capitulated; Debbie Gibson polluting its dragstrip religiosity. The whole shebang was a demoralizing shame. A colossal *'bad trip'*.

An atrocity.

I glanced around Union Ave.

Pastel siding de-beautified everything. Sedans with Pro-Life stickers double-parked near pork-stores. Men bore the fashion guidance of Larry King. The fist hadn't kiboshed Williamsburg yet. All still looked like '83. Turning back to the macaque, I smiled and waved.

The beast blatantly ignored me.

THE VANITY'S COUNTER SEEMED AN IDEAL LOCALE for the staking of a spider's new home. I carpeted the tank with splinters of chips, smatters of rocks, and healthy sprinklings of loam. Neglecting to purchase fresh sponges, scraggles were wrenched from a fraught swab. I prayed the spider wouldn't take distrait for thrift.
(I often overthought on the job.)
Two crickets were already deceased.

Asphyxial ends or murders by peers? Perhaps teeth too long for such harrowing treks had ushered the passage of prairie pioneers?

The surviving party appeared thrilled with the tank, hopping merrily about. One even leapt right onto a sponge, ending a crucible of drought.

While I was loath to rain on such idyllic bliss, it was time for roommate introductions. Ill-equipped to duly proceed, I referred to the care-book's instructions

Having never grasped a tarantula prior,
I desperately feared its touch.
Seeking Dutch courage, I chugged like a friar.
Alas, the hooch helped not much.

As I lowered the unclasped case atop woodchips to let my new ward explore on its own, the mere approaching of soft/pink hands invoked panic/skitters/gores/heaved moans. What kind of *abuse* had this poor creature seen? How could I convey its security? Let it know that its shelter and sanctuary from pits were now all warranted sureties?

Depositing my gun atop a drawer's hungry dust, I scampered Port Authority-bound. Would a day's Alone-Time be ample enough to invert this still-frantic sad frown?

January, 1994

We'd just collapsed onto opposed bed corners when the incendiary device combusted. I stared at long/raven locks, entangled and snared, begging to be comb-adjusted.

"But...but isn't that...isn't that what I just did?"

The lugubrious release of a mournful sigh signaled I'd once again blundered.

"No, Daddy. I want you to RAPE me! I wanna be staked! Pillaged! Plundered!"

"Um...like by a Viking or something? Like I'm Prince Valiant or Tony Curtis?"

"Not like that really. Well...kinda...I guess. But be more like a spic on Avenue D. Like, rough! Dirty! I mean, that's where the hurt is..."

A cauliflowerian lump was rooted just by her nose.

Gnarled sprouts groping in six directions loaned a dead horsefly repose. A hirsute facial tumor on any other woman would've been a borderline unacceptable flaw.

But my dream girl could instill no ill-humor.

(I didn't mind at all.)

"No, Daddy! Not now! I want it to be a surprise!"

Shielding vision atop damp linen, I masked a leaking of eyes. I'd been reared mired in darkness! Nightmares from which I bore scars! The idea of well-poisoning my first healthy rapport was tantamount to shaving with scimitars!

Peering over, I espied tantric breaths focused towards a far ceiling spot. Training my eyes in the same direction, I eschewed sex-criminal thoughts.

Within shadows lurked a tiny spider, slowly weaving
a nest. I stood on the mattress to swat it, inadvertently
brewing unrest. "But...it'll bite us while we sleep...
and they always go for my face..."
  "She won't! Just lay down!"
  Near the heart of an unfinished web,
a pearlish egg-sack was cemented in place.
  Throb-awakened the next morning,
I discerned wounds to my thighs, testes, and penis.
  Elizabeth grinned blissfully unmarked; a blue-veined/
ink-sullied Venus. The ceiling was strung with myriad shells,
mostly of moth-ilk; but even a few rivals had lapsed
perilling; siphoned whilst swaddled in silk.

  "Daddy?"
  Sounded spooked! Was she wise to the scrum?
  Really just playing along? My spur whooped regardless.
She hummed a Roky Erickson song.
  "You there?"
  Sack-laden, she slammed the door with a jolt of
formidable rump. Smacks brazenly danced across my
tongue. A bite bolted impermissible jumps. Bags countered,
orbs couch-darting, she folded in twain to survey.
  Wheeling around, she scuttered bathroom-bound.
  I pounced like a gluestuck toupée.
  A scream! Square kick bruising a plump right thigh,
arms coiled around hers, I wrenched upwards to lattice
a neck, forming unshakeable burrs. She screamed again,
spewing vitriol, booting backwards towards enemy shins.
Piling weight atop the squall, I attempted a dirt-eating pin.
  Alas, the brute was too strong...far too strong...
  Of a thew utterly shocking...
  Dragging me along as it staggered...

Finally collapsing/chin-knocking...

"MOTHERFUCKER! GET THE FUCK OFF! REALLY! NOT EVEN PLAYING! GOT YOU THAT BOOK BY BRAM STOKER TO READ JUST LIKE YOU'VE ALWAYS BEEN SAYING! JACK! JACK! WHAT'RE YOU DOING? YOU'RE SUPPOSED TO BE FUCKING SICK! EVEN BROUGHT CHICKEN SOUP AND ORANGES...YOU GODDAMNED/ MOTHERFUCKING DICK! YOU'RE SUPPOSED TO BE A NICE GUY! A FUCKING NICE GUY! BUT YOU'RE A PSYCHO LIKE ALL THE REST! LEGGO! GET THE FUCK OFF! GET OFFA ME, YOU FUCKING PEST!"

As if transformed to an old gramophone, a lexicon rasped surely not of my own: "I'm going to fucking rape you now, you stupid/domineering cunt! Going to tan your flesh and bury the rest down by the Olde Waterfront!"

She severed this paranormal conduit via knee-to-pelvic-cleft, roaring as I melted like suet.

Beleaguered. Hellish. Bereft.

"RAPE! RAPE! RAPE!"

Somehow I managed to rise once more, palms lifting to concede defeat. "Okay, Stop! You win! I think you may have busted my meat..."

Upon the cessation of holler, a mien cocked to a crestfallen side. Heaving sobs were sporadically cleaved by leaden/head-quaking sighs.

"OH MY GOD...I CAN'T BELIEVE YOU...IT WAS ALL GOING SO WELL! AND YOU HAD TO GO AND RUIN IT! AND, GODDAMNIT, YOU SMELL!"

As she knelt blubbering, I sat beside, simply professing my sorrow.

Clinging that night, koala-tight, as we drifted towards the Morpheus hovel, my last squinting apprised the snide deride of a Moth Graveyard withdrawal.

"I fill this day with hope and face it with joy."

IN AN EFFORT TO MASK THE COMMUNAL RUCKUS, I'd fed the hi-fi *'December's Children'* and cranked it. Alas, Jaggerian wails proved feeble challenge to the roaring/multi-larynxed ear spankage.

'Twas another rollicking afternoon on Bloomfield Ave, the shop teeming with locals of both sexes.

Some shoveled fried rice.

Others slapped toddlers.

Profanities flared through the plexus.

The Ramrod Tattoo Company was located in a lone/poky room, fluorescents peppering an asbestos-paneled ceiling; every inch of wall-surface garishly strewn with laminated sheets of skin-spieling.

A saloon-door counter halved our stations from a bullpen's habitual tomfoolery.

(Scanning the throng, I espied a six-footer. Sable skin/locust limbs/costume jewellery.)

"I hopes dey gives him d'chair! I swears to Gawd I hopes dey gives dat nigga d'muthafuckin' electronic chair!"

"Who, gurl? O.J.?"

"My baby-daddy! Sucka done gone knocked Bonanza up! How he do it in d'visitin' room, I dunno! Now my baby-sista gonna be her cousin too! An' here I thought we hit a plateau!"

A cross-room glance revealed Cliff carving
'*LaChandra*' into a bicep of a girth beyond my thigh.
Cellulite rippled in waves harmonious
with clatterish/clockspringy vibes.

Recollections were dredged of a childhood pond
from which I'd once reeled-in a swan.

In long overdue retrospect, I deduced
the cob housed the brain of a prawn.

MY MONTCLAIR TENURE HAD BEGUN TWO YEARS PRIOR, following cursory NYC-toil.

Still legally verboten within city limits, the
underground had proven too unsound to stanch my
financial boils. It wasn't all bad. There was good coin, a
fine comic-book store, and weighty tête-à-têtes with
Cliff. Best of all, our work consisted primarily of
whetting blue-collar glyphs...*Hearts*...*Daggers*...
Roses...stuff I enjoyed applying, not the overambitious/
chromed bosh demanded by New York's
Yale-degreed clients.

The only major Jersey drawbacks, if I was forced to
suppose, were excessively long bus-commutes
and a monochrome composed of Negroes.

THE LATTER QUANDARY STEMMED FROM NO RACIAL NETTLES, I'd grown up amongst

blacks and was well-accustomed to their presence.

My childhood passions included Chubby Checker,
Mandingo, and the graceful art of Steppin'.

This issue was not political but genetic
in nature, rooted in *Physicality* itself.

(Dark skin was simply of a far greater resilience
than Caucasoid or Mongoloid pelts.)

More troublesome than high density cells was
the all-consuming vortex of Negroidal melanin;
a pigmentation so robust it would obliterate hues
upon entering skin. Even the carbon-based India inks
could read virtually nil from vantages of one-inch
assists; entire designs occasionally going the way
of DC-10s over the Triangle's abyss.

Hoping to stem the *'Where'd it go?'* tide, Ramrod's
owner had procured a batch of luminous inks from
a Texan entrepreneur. Purportedly engineered for
Sub-Saharan husks, these yellow roses
stunk of wretched manure.

Customers returned in droves sporting lumps of
adamantine tissues, inert and near-dead.

(The most heinous calamities were the direct
result of a liquid hurt known as *'EZ-RED'*.)

Viewing the Texas-fiasco as an official last ditch, I
pledged to tread hence with Aristotle, gently
informing black patrons of all likely
disappointments or mottle.

Alas, my efforts were plied largely in vain.

Regardless of warnings of scarring, customers
would *still* request the toxic pigments with
resolves equal parts Sad and Jarring.

These decisions seemed rooted in principle, as if
some believed bright cartoons to be an essential/
Lincolnian right; my good-natured attempts of logical
thought were construed as pestilential/
draconian slights.

A routinely broached point that pastels should *'pop'*
atop darker complexions, as acrylics did on Mexican
velvet, finally catalyzed the Adolfo-transaction, though

Cliff had advised me to shelve it. Needing something tangible to demonstrate that tattoos sat *beneath* one's skin and categorically not *above*, my plan was to lay the brown glass against a kvetcher's selection, providing a realistic tough-love.

A CORNROWED YOUNG THING IN A GARFIELD-THEMED GOWN beckoned with a
digital scythe. Gesturing towards a wall, her voice came in soft lilts.

Shy. Demure.

Childlike.

Her smile, purple and plush, framed fourteen-karat dentures.

"Tattoo-Man, I wants a li'l Tweety on my breasteses."

Discreetly examining an exposed swell, I gauged a pre-counsel venture.

"Okay, no sweat. With your tone, I can make the beak and feet nice and orange, but the yellow isn't gonna work."

Cocking a zigzagged scalp, her gilt grin shriveled; raisining to a nonplussed smirk.

"Whatchu mean? Tweety be yella. I wants him *yella*, way he ass'posed to be!"

Retrieving my pane, wall-leveling the glass, only the bird's outline could be seen.

"But...you sayin' I too *crispy* for a Tweety?"

"No. That's not exactly what I mean, sweety."

"I wants him on my breasteses, and I wants him yella! I gots the money! We clear?"

Febrile shouts of *'Reverend Al!'* ensued.

Up-Down-Far-and-Near.

ONE SCORE AND THREE MINUTES LATER,
miens dimmed as the bullpen surveyed
the fresh wound.

Amongst the counter's wreckage sat a plastic
ink-cap brimming with lemony plume.

"But I can't sees no yella! I *axed* you for yella!"

"You saw me put it in. What else can I tell ya?"

"But then why ain't it there?"

Unruly eyes daggered the shop.

"Truly, sweety, in there it lies.
Problem is — *you're* sandbagging on top."

**SHE REGARDED MY GLOVES WITH ARRANT
CONTEMPT,** sixty thrust forward, thank you
exempt, not even waving goodbye. My station was
still only partially cleared when a rayon-garbed
gent unleashed vociferous cries.

*"Tattoo-Man! Yo! Hurry it up now, boy! Got mad scads
a this workingman's cash ready to divert-and-deploy!"*

While such brusquerie was common in Montclair,
ergo easy to shake, Aloha-ensembles amid
Februarian air did rate double-takes.

Rapping a forearm with two fingertips,
muscles bulged like varnished twine.

A wool flattop was planed implausibly crisp.

Chromed Ray-Bans gleamed untarnished shine.

*"Want a naked bitch riding a big-ass lion! Right here
on my forearm's topside! With colors mad bright!
Like this silk! Hawaiian! Got that? Want it
bright as the Sun in July!"*

(I fought back tears as the pane was unwrapped.)

How was my new friend getting-by?

More bad dreams. In a dark dirty tunnel w/a candle looking for someone named norma. There was a lot of skunks and scorpions and pianos in there and I had a long tail. Then I dont know what happened but I was in a park getting drunk and kaki shorts ran me over w/a big ass horse. Hurt like a bich. Felt so real. His lips were dripping blood and then he turned into her and then she turned into my mother and I woke up shitting water again. Must get a grip bc the toilet is starting to hate me.

Sexy cherrys w/extra juice $60
Panther $75
Panther $75
Yankees logo $65
Panther $75
Teddy bear w/jerome 1995-1996 $60
Thug life $125
Panther in track suit $95
Red barren snoopy w/blunt $70
"Hot black pussy" in fancy script w/sparkles $60

New driver on the bus past few nights. Big fat guy. Fu manchu mustache. Coke bottle glasses. Smells bad. Never say a word to him and he returns the favor. Feel sorry for him bc he gives off sad vibes but I got my own f'n problems.

"My eyes are always open for the future is not as important as the present."

THE CRICKETS WERE CHIRRUPING UPON MY RETURN, balming cells with dopamine soothe.
  Alas, the mechanical flick of a nightstand's lamp
cued the warblers' suspension of moves.
  A glistening cyclone of welcoming dust
swirled in phantasmagorical embrace.
  Orbs swiped clean of brigandry smut,
I espied the vanity's surface.
  The spider, still case-ensconced,
had shriveled to a lifeless furred nugget.
  As I frantically tossed the tank's mesh lid aside,
a cricket leapt...its freedom well-earned...
  Fuggit.
  Despite raps against plastic walls,
the wad endured unresponsive.
  Rigid, frozen, painfully balled.
  An inmate stalled by a thrust shiv.
  Easing fingers beneath, I abdominally lifted,
finding near-weightlessness a shock;
elevation soon conspiring with digital
warmth to reinvigorate arachnoidal pluck.
Spindly legs unfurled and flexed —
the histrionics of an Apollo-assigner.

Wrist held to eye-level, I discerned dwarfish twin
shoots flanking hooked fangs functioning
as virtual pathfinders.

A quarter hour's dawdle led the intrepid moon-
walker to the apex of a thin/bony arm; a collarbone's
hollow was deemed a suitable expanse to
encamp free of a pit-minder's harm.

Studying our refract in the card-framed mirror,
we certainly made for a janky twosome.

The newcomer's fur was luxurious and plush.

Mine:

Scant/scabby/gruesome.

A CRICKET HOPPED ATOP A BRISTLY BACK,

commencing a thorough self-groom.

Was this beast so milquetoast that it might fall prey
to the bullyish whims of its own food?

Climbing in bed with a new *'Blood Meridian'*, three
prior copies dropped amidst throes of transport,
I once again found words cryptic and sloppy
sparking mulls of pursuant abort.

Eschewing a boring paragraph, I surveyed a slow
assemblage of nest — a long/arduous choreograph
— chips carefully dragged as mislaid shards
were culpable of destroying the rest.

With roughly the shape of a cave,
the construct appeared architecturally sound.

Roof.

Walls.

Ingress.

Where in *Tarnation* had this damn thing
found the rudiments of geometric success?

Last night a monkey ran over jesus in the
tunnel.Odd. Only one panther today. Even
odder.Tried the glass 3 more times.
Reactions not great but a big church thrift shop
find made up for all the curses and the spit.
5 good custom 40s/50s suits and 10 shirts plus
pants shoes and stetsons. Just need to have
the sleeves cut down.The name in the coats
is "cornell h. jackson". Cliff laughed and says I
dress like his granpa but he still wears shirts his
mother sends him from louisiana that look like
she sewed them from old curtins.

Honest abe w/blunt $85
Tribal machine gun $90
Night on horse $95
Panda hugging heart $65
Panther $75
Skull w/nappolian hat $75
Dart $50
Dice $50
Thug life $125
Chinese letters for "dark volcano" $55
Why do parents name children after colleges?
To make them sound smarter?
Rented "golden boy".

"I face difficulties with fortitude and courage."

I WAS ETCHING A PANTHER WITH AN ENGLISH DEVICE barroom-purchased several nights prior. The salesman, a former industry-peer — skirting desperation most dire.

Matinée-looks had shriveled to ghoulish grey jerky freeze-dried against a fine skull.

His gaze was now distant, muddled, and murky.

Twenty years had piled in months.

(Hardly calendrically coeval.)

Never handling a single-coiler before, I was stunned by how fast it ran; emitting the angry, piercing, high-pitched grate of a hornet ensnared in a can. American irons were of twin-coil constructs and hummed like wax-papered combs. While the new machine's squeal was vexing, its thrift proved more-than-fair attone.

Chiseling my colleague from eighty bucks to fifteen had required only seconds.

His heartbreak had been a chore to behold 'til horse-banging providentially beckoned.

THE CREEPING PANTHER'S SERPENTINE OUTLINE was primed and ready for shading when my customer (rubenesque/twentyish/copious diaphoresis cascading) reclaimed her elbow from a toweled knee's rest to mull, silently fraught.

Carnauba-smeared lips pursed
as gears slowly turned.
(I hated when customers thought!)
"Tattoo-Man, can this heah pamfer have spots?"
"I mean, I *can* do that...but I'd need some directional
shepard. Just what kind of spotted cat do you mean?
Cheetah? Ocelot? A leopard?"
"Hmph! Dunno now...can't really see.
You be th' artist, use yo' discrepancy!"
As I polka-dotted willy-nilly, the Limey frame grew
increasingly heated. Still I endured, despite
fleshburning throbs, loath to admit I'd been cheated.
Following a smothering of Vaselined gauze, the cold
tap doused ache-beset paws, rinsing away sweat-
sullied talc to reveal ballooning/blistery gnaws.
*"Tattoo-Man! Shit, boy! That's damn clean enough! Got
biz'nix with you to tend! Now hurry yo' flat-ass butt
an' quit talkin' to yo' honky-ass fren'!"*
Turning to heed these meaty commands, I was
astonished to spy female-issue. Plumper than the last,
she was ready-to-fight, glaring attitudinal jujitsu. While
I'd not yet extended invites, she'd already annexed my
chair; a liberty identical to those taken by hordes.
(Such was the Code of Montclair.)
*"I said: hurry it up, Tattoo-Man! Quit bein' so
muthafuckin' slow! Visitin' hour don't last
fo'evah! Gots to be at Rahway by fo'!"*
It soon became clear that the Visitor sought a pair
of sleek/juice-bleeding cherries; fresh fruits, honey-
pots, and other edible motifs being quite chic
amongst her contemporaries.
In a rush so savage as to constrain the apply of

a traditional Thermofax-stencil, I Sharpie-sketched
drupes directly to a breast before hastening a gear-
gathering assemble. Primed to embark, she vised
my right arm, mashing its meat to puree.
  "An' make sho' there be lotsa juice
in them shits, boy! Best fuckin' do as I say!"
  Nodding, I marked another three droplets via dark/
odoriferous blur. Lowering a wingtip atop
the foot-pedal's spring, the machine
commenced a robotical whir.
  "Need this shit muthafuckin' sexual! My man need
motivation to behave! Keep gettin' time added fo' fightin'!"
  Solemnly avowing Salacity, 'twas
an honor to aid such rabid uniting.

UPON A CURSORY GRAZE OF TEAT,

my heart immediately rent.
  The Visitor's flesh was *Kryptonian!*
  Truck-tires would more easily dent!
  Dulled needles bounced awry, leaving no inky caress.
  An unfortunate sigh escaped pale lips
as my guts bouillabaisse-deliquesced.
  "Hurry, boy!"
  My eyes veered towards the Angry Hornet
resting atop the shelf. Digital blisters forebodingly
pulsed...but no substitute presented itself.
  The British import was a spastic runner.
  This task required mercurial power.
  Swapping machines, I intoned *'Okay'*.
  (Her wordless reply was a glower.)
  As if sentient of indignities suffered, the Angry
Hornet buzzed fury greater than prior...febrile,
incensed, pyretic...seams gushing malevolent hellfire...

Glancing up from his own mugger, Cliff squinted
in a raging direction. *"Dang, cuz! Loud fucking bugger!"*
His drawl wielded Cajun inflection.

**IN THE THROES OF THE FINAL
DROP'S FULFILL,** the Hornet saw fit to explode.
Blasted by recoil onto the floor, clasped
hands channeled pitiful crows.
   *"Jesus! Don't let 'em shoot me! Please show me
that you is there! I can't die now! Jus' wouldn't
be right! Kids still be waitin' at daycare!"*
   This humility vaporized swiftly, upon a grasped
quake-transpire. Particles from a capacitor
blown wafted like flakes volcanically sired.
   *"Ain't paying you fo' shit, boy! Try an' make me...
youse can't! Dumb-ass muthafuckin' honky!
Done made me piss my good pants!"*
   I espied an ash-blackened mien brewing within
a mirrored reflection, flanked by a burnt rubber-glove,
fused to an injured infection. Saluting the partition
with a throbbing fist, stares ricocheted sullen, quiet,
rueful. Bursting as abrupt as hand grenades —
the mob cried thunderous approval.

October, 1993

*Dead soldiers lay strewn across the floor.
Some erect, some felled by God's will.
A cabinet card lurked near the closet's door.
(A sepia-toned headshot from Vaudeville.)
A small bookshelf harbored 'Perfume', 'The Bell Jar',
and 'Sybil'. Time Outs and Interviews were wretchedly
deplumed by thickly tarred dry-outs of dribble.*

She was hurling 'Begin the Beguine' from JUBILEE in the shower. I was direly bored. Twirling a nightstand's assigned jewelry, a flower bloomed within an oil-lamp's liquor.

HE HATES MY BAND. I KNOW HE DOES. HE SAYS HE DOESN'T, BUT HE'S A VERY BAD LIAR. IT SHOULDN'T REALLY BOTHER ME, BUT IT DOES. I GUESS HE THINKS HE'S PUNKER THAN ME OR SOMETHING. STUPID, I KNOW. BUT NOT SO SURE THIS CAN WORK. WAIT, IT GETS WORSE. IN BED, HE SPREADS MY LEGS APART LIKE A NEW PAPERBACK AND JUST SHOVES IT RIGHT IN. ZERO FANFARE. NO STROKES, NO GENTLE TEASING, NO FOREPLAY, NOTHING. NO FEELING. NO EMOTION. JUST PURE BRUTALITY LIKE HE'S A MACHINE OR SOMETHING. MAYBE HE WAS A VIRGIN BEFORE ME? I'M USUALLY DRUNK ANYWAY WHEN WE FUCK SO I DON'T REALLY CARE. I JUST WANT TO GET IT OVER WITH AND GO TO SLEEP REALLY. BUT SOMETIMES...IN THE MORNING...I WANT LOVE, NOT VIOLENCE! HE'S YOUNG THOUGH. MAYBE I CAN TEACH HIM A FEW THINGS???   I REALLY DUNNO...

From a sill, Buster glared chartreuse disgust,
a brass heart framing the snapshot behind him.
An agonized man abused a Fender's slung truss
as if the bass was a crackpot who'd maligned him.
She entered the room, beaming and damp.
One towel was a turban.
Another shrinkwrapped curves.
"All clean, Daddy! And creaming my pants!
Better fuck me then eat snatch for dessert!"

Noting the trajectory of my scoffing fret, her padding
wetly smudged wood. "Sorry, not tossing it yet. Don't even
suggest that I should!" Lifting the frame, she squinted.
  "Technically...we're still married too..."
  Crippling with shame, I glinted, unharried,
maintaining a semblance of cool.
  "I mean, we still hang sometimes, though he tried to
strangle me just before last Christmas. That's when we
split. I don't wanna hate him...or for him to hate me.
We'll always share that once-was/past-isthmus. All I want
is neutrality, at least. That and the absence of hatred."
  "Strangle you?"
  "Said something shitty about Buckner. Sox fan.
That kind of madness is sacred."
  A thumb lobbed towards a Mets cap,
suspended above the door from a hook.
  "Almost killed me...says he regrets that. Got him off with
a kick to the crook. Still feel bad about calling the fuzz,
took three to drag him away. You know the riff. Went to
the judge. Restraining order decreed the next day."
  "But...I saw you...with him...just a few weeks back."
  Cracking a window, she addressed
a thin slit of Blue Moon.
  "Yeah...well...SO WHAT, Jack? Sorry to shout, but don't be
possessive too soon. Seamus and I...it's complicated. I feel
kinda bad for him, y'know? Acts so heinously lonely and
devastated. And when I get drunk, anything goes..."
  Thrusting an arm, she released the photo
into the primed gloom of the night.
  Following a pause came shatters of glass.
  Rats sassed like Times-doomed playwrights.

"I regard my friends and peers as blessings, not burdens."

AN UNFURLED ONIONSKIN FLUTTERED — nervous wings of a roadmap-sized fly. Violent trembles echoed each pebbled disruption of the Greyhound's compromised stride.

So very huge was Christ's disheartening visage; hundreds of dashes and dots. Parceling the mirage would mean forty date-slashes spread over a year-long allot.

Wet clucks signaled the next-aisle rebuke of a bearded Hispanic lump. She crossed herself as the vellum was piled deep within my satanic sack's dump.

As we cruised past Exxons/suntan-salons/dilapidated hot-dog shacks, I wondered if Avery's unsavory camaraderie rated such aboriginal flak.

I'D FIRST MET THE LANTERN-JAWED HULK responding to a *'for rent'* classified.

Six-seven. Two eighty. Thirty-odd years. Arms tattooed severely rude to imbue torrential dash-asides. Despite the demeanor of an irritable bowel, he'd made a fine roommate nonetheless. I'd admired his grit, myriad scowls, and overall cleanliness. Fond as I was of the big man, I'd been troubled by skewed priorities. Despite frequent disgorges of racist invective, he'd huddled solely with nude minorities.

AS THE TRACING AGAIN UNFURLED,
I stared and absorbed its pained mien.
  Bulging orbs plead dour mercy.
  Nostrils flared a dying man's spleen.
  A mouth wrenching in obscenely grim
angles showed genuine anguish present.
  My research had required a hand-mirror's
dangle to refract throes of mangled descent.

So this chick at coney island high wouldnt give
it up in the bathroom unless I smoked a kools
w/her first. Later I dreamed about being
trapped in a smokey tunnel w/the retard and
when I woke up I had a asthma attack. Then at
work another lady got furious about the glass.
Said I am a ignorant motherfucker. Got spit all
over me. But then she let me use her albuterol
when I started to cough so maybe she wasnt
so bad after all and maybe I am not as ignorant
as she thought either. Her inhaler
tasted like honey mustard.

Sexy ice cubes $65
Panther $75
Baby boxer w/little boom boom $80
Panther $75
Chinese letters for "sawed off 12 gauge" $55
Lock ness monster w/afro $90
Pistol w/r.i.p. dad $85
Beauty mark $50
Panther $75

Cliff says the man in rayon came back while
I was at lunch. Guessing he likes his woman

34

on the lion and wanted to say thanks. At least someone doesnt hate me. Spider is doing much better to. Perhaps it might enjoy fetch?

> # "My thoughts are my reality and I am thinking of a bright new day."

AVERY'S CHRISTENING BEGAN CALMLY, though the kidneys proved a tad rough, necessitating several pauses of length to purge curmudgeonly rebuff.

"*Sorry*, bro. Shouldn't snip. Know you're just doin' your job. Say, ever tell ya my very first tat was from this crypt me'n my boys once fuckin' robbed? Up in Bronxville we usta hang in these cemeteries. Gettys, Wyckoffs, that rich type a folk. My buds and I was all degenerates. Pissin' up graves like yetis! Rippin' shit off headstones! Sometimes we'd fight over dope..."

"Very gothic."

"Bro, this was fifteen years back! Tweren't no '*goths*' them days! We was just degenerate scum! Typical slothy teenage! One day this hippie drives by, Dead tat hangs from his Dart. *Boom*...instant new craze! Only trouble: no bread for a head fuckin' start. So we rolled this rich Yid who usually had dough and he coughs up a big bag a herb. I get my sister to lug us to Nyack. We kicked the fat kike to the curb..."

"Nyack?"

"Yeah. Heard this *Harker* tatter couldn't scratch 'less he was real fuckin' high. That he'd even trade grass for ink if his connections was comin' up dry. Dude turns out all *sortsa* sketchy, zooted on booger-sugar! Demandin' IDs, paranoid and tetchy, like he thought we was T.J. Hooker! When I showed him the bag, he acts like a prick, tellin' us all to leave. I say, *'Yo, our old man IS a homicide dick...but that ain't no call for aggrieve. I ain't no kind of rat, bro, so your bullshit we don't really need! Word is you dig good smoke, just figgered I'd trade ya some weed!'* He calms some, buds break apart as he sniffs with his big fuckin' schnozz. I snag a Sacred Heart from the wall; sis picks slips from Wizard of Oz. Harker says, *'For those, I'll take the green loot, plus forty five more.'* So I ask, *'Bro, what else you need?'*...thinkin' some jive I can boost from a store. Smile spreads across his face. Says he collects human skeletons. The crew cringes all at once, knowin' I'm gonna bash his dumb grin to gelatin! My bud Phil goes, *'Yo! I know where there's lots and lotsa good skulls!'* Harker asks if there's meat on 'em still, or are they covered in mold? Back in the car, Phil spiels about a crypt-key in Rhinebeck he can loan from some cousin called Angie..."

"Whose?"

"Just some high-neck/ruinin' lives by-the-dozen/ small/slave-ownin' family. So we find the crypt and let ourselves in. Dust. Spiders and shit. Shelves of granite coffins. Even though we pick the smallest, still takes four budgin' the lid. The bones, real fuckin' tiny. Like maybe they was just from a kid."

"And then what?"

"We lift the skull and split as quick as we could!
Dropped the rest off in Throggs Neck.
Scrubbed that shit up real good!"

"Why not just let Harker clean up the dreck?"

"Because that woulda been rude and I wasn't takin'
no chance! *Remember*, this was a sketchy-ass dude!
Hadda optimize things in advance!"

"Ah..."

"Set the thing on the stove to boil.
Didn't figger on it *stinkin'* so bad..."

"Describe it."

"Like I'd scraped Ernest Borgnine's oily dickcheese
right from his hinky-ass nads! Then my old man pulls
up, and I can tell he's stewed from the sound, 'cause
he bruises the garage-door real rough — hadn't
checked to make sure tweren't down. So I rush the
pan beneath my bed, the water still bubblin' and
steamin'. Just then he knocks, three sheets to the
wind, false teeth blood-red and careenin'! *'Boy?
What the fuck's that stink? Smells like cheese
from Ernest Borgnine's dick!'*"

"He actually said that?"

"Bro, how *else* didja think I was able to furnish such
a yore-minded descrip? And I can't let him see the
skull! That drunk, he's liable to kill me! So I fall to the
floor, cryin' earfuls, plyin' all sortsa guilty! *'Sorry, Pop!
Too late! Got myself high on the reefer!' 'Look here,
son, just tell it straight! Was this all on account a some
beaver?' 'Yeah, Pop. Called me a square, no puss unless
we got high!'* Says, *'My bureau has rubbers, don't tell your
sister,'* falls asleep on the lawn outside. Yeah, times was
so *mint* back then! *Now*, they're so fuckin' borin'. Even
the drugs. The dames. The whorin'. The sex..."

Mercy-imploring, the Savior winced.
Mugged. Pained. Perplexed.

Day off. The spider is now happy and
chipper and wants to play all the time. I hope
I can grow to love it. Is loving a spider a crime?
Cold as fuck out but took rides by myself on
the staten island fairy anyway. Went back and
fourth six f'n trips. Sat on the upper deck. Ate
six hot dogs. Drank six beers. Thought about
her all the while bc I really am that stupid.
Afterwards I walked to the babydoll lounge.
Stared at strippers w/dirty feet. One had a
faded straight edge tattoo on her shoulder that
had a fist w/a x that said "you are only young
once so do it right". Another had a tampon
string hanging from her thong. I wonder what
her blood tastes like. Some days belong in
snow globes to keep on your bookshelf
for shakes in old age. Guessing maybe
this was one of them.   Burrrrrrrrrrrrp.

"I find greatness in everybody I meet."

FESTOONED WITH A GREASY RED D.A. and
the throat of an egg-quaffing drake, Templeton
was lording over four drained highballs by
the time I joined Joe's den of snakes.

"*Jackie Bender, public defender! Hey-hey, whaddya say?*"
 The imp's antique shop, Tchotchke-Town,
specialized in mid-century kitsch; gimcrackery
intended for schlocky clowns of a largely Nihonjin
niche. Despite dearly missing the concern's bulging
racks of the aged gabardine genus, I'd shied away
ever since El had confessed covert smacks
to fellate a hypoglycemic penis.
 "*Jesus, dude...look like a hundred bucks! Where the fuck
ya been hiding? Figured maybe you'd just sucked a
blunderbuss after hearing of your ex-cunt's ill tidings.*"

MY RESPONSE ELICITED EARTHY SNIGGERS
unsullied by humor or mirth.
 "Brooklyn, a spider, Jersey, niggers!
All tumors of unfortunate girth!"
 "*C'mon*, Temp...don't use that word..."
 "Why?"
 "Because it's disrespectful and cruel."
 "Had you been *City*-whelped, you'd
not be such a dull-edged tool!"
 "I've known blacks my entire life. They're no better
nor worse than me. We've *all* been yanked by the
same midwife into this Kafkaesque catastrophe..."
 "My bad, Jack, you did say 'blacks'! But at least
concede that niggers do indeed exist!"
 "Meaning what?"
 "Aha! Permit some factual assist! One day, back in
grade fourth, I was entering my building's Otis,
when this bereted beast of a villainous swarth
hops on like an open-mic poetess. I stood at
the elevator's farthest side, as this creature was
nearly an ape, but still I felt eyes scarring my hide
and prayed the scene not end in rape."

"What?"

"As we reach my floor, she says, *'Little baby! You there!
Yo' parents be home?'* Her stare was sore and lazy;
a cent shy of Down syndrome. *'Little baby, you lyin'!
I see that key 'round yo' neck! If they's home, they just
let yo' ass in! Must think I's dumber'n heck!'"*

"Did she follow?"

"Duh! Parks me on the divan. Starts ransacking
drawers and closets like Marxists fighting the Klan!
When I whine, she says, *'Just piss yo' shorts, don't get
offa that couch!'* And she's piling her purse with silver,
quartz, even Maxie's plush Oscar the Grouch.
Next she asks where the jewelry's kept."

"Yeah? And what'd you say?"

"The fuck you think? Stood up and led the way!
When she grilled me about any cash around and I
said I really don't know, she picked up this souvenir
bat she found signed by Joe DiMaggio. Tapped me
once on the head, says, *'Little baby, make me a
sammich!'* So I dug through the cupboards like crazy,
realizing I needed a bandage. Asked what kind she
wanted; mentioned Fluff, bleu-dip, coleslaw. When
she says ham, I hafta explain the cuffs of Talmudic
law. Thankfully, she smiled. *'PB&J be fine!'* I made her
a couple on Wonder Bread while she de-framed my
mom's Liechtensteins. When I told her she'd missed
the very best part by making me disable the crust,
she chopped lines on *'Poker Flat'* by Bret Harte
and forced me to snort Angel-Dust."

As the Imp frothed a switchblade comb and raked
his red pompadour, our staid debate of polemic
genomes was quashed by new breasts at the door.

August, 1994

Two curses passing unbloodied, forsaking smeared sties
of tests, she immediately scheduled an impassioned
study with a nearby abortionist.

Upon my suggest she oughtn't shirk the cheaper
drugstore-apparatus, she jerked a shirt to showcase
peaks of a second-floor's lace status.

"Jesus...look! See how my tits can barely fit in this
fucking thing? Shit's plain knocked-up, alright?
No time for hemming/hawing!"

Verboten beyond the Bleecker Street lobby, I was ordered
back five hours later. Park-whiling by tree-roots
beleaguered and knobby, I spied gaps
swallow rats whole like gators.

Safely home, bed-ensconced, drifting off to a dopey
dreamland, she lobbed a wadded-up missive,
scribbled across a Parenthood's Plan.

'Twas a list of delicacies:

Roasted carpaccio.
Preserved lemon tarts.
Hijiki.
Bloated pistachios.
Yemeni artichoke hearts.

Snorey wisps rasped, 'Please feed me!'

Sallying forth with an industry equal to any beaver's
self-respect, I buzzed about town, snatching all but the
Marzu cheese and its residual maggot-infect. In lieu of
pique, I'd procured turtle soup and a roasted yak penis
instead — burdening my larder yet further with
Jäger and seedy/prosciutto-flecked bread.

Back on East Third, I quietly nestled myriad goods atop
the dining room table, garnishing plates with virescent
leaves shorn from a tall First Avenue maple.

Foraging thick-stemmed blackout candles from the
confines of kitchen-sink coffers, I crammed waxed sticks
into empty wine-bottles and levied digestif proffers.

Ice cubes chimed softly within my hands as I tapped at
the door with a toe. Waiting one moment before
knocking anew, I entered a bedroom aglow.

Oil-lamp flickers revealed nothing save duvet lumps
and a lone scrap-paper note.

Draining both drinks in two frustrated dumps,
I collapsed bedside to grope.

HI DADDY!
FEELING SO, SO MUCH BETTER! THANK
YOU FOR BEING SO GOOD TO ME. GOING
OUT TO MEET SYLVIA FOR A FEW QUICK
DRINKS, BUT I'LL BE BACK SOON TO CHOW
WITH YOU. SHE'S REALLY WORRIED. JUST
WANNA SHOW HER THAT I'M 100% OKAY!
LOVE, LOVE, LOVE.
-E.

An ameboid blob of trapped moonlight
pulsed atop the ceiling.

Strange thoughts coursed of shimmering blight.

A moist womb's glop was squealing.

Glutinous, lumpy primordium.

Was it half-me/half-her?

The phone's bell clappered spastically.

Alas, corporeality had numbed beyond stir.

"I take care of my body's needs."

UPON CHATTING PETUNIA IN JOE'S, Temp stomped at Frigidity's stave. Thirty Imp-minutes comped for *'NO!'*, farewell was a one-digit wave.

Platinum braids. Florid cheeks. A lamb gowned in next-season's Prada. A slumming rich broad, a Greek contessa, the bled seed of a nobleman father. A Moscovian mother claimed less august ichor nonetheless worthy of note; spawned by Stalin's barber/she Warholed with ardor/sponsoring the hip-but-inchoate.

As the lap-perched highborn traced my chin with fingers unmatched to broom, it soon became clear that great vim was derived via ribaldry bashed against groom. Did my erect spur arc left or right? Did my son's apex echo? Did my daughter harbor an Electra-complex? Describe fay sex in the ghetto! Averring my gourd hung by an angle possessing no curve whatever, I waxed of a ward web-entangled/ unswerved by incest-endeavor.

"A spider? How grand! Do tell the sweet darling's name!"

Eyes widened with a snarled scowl's brand.

"Incognito? How abysmally lame!"

Upon the accuse of an endocarp heart, I countered flesh peachlike as well.

Eyes charted forearms green with ink-mottle.

"Yes! And moldy as Hell!"

ABOVE A PLUSH/PEPTO-BISMOL SOFA,
flashed by gold bullion flecks, a fallen matador was
lushly attended by an espectadora's vast/swollen
chest. Hidden bulbs emphasized the black-velvet
tension of a lump in a lavender breech.

The entire duplex was likewise outré,
every shade of vomit beseeched.

"Nice."

Beaming, the Contessa shimmied in a spastic/
cake-mixer fashion. *"Interior-design comes naturally
to me! I'll fix your place next, Herr Jackson!"*

Blonde pigtails flopping as she embraced and
burrowed, derrière fumes were sent upwards.
Escaping its tomb via silk furrows, the gas reeked of
refined trench-custard. Hot tears gathered at
the side of my neck. I queried what was wrong now.

*"Sorry to make you retch, Jackson! You mustn't think
me a cow! It's that time of the month for me,
and I'm a bit more flatulent than custom..."*

Atop a pale shoulder, the Felled Matador shrugged.
Gored. Static.
I cussed him.

**DESPITE FREQUENT TRIPS TO TUDOR
CITY,** and incessantly salty sex-vibes, I was patently
refused the new kitty, no matter how much liquor
was plied. If pressed, she'd sorely fellate, but
these were stunted affairs...withdrawals
enforced pre-ejaculate.

(Was plebe-jizz the Spunk of Despair?)

Several weeks deep into drought, I snapped and
reached for my wallet — my spur barely sheathed
amidst a seizure of spout and screams of a latex
allergy most squalid. Upon noting she'd flushed a

'*Naturalamb*', in light of the simplest facts, Petunia
braced herself against a doorjamb and
declared a steep fright of anthrax.

November, 1993

*My pards in the underground tattoo co-op issued
the ol' booteroo...officially on account of office-sown
sperm...a bowl of pure balderdash stew!*
  *Yes, the janitor had stumbled upon us
unconscious/fully entwined — but no
passionate throes had been thwarted or gleaned.*
  (We'd been dressed and wholly benign.)
  *Upon a drunken behest of re-inked fades,
she'd lain on my torso/leg table.*
  *I'd returned from the sink, scum abraded,
to a snore-show of vexes unstable.*

"Hiya, chief!"
Dawn.
Dry.
Grief.
Blue/smoke-filled cackles.
Frenchie!
Mining tools to pawn...
Gold crags peaked burgundy spackle.
*Blinking in rapid succession, shaking off sleepy cobwebs,
I focused on a forehead's hand-poked cross,
smudged and woefully bled.*
  "Dude...your eyebrows...where the fuck did they go?"
The Janitor shrugged.
  *"You tell me, I dunno! Fell asleep in Tompkins
coupla nights back. When I woke up...they're gone!"*

Reaping the blight of brain-bushwhack,
El spoke amidst pained yawns.
   "Oh Daddy...don't feel so good...
head hurts...any Alka-Seltzer here?"
   My slow dole of deli-funds evoked a dispirited leer.
   "Can't tell you how many times I've caught
that creep stealing tips right off the bar!
Forget about him bringing you change!"
   Too saddened to defend an idol's burnt star,
I cringed like a puppy with mange.

Provisions arrived an hour later, their bearer blissfully
dope-high. Settling in a chair, war-stories ensued,
true tales of bedraggled magpies.
   Coherency flying the coop, nods fleetly commenced —
the heartbreaking/over-oiled case droops
of a salesman's collapsible tent.
   Halting at the brink of each mien-against-knee,
the Janitor jerked as if sprung.
   El squealed, "Avenue D T'ai Chi!"
   My own condemned smirk hung.

"I see everything with loving eyes and I love everything I see."

A TONE MORE FELINE THAN HUMAN
beseeched a rat upon thigh. While Curiosity begged
for illumine, mob-screech distracted all pry.

A brief swivel and curt snort
prompted vents of shrill howl.
  "Spooks. Always gave me pure Hell
on the court. Elbows...intentional fouls..."
  "Athlete, huh? That's pretty cool."
  "I *was*, way back in school. Always the biggest, the
fastest, the best. Always named captain, which brought
on its own type of stress. Daddy usually coached. I
got good grades too. Couldn't help me much
with that...*sports* though, he knew."
  She ogled my 40s oxford.
  (A long-collared thingamabob.)
  "He never cared much for couture...but do *most*
guys, beyond crap they wear to their jobs? Ow! Some
of my *teammates* though, they'd make comments. Get
real teasy and mean. Not to his face — knew I'd cut
out their spleens. But once, after practice, I was piling
soccer-balls into the Blazer, when I saw something
that didn't belong: a Bic disposable-razor. Opened
the net, found a bag with a note/lotsa travel-
sized stuff. Shampoo. Speed Stick. Comb.
Even a nail-clipper and buff..."
  Mulling the yarn for a half-minute's spanse as a
shader pumped a damnable well, I feebly attempted
to transplant myself into Nikes of
tall/blonde mademoiselles.
  "Didja leave the stuff in the bag?"
  "Nah. When he'd watch me shower, I'd be tempted
to finally speak up...but I never veered close enough
to the deed that I actually saw fit to erupt..."
  "What?"
  "Eh, he'd just sit on the toilet and stare, hand me

towels, sometimes blow-dry my hair. Mom felt
bad...'cause he couldn't help it...it wasn't wrong
versus right. He just liked to watch...not to touch.
Just wasn't born very bright. And he, like, *created* me.
I was his property in some weird kinda way..."
  (Inquiring after the dilemma's lifespan,
my guts queered with queasy malaise.)
  "When I was seventeen, I finally told him to quit.
He'd given me a Whitman's box plus a gallon of wine/
I'd screamed Valentine's was shit. After I'd stomped
all over the stuff, I did feel kinda bad, but it was really
all for the best. Left me alone after that. Sometimes,
when I'm home for to-dos, he'll sneak a quick Q-Tip
or tissue. Probably just testing to see if thoughts have
changed...but I'd rather make love to a Shih Tzu..."
  Cat's eyes lingered atop pale knees devoid of
blemish or splay. "Anyhow, I'd never do that! No
freakin' way, José! My mom would be so freakin' sad!
And I couldn't live with it either. What kind of
MONSTER wants to bang her own dad?"
  I rushed to the john for a breather.

September, 1993

I emerged from the Hi-Yella throng,
sideboards freshly shorn.
  "Daddy! No! Why would you do that?
You look like a pesky newborn!"
  Doltishly mistaking chagrin for play,
I sniggered and mussed up her crown.
  "And what's so very wrong with that?"
  "I don't suck infants' cocks!"

(Stung jowls hung nonplussed with frown.)
Surveying the room's smoggy grey writhe,
moist breaths probed a right-ear's canal. Gay rakes of
whiskery scythe fogged my remaining morale.
The offending boor, bent and green,
extended talons lame since birth.
"We've met before? Perchance in a dream?
My name's Allen Ginsberg..."
Lids magnified wistfully closed as a yellow-tarred finger
raised. My pivoting eyes, dodging howls posed,
met lodges of scornful appraise.
"Just understand I've known El a long time!
Long time before your pathetic ass! I resent
your encroach upon what's mine!"
I turned back to the poetic morass.

Chipped black nails lowered a Stella,
foam besmirched via carved-heart.
"Sorry, Daddy. Shouldn't have snapped.
Let's give this night a fresh start."
"Don't worry. I'll grow 'em back..."
"And what'd Seamus say to you?"
"Just that he wishes us only the best."
"Hmph! Woulda guessed more like, 'Go screw!'"

The Moogian strains of '(Get A) Grip (On Yourself)'
hummed through the cranky P.A.
Lagomorphically dashing aside,
Elizabeth scampered away.
Burning in, once again more, Seamus spritzed Jameson
splutter: "She's Eternity's whore...not yours, douche!
See ya soon enough in the gutter!"

"Happiness is contagious, I spread it to others and absorb it from them."

A SCHOTT-BEDECKED LITTLE WHITE HERR
stumbled through the buzzered front-door.
  Weathered.
  Blotched.
  He was a rubbed affair, as if
once-smothered by sacks of dried corn.
  An unmistakably Polish brow
was cleaved via buttery widow's peak.
  Carefully molded into a grieved pompadour,
its mode was utterly bleak.

AS THE POLACK PEELED HIS STUDDED MC,
epidermal sparsity shocked me.
  While he'd seemed the type to prepossess inked
sleaze, limbs hung parched as mesodermal adoptees.
  '*CHINEESE ROCKS*' across a bicep
formed the sole graphic dowery.
  Faded, blue, crooked scrawled pox...hearkening a
T-Rex I'd seen fixed on the Bowery.
  Beneath the lizard a scratch had declared:

' *Nothing Lasts Forever!* '
 "Hey man, where'd you get that?
All those hand-poked letters?"
  Squinting down to the arm as if its presence had
been thoroughly forgotten, the Polack stroked his
scar with a ringed glass eye equally
furrowed and rotten.
  "Oh...dis guy Dee Dee Ramone.
But dat was a long time ago..."
  "Huh. Didn't know he *did* that stuff."
  "Yup, you an' me both. I was out cold an' when
I come to he was jabbin' me wit' inky woiks."
  A shrug pantomimed ancient surprise.
  Cliff razzed from a *'Spin'* Roseanne-besmirched.
  "Cuz, you're saying he started tattooing
you with a *hypo* while you were asleep?"
  "Yeah, dat's basically it. But I was *high*,
not nappin'. We was dope-shootin' creeps."
  "*Dang*, cuz. Crappy. Hope you
at least gave him a slug."
  "Nah. Doin' it seemed t'make him real happy..."
  (A sigh.)
  "Plus he paid for all'a d'drugs..."

REMARKABLY REFUSING TO BLEED, sitting
perfectly still, the Polack revealed a name of *'Kilroy'*.
  Cliff's mien was surlily chilled.
  "Why?"
  "Really dunno...jus' what folks like t'call me.
Allus jus' figgered could be much woise.
Least it ain't *Fuckface* or *Baldy*."

Phone rang at 2am. Woke me up from another tunnel dream. It was just avery telling a dirty joke he couldnt even remember the f'n punch line to. Then today 4 f'n customers came back w/bad EZ red reactions. Keep telling cliff to quit using the crap but does he listen? One day we will get sued by johnny cochran. Maybe even shot. Fu manchu farted garlic the entire ride back to new york. I was the only passenger to. No talking. Just him farting every 5 minutes.

Panther $75
Newark niggaz 4 lyfe $85
Panther $75
Nude hooker $95
Chinese letters for "2 fly 4 dis world" $55
Basketball $60
Panther $75
Tweety $60
Panther $75
EE Comings quote $50
Panther $75

Still thirsty. Keep drinking but it is never enough. Bye bye birdy is on amc and the spider is watching as I write this. Last time I watched it was w/her. When I woke up the next morning she was sleeping naked in the 2nd floor hallway. She couldnt remember how she got there or where all her clothes went. That was wierd.

"I am happy, hale, and hearty."

WITH PETUNIA'S VAGINA ENDURING QUITE LOCKED and my balls bluing to plum, the wining-and-dining proved a right paradox.

Vexing. Goat-stewing.

Dumb.

Upon the arrival of pained-sit junctures, I backhanded Refusal's charade.

Faced with the threat of mane-split punctures, she demanded a perusal for AIDS.

Suckling Sway's boob no longer, Pepto-Bismolically arise, I reached for the battered surplus A-2 condemned to a zipped sack's confines.

In a terrific surprise, she rushed by my side; stroking shoulders, cheeks, and neck; moldering pique via soft squeak and dry/saliva-parched pecks.

"Don't be grumpy! I'm sorry. So sorry. Just stay..."

Tottering across Venetian floor-tile, she piled a sill's plush brocade.

"Just scared. Papa's life has been so vilely unclean. Nothing personal, understand?"

The evening was whiled quaffing caffeine.

Virginal/unplundered/bland.

I BOOKED A TEST WITH ONE DOCTOR KARNSTEIN, foraged from halftone-adverts. While some hooked breasts, the bulk fostered hard miens — tombstone-coarse/sans-shirt.

January, 1994

Grunting swears amidst tissuey tears of every hydraulic
thud/whomp, a stare probed orbs as orphanannically
bare as a Moloch's diabolic blood-dump.
 "Daddy…if…you…were…really…my…daddy…
Would…you…fuck…me…anyway?"
 (Oswald F. Fletcher's star had tanked upon a dropped
cigarette's tinder, scalding cleft vectors of tarred Burbank
to disastrous plaster cinders. Crucified by Jews and
devious Parsons, forty years of obscurity droned,
ere truth-deprived woos trumped previous
arsons to fizz jizz from Maturity's bone.)
 "Tell…me…Would…you?…Would…you?"
 The daisy-pusher's phantom romance struck me as
mighty unfair. Was it a primal imprint? His handsome/dull
glance? A Hun-blighting Croix de Guerre?
 "Would…you…fuck…me?"
 Despite meek licks of oil-lamp flicks leaving the portrait
twilight-ensconced, his sorcerous choler bore the dolor
of a misfortunate/lye-blinded ponce.
 "Tell me!"
 Beneath the scowl a boutonniere
stabbed through a skewed grosgrain lapel.
 A garlic-blossom! Diluted and queer!
 A crude botanical knell!
 "Would you?…Would you fuck me?"
 How could I franchise such a venal demon?
 To even reflect was all folly!
 "Daddy?"
 The fiend's damn eyes wept sepia semen!
 Was it not a spectral Svengali?
 "DADDY!"

"I have a keen capacity to learn new skills that support my success."

LEST I FALL GRIST TO THE COSH OF DESPAIR, Sanity demanded Apathy.
  'Y'all best wash yo' shit, I fuckin' swear!
An' lessee you transit mo' rapidly!'
  'Obsessive-explosive, Ivory Soap,
vagina-faced white bitch!'
  'Tattoo-Man ain't no whitey, dope!
Sheenies be some China-raced type niche!'
  The entry of a tall, pale, ashen
outlier abruptly restarted focus.
  Swathed in supplementary/Yale-fashioned
attire, racquet-jostles split apostles like Moses.
  "Can you inform me of the process here?
How does a man see about being tattooed?"
  His mouth wore a supercilious, jockish leer.
  Was I being clowned?
  Bandied?
  Stooged?

THE KNIFE, COUNTER SET, WAS KUKRI-ESQUE, poly-molded, spade-pommeled.
  "I'd like a panther's head, on my left shoulder,
mouthing that blade a'gobble. Now, listen-up, because

you need to understand clearly: these details require
extreme precision. And, for this, I'll pay dearly.
Can you swing it, Jack? Your decision."
  Webb Fallon's blues nervously
narrowed as I lifted the knife to inspect.
  The grip was timerubbed.
  The edge — bruised/harrowed.
  My parched lips compressed. "No sweat."
  "And put *non gratum anus rodentum* above it.
Or would below look better? I trust ye."
  I palmed some paper and lead to him.
  "Spell it out real bold. My Español's nigh-rusty."

**STARING BLANKLY AHEAD, SPEARING
EVERY FALSETTO,** Webb fifed along to Creedence.
  "Me and her still tread Hell's reverie-ghetto.
That knife and I share a strong allegiance."
  "Pardon?"
  "I was skinny back then...*like you*...so they made me
a tunnel-rat. Charlie's ops were underground...harder
to bomb...that's where the guns were all at. I crawled
in holes, flushed-out what I found, lotsa dreck
swaddled down there. Factories. Farms. Stacks of
Eliot/Pound. Scale models of *LAX* and *O'Hare.*
Scorpions. Spiders. Mines. Spiked ditches. Charlie even
had trained bats! Imagine *that*, Jack! Hordes pouring
in...tides of shrike bitches...an army
of sanguinarian/winged-cats!"
  Gazing up, my blood went cold.
  (The Tunnel-Rat's eyes had melted.)
  *"Saw lanes of mud where skulls were bowled!
Brothels where GIs were gelded!"*
  "All this...beneath the Earth?"

"Why would I lie? To bequeath fucking mirth?"
"No. Sorry, I don't think that.
Didn't mean to imply..."
"Free fucks, Jack! Free corpse-fucks and free corpse-
sucks! 'Twas the day ol' Gaylord died! Y'know, I could ice
everybody in here just with her! Take, maybe, forty
seconds! You...him...these spooks...all a red blur,
if that's how my lady implored me to reckon!"
Dislodging the pommel with five whistling turns,
a piano-wire was neatly unfurled; each expiry of the
oxidized cord terminating with a blunt steely pearl.
"Jack, meet LILITH, a thirsty gal! Used to love dancing
with throats! Always gentle and quiet around vertebral
canals! Never once stump-pranced to gloat..."
A forked tongue cleansed the garrotte.
Honeyed brow-sweat crawled.
Torquing Webb's dung free of wet claret,
I avowed triple-checks of all scrawls.

Built a shrine in the drawer above the gun
last week. It has pictures of us together and all
the notes she wrote and other wierd things
I found on the street like ribbons and rocks
and screws and crack viles. Does this make me
crazy? When I stand in front of the shrine the
ring gets hot like it does around templeton and
avery. So hot that I can smell my skin burning.
And sometimes the skull even talks to me but
I can never understand what it is saying
bc I dont speak good german.
Does THAT make me crazy?

Music note $50
Mickey getting bj from duck $85
Thug life $125
Panther $75
Knife $75
USMC bulldog $80
Panther $75
Mexican panther w/somberero (sp.?) $85
Panther $75
Panther $75

Spider says hello. Haha not really. Just me
pretending to know what a spider thinks.
Would probably just eat me if it was big
enough. Could I blame it? Note to self:
learn more german.

"I only attract loving people into my world, for they are a mirror of what I am."

SLUMMING BEING AMONGST THE FLEETEST OF THRILLS, my spur's sweet luster soon doffed — compelling bores with the deepest of drills to excavate Riis-ian dust troughs.

"*I want to peek in your closets...*
examine your fridge...huff your filthy red towels!"
My resistance held apposite as days were
bridged, apropos to the Dread in my bowels.

THE BLONDE TORNADO FRANTICALLY
WHIRLED, violating with reckless abandon.
Prancing sentry, my wan gusto curled
to the dejection of a feckless Ugandan.
"*Jackson, it's so very dusty in here! I've explored tombs*
in Egypt with less! Tell me, please, is this smut
of intent? A glut for strategic effect?"
True to promulgation, noble laughs
surged as damp washcloths met tile.
"*Phew! Unlaundered since Reagan! How can dirt ever*
be purged with swaths so intolerably vile? Hey, what's
'Clozapine 100 mg'? Can I have some? Does it work?"
As she sped past, sowing pills like seeds,
stiff caroms were snagged by deft jerks.
"Please, Tunie...just knock it off! This ain't
no ant-farm, it's my heart's stable!"
"*Come now, Jackson! I mean you no harm! Look! More*
suits than Clark Gable! And why, pray tell, is this mirror
covered? Sitting shiva for another Negro? And what's this?
Oh! The spider! Gave me a shudder — I'd forgotten you
kept such a wee grove! She's beautiful! What's her
name again? Such a darling biosphere!"
"Told ya, tarantulas don't need 'em.
They don't even have ears..."
"*Charlotte's so tame! So calm! So...so RADIANT!*"
"Charlotte?"
"*Jackson! Everyone deserves a name!*
Even the dumb and unsapient!"

As the Contessa tugged succus from the
furry red ass, more smeared laughs ejected.
  "Look, Jackson! Mucus en masse! Do you
suppose the poor dear's staph-infected?"

Nice day. Getting warmer. Not like I got to
see much of it tho. A rasta mon got very mad
about the glass and tried to start a riot. Kept
yelling "you is some pig" but the riot never got
going bc nobody wanted to loose their place in
line. So I had jerk rabbit from a jamaican (sp?)
place for lunch w/rice and peas. Good but the
garlic made my stomach hurt. Puked it out the
bus window later. Fu manchu has been very
talky these days. Says a lot of personal shit to.
Asked me if I believe in love. I said it depends
on how many drinks and he laughed and farted
at the same time. He asked me if I think god is
real. I said probably not and he said what about
jesus. I said oh yes he is certainly real. A real
pain in the ass. He laughed and farted some
more. Then he asked me if I know that the
reflection in mirrors is just a rippel from
another dimension and he said sometimes he
doesnt even see his own and thats how he
knows bc he is a boat rocking guy who makes
big waves. I had a good joke ready but the bus
was smelling so fowl that I just said yes I
totally know what you mean. He also claimed

he fucked atlantis morissette n a parking lot in toronto once. That seems totally ridiculous to me for obvious reasons but the way he described the details seemed to real to be made up. Then blossom finkelstein was on the subway and I waved hello and she just stared at me all blank. I said "hey dont you remember me blossom. Its jack bender from cabin 3 eagle force. We went out all summer at camp ballibay once and I have never forgotten your tits." She said "oh thank you for remembering" and introduced me to her husband who was this tiny chinese guy sitting next to her.

Naked girl w/whip and guns $115
Panther $75
Teddy bear in death row orange $65
Snoopy w/machete (sp?) $85
Sexy honeypot $65
In loving memory of my darling claudia $55
George washington w/axe in head $70
Panther $75
Panther $75
Crucified clown $90
Beauty mark on butt $50

Oh yeah. Last nights dream. Riding in a 1971 dart. I was the loan ranger. Tonto was driving. We ran over the retarded black girl in the lincoln tunnel. I looked behind us and there was a bloody leg flying in the air w/a ruby red slipper on it. I asked tonto to stop so we can put the leg back and he just said "how"? I woke up to the phone ringing at 5am but was to afraid to answer. Also rented "sabrina".

"I attract wealth effortlessly."

LUIGI'S GAL-PAL WAS TALL AND PORCINE, friz sporting polymer bow. Bedecked via moist singlet and acid-washed shorts, the Troll was homologous to cargo. Beaming with pride as he ushered his bride through the swarm of Ebonic chockablock, excited frog's legs spryly can-canned like a chthonic/shopworn Offenbach.

"*My man...sorry we's late! Fuckin' bus-drivers can't do their jobs...marrone!*"

Chair-slumping deep, cremasters contracting, I barely suppressed a sobbed moan.

In order to streamline certain calamity, I'd pre-wrangled our parrot-flock, a move soon issuing curtains to amity when the bird hatched a 10-karat hawk. Spinebent to stencil a buttermilk calf, ovulation blitzkrieged my nostrils — the pursuant retch tensiled by Stiff Stuff-wafts/lactation/spritzed siege of sweat-fossils. As I reared back, Geraldine leaned heavily into a counter-perched, hi-topped Pony. Cursorily appraising the violet besmirch, she hawked glops of phlegm-macaroni.

"*Yeah, looks pretty good. Just how I like 'em since my divorce...long, solid, and thick!*"

Freshly punched, Luigi spat sniggers obediently
forced, fearful of strong/squalid kicks. Upon
my request for a preferred color-scheme,
the Troll was tasked arbitral duty.
   "Jeez. Dunno. Tough fuckin' call.
Um...how's 'bout Tutti-Fruiti?"

I'D ONCE HEARD AN INDUSTRY ADAGE:
'People get the tattoo they deserve!'
Geraldine's bird timpani'd brays savage.
Fecal.
Shrewd.
Berserk.
When the macaw's outline began to spawn an
electrocardiograph quality, I begged for calm,
invoking harsh/epitaphic causality.
   "Stop moving! Remember, this shizzle's forever!"
Alas, construing her *'cocksuckers'* for humor
soon proved a fizzled endeavor.
   "Yo, babe...I fuckin' swear...gonna knock this douche
out if he don't quit it! He's *hurtin'* me, Louie...
so fuckin' bad! Yeah, that's right...I admit it!"
   "Hon, my man's jus' doin' his job!
Gotta sit *still* for a while!"
   "But...*damn*...Lou, this really hurts!
Youse know cryin' ain't my style!"
   Acid-washed thwacks liberated plumes of
densely-sown/vaginal-funk. Pungency roamed thence-
and-whence, blooms of dildoed/sandalwood punks.

LEG MUMMIFIED WITH TRANSLUCENT
WHITE TAPE, her wallet emerged from a purse.
   Upon a claw's brusque attempt to stall it,
eyes glared the curse of a hearse.

"*What?* Kid did his job an' I'm gonna pay him!
Youse got some kinda *beef* with that?"
   A male-patterned mullet quaked side-to-side.
   Orbs queefed magnanimous tact.
   Redirecting his gaze, the Troll winked slyly,
peeling Franklins from an emerald cluster.
Smearing the moolah across my counter,
he presented a Jackson with bluster.
   "Hon, if youse thinks youse can *walk*, go get us some
cigs an' some joe. Grab the News an' Post too.
That bus'll be runnin' real slow..."
   He patted my shoulder. Garlic belched forth,
filling me with Nausea and Dread.
   "Fuckin' meatball parm! Want some
joe too? Maybe a Snapple instead?"
   Choking back bile as Geraldine
limped, Sickness hijacked my frame.
   (Five panthers danced from Cliff's lamp like pimps.)
   A slam triggered the Troll's greenback-reclaim.

From sugar packet: "if this is coffee please bring
me some tea but if this is tea please bring me
some coffee." — abe lincoln. I dont really know
what that means but I like the sound of it. A
dude at work told me that lincoln is part black
and thats why he freed the slaves...so his
family could be free. He said that babe ruth
is part black to. I asked where he got this info
and he said spike lee. Maybe there is something
to it? I always thought lincoln was jewish bc his
name is abraham and everyone hated him etc.
Speaking of jews isreal just killed a bunch of
arabs and they called it something about the

grapes of wrath. I wonder what john steinbeck
would think about that. Would he be proud?
Is he jewish to? Steinbeck sounds a lot
like steinberg. Probably jewish.

Betty boop farting $85
Panther $75
Mexican lady face w/roses $90
Chinese letters for "prince of zanzibar" $55
Mister lucky $75
Heart w/wierd name "paraphilia" (sp?) $65
Gorilla warfare $70
Panther $75
Phresh jamal portrait of self on arm $95
Panther $75
Panther $75
Panther $75

The dust is choking me all the time lately.
Asthma etc. Silver lining: it chokes
escaped crickets to.

"I see everything with loving eyes and I love everything I see."

**THE THRESHOLD-PAUSED POLACK
LOOMED MOTIONLESS** — stiff, apprehensive,
braced — as if surveying the drift of a volcanic
eruption from a distance adjudicated safe.
  Cliff's drunkenly harrumphed hello
was only a shorthair past fuzz.

My own regard belched likewise inchoate.
We were stuporous.
Threadbare,
Buzzed.
A young gay pimp had doffed a Havana Club
flagon one shitty/ho-raucous evening prior.
Our Sunday had been drubbed off-the-wagon.
Kitty Dukakis smote the TV-amplifier.

**KILROY ACCEPTED THE JOSTLED
CONTAGION** before waiving his right to sup,
sparking a thunderstruck/spitty rebuke
from a Cajun raving in cups.
*"Hey, cuz...what the fuck? Our rum not good 'nuff
for you? S'the Real McCoy! Bring ya luck!
Make all your woes say Adieu!"*
A pompadoured wisp wince-ruptured.
A nub smothered a hollow with shame.
Hangdogging eyes followed Sears engineers
asphalt had pothered 'til maimed.
"Sorry, Cliffy. No 'fense. Love some. Really I would.
I t'ink rum's real spiffy an' youse guys is great.
But...AA...wouldn't end-up too good..."
Pulling a chair aside, patting its tinny seat,
Cliff's glare nullified. A gaze glazed bittersweet.
"No, cuz. *I'm* the one who's sorry. Didn't know...
apologize sincerely. Takes a shit-ton of guts to assume
control and face the world so damn austerely.
Absolutely respect it. To me, you're
a real fucking man..."
My own pickled pea dissolutely reflected
a Catastrophe's caravan.

February, 1994

"Don't be cruel, Daddy! Give a sister down on her luck a
little bit of a break. Sick of this shit I already got! Houston
to Bender! Girlfriend's arm needs freshening-up!
Earthly contentment at stake!"

Botched knuckle repairs were one thing,
new engravings another entirely.

I'd never much fancied past-work revisits —
moments strewn with Hebraic anxiety.

Tech-imperfections would jailbreak skin
to torch cauldrons retaining self-loathing.

Thoughts of ogling ineptitude hillocks
raked brains like hair-woven clothing.

"Buster, Daddy! Give me Buster!
And jam a knife through his skull!"

"Okay," I sighed. "But where would you want it to go?"

The chalky white meat of an inner left
forearm was stroked post three-second lull.

"Here, Daddy! And do a good job!
Need something cool to flaunt at the show!"

Jotting the cat in 'Draw Tippy' fashion,
I imbued raw kernels with life.

Mulling future paths, fingers rushed mid-draft,
prophesying Doom down the pike.

The fleeting novelty of my slavish
devotion would soon indubitably fade.

David Bowie-types would spirit her off
on 'lude-and-champagne escapades.

Or perhaps Rockstarletry's soaring orbit
would render Love a Fahrenheit-mooted point?
 O cursed Spite...
That ever I was born to set things right...
Was Time not shorn out-of-joint?
 Sufficiently desperate to land a staid purchase,
I chutzpahed a Voodoo-sketch, concealing my name
within a blade's surface, scrimshawed via curlicued etch.
 Dispersing the glyphs skewed and far, to be discerned by
none but myself, 'twas a cloddish/unmystical/woebegone
riff swiped from an imbecile's mold-blossomed shelf.

 She feigned weepage upon each linear dash,
an exceedingly disruptive tactic.
 My pleas for repose were answered by Bronx
Cheer splash, restraint being anaphylactic.
 Was she somehow wise to the anchor install?
 Was this mockery in the face of my pathos?
 Despite bearing down like a Neanderthal,
aches clocked with the grace of a stray ghost.
 "Daddy...ever tell ya 'bout the time me and Jane
snorted-up all of ol' Oswald's ashes?"
 Could this inhuman creature even court pain?
 Sadness?
 Forgiveness?
 Compassion?
 Bending forwards, dipping its head, licking its flesh free
of clots, the dream girl beamed a gore-red smile
while my viscera twisted in knots.

"I glide through my days like a drake on a lake."

**A DRAGON-EGG LAURELED BY NEAT
HOARY WOOL** comprised Quincey Morris's head
— a codger of panache implying freeheld grasp
of the six molls mincing his tread.

Drawling backwoods, the black Hercules adjured
a scorpion veiled on his chest. Not as a totem of
pimp-diocese, but to bewail cautionary attest:

*"Mah ex-missus, boss, she were a scoipio! Dat dang
ho stung me all up! Put mah best shit in escrow!"*

Beneath the drill, the ponce confessed to bank-
heists of the 1960s. Halcyonic recall imbued
dank eyes with maudlin pines of quick-seize:

*"Such good clean fun it were too, boss! Tweren't all
brouhaha though. Hadda scram afta ev'ry job! Lay real
Gawd-dang low! Reckon ah hit fitty vaults, but ah was
allus real careful! Nevah did get caught! Sunday choich
kept me prayerful! Den ol' Sam...he come a knockin'!
Sunnovabitch done draft me! Put me in boots! Say
you a Marine! Shipped me off wit d'infantry!"*

Ogling the 'pen, the dragon-egg flailed
in tandem with packets of laughter:

*"Kids t'day dunno 'bout no shoots in no nails! Tantrums
a faggot-ass captors! Shit was rough, boss! Hadda clean
mah dingaling alla dang time or jungle-rot eat it
alive! Evah hafta kill bloodsuckin' leeches
by stickin' yo' thang in a hive?"*

"Um...define leeches."

*"Ya loin what a leech be dere foist — ain't got
no choice t'be lazy! Next ya loin Chinese food's
d'woist! Den all Peckahwoods is crazy!"*

"Pecker-what?"

*"Smaht boy like you dunno what no Peckahwood be?
Oughta be Gawd-danged 'shamed!"*

A coral palm rubbed my pitiful scalp
with good-natured/fatherly aim:

*"Peckahwood what we call a hillbilly — mo' propah den
Cawnpone an' Po'Trash. Mind ya, ain't got no truck wit'
whitefolk in gen'ril...jus' a fun way a slingin' some hash!
But ah tell ya, when we in dat jungle an' see dem V.C.
all fixin' to trot-up a ruckus, Peckahwoods jus' go runnin'
right at 'em, gettin' all shot-up in d'tuchus! Right at 'em!
Like dey be a big Christmas toikey! Sent dem fools home
t'dey's mamas all lookin' like boxes a joiky!"*

The grey brow furrowed with jagged grooves
upon queries of Tunnel-Rat peers:

*"Oh, let's not discuss dem niggas if'n ya don' mind...
crazier'n Peckahwoods ah feah! Jus' heed mah advice and
stay away from dem liahs should one evah cross yo' paff!
Bettah off rappin' wit' hairy-ass spidahs den
dose Gawd-dang snakes inna grass!"*

Called in sick yesterday which is never good
but more wierd tunnel dreams made me very
deppressed. The retard again and also ronald
macdonald. Kaki shorts was there to but he
looked different. Skinny and old and dried up.
He was leaning over the retard and I said hey
buddy get the heck off of her she is only a kid

and he just laughed and said Im ready for my close up. I said who the heck do you think you are asshole and he laughed some more and pointed to a mirror. Then ronald macdonald started singing "working to hard can give you a heart attack ack ack ack you ought to know by now" so I got the gun from the drawer and put a bullet in his left eyeball to shut him up. When I turned around the retard and the old man were gone and all that was left was broken glass and dust blowing around like a little oz twister. Next thing I know I am wearing the bloody clown suit myself. Charlotte and I spent the rest of the day doing exercises from "you can heal your life". This morning cliff thanked me for not showing up bc he set a new record. 23 tattoos including 9 panthers. And he keeps talking about bossnia like I should care about some place I never heard of. Also said the man in rayon came by again asking for me to. Its nice to be appreciated I guess. Gloria estefan is on leno now. Not very pretty but there is something about those hips. Petunia does not shake her hips like that. In fact they hardly move at all.

Panther $75
Beauty mark $50
Lickable honey $60

Yankees logo $65
Nubian teddy bear $70
Lipstick on butt $65
Golden glove champ $85
Panther $75

All the customers keep talking about some new yankee called cheater. I feel bad for him. Must really suck to be a athlete w/that name. How will anyone ever take the poor dude seriously? Also blood meridian is really f'n stupid. Just a bunch of gobbly gook. The picture on the back is wierd to. Doesnt look much like a writer. More like a guy who eats whipped cream for dinner. Rented "stalag 17". Eh.

"Thinking positively in tough situations is just something I do naturally."

RUPTURING IN TWAIN LIKE A COBBLE-STONED PEACH, the throng wailed before piping shut. A jettisoned bane of cellulose liege flew as gales sniped trees full of nuts.

The six-foot globule of natty jism scowled upon a landed survey. Within the rayon hull of a wacky prism, a mien troweled candid dismay. Cloaked beneath an aloof tarp, I soldiered-on with the task at-hand:

An obtuse teddy...

Strangling a heart...
Emboldened by simpleton-glands.
Whilst ink-charged tusks still stabbed away at ninety
snips per-second, a forearm was thrust flush with my
schnoz, eclipsing residual reckon. The naked bitch
riding the big-ass lion had healed beyond hopes
allowed, nary a hitch of keloid-scion dotting
the brown slope's corral.
"Sweet! Came out great! Thanks
for coming back to show me!"
Alas, the sprout failed to abate.
A stunning Rolex clacked slowly.
"That shit look *mad bright* to you? You think
that shit look *'sweet'*? Done *told* yo' ass I need
mad colors...not crap niggas can't see!"
Warily lowering hefty brass, I peered into
bristling orbs. Chiming in, my customer sassed —
resistant to leered platforms:
"Brotha, can you jus' let this man finish
mah deal fo' you go causin' a ruck?"
(A Vuitton billfold flashed a gold shield.)
"Bitch, shut yo' nappy-ass up!"
Peeling off gloves, I rose, commencing
a whispery attempt to assuage.
"Sir, understand my sole motive is Love, not
Dickering, Venting, or Hate. I'm not giving you a
runaround, and I'm not leading you on — your
satisfaction is paramount — but that's the best
freaking tattoo I can spawn! Remember how I used
the *glass* to beseech your ken even before we got
started? Regretfully, we've reached an impasse,
but it pains me you're so brokenhearted."

"*Listen,* I paid good money for this, and now I want the shit done right! You gotta realize that I ain't some *stupid-ass* nigga...I'm respectable/strong/polite! I work muthafuckin' *hard* at my job, and my money's damn green as yours! Same bright-ass paint the *white man* gets, that's all I'm askin' for!"

"But I *do* respect you and I *did* use the same inks... I'm sorry if it seemed to be contrary! That said, how can I eschew a physical jinx? I'm not a Houdini or Bradbury!"

CAUTIONING THE RAKE OF A FRESHLY HEALED WOUND being tantamount to a cicatrix invite, fearmongering staked a brief yield of Doom as Porsche-keys flickered prim spite.

"Okay, Tattoo-Man, no hard feelings, but gimme my *money's worth* when I'm back! I want every fuckin' paint on that damn shelf jammed-up in these crannies and cracks!"

WORMING MY WAY THROUGH THE BULLPEN BUSTLE, I spied a youth by the Unicorn-flash.
Gnawing grey ribs.
Chewing Byzantium muscle.
His castoffs fell forlorn/slapdash.
"Hey, buddy. Those'll get stuck to the carpet. Can you just toss the bones in that bin?"
"BITCH, THIS AIN'T BE NO FUCKIN' SLAVE-MARKET! AIN'T BE NO GONE WITH NO WIND!"
Reserving comment, I returned to my chair. Warm eyes brimmed at my shrug. As I spritzed green-soap, cleansing her bear, she leaned in to coil a hug.

Found a old dilldo on union ave the other
morning near the bicycle repair guy and put it
in the shrine. It is getting to be a 1st rate job as
far as shrines go. Lots of healing energy. Every
time I open the drawer and stand there for a
while I get a big hard on no matter what I am
thinking about. Every single f'n time. And if I
wake up w/a hangover then I just open the
drawer and boom it is gone to. Plus a new
hard on. Then after I close the drawer and read
the cards charlotte just stares at me and my
hard on like I am lincoln at gettysberg until I am
done speaking and if she is sat sfied that I have
done it right she goes back into her hut. If not
I just read them again and usually the 2nd time
is the ticket. That dilldo will probably be the last
new piece I add for a while bc I have not been
walking around so much these days. It is getting
to hot outside for me to go look for stuff. Less
about the heat really and more about the sun.
I mean I cant really stand being in the f'n sun
anymore at all. Sometimes it feels like I am just
about to bust into a big ball of fire. The ring
laughs at these moments to. Its pretty creepy.
Oh well there is always the shady side of the
street I guess and all my old wind breakers and
stetsons and ray bans to. Me and the moon are
still cool tho. Anyway I went to billys topless w/

avery after work. We smoked loco weed w/
some of the girls in the bathroom but then we
got tossed after avery pulled out a switchblade
and started stabbing the stage and a girls toe
got a little nick. He had to pay her $100 just
to shut up. What a nut! On the walk to his car
he took the knife out again and started cutting
up a pearl jam concert poster on the wall and
turned to me and said "jew". Didnt know what
he meant by that. Like if he was calling me a
jew or pearl jam a jew. But then I realized it
was me. On the drive home I told him about
my kaki shorts dreams and my old man dreams
and the tunnel dreams and the retarded black
girl dreams and my deppression and sadness
and hopelessness and deep feelings of being
lost and he just called me a jew again. I asked
him if he ever saw "network" bc I rented it
from kims the other night and he said no bc
that is a jew movie. He also said only a jew
would have a pet spider. So we talked
about cheater and the yankees and
porno mag 3 packs instead.

Beauty mark $50
Frankinstein monster w/dreads $90
Dice/cards/flames $65
Sexy cherrys $60
Panther $75

Outline of africa $60
Pit bull in diaper $80
Panther $75
Chinese letter for "newark" $50
Panther w/gester hat and blunt $85
Panther $75

Gotta start trying to get more rest bc I have been yawning a lot at work. It would be ok if I didnt drool so much when I yawn. Crickets are chirping. Nice bc it makes the bqe seem not so loud. I keep wondering who that dilldo belonged to. It is very long. Maybe a tall person? Tried to sniff it but my nose was to stuffed.   Kinda sad.

"The Universal Force is in every cell of my body and easily restores me to wholeness."

THE CONTESSA'S MAULISH/SOB-MANGLED YAWPS forced a yardwide phone-buffer. Alas, the cocked angle flopped solace-bereft.
   Such was her floodtide of suffer.
   Galvanized by maternal birthday-soirée, she'd chartered a Parisian Concorde; ushering skies duly stargazed to fit gowns Abyssinia could ill-afford.

With the gala now in close gawk, she was still
remiss of all togs. The Fedex DC toting her frock
had swished amidst chilled English fogs.
  "Listen, gotta bail, see?
Someone just sat in my chair."
  'Jackson! You're not being THERE for me!
  It seems like you don't even care!'

**THOUGH THE FLATTOPPED HISPANIC'S
MANNISH CLOBBER** clearly earmarked
Bulldaggery, this veneer was sheared by the
plexiglass topper of a below-the-knee amputee.
  "On my left wrist...I want a dolphin...
Papi, what all Flippers you got?"
  With the dogged persist of a smallish goblin,
her sapling outstripped mom-éclat.

**THE MADONNA AND CHILD ENDURED
CORPSELIKE...**rigid, blank, sans howl...vitality
seeping only through frigid eye-darts towards
a rank/gore-blighted lap-towel.
  "Let's just get this outta the way.
You been wonderin' strong on my leg..."
  Vigorous shakes of my pathetic scalp may as well
have belonged to fried eggs. Despite her son's
squawked farts, dull barks soldiered absently.
  "So I'm walkin' to work...near Liberty State Park...
when this maricón Dart just smashes me..."
  Vented skin below my face bled red-pelleted
deacons. Flaring fluorescents bestowed the
glaze with all-enveloping beacons.
  "Shit got really weird and calm. Kinda like almost
peaceful. Like I was already in the coffin embalmed. A
Stephen King novel...evil. Worst part about the recovery's

been just seein' my baby in danger. Carajito's been rippin'
the right legs off all'a his friends' Power Rangers. Says he
thinks I got hurt on purpose, so the doctors can take me
away. Padre tossed us from service last week for
dropped turds in the offertory plate..."

As I obscured pricked signals with
soaped Bounty, spermy brims renewed.

Perturbed brick vigils screamed:

"Revoke thy foul meat! Swim amongst germs unglued!"

September, 1993

After a quick East Fifth looksee, El decreed once quite
enough. Whoopee there was simply not meant to be.

(She beseeched a strict lighten-up.)

Deep within my fuselage, I pegged her reluctance
on Avery — the non-decorum and brute's visage
had steered a conductance of knavery.

She just doesn't get him, I solaced, thumbing the brass
ring for strength. His brusquerie though, to be fair, did
warrant some exegesis of length. Admittedly, I deemed, he
ain't too pretty. Certainly, I observed, he ain't too proud.

He might, I surmised, laugh a bit too loud.

But that never hurt no one.

Bellicose evenings slowly crept as I honed the blade of
a spade. Battery charged, I ordered sheets marred or
Hell duly be paid. Punctuating the edict via thunderous
thwacks of an indigo-suede wingtip, the magnificent
beast's vim only increased to waylay staccato guilt-
trips. Propelling me to the brink of rout,
she yielded at lachrymal droplets.

Alas, my glandular coup was a pond sans trout.

I'd thrown a rat's venal gauntlet.

As coarse jet locks absorbed saline,
she counseled maturities due.
  It was finally time for a crib of my own.
  To slay Youth's bugaboo.
  Her suggestion: North Williamsburg.
  A veritable No-Man's Land!
  "But why? There's nothing there.
I'd have no friends. I don't understand."
  "Because, Daddy...rents are cheap. I read all about it in
the Times. Because it's a good starting point for folks like
you...you're the write-up's true paradigm! Because
every man should have his own den. Because
a river should run between us..."
  Too preoccupied decoding 'folks like you,'
the night careened unlibidinous.

"It is normal for me to be completely relaxed and confident in social situations."

AS SLEEK AS A GOUACHE ERTÉ, palatially
Carlyle-ensconced, the birthday girl's posh
repartee was dialed via child-response:
  "Petunia, would your friend care for a fine cognac or
might he prefer a pale lager? Inform him that I had
Juan acquire some Trappists if he's familiar
with the handling of augers."

Like Maenad, Thylacine, Pixie, or Smurf, this was a
mystical thing. A creature ripped from the regal/
pulped turf of Blueblooded/Whartonian bling.

A spoon's crisp clanks against clear crystal
spurred swift/swank/swiveling leers.

"Meine freunde! Danke! Lend me thy sniveling ears!"

The Count! Tall. Yacht-burnt. A wiry auburn-fleeced
globe. A stout frame hurt by a tiny tux-frock
beseeched a boxcutter-disrobe.

"How my heart so very much swells to share
this momentous occasion! It swells and it swells
and it swells! Beyond all orgasmic pervasion!"

Wrenching free from gravity, arcing legs felinely,
the noble fop flopped atop a bergère's ancient
finery. Oblivious to fragility, heels Whitechapel
rippers, clouds of pink particulate
blighted patent opera-slippers.

"Hail terse codger Blake! Radiguet! Lincoln of
the schvartzes! Cursing slaves with Freedom's
goo and craves of Golden Arches!"

Searing brands within my hand stoked fleet exams
of source. Red orbs coked volcanic damns.

Daily heat of small brass corpse.

"Hail an ex-wife so divine! Fifty years above Terra!
We quoth the raven to screech L'CHAIM
and cheer our beloved chimera!"

A CELEBRATED JEWISH LESBIAN had not
much to say. A truncated/shrewish thespian's snoot
was surgically snipped away. A confident Roman
wearing multiple hats was of obvious patrician
descent, vending Fiats to Russia, 'X' to Larvotto,
and landmines to the Near Orient.

Another guest was a stretched monsieur of my own
approximate age, performing profane legerdemain
of a farfetched/high-calibered sage. With a tired,
humdrum approach veering nigh-prosaic, the
necromancer yawned whilst an astonished
Bichon hovered past Byzantine mosaics.

My admiration for the skilled craft distended
beneath opulent coffers, where a fly suspended
to release swilled draughts revealed a
Spaded Ace lodged within boxers.

Despite the mirth this plant provoked, there was no
suppressing shudders. Such devious traits, unbound
by yokes, were immune to Morality's udders!

**DURING A PARLOR-DOLE OF COFFEE AND
SCHNAPPS** I was smashed against damask paper.
Seizing my wounded right paw, the Count
splashed my tragus with vapor.

"And *why* is this canary so damnably blue?
Is it so very unhappy to be there?"

"The reason primary is you've misconstrued.
It's a barn-swallow. Half a matched pair."

"Ah! And *what*, may I ask, do they symbolize?
Nothing's accidental, you know? The Jungian
in me is inclined to analyze. I take it
you're a *swallower*, Romeo?"

"Um...they just, like, keep my fists flying. I guess..."

"*A fister!* I see! The daughter's fruit stayed snared
to the tree! Should've expected no less!"

Without warning, falling pants unsheathed
a pompadour-shaped hip nevus.

Beneath the tumorous coif, William Holden's
mien was mole-toupéed amidst a scape of stiff penis.

"Your thoughts, junge taube? Do you LIKE it? Tell me now, please, with candor. You think what? Höflichkeit verdammt! Does it fall in accord with your standards?"

Gawking with shock at the botched smear, I took note of etched eyes unstatic. Greywashed blears darted madly about, defying all logic emphatic!

What *witchery* had condemned a poor soul to this foul cell of courtly groinflesh?

A karmic atrocity?

God's ballroom monstrosity?

Beelzebub's purloined Hell-crèche?!!

There were some words fingered into the dust on the mirror this morning that I dont remember putting there. Does not look like my hand writing but who knows bc I was pretty drunk last night. 'INVALUERIT PURITATEM'. Must have copied it off the back of some money. I meant to ask cliff what that means but I forgot. Hot as chicken grease today. Triple whammy to! More glass complaints and EZ red disasters and rayon man. Yell yell yell! Yell yell yell yell yell! Everyone yells! They all yell like its gonna change things that just cant be changed. Or maybe they are just blowing off steam. I do understand the need to do that. I just wish it was not right in my face. Pretended to be asleep on the bus so I didnt have to talk to fu manchu then went to coney island high. Thought I saw eddie heartless and went over to say hello but it was just that matt dillon creep again. His pick up line is "hi Im matt dillon". I saw him lay it on a bunch of different chicks. It worked w/the 5th. At least she was the 5th by my count bc there may have been more before that. Just for fun I went up to this one bimbo w/big cans and said hi Im matt dillon and the dude tapped her on the shoulder and said "no he aint bc I am". She was the 5th btw. That was the girl he got.

Panther $75

Chinese letters for "long tall sally" $55

Rest easy now mama $60

Dragon w/opium pipe $100

Broken heart $60

Panther $75

Nubian julian $65

Panther $75

Panther $75

Panther $75

Sexy cherrys w/extra juice $60

Panther $75

Found a 1933 wheat penny in my change. Put it in the shrine between the broken switch blade and the purple lace panties. Also charlotte is out of crickets. Note to self: buy crickets.

She says she prefers the little ones.

"The more I give to others the more I realize I have to give."

IT WAS A DARK AND STORMY NIGHT,
teetering on the brink of raging. As our clientele
largely inclemency-spurned, eventide had crawled
sans engraving. Cliff and I sat twiddling our thumbs
whilst Roy Orbison waxed turmoils feminine/morose.

The poor sap sounded yet sadder 'neath rain.

Pathetic.

Lachrymose.

With Ma Bell's clang a masculine voice expressed
matters of grave concern; the asylum absconsion of
a Nutley internee, a schizoid of insalubrious yearn.
Allegedly consumed by the blazing recall of a sister
erstwhile chewed-up and carved, the escaped had
declared a sororal memorial as the object for which
he most starved. With the precipitatory fusillade all
but crippling John Law's vigilant trawl, every Essex
County scab-vending annex was being alerted
to the walking psychotic pitfall.

Thanking the 'doctor' sardonically, lowering the
wireless-receiver, I précised the tidings to Cliff,
who deemed them a craft of deceiver. We rarely
minded such rudimentary jeers being riled by the
competition, a supplementary wit-veneer being our
lone criterial condition. This stab, however, so reeked
of quiescently uninspired bosh, that I swiftly divined
it the mental flab of the recently hired or sloshed.

BURSTING AJAR WITH SUDDEN ERUPTION, the threshold admitted torrents of rain and debris, immediately snuffing our reciprocal launch of warranted tomfoolery.

A tall/gaunt/Karloffian obstruct lurked drenched within the portal's gape; cardigan cryovaced, eldritch eyes glossed, scalp shorn via straight-razor scrape. Bolts striking, clouds growling, the wizened ghoul ambled forward; stalling with the room only half-traversed; his bawl — stern/stoic/stalwart.

"MY FATHER IS IN THE AIR FORCE AND HE SAID I CAN HAVE A TATTOO THAT SAYS 'LINDA' FOR MY SISTER! I LOVE MY SISTER! I LOVE MY LINDA! I WANT A HEART WITH LINDA! MY FATHER IS IN THE AIR FORCE AND HE SAID THAT I - I - I - THAT I - I - I - THAT I COULD HAVE MY - MY - MY LINDA!"

Mandible sinking in double-take, I slipped Cliff the 911 hi-sign, approaching the counter with hand extended for shake as my peer john-dashed to hail swine.

"Hi, buddy...I'm Jack. What's your name?"

"RONALD! RONALD! I AM RONALD AND I WANT LINDA HERE! HERE! HERE!"

Punctuating his words autopugilistically, with genuine force applied, I feared for both the lunatic's left arm and my own homicide. Fang-honed canines spied, I envisioned my face as chewed meat, fearing too for a countenance already challenged sans Necrophagy.

"LINDA! LINDA! LINDA!"

Time's unfurl found my friend phone-fettered.

Acuity was ransacked for plans.

How did one stall an incestuous head-case... a wet/wroth/windigo-man?

Settling upon a townhall approach, let's-talk-about-you blarney ensued, the Lunatic responding at Gatling-gun speed with salvos of verisimilitude.

"I like your haircut, Ronald."

"TYRELL CUT IT! COLORED, BUT I DON'T GIVE A HOOT! HE SMELLS LIKE POTATOES AND I LIKE POTATOES! THAT IS MY MOST FAVORITE FOOD!"

"What's your favorite movie?"

"BILLY JACK!"

"And who's your favorite ballplayer?"

"MUSIAL!"

"Aha. So you're from St. Louis then?"

"HACKENSACK!"

"Hmph. That's unusual..."

Spotting a soft lime smudge beneath a right wrist, optics automatically squinted. My chin tucked tightly with the claw's shrivel-to-fist.

An old fractured Hamilton glinted.

"And...um...what's that signify, Ronald? The cross on your hand, I mean."

"CELTIC FROM IRELAND! THAT'S HOW COME IT'S GREEN!"

"Ah...so you're Irish. Yeah, that makes sense."

(Like a Reaper sowing virus-galore, the mien grew forebodingly tense.)

"NOT IRISH! POLISH! SAME AS STAN MUSIAL! NICKNAME: THE MAN!"

"Favorite food?"

"BLACK PUDDING!"

"Democrat?"

"I LIKE IKE! UNDERSTAND?"

IF THE LUNATIC FOUND MY INQUIRIES 'OFF', his unflinching demeanor betrayed nada. I was pondering the same coolness ushering Linda's quietus when Cliff's resurface blazoned a rallied armada.

Thunder! Lightning!

Moist air pinkening with blush.

Three cruisers glided to calcified halts as the Lunatic surveyed the fuzz-crush. A puddle of gold seepage haloed ruint loafers as six dampened blueshirts entered. A serpentine 'O' formed as they fondled truncheons and holsters.

The terrified fugitive was centered.

Diving partition-bound, he grabbed at me wildly, teary-eyed/sanctum-imploring:

"NO! NO! NO! PLEASE MAKE THEM GO AWAY AND LEAVE ME BE! I AM RONALD AND THESE MEN ARE BORING! MY FATHER IS IN THE AIR FORCE! HE SAID I COULD HAVE LINDA! HE SAID I COULD! HE SAID! HE SAID! HE SAID!"

Snubbing the pleas with a curt swivel, my blank sternum flooded with Dread.

CONTRARY TO RONALD'S VAST AGE AND HEIGHT, the bulls addressed him as a tyke of pubescence. As glib tones prodded and mocked, my conscience beamed a shrike's phosphorescence.

The *spider*, I lamented, would be shocked at the depths of my finkness. Verily, I am a Judas.

"No! You have been my friend," Charlotte vented.

"That in itself is a tremendous thing, in a world rife with barracudas!"

A constabulary conferment deliquescing to skirmish sparked a graceful act of Defiance; Ronald's *'Billy Jack'* homage was a threshing dervish, decking faces with painful sweet-science. Landing kicks and chops with precision aplomb, he'd transformed to Laughlin's oracular halfbreed — even Mace, Taser, and FlexiCuff qualms unable to retard the valiant warrior's creed.

Breathing fire upon his fated extraction...

Airborne-ensnared and spread-eagle...

Declarations resounded as magnificent combustions...

Cherry-red.

Dead regal.

"MY...FATHER...IS...IN...THE AIR FORCE!"

Uncoiling a nervously coshed issue of *'George'*, Cliff gassed as he examined its cover, fingering the Hitler-faced penis I'd scrawled on Drew Barrymore's chest, who'd struck me as desirous of lovers.

"GOT US A SITUATION HERE, FELLAS... turns out the gent's a voluntary internee...free to leave as he sees fit. We lift one more finger, *boom*, scary attorney. Sorry, can't really do shit."

"So...you're saying what exactly?"

"If you *wanna* give him a tattoo, no law says why you can't. But, hey, buddy...wouldn't recommend it. I mean...*you saw*...this guy's violent!"

SHOULDERING HIS WAY THROUGH THE STREAKY GLASS DOOR — uric, orbs cayenne-grazed — a rope of cochineal drool stalactited Ronald's fine chin, yet he was calm/mayhem-unphased. Lowering himself into a chair, our interview duly resumed, answers emitting quietly hoarse, his larynx bellow-consumed.

Favorite animal: *Moth.*
Favorite bald man: *Phil Silvers.*
Favorite rock-group: *The Adirondacks.*
"Want some java, Ronald? Good for a cough.
I take it when I have asthma attacks."
　Bloodied saliva echoing jerks of its source,
Cliff flicked Mister Coffee on.
　Religiously unkempt for Flavor's sake,
the machine pissed a thick Cuban spawn.
　Slurping his Bustelo peacefully, slobber
sundering with a cup's crumple-and-toss,
Ronald droned along to *'Sweet Caroline'*
while I sketched in homage to love-lost.
　As I squinted to erase a mistake,
screels rattled Sanity's chains.
　"Are you a worm or a snake, Daddy?
Are such schlemiels not cosmically ordained?"
　Slithering to Cognition's forefront, venomous
memories swarmed...fly-specked byproducts
of long-ago yarns imparted by an
oldtimer fistically formed.
　According to the codger's eyewitness-
account, Charlie Wagner, a debauched purveyor of
scab, was digging a dagger-pierced heart in a swabbie's
forearm when synapses whiskied mid-stab. Upon the
final smearing of sponge, the sailor's lead jaw dropped
— his spirits tumbling in precipitous plunge as he
fathomed a knife's blade arrowhead-swapped.
　My drawing, of course, was a faithful
tribute to Yesteryear's inglorious error.
　Ronald approved sans any rebuke.
　Cliff gaped with censorious terror.

AS THE LUNATIC REFASTENED HIS MOIST CARDIGAN, I proclaimed the funds-due a mere fifty, having discounted the price by some twenty percent to temper my ignominy.

Swollen knuckles groped about pockets.

His return gaze wore a veil of Mistrust.

(I telepathically implored blazed saw-cuts.)

Alas, two rubbed quarters were thrust.

Wierd one last night. Almost like a news reel narrated by walter windchill. Starts off normal then turns into the story of holden joining a cult. So I was holden and saw everything thru his eyes. It is 1949ish and the cult is focussed around the worship of ventriloquist (sp?) dummys in the form of little retarded black girls. The worshippers hold the dummys as they pray. There are tape recorders in the dummys that lead to head phones that play loops of a choir singing the words "happiness, Ill do my thing" in a slow chant. Subliminally in the chant are rules of the cult. There were a lot but I cant remember them now. I think one was "only eat the guilty". They gather in a large oval shape in a tunnel w/lots of bats flying around. The walls are mirror lined. They stare at their own reflections as they pray and kind of shift in place like those jews from the south side w/the charles dickens clothes. Then holden quits the movie biz and moves to asbury park. Its a misty fall morning. Walter windchill explains that holden is a solid citizen as we see shots of him picking up stray pieces of litter. Some of the trash he throws into a drawer shrine. Some he tosses into the ocean. Shots of the cult in the tunnel are scattered around the garbage collecting bit. The "happiness, Ill do my thing" chant can be heard all the while beneath the sound track. He walks down the boardwalk and stumbles on a outdoor flee market filled w/unfinished art projects and sideshow banners. There is one w/my picture that says "see the worlds loneliest boy! is he alive or dead?" It gives him the willys and he begins to feel ill. Now it is 1981 and we are in nyc. Its like reenacted footage from americas most wanted. Hes been filming his comeback movie on location and hes very resentfull of the term "comeback". Billy wilder has ended his retirement to direct the film. Billy wilder has also joined the retarded dummy cult and has become a out of control drunk and is constantly provoking the actors and crew into violent misschief. A bunch of clips illustrate this point. After billy wilder molests the key grip holden is fed up and steals a dodge dart from the set to drive around manhattan. He breaks every traffic law imagineable. The cult chant gets louder in the background. He begins to sweat like a candle melts. His head bleeds. There is tissue stuck to the blood. He turns the wrong direction on a one way street and floors the gas. The sedan can be seen from a aireal (sp?) view w/a spotlight from a hellicopter shining up the night. As he speeds towards brooklyn he somehow climbs ATOP the w'burg bridge driving OVER the cables and support beams. That he is saying FU to the laws of physics seems not to matter. The only thing on his mind is buying wine to distribute to the cult members who are all dying of thirst. The car can be seen from a long shot. The city is glowing in the background like a cheesey model. The car veers off the bridge and dives into the river hood first. The dream ends w/me (as myself) finding a empty spot in the tunnel cult oval. The one left empty by holden. I pick up his dummy and put the head phones on. El is next me w/tits bigger then ever. She looks at my dummy and says "would your friend care for a glass of fine cognac?" I look in the mirror to pray but see only the dummy and kaki shorts floating.

Panther $75
Liberty bell $75
Alf w/afro $85

See low dice $50
Panther $75
Jesus saves $80
Panther $75
Nefertiti $65
Panther $75
Heart w/shaniqua $60
Garfield strangling od $80
Panther $75
Beauty mark $50
Panther $75
Panther $75
Panther $75

Fu manchu was sad bc his wife is leaving him and she is not taking their baby son who has down syndrome w/her. She says she is to young to be living in hell. He explained that she doesnt understand the meaning of family bc her people are from norway where everyone is born with a frozen heart. He asked if I would tattoo the words "think twice" on his wrists sometime for a discount. I said ok bc I felt bad for him. I told him about my dream w/o describing the retarded dummies bc I didnt want to make him more sad. He pretended to be asleep and snoring while I was talking even tho he was driving a bus. Maybe he should think twice about sitting in my chair.

"I am secure in my body and celebrate its sexuality."

FESTERING WITH RONALD-SOAKED GUILT,
antidotes were mulled on Fu Manchu's rolling
Greyhound. Gristedes? Hooch? Sweat? Colonics?
   Karaoke at Winnie's downtown?
   Coitus comprehensibly conquered the confab,
concluding consecrated champeen.
   Climaxes, Cliff clarified calmly,
were analogous to spiritual aspirin.
   "Yeah, dude," concurred our chariot-captain's
corpulent/crag-creviced countenance.
   *"Nothin' livens me up more than fresh poon! But only
top-shelf! Got a rep to maintain! Like some regal-ass
broad from France! Tellin' ya, stupid Weegie cunt has no
fuckin' clue what kinda animal she's unleashed! Biggest
favor she coulda done! I'm an esurient sexual beast!"*

FRAZZLED FINGERS WEARILY WALKED to
reach out and touch young Petunia; five faulty phones
filching ten full bits 'fore finally striking mechanutia.
Slamming handset-to-cradle, I spat and I wailed,
overcome with Ludditian ire; yuppies dodging my
maledictory flues, leery of lexiconical fire. Stalling,
pausing, breathing, believing, I affirmed 'til Temperance
regathered. Dialing anew, I message-imbued digits
dictated from a receiver germ-slathered. Booth-
perched, I awaited callback whilst wooly Authoritites
oozed bile; overtly disdaining Caucasoid-trespass
as they slithered past mop-deprived aisles.

An hour passed before stakes were pulled
and I sniffed at a dull/pallid palm.
   Red eyes burned amidst a semen aroma.
   "Least it ain't scat," I wisped, not
assuaging the skull's valid qualm.

THE BEAUTY BAR, A DIM-LIT SALOON,
was populous, smoke-blued, and raucous. Eno's
crankage begat mystery — his croon hardly
warranted amperes of Bacchus. Fortuitously
procuring a stool unmanned, I glimpsed two girls
parked adjacent; though such nominal-design was an
affront to Fact's span, mere linguistic complacence.
   A brunette was closest. Waxen, pulp-crushed, and
painted. False eyelashes mushed by bangs perilously
low bespoke lineaments promiscuity-tainted.
   "Buy you gals some drinks?" I asked as she leaned,
spying roots frosted with silvery hoar. Braying akin
to a Tourette's pony-din, she whinnied several times
more. Examining a smile likewise equine — broad,
toothsome, gummy — I surveyed an inferno-haired
chum wielding a pan more winsome,
alas shading bosoms less plummy.

**CABBING TOO FAST TWIXT-BOROUGH/
CROSS-BRIDGE,** neighs sprayed bereft of
pulchritude. "Brooklyn, eh? Like, who the *fuck* lives
there? You some kind of *poor* little dude?"
   That a Canuck-cadence had slinked by detect left
me abjectly crestfallen. Bloviation spiking like a sonic
brain-hammer soon forced behests of Ghost Stalin.
   "Comrade, be quiet! Show some respect!
   There are lyudi here old and asleep!"
   (Alas, this vygovor proved only snigger-bait more.)
   "Bah! You act eight fucking years-old!
Don't be such a ninnyish creep!"

Door scarcely locked, keys still jingling, a crotch-slap
was peppered with barks. *"Fancy slacks, eh?*
Off with 'em now! Got business to tend in the dark!"

Dropping trousers for Comfort's sake, not that of
mindful compliance, I folded and hangered whilst she
scanned affirms, scoffing at blind pseudoscience.

AS MY CLOSET SLOWLY SLID SHUT,

a crepuscular sight hewed dumb. Shorn wrappers
and binds exposed dyad juts blighting the doctrines
of Newton. Wales of blind-sifted luminescence sliced
at the flesh of an obscenely molded baguette. Yanking
down at the ceiling-lamp's chain, a spotlight raked
veins sheened by Mortality's debt.

Unmindful of the gesture's innate cruelty, I jerked
the chain once more, sundering my shirt with a
truant's glee, pearlized-discs ricocheting the floor.

"How's a stringbean like you gonna give
a gal like me anything close to a good lay?"

Open-palming with all needed force, she sunk like
a ruptured soufflé. Scooping aloft, pivoting heels, I
loosed the heft to the bed. Teats flopped like custardy
meal. She bounced whilst underwear shed.

LABIA-PROBING WITH CURSORY STROKES,

I discovered pink folds pre-slickened. Plunging my hilt
with a decisive poke, her mollusk reduced as pace
quickened. *Not too shabby,* I mulled. *Not too shabby at*
all! Perhaps year-forty wasn't Death's indisputable moll?

With the violence of thrusts, breaths became
screams, exposing teeth bloodied and fulvous;
transmogrifying my spur to a unicorned-lance.

Ivorian! Inflexible!
Bulbous!

*"God! Like, oh my God, eh! You're
gonna break me in half, Moosedick!"*
Another backhand kiboshed this insipid jibjab.
A lower-lip split with the flick.
She beamed beatific as I vacuumed the wound,
spitting gore to vast pallets of breast; garlanding
her sternum with an apoplectic festoon.
(A hemophiliac's heraldic crest.)
*"Hear me, Hercules? Said
you're gonna break me in half!"*
"My name...ain't...Hercules...it's *'Daddy'*, you fucking
whore! Get that straight and remember it
fast or I'll thrash you raw thrice more!"
All of a sudden, vaginally entombed, I felt so alone.
Adrift and marooned. A moonwalking stray,
floating in space, forever at bay, the last of a race.
Glancing to Charlotte for speedy relief, my gaze was
greeted from within a hut's reef — progress minded
by eight resolute eyes — accepting/non-
judging/adoring/cute/wise.
"Salutations," said she, standing placidly still.
Spinning away, my brain went blank,
rancid with red/harlot swill.
All around us, dust-motes swirled.
A vest-pocket cosmos. Miniature worlds.
Flaunting, taunting, dangling escape.
Not in want of further haunt, I continued to fixedly
rape, flipping the body around, pillows flushing
with garnish, mooring the mien firmly down,
ignoring sad bellows mid-carnage.
This was surely no aspirin, I'd now assiduously
learned. Damning Cliff's scowling grin,
I adjured Charlotte to turn.

November, 1994

Along came the night of the Spitbacks showcase at
Greenwich and Spring Street's Don Hill's, an affair
of which I'd heard such copious prate that
I'd ceased scraping ear of wax-pill.

A new bank account, Hudson-corpse bloated, would float
all the Pat Field's that she pined! A Fire Island timeshare,
blazed queens included, consumed her fame-famished
mind! A&R bigwigs waving covenants fat would skew her
life this way then that; rocketing her past the dull echelons
segregating Guttersnipe from Aristocrat! Accolades...
rightfully hers all along...finally flying home to roost!
Just deserts chiseling her name beside
Piaf, Picasso, and Proust!

Alas, I thought, it was myself alone who'd enabled such
fraught. Utterly complicit, I'd been an open wallet; a
walking Fort Knox, silently dream girl trailing, green
blanketing every comfort sought with a prodigal
fidelity's unfailing. Despite this staunch/unwavering
support, I didn't even rate the guest-list. Eight bucks
admission to see my own girl's band; pique
quickly granulated to cyst.

A thumb/finger clamp folded protests shut like a small
waxed carton of milk. "Shhh-shhh, Daddy-Daddy!
Tut-tut! So tacky to cover-charge bilk!"

Asking myself what choice did I have but to simply ingest
such flaws, I rationalized eight dollars as a meaningless
speck. One panther's perfunctory claws.

Though the stage was Stygian and the drums spread
pell-mell, the club brimmed early wanton and rake.
Bolstering a forbearance diaphanous at best, I quaffed gin

with the vim of a hick-fleeing snake. A passing stranger,
Camel Lights 'twixt folds, muttered of a liquored-up/dizzy
broad; the gash in his forehead a sight to behold,
leaking red with each quake of his jaw.
  "Oh, she's in the fuckin' basement, yo! Just decked me
with a fuckin' ashtray! Dunno how you're so patient, bro!
Bitch wrecked the whole pre-show soirée!"
  Alas, my progress was nipped at the stairs by a sentry
gargantuan and homely. "Whoa there, whiteboy!
Whatchu got? V-Eyed Peas an' delivery-boys only!"
  Two drinks further, feeling sloppy enough, I shadowed
some skins to the head. Both short, twig-lean, full-sleeved,
shrew-mean, their grins underpinned sins left unsaid.
  A glass vial's stall-shaded reveal spurred fingers to
bill-coiling action, narc-fueling a Somnambulist's zeal,
heralding rampant stupefaction. Snooty runts proved
snotty cunts! Combed scalps went muss! Shattered
chalices shrilled! Quips oozed like lewd pus! A foreign
barman implored sex! I punched his pierced nostril! An
outraged donnybrook swiftly ensued, crestfalling
the spurned Austral! Fleeing the sweaty/scary ruck, I
smashed to a clamorous halt. Debbie Harry glared,
angry as fuck, a pillar of glamorous salt!
  The old star paused, smoothing her blouse as eyes shook
free of cornsilk. Stroking my hand, she curbed our
rouse with a wry familiarity of low ilk.
  "Hey, go easy on the mambo-dust, toots!
  Shit can kill ya, y'know?"
  Pressing lips to a leeward left lobe, inspiring florid wafts
of Chanel, gentle murmurs imparted desperate probes of
a childhood's memorial knell: "Listen, I've loved you since
nine! Even recall first hearing 'Parallel Lines'! See, my
mom was always fucking these strange dudes and —"
  The Old Star's right palm caught my left ear,

installing a dog-whistle pitch.
"Thanks a mill for sharing...you insensitive/gristly bitch!"

The introductory strains of 'CRIME DE MENTHE'
strummed — an anthemic ode to poisoned rapists.
Fifty palms dais-raised a messiah buxom.
Loads of pit-moistened papists.
Boot-gazing, mane hanging, pallid arms stretching taut,
vinyled thighs echoed the discordant clanging
of four three-chord juggernauts.
Grasping the mic, caressing its shaft, lids clenched for an
eon's expire. Carmined lips bleated obscene telegraphs
of stepfathers and daughters strife-mired. A claw crushed
a crotch 'til knuckles paled white. Its owner reflexively
screamed. The audience blared in orgasmic delight,
beerjaculating a hundred vexed streams.
Above the throng, a puck shrieked from Beyond:
"Not yours, chump! She's Eternity's!"
Dying for grog, I'd commenced a bar-slog
by the dubious words of verse three.

Siphoning nostrum from a Rolling Rock's gape, a stray
bottle's heel smashed my own. Stumbling asswards, my
tongue surveyed reshape sufficient to stoke sad groans.
Too stunned for true anger, I warily rose, fists balled/brow
furrowed. Spying no certain smoking-gun languor, into the
crowd I re-burrowed. Spitting out gore as I shimmied,
a payphone provided quicksilver. My left front tooth
was an abject bust, cleaved diagonally off-kilter.
A firm shoulder-thwack broke a deep trance of Self.
I spun to face its source.
Heinie a'jostle, the Old Star belched.
Triumph obscured all remorse.

"My faith flaps free of all sully."

TIRE-KICKERS FLITTED LAZILY ABOUT,

horseflies skirting manure. Rents being due, thirty-firsts meant drought. A most fortuitous lull to be sure. It was once again time to face Damnation.

(And Avery fared best amid isolation.)

Sunlight stabbed through a shattered glass door.

AS THE SAVIOR'S WHIPPED SHADES DULY COMMENCED, the Detective's spirits ran spry.

Freckles jiggled as giggles dispensed.

He regarded a beleaguered hi-fi.

"This 2 Tone crap makes me think a this black broad usta be 'round CBGBs. BimSkaLaBim and Toasters gigs mostly. Always fronted like she couldn't see me..."

Glancing towards the bullpen's gape, the big man shrugged and spat. A fat woman beating a toddler's nape was swinging a plastic Rugrat.

"Wasn't like these jigs out here. Had a nice mellow/yellow pelt. English was impeccable too. This nig tweren't raised in a veldt! Tried mackin' it a million times. She always just shoots me down. And it's wrackin' my fuckin' *pride*, bro! Even tried losin' some pounds! So one night again at CB's, when I'm near three sheets to hammered, I spot this broad drinkin' a Sea Breeze, and get totally fuckin enamored! So I stroll to the bar, slide next to her, order a beer from the keep. Ask the bitch if she wants another. She sneers like I'm some kinda creep! I'm like, 'Yo! What the fuck's your problem? You act like

I'm Jack the Ripper!' And she looks at me, real fuckin'
solemn, asks if I dig Squirrel Nut Zippers. And she
talks with this real *hifalutin* voice! Like Alexis fuckin'
Carrington! I wanna say 'FUCK NO! SCREW THAT
NOISE!' but instead just play good samaritan. I go,
*'Why ya always gotta shoot me down? I asked you out
one million times! What is it? I'm just a big stupid clown?
Is bein' Irish a fuckin' crime?'* She says somethin' about
hatin' cops. I go, *'Yo! I hate 'em too! Ten more years and
ka-boom! Pensioner in Malibu! Can't blame blacks for
hatin' us! Most fuzz think your people are junk! Shameful
way to do the good folks who gave us Willie Mays and
P-Funk!'* She nods. *'Brother, you really have no idea! Even
though my father's a doctor, he's treated like diarrhea!
Pulled over all the time! Least once every week!'* She says
he drives a Volvo. I tell her the dude's oblique. *'If he
got hisself a maroon de Ville, his problems would instantly
vanish!'* She covers her grin with some swill. Says, *'I'm
Linda Lee!'* in Spanish. We stay for another round,
then blow CB's for tacos. Yo, bro! Need the
john! Cool your jets, Picasso!"

SCOOTING IN DEFERENCE TO VAST GIRTH,
I wheeled towards the bullpen and squinted.
  The Ogress was past thrashing her birthed.
  (The Bruised Wren disconsolately glinted.)
  *"Need me some shit on my left titty!
  How long Jesus gon' be?"*
Scanning a wrist of impenetrable pith,
I forsook the scabbed crudity.

A ROARING FLUSH OF BROADCAST RELIEF
heralded a triumphant young crapper. Shimmies
slushed the Savior's mien as Avery
burlesqued a punk flapper.

"So we go to her fuckin' place, and her bed's got
these _mint_ fuckin' sheets. Thick, smooth, creamy silk
satin. And whatever I say she repeats! Like, if I go, '_Oh
God!_' she says, '_Oh God!_' If I say, '_Feels good!_'...the same.
And I kinda wanna test things out...tinker around
with her brain. So, '_Just like that!_' gets a '_Just like that!_'
'_You're the best, babe!_' echoes too. Then I yell, '_I fuckin'
love waffles!_' just to see what she'll do!"

"C'mon..."

"_Yeah_, bro! Screams about waffles all sortsa awful
and I'm feelin' real bad for her neighbors! But when
she hops on top and starts caulkin' my stalk, dudes
upstairs begin blastin' Slayer! To get even, I tell this
broad, '_Fuck my nigger pussy!_' Sure enough, she starts
screamin' that shit with a vigor that soon overtook
me! She's ridin' real hard and fast, like I'm some kinda
Quarter Horse — yawpin' that shit over-and-over,
battlin' those douche power-chords! And she's shakin'
around like a fuckin' jackhammer, makin' Seka into
Shirley Temple, still screamin' away about her
nigger-ass jammer! Shit was absurdly mental!"

"Classic..."

"Hold-up! So, we finish, her breathing slows down,
then she gets up for a shower. And I'm layin' on silk...
all wet from sweat...feelin' like I got super-powers.
I mean, _finally_, after so many months, I got to nail this
black cunt! Felt like I'd scaled ol' Everest or collared
some perp on a hunt! And she yells out from the
bath. '_Hey copper, come fuck me in here!_' But then
when I stand, the sheet lifts with my ass,
and I realize my luck's disappeared."

"..."

"So I cross myself, pray real quick, and yank the damn thing from my cheeks. You can probably guess what came next...let's just say an unfortunate leak. I think about rinsin' it off in the kitchen, but don't wanna discuss why it's soaked. And she's still howlin'. *'Get in here right now, copper, or your license to thrill is revoked!'* So I throw on my gear, crack a window, and toss the mess to the street. And in the stairwell, I'm fuckin' chucklin', thinkin' I pulled off a feat. But as soon as I hit those cobbles, all a my blood lags cold."

"Forgot your wallet?"

"Nope. Shitty sheet was snagged to a lamp, blowin' like a flag from a pole."

Yet another stupid dream! Will they never end? Woke up covered in horse flys drinking the sweat off me to. This fan is just not cutting it but I cant even run the blender and the radio at the same time w/o the goddam fuse blowing so just imagine what a ac wou d do. At least charlotte likes the heat. When I let her out on the floor she runs to wherever the sun is and does a little boogie. Speaking of boogies we were listening to the terry gross show today on wnyc when the customers started complaining like we were spooning out castor oil. Apparently noble prize winners are not interesting enough for them. So I put on jackie wilsons greatest hits and you should have seen the dancing that broke out in the waiting area. Even cliff and his customer joined in w/her arm all bloody and everything.

Panther $75

Smurfs fucking $80
Panther $75
Gangsta Pryde 4 Lyfe $90
Panther w/yankees hat $85
Taz smoking spliff $85
Juicy cherrys $65
Panther $75
Pochahontas (sp?) $80

Seriously thinking about getting rid of this gun.
Sometimes I wake up at night and its in my
hand even tho I always put it away in the
drawer. One time there was even a shell empty.
But where did the bullet go? There were no
holes in my walls. I wish I could get charlotte
to eat these f'n flys. Will discuss it
w/her when she wakes up.

"Every day I find it easier to empathize with people."

THE RATTLE OF A PRIMEVAL BUZZER
signaled grub's arrival. Through the intercom
came flubs of drubs thwarting one's survival.
  "Dude, just a few flights up. Want your pay or not?"
  'Prease! You come down! They hit and scale a rot!'

MOUNTED ON A BROWN THREE-SPEED,
the man proved just a boy.
  Lardy nettles crowned debris.
  An unlit tube harked Freud.

Sliding sacks from handlebars,
I thrust a herd of bills.
  Eyes chided me like mason jars
of turd-fermented swill.
  "Three bucks on just five clams...
  Pretty damn good tip..."
  "Prease don't reave! Prease!
They want bike! They hit!"
  A tomcat gnawing pigeon-guts
was the block's lone sign of life.
  "Some kinda flaw to vision, bud?
  See a doc about that sight."
  A thumb jerked towards Lorimer.
  'Bad Boys!' yawped. I squinted.
  "Um...er...no one there."
  A sad noise dropped. A Schwinn rid.

LILLIPUTIANS SWARMED THE CORNER —
throwing knuckles/shoves with mirth.
  A Confucian bike was swiped by hoarders
bucking feet above the Earth.
  As I grasped dwarves as preteens, they suddenly
dispersed; coursing with the random
flee of a pea-green/tile-scourge.
  Shorn of threads save mismatched socks, violence
flowing from ten wounds, the Boy cursed God's
whiplashed pox like Elias in *'Platoon'*.
  How much had his smuggle cost?
  What horrors had he endured?
  My noodles went the way of tots
wielding dampened two-by-fours.

Ran into templeton at the beauty bar and he said some real funny stuff about america using giant pink poodles w/grenades in them to confuse and kill the communists (sp?) in the korean war. I was thinking about that on the way to the L train and I guess I was smiling bc when I turned my head I accidentally made eye contact w/this little yellow haired dworf in a busyness suit walking past. Then he gave me the finger. Maybe he thought I was laughing at him? Felt horrible about it. I called petunia when I got home and of course instead of making me feel better she just flipped it around to make it all about herself. She said "well you know when I was at brown I used to date a dworf. All of the girls liked him bc he was very handsome and witty and we were all very curious." I said Im sure he had a big dick right? And she says "bigger then yours." Then she said "I take that back. Yours is longer but his was thicker, Like a soup can." I said thats nice but what about MY feelings and she says "oh dont be so quaint with all this feeling nonsense. The little darling probably just doesnt approve of tattoos." I said ok but I still feel bad bc even quaint people have feelings to. Then she asked me if I want to see the phantom or cable guy tomorrow.

Panther $75

Black widow $65
Aligator eating baby $85
Panther $75
Popeye smoking blunt $80
Pyramid w/palm tree $70
Panther $75
"Asanbosam" in fancy script $50
Snoopy burning american flag $80
Panther $75
Panther $75
Panther $75

Found another empty shell the other day.
Definitely gonna give luigi this gun. Just hope he
doesnt do anything stupid like shoot his
mother or gf. Thinking maybe cable guy
would be better. Charlotte says kazaam.

"I make the necessary sacrifices to achieve my goals."

***AMIDST A PULSATING, CANCEROUS,
PANTHER-RAVENOUS CLUSTER,*** the
Necromancer made the scene, orating catalysts with
bluster. "Don't look so damned *surprised*, Jack! I grew
up in Montclair! Back in town 'cause my ma died!
Week's been a long/brutal/bland nightmare!"

"Sorry..."

"Eh. Anyhow, reason I'm here is my new chick's setup is much too sweet to let go! Cute! Dumb! Loves suckin' dick! Folks got *shit-tons* of dough! What I need is some kind of ink to hip Tovah I'm down for the game long haul! But logic says may as well claim two birds, long as I'm stuck with the scrawl..."

"I don't understand."

"Here's the thing: T's pop — dude's real tight with Phil Knight, see?"

"The basketball coach?"

"That's *Bob,* you dope! Talking 'bout the founder of Nike!"

"Ah."

"Deep in my heart...I'm an *illusionist*...on the grandest of all fucking scales! If I can con this creep into bankrolling my start...Houdini's sad shit'll look pale!"

"Like what?"

"Freeze me in ice! Bury me! Throw me chained into the ocean! Long as it's televised on MTV, my pain requires due promotion! It's not all about *money,* Jack — success feeds on powerful sway! The best connections just can't be bought! Devouring souls is the way!"

APPARENTLY NOTHING AROUSED THE C.O. more than an über-loyal douche.

Thus sparked a drive to crown an uno with a royally tumorous Swoosh. While the device could be piped to olde Herr Knight as *'Nike is Number One!',* Tovah — not quite as bright — would discern only a T's titular stun.

"And make it *extra-good*, Jack! Gimme your finest work! Free yourself! *Journey beyond!* Do it for our kind of jerk! Guys like you and me, Jack, we gotta stick together! Don't think I can't see why *you're* with Tunie! Fact is...we're birds of a feather!"

AMBUSHING THE JOHN FRANTIC, raining hot suds across hands, I rushed to degrime all mojo-satanic even before draining my glans. Wiping dry, prying my fly, orbs gaped disgraces uncool.
Fluttering loose from my boxers,
Aces-and-Eights dove in the pool.

Went up to petunias mothers house on long island. Her driver took us in a jaguar (sp?). Not a limo but still some nice wheels.
Petunia tried to get the shofar to smoke pot w/us but he politely refused. He is a tough puerto rican named juan but she calls him obi juan. She made some joke about his dick to. I guess her mother said he has a big one. I didnt like it when she did that. It was rude and could get him fired or something. The pot smoking I mean. The house itself is on a big estate in a seashore town called mount hawk. Looks like a park w/big green golf course lawns and nice trees etc. There are a bunch of houses on the property and maybe 10 dogs of all varietys

that basically do whatever they please. They
like to swim in this big pond. There is a pool to
but they are not allowed in that on account of
pissing. There is also the ocean but they are not
allowed to use that either bc of sharks. One
dog named orlok (sp?) is kept caged up tho. Big
scary rottweiler. He is caged bc he killed 3 of
the other dogs and even ate one. The one he
ate was a weiner and all that was left was her
ears. I waved at him but he just growled. One
of the houses is basically a private theater and
we watched "panther" about hugh e newton in
the 1960s. Pretty neat to see a real movie w/
popcorn and everything w/o having to sit in a
room full of nyu students saying "note the
superb composition on this shot" or listen to
chinese babys screaming for milk. I fucked
petunia in a hot tub to. While I was fucking her
she told me that her mothers old boyfriend
built the sauna room and hot tub. He was the
ex drummer of brownsville station or
something but when his band flopped he
became a carpenter. After he was done w/the
sauna her mother dumped him. That seemed
a little harsh. I wonder what petunia wants
me to build for her. The next morning we sat

around the pool w/some other rich people.
I stayed under a big umbrella oc of sun. The
girls were all topless like it was no big deal. Tits
everywhere. Her mother came to the pool in
a white robe and sunglasses and a big white
towel around her head and didnt say a word
to anyone. Not even "good morning". Then she
took off the robe and did laps w/the towel still
around her head like a turban. 30 of 40 times.
When she got out and walked away the
turban was still completely dry. Strange. Cliff
said that sounds sexy. But trust me it was just
plain strange. Good to be back now. Charlotte
was very happy to see me. She made a heart
in the dust w/her butt. Today the shop was
festive bc the olympics are starting in atlanta.
Everyone was wearing olympics t shirts and
hats etc. A pretty good day. No glass
complaints. No rayon man. No EZ red etc.
In fact the only bad thing that happened was
when I was shaving this blonde girls chest to
put a stencil on a hair came out of the bic and
stuck to the soap on her tit. She was so pale
and the hair was so black and thick and curly.
She saw it to but didnt say anything. Just turned
her head and looked away like she was going

to cry. The boss has been making us re use the
razors for a few months now. Why? They cost
less then a dime each. This was a pretty girl to.
Now she will never come back and I cant really
blame her. I am just going to start throwing the
razors away and pay for the extra dimes myself.
I dont want people to think that I am dirty bc
I am the type of guy that takes a shower
almost every time he shits.

Panther $75

Smurfette w/blunt $80

Olympic panther $85

Dolphin $65

Panther $75

Prez clinton toking up $80

Panther $75

Butterfly $65

Beauty mark $50

Beauty mark $50

Panther $75

Indian feather $60

Hambone loves sally $55

Drinking schlitz now. Disgusting but all I have in
the fridge. But how did it get there? I dont
remember buying any. Atlanta is such a
shitty place to hold the olympics in.
I hope it blows up.

"I look challenges in the face and laugh with reckless abandon."

WITH RAYON MAN'S STOMPS FAILING TO CEASE, I commenced mulling different careers.
As lads braver than I chomped a mouthpiece,
dust whispered insensitive jeers:
  "Flapdoodle! Pipe-fodder! Boxers are spartan — you're lazy! Be snuffed in a round by the worst prelim plodder! Best stick to Martin Scorsese!"
  Charlotte scrambled atop my palm.
  I blew lint-barnacles free.
  Fine hairs parted.
  Eight eyes spied calm.
  An ad barked recruits of Marines.
  "Hmph! Well, there's an idea.
At least they'd buy all my food..."
  Several plump moments were sheared.
  (My beloved's reply was subdued.)
  "Okay. But first, make sure you get plenty of sleep. Please try and stop worrying. Keep fit! Don't lose your nerve. And no more phantasmagorical dream-scurrying!"

BOGGED IN THE GUTS OF A GRANITE BEHEMOTH — dark, dismal, tired — flyspecked
smut and coffee-splash zeniths robbed
the room of all pill to inspire.

Contrasting the squalor, two Leathernecks stood.
Handsome.
Strong.
Picturesque.
 Tan-and-blue clobber belied the
dolor of my sickly/pigeon-shat heft.
 "Okay, Benda, you scored high on this test fo' aptitude,
but what's up wif them tattoos on yo' hands?"
 "Um..."
 "Don't be rude! Tell it real straight!
Y'all in the Ku Klux Klan?"
 "What? No. Listen, sir, would these
really preclude from the Corps?"
 "Dunno. Can't really say. All upta the view a the board.
Now, get Grandpa's Sunday-suit off!
Hafta take us some pitchas!"
 (Slowly removing my jacket and tie,
I paused at a buttoned groin-fissure.)
 "Yup. And also them skivvies."
 "But I don't have tattoos on my legs."
 "Board don't know it! Off with that shit please!
Dang...paler'n hardboilt eggs!"
 With an Instant of Nixonian vintage,
photography blithely ensued.
 Documenting a moldy/thin mintage.
 Pornography of wry rectitudes.

Coney island high again w/avery plus some
strange fat dudes who I think were mostly
cops. Some old guy in the bathroom made
fun of me for the book I was carrying. "Call it
sleep" by henry roth. He said "what is a kid like

you reading that book for? That book is only
for fags who want people to think they are
smart." I said that I found it on a garbage can
lid. A lie but what else could I do? When I am
a marine people wont be so f'n loud w/me all
the time. Then some frizzy haired bich w/big
cans started talking to me and avery etc. So we
bought her some drinks but avery kept sticking
wet gum in her hair from behind. Just for the
goof I guess? After about a hour there was a
full pack in there. Cant imagine her reaction
tomorrow. I guess I will ask avery later bc he
took her home. He loaned me some good
movies to. One called "the mack" is about a
pimp who dreams big. The other is called "hard
times" and it has charles bronson and that guy
who looks just like lee marvin but isn't lee marvin. James something or other. I always forget.
That must really suck to look just like somebody else and even have the same job as them
to. Or maybe not. I guess it worked out for
james whatever even if nobody can remember
his name. He still probably bags a lot of ass I
mean. Cliff said that charles bronson was so
poor he had to wear his sisters dress to school
sometimes. I said how do you know that and
he said he has read 3 books about charles

bronson. I cant understand what cliff was doing
reading even 1 book about charles bronson
but 3? I said where did you get these books
and he said that ronald gave them to him when
he went to visit him in the loonie bin. Wtf?
What other dark secrets is this
guy hiding from me?

Grim reaper shooting craps $95

See you in heaven granma $55

Panther $75

Garfield w/tec-9 $70 (This guy brought his tec-9
in as a model and also his garfield doll.)

Panther $75

Fight the power $60

Hand flipping bird w/diamond ring $85

Panther $75

Just took some zanax that cliff gave me bc I
think I may have been sleep walking lately. Luigi
said yesterday I walked right past him in the
hallway at 5am w/my eyes closed and my shirt
on backwards. Also charlotte was acting kind
of strange and nervous tonight. Running away
from my hand. Made me feel sad. I shoved a
little crumb of zanax down one of the crickets
mouths to calm her down. I guess I should have
shoved crumbs down all of them but I
already swallowed the rest.

"My chief weapon is double-barreled compassion."

"HIYA, FELLAS...NICE T'SEE YOUSE...
Alright if I come on in?"
  "Free country, cuz! You know better!
Don't be a stooge or curmudgeon!"
  "Youse eat lunch? Got ya some pastry and cocoa."
  "*Jeez,* dude — where'd you get punched?
Your face wreaks of Quasimodo!"

*"WELL, DERE WAS DIS OLD MAN AT AA
NAMED GARY* — an' I's thinkin' he's a real nice
fella. Tough plan at dat age to quit drinkin'. Just lost
his wife, Daniela. Ast me t'drive him ta Oivin'ton. Says,
'Wanna see medals from bein' a Legionnaire?' So, one
minnit, he's squawkin' 'bout da boinin' a Dresden...
suddenly, I'm reelin' downstairs."
  "*Shit.* That fucking blows.
Guessing next he robbed you?"
  "Didn't have much dough really...
Just took my Timex an' kazoo. "
  "What about that ring there, cuz?
The one with the hairy glass eye."
  "Tried but quit. See dis big cut?
Ain't come off in a very long time."
  "Well, today you're gettin' a *free* custom
piece! Don't even think about griping!"
  "*Nah,* Cliffy. But t'anks alla same."
  "Humbug! Cease thy insolent sniping!"

"COPS EVER NAB THIS GARY DUDE?
Did a real job on your throat."
  "Nah. Hadda stop scrabblin' for clues 'cause his
buildin' was condemnt t'be smote. Wreckin' ball fella
foun' me dere. He was tendin' da very last sweep.
Nice guy, called 911. Said I was cuddlin' a rat
while I sleeped."
  "Alright, cuz! Done!"
  "Nice one. Love it. Only...what's it s'posed t'be?"
  "Why, that's *Hot Stuff* on the john reading
Playboy! Here, see the bunny?"
  "But what's dat dere in his palm?
Is he scarfin' a weenie?"
  "*Seriously*, cuz?"
  "Ah. Good t'ing Ma's gone. Too old-fashioned.
Thunked modern art was for sheenies."

Day off again. Cleaned the spider tank. Then
luigi started following me around the sidewalk
waving these yankees tickets the sanitation
(sp?) department gave him for being garbage
man of the month. Said cheater is on a real
hot streak and did I want to go to the game?
Told him I was going to work just to shake
him but he rode into manhattan w/me on the
subway so I said fuck it and just went to work
anyway. Afterwards I went to this loft party
where everybody was a "film maker". Even the
catering person who was a japanese sushi guy
w/dread locks. What is a film maker? Its not a
director. Its not a screen writer. Its not a actor.

Where are all these films that all these people
are making? Is that the 8 minute crap they run
at 3am on channel 13 when nobody is
watching? They asked me what I do and I told
them I am a tattooer and they ooed and ahed
like I had just said the most fascinating thing in
the world. They asked me "what is the most
unusual tattoo you ever did?" So I told them
the truth. A green stem w/a leaf coming out
of this bichs dialycist hole bc she thought it
looked like a cherry. They said oh that is so
neat making something beautiful out of a
tradgedy. Then I explained that she killed three
kids while she was drunk driving and thats why
she is on dialycist but she didnt go to jail bc she
is rich. They should make a film about that.

Panther waving ethiopeon olympic team flag $90
Mets logo $65
Panther $75
Winnie the poo $85
Colt 45 w/smoke spelling "gotcha" $70
Miss piggy $80
Panther $75
Panther $75
Panther $75

Saw holden in the tunnel again. Laughing in a
river of blood. Really starting to wear on me.

"Nurturing a healthy relationship comes naturally to me."

FOUR BANSHEE DISPATCHES ILLUMINED DUST RED — each one increasingly piqued.
'Ignoring me, Jackson? So ill-bred! Must be fun reaping my shrieks!' Feeble protests of panther-fatigue collapsed against a will of pure steel: *'Unacceptable! Get amped for a shindig ripe with intrigue! Tonight you meet the real deal!'*
"Anna Nicole Smith?"
(The honoree, alas, was not Mexia's droll myth but a lad smitten by maladies yet christened.)
"Bummer. The symptoms are what?"
'Beyond boredom, no one's quite sure! The specialists have all reached their wits' ends!'
Stoking the tragedy was an inkhorn éclat educing bays of Fitzgerald's odd fame.
"Can the pageantry, sure his stuff's snot! So what's this imperiled sod's name?"

'LARCENY CHLORINE' WASN'T MUCH OF A LAD, nor that much of a man. Glum, fuzzy, and tender-limbed with a warmed crap shaking of hand.
Nor did he strike me as singularly beset.
Repulsive, but of a hearty pink shade.
"Word is the street vets you the new Fitz. An explosively arty renegade."

Babylonian shoes shuffled and slapped moves
awkward/ungainly/crude. Palms begat Jolsonian
flaps. Grooves proffered depraved turpitude.
 With Nihility's spin, a mien fell grim.
 Young ladies and lords thundered.
 "Scotty didn't hoof and I slay on the boards!
Call me the Golden-Heeled Wonder!"

BENEATH THE MATADOR'S DYING LEER,

'Larceny!' hewed upon climax; a crying surely
pre-engineered, Bliss being noob to unlubed anal-
hijack. Silently sweating atop Pepto fabric for
an interminable/post-sex expanse, fingers pet
a stretched globe of fat prick as cabs
blared vexed Arabs' rants.
 Lips brushed my throat's apple.
 Whiskers grated her nose.
 "Sorry, Jackson. Forgive the rattle.
You're frightfully hurt, I suppose."
 "Sorry for what, babe?"
 "For screaming *LARCENY*, you twit! For being a slut!
Craving a knave! It's beyond all parse of acquit!"
 Shrugging, sighing, staring ahead,
I liberated a coppery belch.
 "Ah. That. No biggie.
Let's just consider it squelched."
 "Jackson, what exactly do you mean by *'No biggie'*?"
 "Just that: no big deal."
 Clawed at the jaw by two tiny paws, a dome
wrenched sideways met screels. "*Jackson!* You mean...
you...you...you don't...*you don't even care?*"
 Coins clattered across Venetian
floor-tile as I lifted my slacks in the air.
 "Fine then! Just leave! We clearly need some kind of
détente! Rush back to that hovel to watch your sad insect
toddle for the rest of its meaningless haunt!"

Charlotte is still being skittish when I try to touch her. Maybe she is afraid that I am abandoning her bc of the marines? Could I bring her along? Bad bad bad bad bad EZ red mess came in today. Huge scar all swelled up like a pile of raw meat. Felt awful for the guy but what could I do? Boss wont even let me throw it away. And cliff had a very obvious boner for the entire day to. He said it was a rubbing cocaine on his dick last night thing. Wierd right? Also heard that my friend laird from grade school died. Heroine od. He was a good guy and I feel pretty bad about it. Used to try to get me to read "catcher in the rye" but I never did. Once when I was 15 he called me up and told me he was gay. Said he had been looking at himself in the mirror while he jerked off. We never brought that subject up again. Another time I took him to trenton to get a tattoo and he got the cat in the hat on his ankle. I asked him why and he said the cat in the hat represented neil cassidy. I said who is that and he told me to read "on the road" so I did and there was no character named neil cassidy nor was there the cat in the hat. We didnt talk much after that. Now we never will.

Sexy cherrys $60

Rest in peace cornwallis and cool clark $65

Panther $75
Piece sign $60
African fertillitty mask $80
Panther $75
Panther $75
Little elroy $50
Panther $75
Chinese letters for "mad money" $55
Mini mouse $75
Sniper w/afro in hot air balloon $95
Note to self: buy cocaine.

"I accept rejection with a positive attitude."

ONE WEEK PASSED SANS WORD. A second
leaked gas to a third. Ruminations of rappelling
to abysses unknown sped swiftly along undeterred.
  Slumbering beneath patched canvas tarps.
  Awakening to wafts of woebegone farts.
  A pile of bone in Bedouin sand.
  Arguing Stallone over Jean-Claude Van Damme.
  (Admittedly eldritch or not, such
reverie rallied and spurred!)
  'Marine Corps!' "Hi. Jack Bender here.
Came in four weeks back."
  'Yeah?' "Um...I took a quiz to join-up."
  'And?' "Then you took pics of my tats. Mentioned
some board...a review...passing muster..."

'Wait, cold sore? Bald dude? Y'all D.Q.'d!
Said yo' wan ass be lackluster!'
  Spiraling earthbound, a heart careened past lungs/
liver/spleen/and cock. Rioting within a scrotal
dogpound, it swung like beans in a sock.
  Lowering the receiver, staggering cross-room,
  I tugged at the vanity drawer.
With one blue twink, a snubbed nose winked.
Insanity's come-hither allure.

May, 1994

'Live at Five' blared while I nursed her DTs, a slop-bucket
readied bedside. The day's big scoop: the Menendez hung-
jury and a subsequent bid to retry. Amidst a spiel of Axel
Foley's third romp, I divulged a juvenescent camaraderie.
  "Went to prep-school together. Thinking of 'em as
cold-blooded killers is kinda beyond my capacity."
  (Squinting mum at televised chums, I espied
Erik pulsing brave fettle. Lyle cried — toupeed,
numb — a human Cossack-razed shtetl.)
  "Daddy, I went to a snob-factory too!"
  Hacking globs anew, pail handheld, a fine
chin furrowed 'til mucilage quelled.
  "Just gonna assume you were expelled..."
  "English teacher. Pothead. Forty one. Wife left him for a
Chinese conductor. Could read and write hexes in
Sumerian! Once summoned Satrina and fucked her!"
  Clairvoyant florets blossomed sparklike
across the smogged expanse of my dome.
  ...pigtails...halters...braced teeth against Bics...
a clog-dance of fiery hormones...
  "We'd sit by the pond and he'd
tutor me. Every weekday at dusk."

...an armor of tweed...scarf-swaddled jowls, pipe-shadow cleaved...a spirituous paternal musk...
  Slushing again, she thumped the results,
which I dutifully hauled for disposal.
  "For such an old man he humped like the Hulk!
Truly a walking Chernobyl! It was when I returned his
'Usher' by Poe that I saw him hung from the door!"
  Dumping red slop, I churned a sanguine flow.
The flusher flung clots to the floor.

"I may not always be aware of the choices made by my Higher-Self, but I can always trust those choices."

TRAILBLAZING A PATH TO THE CENTRAL-PARTITION, grip mimicking the color of soot, broad lips ornamented by keloidic beads emitted a metered/King's English output.
  Were it not for his tribal-cicatrices and bright pagan clobber (bejeweled-fez, dashiki-mate) one might've assigned such aplomb to an Anglican bishop or an august Tuskegee potentate.
  Instinctually reverent of manifest grace, I traversed the counter — enacting a guided flash-tour — ebulliently elucidating each Jungian trace like a hook-nosed/talking brochure.

"*Take this daggered rose here! What's plain to
see is that it represents coitus or fertility!*"
   While the African projected politely obliged,
if borderline mirthless, a finger's spear of a panther's
sleek hide proved my toil intrinsically worthless.
   Though the feline selected was a standard fist-span,
grave concerns were expressed: "I'm in academia,
understand, and can't be judged. Let's reduce
it to just a smidge less."
   Upon a beseech of peach-stone dimensions,
I retrieved my brown glass to dissuade, evoking
pained groans from bystander-tensions
lining the counter-stockade.
   "Now see what it looks like through this? Please,
just *hark* what I say! Your melanin is dense and the
larger the piece is the clearer it'll read anyway!"
   Irritation jailbroke its corral.
   My counsel was stripped by gut-feelings.
   A stentorian roar of righteous morale muted
a covert pitch of drug-dealing.

ANXIOUSLY YAKKING AMIDST GEAR-ASSEMBLAGE, he cast forth a line of smalltalk.

   "A gift to myself for a doctorate logged!
Now it's back to Nairobi's gridlock!"
   "Oh neat, congrats! Very cool, man.
And what was your thesis?"
   "*Sex, Sensuality, Cesspools, and Vampirism
in James Aloysius Joyce's 'Ulysses'!*"
   Soap-gluing the vellum to a heathen husk, my chest
succumbed to vexed tightening. Juxtaposed against
veldt-seasoned dusk, the stencil's caliginosity was
frightening! Even with my gooseneck hideously

angled, I gawked nary the meanest of guidelines.
Relying upon a bulb's refractive dangle, my schnoz
dragged like a policeman's canine.

All for show! A corpulent farce!

The inefficacious polish of mere turd!

An anemic capitulation to a haughty black arse
rending me typist of Theater Absurd!

**FOLLOWING AN HOUR OF THUMPING
DESPAIR,** and a gentle de-gore with witch-hazel,
the African wound-gaped and slumped in
a chair to bitch and roar at his navel.

"But sir, I can't see it! It's as if it's not there at all!
Are you *certain* that your needles were sharpened?
Perhaps your tools require an overhaul?"

(I nodded; sympathizing/despising/disheartened.)

"Dude...dug way hard enough...it's in there alright...
just look at the fluid that's rising! But it's *beneath* your
flesh, not on top, so this shouldn't be at all surprising!
I explained it to you before we got drilling! Stratum
corneum? Tyrosine? Various skin-types unwilling?"

The African grinned, arcing scars as thoughts
gathered, as if steeling to quell an armed moppet.

"Come now, sir! Might we not inject some
cheeriness here? Some fun-feeling pastels atop it?"

A wand-like finger swirled at soft-hues.

"Perhaps a creamy lemon
or minty green would do!"

Lids slowly clenched, lungs deluged with grief, my
soul idled adrift in search of psychic relief. From a
vast height, way up in Valhalla, a great-great
grandfather stared down; bicorne-plume trembling
with unbridled disgust; mien blazoning
antebellum frown.

Verily, I was of no kinship to he!
Adopted perhaps? A rape's progeny!
Certainly not of the same lifeblood!
'Even those consarn Marines recognized a
conglomerate of horse-dung and sewer-piss mud!'
"TATTOO-MAN! WAKE YO' ASS UP! HURRY UP
WIT DAT GODDAMN NIGGA! WANT MY BOO'S
NAME IN GUNSMOKE GETTIN' ALL WISPY
FROM A BIG OL' WESSON HAIR-TRIGGA!"
Unfolded lids met a nightmarish sight:
A deadpan African...garish fistfuls alight!
"Now then, sir, shall we commence with the
implementation of additional ink? I've taken the
liberty of pre-selecting a few choices. What say
you to a tongue of bubblegum-pink? White
highlights to implicate moistness?"
Snatching the vessels, shaking with vigor, I attacked
the scrawl like a hellbent gravedigger; raking each
section five or six times, bearing down with all
summonable force; impregnating the panther
with a star-crossed rind virtually jack-in-
the-boxing a jet/dermic source.
As the African stood, draped with thick gloat like
a dowager's askew schmatte, I tempered my choler
with visions cutthroat of a chaotic Avenue Kenyatta.
The inappropriate swaths would be duly consumed
within only a matter of hours, by which point he'd
be dodging ape-crap, continents zoomed,
hubris transmuted to glowers.

EYES RESEALED, A COB TOOK FORM, skirting
an unbroken lake-pool. *'I maintain control, never get
riled, and always stay effortlessly cool.'*

A canon blasted. Down feathers puffed.
(The partition had been thwacked a mite hard.)
As my vision was ground, tethered, and cuffed,
Rayon Man fumed like a Jacobite charred.

So they bombed the f'n olympics. Now the
$64000 question is who are "they" the arabs
or the irish. Cliff thinks the north koreans. One
of my customers said it was the kkk. I told him
maybe it was the martians (sp?) and he
shook his head and said no it couldnt
be bc mars aint real.

Panther $75
Panther $75
Whip w/"resist/submit" $85
Panther $75
World's phreshest dad rip $65
Vain wayne $50
Cross w/rose $80
Garfield w/dreadlocks $75
Forever tyrone $50
Panther $75
Snoopy w/gunshot $80
Panther $75

More bad dreams. Tunnels. Retards. Holdens.
Horses. Polish bakery has pink cakes in the
window. Sun so bright it hurts. Charlotte please
stop being wierd. We are supposed to be
friends. I love you. Sadness. Drunk.

"I am trapped within an immense blob of joy."

AN IMP STEERING GREASE-MAULED LOCKS

sneered at an exiguous coif. *"Jesus, dude! Killing me
here! Near as bald as Mikhail Gorbachev!"*

We'd convened at Thunderbirds, an upstairs
saloon overlooking Second and A —
Templeton's wan, blurred, ginger-haired festoon
invoking a cherry-daubed/creamy parfait.

A winsome-if-fearful brunette approached,
vetting Stygian pleasures. A tight cotton tee clung
to sphered hulls hefting beyond Darwinian-measure.

(A pink spit-bubble fled the zing
of a lewd/rodent-gapped whistle.)

"And that *ring*...shit! Trouble! Why's it still
there? Dontcha think it's due for dismissal!"

"Eh, just sentimental, I guess."

"Bullshit! Quit being a pussy! Just finally toss it!
Enough already with the phony distress!
Just let it dive down a faucet!"

I unfolded the Western Union missive the Contessa
had recently wired, purporting our traffic had duly
emboldened an indecent flea-infestation quagmire.
Failure to reimburse said costs would
result in swift litigation pursuant.

"Scabies, eh? *Jack Bender*:
lost/semi Caucasian truant!"

Yakking the latest news from Bloomfield Ave,

I decried bountiful spleens of black cops.
 "Spitting-mad, doom-filled nags!
 An insurmountably mean paradox!"

"ONLY BEEN TO MONTCLAIR ONCE...
birthday-thing back in fourth grade. I was in
private-school then. Some janitor had raped a few
twerps at P.S.11 and my folks were kinda dismayed.
Lotta the kids were from over the bridge. Fort Lee,
Leonia, Scotch Plains. Often they'd have these stupid
parties that required cars/buses/and trains. So this
dipshit Barnabas turns nine, and I get fucking invited.
First said *NO*, but he moans and whines, still dunno
what made him excited. It was *scary* going under the
tunnel myself; Etan Patz had just been kidnapped.
Remember that creepy-ass stare? Didn't wanna get
roofied or sapped! Anyway, we play hide-and-go-
seek. Never been there before...first fucking time...
all the spots got sneaked quicker than whores on
the street fall prey to organized crime! Pantry: *taken!*
Broom-closet: *taken!* Not one bed-underside left
alone or forsaken! In the john, I find the tub empty,
but step ankle-deep into cake! It'd been the *Greatest*
too! I'd wrecked Muhammad Ali's sweet face!
Ran straight back to the bus-stop trailing
moist footprints of frosting!"
 "What flavor tracks?"
 "Jesus, Jack! Your failing clairvoyance exhausts me..."

STUMBLING WITH DRINKS TRAY-
BALANCED, the Waitress served comically dour,
responding *'Miss Anthrope'* upon my name-challenge
with a primness designed to faux-sour.

A serviette-scrawl beneath the next round
lured hypoglycemic slits. *"Number put down?"*
  "Just a name is all."
The Imp crumpled pulp as he spit.
An ichorous blossom slowly unfurled,
crying out *'DAISY!'* to a grim world.
  Just as I espied the I's heart-dot, and the Only Ones
commenced cooing piffle, I rushed to swat the napkin
aside before Temp could eject further sniffle.
  Ulcer-blood glazed dinged teeth.
  A pompadour wavered with ire.
  "Such a pussy, Jack! Even that RING agrees!"
  Enameled eyes blazoned red fire.

Boss chewed me out for re using razors. I said
but Ive been paying for them but she said thats
not the point its the principal of the matter so I
quit and got drunk at the bowling alley in port
authority. When I finally got home there was a
message from her on the machine. I think she
was crying. She apollogized and said I could
come back. I will think about it.
Charlotte still wont let me touch her or even
talk to me. What did I ever do to her but buy
her nice presents and whisper sweet things?
Sound familiar? Rented "the wild bunch"
and also "breezy".
Li'l eliza $60
Graffiti letters $70
Tiger w/big dick $90
Puked up a hairball like a cat. All blonde. Wierd.

"I engage the opposite sex with composure and grace."

RETURNING TO THUNDERBIRDS SANS IMP CHUM, my stalk lured a likewise smitten imbiber. Plump, goateed, reeking of scum — he flung equal parts Seagram's to cipher:

"Smokin' hot, right, bro? Dig how she always looks scairt! Weird thing's my boy Enzo swears her sister's some star! Big fuckin' house in Bel-Air!"

CASTING FAUX-FEAR, DAISY TAPPED A HUGE BREAST boldly pinned World's Best Mom!

"Case it ain't clear, that's from my girl — lest you pursue solely virgin pogroms."

Behind an honest, mononuclear smile, her face bore a fraught veil of terror; a mien akin to one awakened by roars following a zookeeper's cocktail-steered error.

Watched "bridge on the river kwai" (sp?) last night. Good stuff. Then today some long haired hick wearing a lynird skynird tee shirt came in and asked me if I would tattoo a black mans head on him w/a cloud over it sending a lightening bolt down splitting the head in half w/the words "white lightening" under it. This was in a room filled w/maybe 35 black people.

He also had a carton of orange juice and a
bottle of vodka. And the wierd thing was that
nobody got upset. Some laughed even. If I had
said that they would have just killed me. Cliff
said its ok for red necks to say that in front
of them bc they are equal in terms of socially
economical static. He said that even tho I am
uneducated and stupid that I dress to
ecentrically to pass for oppressed so
different rules apply. Anyway when I told the
hick the tattoo would be 75 bux he screamed
and stomped bc he only had $15. He was so
drunk that he forgot to take his oj w/him and
cliff drank the rest. I warned him the guy was
chewing skoal and drinking from the carton at
the same time but cliff just said "fuck it. I have
put my mouth in much worse places and lived".

Sexy ice cream cone w/extra drips $65
Panther $75
Reggie bar wrapper $90
Tombstone w/big daddy $60
Panther $75
Dominican flag $80
Panther $75
Panther $75
Yankees logo $65
Chinese letters for "I like big donkeys" $55

Another bullet was missing the other day. I told

luigi I might give him the gun and he acted like it was really no big deal. He said "ok maybe I will take it off your hands but I dont know tho bc I have to much stuff in my room as it is". Maybe I should just drive out to los angeles w/ it. Charlotte wont even look at me anymore so I have nothing to lose anyway. Ok good night.

"Change allows me to experience my true nature."

RENDING SLEEP-CRUST FROM LASHES BONDED BY DUST, I reeled with injurious horror.
   Lids clenched, I paused to regather,
beseeching my inner rip-roarer.
   Hands peeled from eyes, I squinted and scanned;
alas, detecting no change. Across a linty expanse,
two tarantulas skulked, crowding the
dusted vanity's range.
   Charlotte and...someone else!
   At Panic's brink, Ration wrested the wheel,
commencing a likelihood-inventory.
   Surely this was some form of consumption-mirage
dredged from a claret-drenched quarry?
   Was my hangover not perfidious?
   Cruel, merciless, stabbing?
   Perhaps my swill had been insidiously spiked
by a cad disliked? Some ghoulish herpes-
virus of the brass ring?

**WITH NO SMALL EFFORT, I MANAGED
TO RISE,** lurching aquarium-bound. Finding the lid
securely affixed, affirms framed a hurt/carrion frown.
   Spine arching south, eyes scintilla-soaped, my pulse
slackened near-static. Too ossified to blink,
much less manually probe, lungs mugged by
anathema asthmatic, I screamed.

WAILS DULY SPENT, A RENEWED SURVEY
was flummoxed by a startling/uncanny congruence.
Looming beneath, virtual Doublemint Twins nestled
on chips...albeit of a far leggier influence.
   Tension waning, alarmed thrums shifted
to effervescent streams of fascination.
   Perhaps Magic bore verisimilitude indeed?
   Perhaps Aces-and-Eights confirmed Shamanation?
   Perhaps someday I might travel through Time!
Become a Marine after all!
   Even dare to pry Loss from *Eternity's* gape!
Had Columbus not conquered such squalls?

WITH DAMNABLY ACUTE PARALLELS
hindering detects of doppelgängers, my fingers
ambled with a drake's slow dwell —
respectful of topples with fangs near.
   While left-side pokes roused only insentience, the
subject proving utterly inert, a gentle tapping of the
right's rear-hide stoked a five-inch vault above dirt.
   Scurrying hutbound upon an inaudible crash,
the beast was fueled by palpable pain.
   Phew, thought I, thankfully ungashed
through the grace of Thaumaturgic Legerdemain.
   Squinting once more, I cringed and recoiled.
   (Orbs had fallen prey to anal-rupture!)

Had sweet Charlotte expired within Sodomy's throes? Had this infiltrator dared to touch her?

AS I PONDERED MY BELOVED'S TERMINUS, the killer trembled in a markedly mammalian fashion. When a cricket flopped atop the other furred truss, the corpse teetered with a stiffly unified dispassion.

Heaving weightless remains to a tusk of a nose, perceiving only a hollowed-out shell, it came to my brain that I grasped a *husk* deposed.

A crux of metaphysical groundswell!

PEERING DOWN, I SOUNDED SORROWS... feeling finky...abjectly unwise...

Kneeling as still as Mount Kilimanjaro, Charlotte winked eight shiny jet eyes.

May, 1993

One balmy, moist, moonswelled Spring eve, chilling buzzed on Avenue A, I was calmly observing gazelles as they grazed when a shrill cuss harked new affray.

Through the yawning gape of the Hi-Yella saloon, a raven-haired mess careened — hexes grouting gaps 'twixt chortles pursuant to a brutish ejector's quarantine.

Goosebumps!

Angina!

Fuck! Shit! Gadzooks!

Her! Yes! Indeed, 'twas she!

The girl with the scab-crusted dukes!

Palm spiked in high salutation, I descried one arm coiling another, hastily abjuring my trite elevation upon prejudging a foil beyond brother.

Blackguardly, big-nosed, balding — waist cartridge-belt
draped — the boor and I shared a preternatural
resemblance despite a shambolic/sprawling/swelled shape.
Noting the toting of a tall/clear pint, barren save plumed
foam, I shuddered and muttered perturbed forebodings
of doomed/jackbooted chromosomes.
  The duo doddered hurriedly past.
  (A compulsive leer escaped review.)
  Invisibility proved a grim liability when a lager glass
raped a new Alden shoe. Unburdening besieged
trouser-cuffs, shards tinkled like sore chimes.
  Ten yards ahead, the Raven-Haired Mess
heaved a flaming, whatsit, yuppie-rebuff.
  A Gin Sling-fueled war crime.
  Two seconds ticked.
  A 'Vette combusted — blazed to a lustrous inferno.
  Damning all spics, the scalawags gusted.
  Silhouettes maladjusted and vernal.

"Others see me as someone who is passionate and exciting."

**DAISY'S HARVEST WAS EMBARKED ON
A ROOF,** above an uncle-allocated townhouse;
a Bleecker Street nest harking lavender truths,
brimming art from *Ashcan-to-Bauhaus.*
  Portraits of Sandow and stuffed Poodles
cluttered an oodle's breadth of dusty/old shelves.
  A Smith Corona was avowed the rich persona
of one of Death's unjustly held elves.

"So, this Butch fellow writes often it seems?"
...I asked, meeting a swift wrenching of eyes.
"Impolite to make fun of old queens!"
the fear-mask trenchantly surmised.

PUMPS TATTOOING IRON ROOF-RUNGS
riled sneaking suspicions.
  Had she planned this seduction, step-by-step?
  Was her atheism a herring of recherché
intromission? Was I being played for a bruja's
stooge — led like a gullible foal?
  What was her object?
  Moolah?
  Spooge?
  To swallow my mudpuddle soul?
  Wasn't vigilance a must in this tractable state
of viewing things through molt-lenses?
  Was my reverie not such to invoke awkward
combusts of odd/chart-topping cadenzas?
  'I belong, a long way from here,
  I put on a poncho and played for mosquitoes,
  And drank 'til I was thirsty again,
  We went searching, through thrift store jungles...'
  Had I not merrily splurged a century-buck on
garlicky slugs and wines of unpronounceable
vineyards? Had I not verily purged the same
harsh muck as mephitic upchuck into a
chain-toilet's redoubtable innards?
  Yet still I sang, strolling post-meal, as if nothing queer
had transpired. Indubitably/unequivocally/irrefutably:
  I now found myself hex-mired!
  'Geronimo's rifle, Marilyn's shampoo,
  And Benny Goodman's corset and pen...'

THE ROOF'S ATMOSPHERE WAS COOL AND CLEAN, the Moon fat against gristle-flecked Phthalocyanine. We leaned against bricks overlooking Olde Greenwich.

Pitch mansards sowed Dickensian vibrancy.

She kissed adeptly, a real pro in fact, verging on free of all slobber. Casting me aside after a minute's tongue-lunge, she dislodged pink genital clobber. As she kicked lace loose from an ankle, I glanced with a curious squint. Twisted and damp like an abused cold-cut, it pulsated Luna's soft glint.

"Pretty..."

"Aren't they though? My sister brought 'em back from a shoot in Paris."

Spearing the knickers with a vamp polished black, I booted them right over the terrace.

"But — you asshole! Those were brand new!"

A roar sassed from below, wielding verbal Kung Fu.

"OH...HELLZ NO! HELLZ FUCKIN' NO!
KEEP YO' NASTY-ASS UNDIES TO YO' OWN SELF, HO!"

Scampering off to an opposing wall, Daisy leaned atop it face-first. Despite elbows ledge-pinned and a derrière's wag, I held firm against being coerced. Surveying the posterior for hail-damage scars, I detected myriad dimples.

How old was she really? *Thirty five? Thirty nine?*
(I swallowed a bug.)

Why couldn't things ever be simple?

AMBLING FORWARD, UNLATCHING MY BELT, detaching a cotton crotch-rind, I plunged in sans ado where the happiness dwelt, attacking the half-rotten behind.

Through an unpadded bra, large mounds seeped
like watery/putrefied fruits. My grasp shifted to
her larynx instead, simulating a suicide-noose.

While she sputtered and hawed, I battled urges
to gnaw, phantasms plundering my eyes.

*"Be a man and do it, Daddy! Throw the
sorceress over! The World's so sick of her lies!"*

(Shut up, I say! I simply cannot! This is a nice, pretty,
very sweet girl, and what if I fucking get caught? And
hey, I want her to *like* me! I'm concerned, caring, and
kind! Who gives a fuck about being a man? I'm
Nature Boy! There are worthier endeavors to mine!)

Disaster impending, thoughts prudently shifted
to the old standby of Grandmother's corns.

Withdrawing to wheeze, I examined veins
thrumming like serpentine vascular-porn.

Eyes!

Yes, *EYES* were required to quell this
execrable/mounting bloodcrave!

Was it not as onerous to snuff those who
watched as roasting turkeys in microwaves?

Venturing to swivel the petite frame around, pumps
held with polarity strong. Stroking sleek hair
with dogged persistence, I sighed
and queried what's wrong?

Slowly pivoting on her own accord, palms fixedly
skirt-smoothing, the fear-mask sagged
with vast self-abhor.

This was an inwardly black-and-blue thing.

"No, Jack. We can't fuck from the front. At least...
at least not yet. I have *scars*...from giving birth to my
daughter...and I don't wanna make you upset..."

Suppressing a twitch, I squashed guffaws.
This lily-white *lamb* was my witch?
Such nincompoopic chutzpah!
Such bubonic folly!
Was Idiocy not a son of a bitch?

**ARGENT STRETCH-MARKS FORMED
A MUMBLETY-PEGGED VEIL,** tragic stigmatas,
far beyond pale. But should I have fled?
Hatched-up a lie?
'Twas time for bed? Scratched my danged eye?
Indict escargot for acute diarrhea?
Invoke Jacques Cousteau or a sub in Korea?
Instead came my worst crime thus far/staying dead
put/soles anchored to tar/stroking rose-florid cheeks/
soothing rampaging cries/appraising stone-horrid
physiques with assuaging disguise:
*"Those aren't scars, babe.
They're a badge of Experience."*
As she melted within my disaster-embrace,
I re-entered Daisy's moist cleft. Belting ballads of
the Master Race, the brass ring voiced crazy behests.
*'WENN ES DICH GLÜCKLICH MACHT,
ES KANN NICHT DASS SCHLECHT SEIN!
WENN ES DICH GLÜCKLICH MACHT,
DANN WARUM DIE HÖLLE SIND SIE SO SAD?'*

So I finished "catcher in the rye" on the bus
in honor of lairds memory. Holy shit! Just got
worse and worse and worse! Not even good
enough to line charlottes tank! Fu manchu
didnt even want it so I gave it to a bum
at port authority! John lennon got

f'n shot bc of that book? Jesus!
Panther $75
Strawberry w/extra juice $65
Beauty mark $50
Hindu elephant w/mouse $80
Sexy pit bull w/yankees hat $85
Pope smoking blunt $90
Panther $75
Holdin on 4 dear life $50
Panther $75
Back to blood meridian.

"I may not yet understand the good in this situation, but it is there."

CARNAGE OUT-SLASHING CRAPULENCE BY YARDS, lids swiftly re-clenched to quell.
  Wine-glass shards!
  Wall-hangs askew!
  An intransigent vent of loosed Hell!
  Even my compendium of slipcased ECs
(a veritable almanac and bible) had been de-shelved,
strewn loose, and wretchedly creased as if
beset by some paranoiac reprisal!
  Compounding this pain was the hazy
recall of shitty cants and nocturnal dials.

I groaned, hoping Ivanhoe Drive had been
spared of rants pithy with rancorous revile.
  Unswiped sight still rimy with motes,
I needed to affirm posthaste. Blazing trails through
grimy sown oats, toes stubbed thrice as I raced.
  But...*NO! NO! NO CHARLOTTE NO!*
  Verily, a nightmarish manifest!
  The tank! Capsized! Contents demised!
  Nary a mite spared sans molest!
  Reeling with Angst, my palms sieved the farrago
upon a threadbare/carpeted floor...discerning
nil...save crickets quite ill... embargoing
to spare chirrups no more!
  From across the room issued a gurgling
purl, capped by a hawking of phlegm.
  Through a squint still muddy, I espied
a pale nude, plush from sternum-to-stem.
  The Canadian!
  Throat scurfy with scabs! Gash smitten with bruises!
  Blitzkrieged by Dread, mulling Charlotte in bed,
I trawled linen for corporeal abuses.

SWISHING A MUG OF JAVA-SMOKE

engendered no apparent avail. An effluxion coma?
  ('*Xanax?*' I hoped, hankering no sojourns to jail.)
  Flummoxed and bored following an exhaustive
pad-scrub, I diddled Sleeping Beauty twice more.
  Despite a vexed salt of sundry mad drubs,
little seeped beyond suety snores. Upon a
clement arousal, at half-past four, I appraised
her of Charlotte's manhunt.
  Reaching down, the Canadian winced.
  "Oh *fuck*...think it may've died in my cunt..."

Its my own stupid fault. I should have treated
you better. I should have spent more time w/
you. Shouldnt have gotten drunk so much
w/strangers. I am such a fool. I am a
stupid selfish ugly ignorent bald fool. I am
nothing. I dont listen. Always messing things up.
I am a f'n asshole.

Panther $75

Panther $75

Piglet $65

Panther $75

Liberian flag $80

Chinese letters for "gin and juice" $55

Mcdonalds logo $60

Betty boop naked $85

Yankees logo w/sparkeling diamonds $70

Beauty mark $50

Panther $75

Been having bad dreams every night w/retards
and old men in tunnels and they scare me.
Only you had the power to keep me calm.
Please please please come back. I need you.
I promise that I will never ever let you down
again. I promise I promise. I will pet you more
to. I am so so sorry. I love you charlotte. That
daisy chick called again. Been like 4 or 5 times
now. Should I call her back? Could really use
your advice. Please come home.   Please.

"I am never lonely for I am always standing beside myself with joy."

DESPITE MANY DAYS SPENT SCOURING,
my beloved was not to be found.
  The Withers Express grew increasingly wrecked.
  Shoved. Torn apart. Flipped around.
  Closets were ransacked. Pockets were probed.
  Each shoe received vigorous shakes. Treed vamps
offered naught but hoared gobbets of dust as tokens
of concessionary forsake. Even a ceiling of tiled
pressed-tin, inviolate since Grant bested Lee,
fell prey to disconsolate wrenchings;
edges julienning fingers with glee.
  A perspicacious man had long before logged:
  "Despair has its own calms."
  How I so pined to flood the savant's gay pan
with revisionary/brass-knuckled bombs!

GONE! GONE! INDISPUTABLY SCRAMMED!
Only her shorn husk remained; a morbid shell
relocated to the bark shanty's jamb.
  (A structure re-erected in vain.)
  And there the death-mask blankly endured,
collecting motes like an octavalent Mark of Cain;

constantly harking to some mysterious crime
borne of a heinous/bacchanalian campaign.
  Just a matter-of-course.
  Another belt-notch.
  Was my butchery of Health not a given?
  Was I not the Midas of Shit?
  A glue-drizzling fiend?
  An offender beyond all reach of the shriven?

**BALL-BEARINGS SQUEALED AS THE
DRAWER BREACHED** to reveal
a burden cool and firm.
  All for the best! When it's time it's time!
  Oil meeting drool, I squirmed.
  Perhaps it'd go smoother up on the roof?
  One last Lunar-Farewell?
  Should I even bother with a note's
lachrymose proof?
  Was finding takers not doomed a tough sell?
  But wait! What's that?
  A flutter in the tank's open gape?
  Quickly...Jack! Drop that damned lid!
  Risk no more eight-legged escapes!

LIKE A FELLED GOOSE, hope shriveled and
flopped. The flits belonged to a thirsty cricket.
  As it lapped from a sponge kept perpetually
moist, I resisted strong urges to flick it.
  Shifting its attention to the flecked chips, unearthing
a chum's chucked limb, the tiny bugger employed
a most dexterous grip as it supped
with a turbulent vim.

Rainy day finally. Everybody was yelling about "wcw nitro". Even cliff. Talking about it like its a real sport. They all love fake wrestling and a baseball player named cheater. Surrounded by phonies (sp?). Still no sign of her. Every time I pass the tank I look inside and see that stupid corps. Told daisy about it and she said "I cant believe you are so broken up over a dumb spider. Its just a bug dummy." At least I found a nice piece of purple ribbon to add to the shrine. It tastes young.

Mary mother of god $70

Sexy strawberry w/extra juice $65

Panther $75

Lashawnda $50

Shark biting taz $85

Panther $75

Yankees logo $65

Skunk holding flower $60

USMC bulldog $free (bc he only had one arm)

Panther $75

Panther $75

Lucky dice $50

I believe in miracles I believe in miracles
I believe in miracles I believe in miracles
I believe in miracles I believe in miracles
I believe in miracles I believe in miracles
I believe in miracles I believe in miracles

I believe in miracles I believe in miracles
I believe in miracles I believe in miracles
I believe in miracles I believe in miracles
I believe in miracles I believe in miracles
I believe in miracles I believe in miracles
I believe in miracles I believe in miracles!

"The greatest thing that one can learn is just to love and be loved in return."

THE ACCURSED LORD'S DAY ONCE AGAIN DAWNED, marking advents of crippling things.
A beer-sale embargo fueling hangover-sorrow.
Bus commutes tripling D.T. stings.
The pained clairvoyance of Polish annoyance obstinate since a hospital-release.
(Though we'd thrashed Kilroy hither/thither like a frayed shuttlecock, our Sundays still bore the stalwart allure of illogical follicle-grease.)
In lieu of cudgels with phone-book spines, we'd trod a more pusillanimous path; anointing pallid arms vulgarity shrines, daring Longanimity's ceding to wrath. Bert cannibalized Ernie's cadaver.
A bishop lap-hosted Jay North.
Connie Chung tantalized a turgid Dan Rather.
Snarling Negroes bedecked a panther's flexed swarth.

But still, the Polack proved a scissorbill, hermetically sealed against hints; contrarily besotted with scrawls solely plotted for the singular evocation of wince...
'COULDA NEVAH COME UP WIT DIS ON MY OWN! YOUSE ALWAYS KNOWS JUS' WHAT I LIKE! SOMEHOWS, YOUSE TWO CAN READ MY MIND LIKE OTHA FELLAS PEDALS DERE BIKES!'
Our skills had apparently transcended mere craft, blossoming to art extraordinaire...
'PICASSO WHO'S? I'LL TAKE YOUSE!'
Worse yet, we'd become his best friends...
'DESE TATS MAKE ME FEEL LIKE I'S WALKIN' ON AIR!'

DISDAINING VIGILANTLY VESTED VENETIAN FULL-TURNS, solar ambuscades sallied slivers and cracks, gambolling atop dust with the dogged resolve of a flesheating/microscopic wolfpack. Broiling bedbound 'til eleven half-past, when the cloud cavalry finally stormed, my only solace was found through a cable Noir-Fest.
(An unflagging parade of the forlorn.)
'Detour' was on, albeit Turnerized, the tale of a Doom-betrothed hitchhiker's trek; Tom Neal's bit as an undisguised twit wielding an abjectly disquieting effect.
So he'd blundered minding a dream-girl's sake!
Was Perdition condign for one simple mistake?
Rankling! Insulting! A flagon of gall!
Had Herr Ulmer never crossed the path of No Good Reason at All?
Even after buffing the Trinitron's lint, sherbert-hues resembled digitized manure.
What kind of clod would greenlight a Grade-C quickie with such a fruitlessly stylized restore?

As if eavesdropped by some mysterious force, the
offending visage commenced a phantasm's hover;
phlegmatic vapors spitting-up an amoral right
palm whilst ogling a Baby Gap catalog-cover.

Mind wearily drifting from Sodom to Problem,
mulling arts of strategic departure, I invoked
Tardiness to absolve Kilroy's approach
with the aim of an analgesic archer.

**LANDING IN THE SHOP AT THREE'S
BURNING CUSP,** my satchel plunged with abrupt
despair. While Cliff attended a fat brown shoulder,
a Polish rump obstructed my chair.

Calm, patient, and fixedly pleasant, right-handedly
clutching a paper carton, his ring's fissured glass eye
refracted fluorescent descry as I studied
a Greek diner's garnished Spartan.

*"Sorry if dis went too cold already, Jackie.
One an' a half sugahs though...right?"*

Breezing tacitly past, I raided the bathroom,
guts reeling with braky/cold blight.

WIELDING A BROADSWORD'S PURPOSE,
exiting the w.c., the edge of Skuld was promptly
dulled by a paperbacked bull mugging
a counter's debris.

> To JB, a hell of a baby!
> Good luck with the broads and the chicks!
> Tuck that chin and keep on punching!
> — Jake LaMotta, 1996.

Dumbstruck and dazed, my gaze butted orbs glazed
and partially cowled; Lilliputian Jacks staring helplessly
back like pupil-ensnared gamefowl.

"Youse says youse was a real big boxin' fan, ain't dat
kinda right? He's my pops ol' pal, so's I got him
t'sign it when he was ovah f'dinna last night."

Fighting back tears, vision shifted to Cliff as gore seeped from a licorice pelt, polluting a crude but unambiguous Lincoln in the form of an afro-wigged welt. Upon a copious green-soap spritz, I detected a cursive inscription, Kilroy's blather availing no matter as Tom Neal's ethereal squeals consigned it to virtual Egyptian.

'ALL MEN IZ KREATED FUNKY!'

Busy busy busy. Worked on averys back today and its looking pretty ok now. Showed me a binder full of crime seen photos. Big and glossy in color. One guy they fished out of the hudson. His skin was puffy and pure white and his eye balls were gone. They took a shot of his corps next to his drivers license (sp?) for the before and after stuff. Not much resembalance I must say. Ave says they call them "floaters". Another was a teen age black girl who committed suicide in her bathroom w/a shot gun. There was a photo of a kleenix box w/just one tiny piece of brain on the top tissue. The scrap of brain was colored like pink corl and shiny like a glayzed donut. Almost pretty. She had corn rows and in another picture where her scalp had peeled back you could actually see the pattern of the braids on the inside of the skin. Looks like it might hurt even more to have corn rows knotted then to have your

head shot off. The note said she was sad bc her
pimp had given her aids. Then rayon man came
in but as soon as he saw averys badge and gun
on the counter he just turned around and left.
Or maybe jesus scared him?

Panther $75

Panther $75

Panther $75

Sexy cherrys w/extra juive $65

Brick shit house $75

Averys back $free

Panther $75

Eagle and snake and cactus w/mexican flag $95

Tribal ak47 $90

Panther $75 (on a dworf)

Panther $75

"Li'l hakeem aint so dam mean" $60

Beauty mark $50

Def jam logo $65

Devil $80

Panther $75

Sexy honeypot w/bees licking drips $65

Panther $75

USMC bulldog $85

Watching news now. This ross parrow guy
seems pretty all right to me. Why does
everyone hate him so much? Charlotte please
come back bc I miss you. I didnt kill you right?

"The family I will have is more important than the one I come from."

NEAR BUBBY'S TRIBECA CAFE, home of the twenty-dollar waffle, a passing cluster of overhead gulls squawked schadenfreude unlawful.

Sidewalk-ensconced beneath a Perrier gamp, the duo beckoned and waved. Identically accoutered in middies and shades, each was supping a lemonade pint. Ice tinkled betwixt mint flakes.

As I withdrew a chair and forced a grin, a challenge beneath beams of pure murder, the overgroomed child (locks silk-ribboned) scoffed like a Brahmanical sirdar. While a heart-shaped hairline and delicate features extolled triumphs of matriarchic gene-sway, her default visage brimmed Disgust over Fear.

This one...I surmised with abject surprise...

Will be a true maneater someday!

ALTHOUGH 'SPROUT' HAD LOOMED AS MERE DIAPHANOUS THEORY, only occasionally regarded in passage, evidential corollaries had branded her mother with an unkind and savage embassage.

Low-slung and wrinkled bosoms.

Dark grapely nipplish hues.

An atrophic roadmap of silver-sheened trenches crowning a cavernous flue.

Despite an otherwise fine fettle (like her quondam mate, she'd harbored Olympian aims) I'd routinely inflicted the spiritual bruise of blouse-encased screws, plunging deep before any peeps/protests/ obsidian-claims. While this repugnance indubitably saddened, she was far too timorous to get tough; padding harsh truths with goose-down delusions; suffusing Reality with Fluff.

LEERING, THE FEAR-MASK FAUX-GULPED, hands sailing to-and-fro.

"Sprout, this here's Dummy! Dummy, this here's the Sprout! Ain't she a darling though?"

A clear relish of discomfiture sparked swift thoughts of belt-flagellation — siphoning ichorous sap from perilous traps, awaiting swift/police-dealt truncation.

"Howdy! Nice to meetcha, dear! But why so glum? Got yourself a nice mama here!"

Consenting to relinquish the tube from her lips only upon a hand's tottered secession, a glance towards Daisy then back to myself prompted grim/Foster Granted reflections.

I was decomposing with appalling haste!

Balder than within Kilroy's purulence days prior!

Wan!

Withdrawn!

A galling waste!

Would a twenty-sixth year stoke the calendar's jeer before falling prey to scalding expire?

Phlegm cleared, the Child's thin voice wielded considerably less throat than I'd guessed:

"My daddy runs faster than you..."

I beseeched God for cardiac-arrest.

Guy comes in today and says he wants a "portfollio" around his arm. I ask him if he means a tribal and he says no so I draw him a nice big portfollio w/a zipper and a handle and the guy says "what the fuck is that white boy?" and I say it is a portfollio just like you asked for and he pulls a blue bandanna (sp?) out of his pocket and puts it on the counter and points and says "no mother fucker! I want a portfollio like this! dont you know what a f'n portfollio is?" But I could not argue bc he was a crip and you have to be very careful w/those types.

Pit bull howling by tombstone $85

Panther $75

Small rose $50

Thug life $125

Panther $75

Nubian princess $65

Knife thru basketball $85

Portfollio $100 -$50 crip discount

Panther $75

Micky boning mini $80

Panther $75

Panther $75

Now that she is gone nobody understands me except the little black retard and holden and I had to f'n dream them up.

I don't even understand me myself.

"I share a strong spiritual bond with my maker."

CHRIST'S EBONY SHADES SKIMMED SWIFTLY ALONG, begetting both Pain and Lifeblood, imbuing the Semitic visage with a queer lucidity and an uncannily cognitive flood.

Forsooth, I'd wrenched the Savior south from the heavens to tether the dorsal of a coke-sweaty hide.

Was it maudlin that this feat promulgated self-love?

Did it not rate scant morsels of pride?

Avery, however, was faring quite poorly; skittishly jerking with shake. Reluctantly, I queried the thew of his opiate cache in the midst of a five-minute break.

"Nah, bro. Nah! Got plenty still. Always fuckin' do! Just been my roommate, Pat! Douchebag's got me all *sortsa* antsy. This fuckin' guy...wotta prat!"

"With the braided goatee and the Sub Pop hoodie? Who sells tickets? The trendoid dip?"

(Having glimpsed my successor only twice-prior, I'd not found him particularly hip.)

"Yeah, scalper all right. That's how I met him actually. Rangers game...outside M.S.G. Flashed him my shield and said I wouldn't book him if he threw me a fuckin' freebie. Only had two stubs left, so we both went in and he just watched the game with me. Good seats too! Dead-center behind visitor's goal!"

"Um...so...what's the big problem then though?"

"For *one*, he fuckin' snores! I mean, I can hear it every fuckin' night! All the way through a buffer a two

shut doors! Drives me fuckin' nuts! So impolite!
'Nother thing, he's got a cat..."

"But what's wrong with that? It's always
seemed like you've thought the best of them."

(Inhaling belches fetid, I reactively fretted
in tandem with the Son of Bethlehem.)

"Pardon. Well, I do like 'em. But *this* one...I dunno.
Stares at me real fuckin' funny. Kinda like Heathcliff
meets Cujo. I mean, clawed-up the couch. Kicks litter
'round the john whenever it pees! Shat on my good
leather bomber! The Avirex, with the nude broad
on back! One that says Pistol Packin' Mama! I mean,
someone offers you a room, dontcha think it's *right*
to inform 'em there's a pet in the mix
before you decide to accept?"

"So why didn't you just kibosh Pat on
move-in day? Seems like a valid intercept."

"Dunno. Guess 'cause it's cute? Still just a kitten.
Hold-up, ain't even mentioned the worst!"

"*Whoops*...here it comes...twice bitten!"

"Shut it, bro. Lemme set this up a bit first. 'Bout a
month back, chick gives me a little green scorpion.
Present for my fuckin' thirty fifth..."

"Oh shit, man. *Honestly*, didn't know.
Would've gotten you some kind of gift."

"Eh, don't worry none. You give me plenty enough
just bein' my motherfuckin' friend. I don't expect
nothin' from no cheap Yahudis neither. But *yeah*,
said she bought it from some Ricans. They fight 'em
against spiders! Kinda like fuckin' *roosters*, I mean!"

"I've heard."

"*Sick!* Degenerate spics! Intrinsically morally
diseased! Anyhow, she made a display for it too. Like,

a little fuckin' mint diorama! Round tank! Rainbow gravel! Even had a cactus with a flower on top... yellower'n a Cuban banana! Couldn't fry an egg with a Glock up her twat, but she did a good job on this at least. I mean, I really liked it! But the fuckin' cat... all sortsa distraught...and I'm like, *'Yo, Pat! Keep that hairball clear a my beast!'*"

"And what'd he say?"

"Bro, calm the fuck down, I'm gettin' to that next! Says, *'Course I fuckin' will! Think I want that thing all stingin' her up? Can you imagine the fuckin' bill from the vet?'* So, figure he gets it, and everything's jake, 'til a few days pass and I wake up to this huge fuckin' racket! Somethin' crashes and Pat swears! Pretty clear the cat's finally reached the bowl and attacked it! And I'm *pissed*, bro! Pissed! But I stay in bed, 'cause if I get up, I'm just gonna fuckin' smack him! And I can't afford that shit! First roomie *ever* that pays rent on time! So I stay mum...diplomatic...like my Grandpa Mike, the old-timey Tammany sachem! Just listen to him sweep. Pickin' shit up. Cat screams once, but I figure he's just kickin' the dumb thing. Soon as he splits, I check-out the livin' room shelf and see Pat shoulda been a janitor or somethin'! All looks fine! Like nothin' bad took place! Even the flower ain't got no fuckin' bruises! And I'm thinkin', *'Okay, well...maybe I was wrong.'* Like, maybe somethin' else fell; good thing I didn't start accusin'! Then the cat comes over and starts rubbin' up on me. All fuckin' kinds a happy and sweet. Just purrin' along while I checked the bowl out, makin' sure the scorpion ain't deceased. 'Cause it's *frozen*, bro! *Motionless!* Like an old spook hauntin' a bus-stop. So I ding the glass, but fuckin' nothin' happens'. Still as a bucket a slop! Usually when I tap,

the little fucker starts hoppin', 'cause it knows
it's gonna get fed. So I take the lid
off and give it a shove..."
   "With your finger? While you
still weren't sure it was dead?"
   "Fuck no! You *loco*, bro? I used a fuckin' plastic fork!
Go beneath its belly, give it a lift, and the thing
tumbles like a fuckin' flicked cork! And I'm thinkin'
motherfucker. That motherfuckin', cocksuckin'
weasel! No apology! No fuckin' note! Dude's all set
to play fuckin' dumb like the poor thing died
from lung cancer, syph, or the measles!"
   "Um...do scorpions have lungs?"
   "Dunno, bro! Go look it up in your fuckin' Torah!"
   "Sorry..."
   "So, the cat's still rubbin' up like we're best fuckin'
pals, and I'm tryin' not to go Sodom and Gomorrah!
I mean, *straight-up*, I'm itchin' to kill it, but change my
mind pretty fuckin' quick. Didn't know no better. Just
a dumb beast bored outta its skull lookin' for any
kinda kick! Then I think 'bout fuckin' up Pat some
more. But, like I said, he's been an alright roommate
besides. So I take the high-road. Classier that way...
lettin' things fall wayside in stride. Still owed him an
eighth for some Motörhead tickets, so I weigh-out
my stash and drop the dead fucker in the doob..."
   "Then what?"
   "Then I shake it around, 'til the shit's real hidden, and
plant it on toppa his faggot-ass/gay Rubik's Cube!"
   "No. I meant, did he see it?"
   Rippling with convulsions of Avery's laughter,
the Savior implored a tender mercy.

"'*Course* he fuckin' saw it! This was two weeks back!
Dude just can't handle no controversy!"

"Hasn't said anything?"

"Zilch! Ain't got the balls! Fuckin' *cat's* got more
balls, and *he's* a fuckin' *she!* Tellin' ya, Jack, only thing
in life you gotta have is balls! Otherwise,
what's it all about really?"

Beleaguered eyes scarring the gargantuan
back gawked like an exasperated wraith.

"What about Family? ...Friends?
...The Ecstasy of Unmitigated Faith?"

Hunching abruptly, the Detective
shuddered, trumpeting a garlicky fart.

"Listen-up, bro...I put faith in *nothin'*...
'cept Uncle Sam's a stingy-ass kike and
nobody dodges Fate's free-wheelin' Dart!"

November, 1993

*Noonday beams callously sliced. Scratches raked the
bedroom door. Oppenheimer blossoms of neuralgia diced.
Ark-raiders baked in flames of messianic store.*

*I judged the pillowcase beneath my cheek aberrantly
flaky and dry. Weightless scales of vomitus crust
aspirated with expulsions of sigh.*

*Buster and Elmer stormed a freed threshold, desperate
for comfort/caress. Talons hypodermically stabbed three
toes, birthing pirouettes of hurt and distress.*

*Basking in El's unalloyed cat-bliss,
my heart pulsed preposterous ardor.*

*A fat kiss banished pain to regions unknown
with a meteor's phosphorus larder.*

How I relished such delirious bursts!
How I lived for such rare manifest!
"Smiling, Daddy! That's kinda strange!
Usually look so damned depressed!"
  "Sorry about that. Just couldn't
help it. I...I'll knock it off..."
  "Silly! Perfectly okay to look goofy sometimes...just don't
let it poison your trough! Like Queensbury said, protect
yourself, yeah; but you'll suffocate in a house of
windowless brick! Best permeate that husk
with some Nature Boy logic or huff
the fate of a mouse in aspic!"
  "Nature Boy? Who...who the fuck's that?
I ain't never heard of him!"
  "Oh...ignorant, uncultured, foolish young Daddy...calm
down! Cool that rascally vim! He's the fellow from that
Nat King Cole song! C'mon, you know the one! Ugh!
Makes my eyes fucking fog! Champion
tearjerker bar none!"
  "Hmph! Got a copy on hand?
I wanna hear what's so damn great..."
  "'Course I do, you lowbrow brigand! My mama's old 78!"
  Flashing a mad grin as she dashed aside — jiggling,
naked, pale — she returned moments later with a
disc of shellac, wielding a basement's mildewy veil.
  Gently tabling the treasured heirloom,
she paused with a tonearm half-raised.
  "Words are important, ignore the tune!
This lesson'll stick 'til your dying days!"

'There was a boy —
A very strange enchanted boy —
They say he wandered very far —
Very far, over land and sea —

A little shy and sad of eye —
But very wise was he —
And then one day, a magic day —
He passed my way, and while we spoke —
Of many things, fools and kings —
This he said to me —
The greatest thing you'll ever learn —
Is just to love...and be loved in return.'

The disarmingly brief, mysterious song left me hunched
in bed and dumbfounded. Mortified with
incomprehension, I gaped like a
teetotalist rum-hounded.

"That's it?"

Quaking, shaking, she collapsed face-first,
in time with my innards' cloy.

"Oh Daddy! Daddy! How I love you so!
You're my goddamned Nature Boy!"

Still unable to discern any congruence between myself
and some serene Swazi waif, fevered dream girl tears
glazed my sternum. Blood from a Nazi air-strafe.

"I enter new friendships like pools of water on hot Summer days."

**'TWAS A SUBTLE CHASE, BUT REAL
NONETHELESS,** my blood wintry with brumal
affright; tail-scorching since a bus-debark — four
dusky eyes loomed ruefully glued with
the grit of a cruel snakebite.

Glancing back on the escalator, I mulled the stalk's enigmatic fuel. What on Earth had I adventitiously done to lure such problematic ghouls?

Did I project the millionaire playboy-type, toting verdant scads to while? Was it the brass ring? Possibly my watch? An early Fifties *'Mystery-Dial'*. Both shiny, yes, perhaps even scarce, but of peripheral value at best.

Where were these *balls* Avery pledged I possessed? Where was my Nature-Boy wisdom?

Did these grim assailants conceal *stakes* on their persons? Was my fate slated Van Helsing victim?

AS THE DIAGONAL LIFT HIT PORT AUTHORITY'S GROUND-LEVEL,

I absconded as brisk as I could. Many years past my last feardriven dash (wiped from an onerous workday besides) lungs singed as I strove to forge distance, barreling those clotting my stride. Though caterwauls peppered my wake, I took no pauses for heed, inveigling ascription to Big City wonts, balking at the huntsmen's great speed.

Damn! Damn! Doubledamn!

Much too close and gaining!

I kicked-up my pace to the paramount notch — these rogues were dead-set on maiming!

They'll pierce my foul heart! They'll lop off my crown!
They'll dump me in Potter's...bones facing down!

Though outwardly, I welcomed such gore, I deserved the bitterest of ends, my craven kernel beat feet with the ardor galore of a hatchet-man's targeted hen. For I was an insipid bug-slayer! Morality's twilit gnat!

A wretched wilter of daisies!

A vile/Knicks-ticketed 'Pat'!
A/C/E stairs sighted! Yes, turnstiles at last!
Commencing a full-throttle sprint, I burrowed
frenziedly fast. Plowing through a flock of old Chinese
hags, I chuckled, bitterly ironic; continuing skedaddle
amidst Cantonese babble with a haste
bordering on the subsonic.

**AT MY TOKENLESS HURDLE'S HIGH-
KICKING APEX** came a staccato of titular-burst:
*"Jack! Jack! Hold-up, it's me!
Just lemme talk to ya first!"*
Back-up! Providential relief!
A kindly if star-crossed arrival!
'Twas a spiritual hoist to meet such philanthropy...
a shame there'd be no survivals!
Turning to face the heavensent pawn, finding only a
panting Crip-dyad, I scrutinized miens asthmatically
wan despite complexions echoing La Amistad.
Observing an arm thrust into view, fluorescence lit
contours more swish than tattoo. Slapping the mark,
the short Crip beamed, even as he labored for breath.
The voice: friendly/proud/keen.
Rife with Ebonic shibboleth.
"Healed-up mad phat, dawg! Shizzle's th' fuckin' bomb!"
Squinting at the quivering/hickory mass,
I marveled at the Short Crip's aplomb.
This was certainly not my glyph.
Perhaps he'd mistaken me for Cliff?
"Um...you sure I did that?"
The grin fell as piteously flat as a harpooned
weather-balloon. *"But...Jack...you done ALL my cartoons.
You...you...you done it last June..."*

Shitty day.
Daisy called me at work crying and said
that her neck is infected. Then another
customer came in w/a bad EZ red scar on a
tattoo cliff did like only 2 weeks ago. Why does
he keep using that crap? Then I had a wierd ass
dream on the bus. I was in a 3rd floor condo at
the jersey shore. There was a pretty black slut
w/me and I was reciting poetry (WTF?).
Holding the outside window sill my deranged
(sp?) malicious (sp?) half brother clawed at the
glass and begged to be invited in. His name was
josh. I refused and just cracked open the
window to smack his face w/a copy of catcher
in the rye. He fell to the 2nd story balconey
but landed on his feet and looked up at me
w/a evil grin. I turned away when the slut said
something to me about president rosenfeld
being a spy for the international jewish bankers.
When I looked back out at my half brother
he had mutated into some kind of hidious
monster. Half panther/half human. I somehow
knew that he could not enter my apartment
so I laughed at him and dared him to even try.
Moments later there was a knock at the front
door and I reached for the book but it had
become the brown glass.
          At least there was no tunnel.

Sexy watermelon slice w/bite $65
Heart on rollerskates $75
Yankees logo $65
Panther $75
Phat p'gell be raising hell $50
Taz in girls underwear $75
Fuck the police $85
Beauty mark $50
Beauty mark $50
Papa smurf w/blunt $65
Panther $75

Fu manchu keeps saying that if jesus didnt exist he would sufficate his motherless son.

"My heart's aflame, burning with white-hot love."

UPON AN ATTEMPT TO VEIL A MANILLA DISPATCH as we scaled unpleasant pine, her pique flared like a friction match amidst creaks protesting our climb. "*Jeez-Louise*, Dummy! What the heck *is* that? Just *tell* me already, okay?"

"Nothing, alright? Just a debt-notice! Get 'em every fucking day!"

A vexed frown haloed a withdrawn key's stir of achromatic whit. "C'mon! Please! Be honest now, Jack! It's from *her*...isn't it?"

Swiping sully from shirt, a brushed *'Shadow Plaid'*,
I traversed my apartment's front-door,
entering the World of Hurt.
  The Dust Stalingrad.
  The chute to Poe's Nevermore.
  Exasperated, I glared, carefully
avoiding the gauze clotting her throat.
  "Look, Dee…it's a surprise to me too. Sorry if it's
gotten your goat. Truly, I am — but it's really not such
a big deal. Probably just an *'I hate you'*-note…
or *'Eat shit you stupid schlemiel!'"*
  "It's okay, Dummy. Not jealous or nothin', but I
know that you're dying to open it. I know what she
means to you and I totally get it. My skull
isn't filled with coconut!"
  "I think you mean: *meant.*"
  Hands thrust in God-beseech
fashion aped a Bayou-plea to repent.
  *"You clueless schmuck! Motherfuck a duck! Just open
the goddamned thing! Trying to be fucking magnanimous
here! What aren't you understanding?"*
  Fishing within a linty hip-bag, extracting my father's
old knife, I ripped at the envelope's provocative
swag as if impacting a slattern's shelf-life.

**ALAS, THE MISSIVE CONTAINED ONLY TWO
BLANK POSTCARDS** cloning dated fruit-crate
labels. *'COMBAT'* shaded corsairs amidst a plank-spar.
A burro filched *'JACK-S BRAND'* globes with
a snout covertly de-stabled.
  Groping the envelope blindly, seeking the escorting
epistle, my fingers exhumed a lone *'Post-It'* note
whilst the fear-mask loomed forlorn and abysmal.

> Saw these at a rest-stop in Fla on the last
> tour and I knew you would like them. Just
> wanted to say hello and I hope you are well.
> Was thinking about you.
> Write if you like.
> Hope summer was nice!
>
> Love El.

Electric twinges skewered my pith!
Acute pangs of pleuralgia!
Was I already the faded old pal of a relic-corral
beneath a rustproof roof of nostalgia?
"Well? C'mon! What'd she say?"
"Nothing. Said nothing. Just drop it, okay?"
"Probably just wrote because of me!
Catty! So damn *unnecessary* too!"
"Honestly, Dee...don't think so this time.
This has nothing to do with you."
"Nope, Dummy. Nuh-uh! Probably just heard you're
dating a movie-star's sister and got all kinds of
jealous! Trust me, I know how *girls* think...
you really only get the fellas!"
Lips shriveled grimly as mascaraed orbs
scanned ephemera torn from my grasp.
"Huh? That reminded her of you?
What the heck? So fucking mean! *'Jack-S'?*"
Eyes pelted the sentry of Charlotte's hut.
(A dusty, unforgiving shell.)
*"This harlot slut you're so fucking
hung-up on is making our lives living hell!"*
I wondered what Ivanhoe Drive was like.
Did motorists joust Rights-of-Way?
"JACK!"
Did they share old records on hungover mornings
in tattered white lingerie?

"Can you PLEASE just move beyond this already?"
...was Los Angeles not a pavilion of despair-
coordinates the Map should oceanically abort?
"JESUS CHRIST! ARE YOU EVEN LISTENING?"
...purging the World of four million nightmare-
subordinates and hordes of starched khaki shorts?

Well it turns out that daisys sister is now a junky so they put her in a rehab for scientologists (sp?) only. Her bungalow (sp?) mate is lisa marie presley who is there for pill popping and wine cooling. Daisy made me talk to her sister on the phone and got mad when I asked her if woody harrison got boners during the naked bits in that serial killer movie but her sister just laughed and thought it was funny. I asked her if I could talk to lisa marie to but she said she was on the golf course. That was a shame. She also told me that heroine is the devils candy. I told her I always thought of the devil as more of a malomar (sp?) guy and she said no he definitely prefers heroine and I said how do you know that and she said
"bc we are fuck buddies".
Panther $75
Broken heart $60
Panther $75
Virgo symbol $60
Beauty mark $50

Lipstick print near cunt $50
Panther $75
Panther $75
Beauty mark $50
Tweety w/afro $65
Panther $75
Chinese letters for "dead police" $60
Hebrew letters for "black jesus" $55
Yankees logo $65
Sexy hornet insemenating flower $70
Panther $75
Spider on earlobe $55
Panther $75
Panther $75
Panther $75
Beauty mark $50
Panther $75

Rayon man honked at me while I was waiting for the bus. He was wearing a yellow fedora that matched his yellow shirt and his yellow porsche. Even tho he gave me the finger when I waved back I have to admit that his hat was nice. Reminded me of that time when I bought a old stetson and el told me to never wear it bc only faggots and english men wear them. I said "what about holden?" and she just knocked it off my head.

Then a police horse walked over it.

"I never prejudge people based on their age, race, or reputation for my mind is an open one."

**NEAR THE URINAL-TROUGH OF
THE TURKEY'S NECK TAVERN,** at the tip of
North Twelfth and Bedford, I was accosted by a chap
colloquially dubbed *'Heartless'*, but known to staunch
pals as Edward. Amongst his fame-claims were a
childhood perch upon Jim Morrison's lap, a cursory
resemblance to Matt Dillon, signed plywood hurt
by Chuck Norris's love-tap, and churned turns
as a Bob Mapplethorpe mannequin.

"Yo! Jack! Your mouth's fuckin' bleedin'!
Your *teeth* look real long! Your gums are recedin'!
Been bangin' a Chinaman's gong?"

"Hey! Nix that noise! I'll have you know I'm just
fine! Nothing that a well-placed bullet won't
cure, provided not borne from my shrine!"

"Dude! Stop! Seriously! Don't even fuckin' kid
around! Nuff'a my buddies have OD'd already,
can't have you be *next* in the ground!"

"Calm down. Told ya...I'm fine!"

"And what about that *girl,* Jack? The one with the
rack? She know you're hooked on this stuff? Maybe

she could put you in Bellevue at least? You can
kick, man! Just gotta believe! Even
when the goin' gets rough!"
  Shaking my head, rinsing piddle with soap,
my voice twanged like an untuned guitar.
  "Not faking, Ed! Since when have I *ever* fiddled with
dope? And I've been marooned a year
and counting thus far..."

**HERR HEARTLESS RANG THE
VERY NEXT EVE,** proffering remedies
from Roosevelt Isle.
  With internal fear-masks inculcating Guilt,
I declared blind dates out-of-style.
  *'But listen, dude...just trust me on this! This is the best
friend of Lucy's little sister! Smokin' hot! Bangin' bod!
Tits juicy as King Kong's dick blisters!'*
  "Sorry, man. Can't do it! Reading a dense book.
But...wait! Hey! Look, man! I said no!"
  *'Jack! Please! She's on the tram now!
just do me a solid? Already told her you'd go!'*

**THE LOFTY APPRAISAL FARED
CURIOUSLY PRECISE** when my
castor-oil surfaced usuriously nice.
  Long copper hair! Whisky-flecked eyes!
  A jutting thorax! Silk-stockinged thighs!
  Subsequent to mussels at Arturo's on Houston
came a near-empty midnight matinee.
  Commencing to neck two reels in,
Rose blazed an incandescent bouquet.
  As my fly was unsnagged, and she spit to lube,
Zoë Lund huffed skag through a tinfoil tube.

ADMIRING THE RED CROWN'S RHYTHMIC HONE, a devilish thought made itself known. Glancing north, she squinted, nonplussed, gape glazed thickly with drool.

"Hey...Rose...how old are you now?"

Giggles hearkened hooky from school.

"Oh. Weird. Ed said you knew. Fifteen next week. Said you'd do me a tattoo."

While I remained calm, an internal storm zinged, condemning Herr Heartless to Hell's Lizard Kinged Ring. Cosh-wielding brothers pounded Withers concrete, steadfastly focused on slaughter.

An outraged father, hose-length clutched, avenged the besmirch of his daughter.

A cell-door! Slamming shut!

Felonious prongs deflowering my butt!

Wafts of gas! A Shelby's roar!

Khaki Shorts' Mustang! A lance tarnished with gore!

Pausing again, eyes opened wide.

Rose beamed Innocence.

I mournfully sighed.

So cliffs gf caught the crabs and passed it on to him but he says its ok bc its from another chick. But the real big news in the shop all day long was that they shot tupac. Like that is a big f'n suprise? Why wouldnt he get shot? I thought that the first time I saw him on mtv. "Just look at that dude! There is a man begging to get shot!" Still no word back.

Should I write another letter?

Rip tupac $50

Panther $75
Preying hands $75
Beauty mark $50
Chinese letters for "thug life" $55
Only god can judge me now across back $100
Dead babys footprint $50
Heart made of ice $65
Panther $75
Surfing pit bull $85

Speaking of shots this was wierd. Dreamt
that me and the retard were coing it and she
turned into a man and wouldnt stop laughing
so I ripped his/her throat open w/dads old
knife. Then I felt bad so I went up to the roof
and put the gun in my mouth and pulled the
trigger. This morning when I woke up there was
another bullet missing. Cliff thinks I was
making this up and got very mad. Said
he is way to itchy for malarky (sp?).
———— But what does malarky mean?

"I am mired in cosmic glue and loving it."

**THE SAVIOR'S TENEBROUS WHIPPAGE
PETERED,** conjoining the next stage-arrival,
goading me to implore miracles more like
fate-cheaters at a tented revival.

The color-tinting of Celtic pelts was a typically grueling endeavor, satisfactory results as evasively fleet as upon those suntanned forever. Despite being lily-toned beasts, emerald blood ran unfeasibly thin; an unchecked millennium of rampant hooch-feasts divesting coagulum. Avery's acromegalic hypertension only further compounded our hurdles, copious ink *'holidays'* bearing pockmarked tribute to such demoralizing girdles.

A thorough weighing of options adjudicated nether-commencement most prudent.

"If we knock out the kidneys first, the rest's a cakewalk. Congruent?"

"Roger that. But should the cloak at his neck be red? Perhaps a nice baby blue?"

"Nah, bro! Purple! Gonna be enough red as-is between all the blood and the spew! Purple's the color a royalty! King a Kings you're fuckin' with here!"

"But *was* he a monarch? Always thought him a rabbi. Or some kinda preacher or seer."

"You fuckin' *deaf*, Yid? Just said he was the *King* a fuckin' *Kings!*"

Sovereign demands of only the best compelled duly amplified stings. Penetrating with depth and clarity, needles raked lush burgundy tones. Irrespective of serfly discomfort, Temerity surrendered to moans.

"MARY, MOTHER A COCKSUCKIN' GOD!"

"So, um, how's Pat?"

"Dunno. Alright, I guess? *GAH!* His new broad's eyes are spaced kinda far! *UMPH!* Tragic trout-face. Least she has a nice car, I guess. Least there's fuckin' that..."

"How's the cat! "

"*DAMN!* That fuckin' thing! Eh, last week it was constantly rubbin', yowlin', and howlin'. Like a fuckin' hayseed on crack it was! Wouldn't quit creepin' and prowlin'!"

"Just a kitten, right?"

"Yeah..."

"Probably in heat, I'd say."

"Yeah, some cunt said the very same at Billy's just the other day! *HOLY CHRIST! FUCK! FUCKENSTEIN MONSTER!* Bro, just fuckin' hold-up! Need a breather here! You're *killin' me,* slow and steady! Get yourselves that little fridge I suggested and fill the fucker with beer already!"

The Detective mopped sudor from a broad forehead using a wadded-up Messier jersey; the Savior oozed a plodding slop hearkening foreplays of immutable heresy.

"So, yeah. Fuckin' redhead gets off the stage, I buy her a gin, and then we get fuckin' talkin'. Drink too much 'fore I know it and I start babblin' and squawkin'. *'Oh, the cat's just in heat.'* And I'm like, *'What? You some kinda expert or somethin'? You ain't just a fuckin' stripper?'* Then she claims she part-times as a vet's assistant on account a Billy's Jew-ass tippers."

(Lifting the shader to resume my chore, I lowered a brogue to the pedal; the somber scowls clouding the counter were too magisterial to shun meddle.)

"*Ow! Ow!* Fuckin' stop! Jesus, last bit just hurt too bad! Maybe his cloak don't need no color? Good thing I didn't choose plaid!"

"Sorry..."

"Anyway, broad says the only real way to calm the damn thing is to just satisfy it sexually. And I'm thinkin' more fuckin' kittens is the *last* thing I need, so I ask if I can do it intellectually. And she laughs and says, *'Well, no...but here's what you CAN do! Shove a Vaselined Q-Tip up her sweet little flue!'* So I give her the mad stink-eye and she says, *'Truth...even though it sounds like I'm makin' this up!'* And I'm, like, *'No fuckin' way!'* I mean, that's *unnatural*, bro! Basically a zooerast schtup!"

"Does sound weird."

"Anyway, I buy us more drinks, then head home 'round five. Strippers: all filthy/lyin'/two-bit whores fulla cockteasin' jive! My own fault though, I wear long pants; I shoulda fuckin' known better! Get home all wrecked, rip off my threads, write the old man a hate-letter. Then I'm standin' in the bathroom, naked, just brushin' my fuckin' teeth, when the cat wanders in; starts rubbin' on ankles, lickin' at fuckin' feet. I kick it away, but it comes right back and just whines like a dyin' whale. So I look down to it, and 'fore I know, my guard drops like crap from a Clydesdale! I'm all like, *'Awww, li'l kitty! C'mere, you! Daddy gonna fix his baby lamb!'* Then I root 'round the cabinet, toss shit around, 'til I dig out the Q-Tips and wank-jam..."

"No."

"So I pick the cat up, and it starts purrin' right off, like it already fuckin' knows. Waddle to the couch with the whole shebang, still not wearin' no clothes. Set the cat down, onto my lap, and her tail sticks up like a pole..."

"That's called *'flagging'.*"

(The big man's eyes shuttered thrice in protest, then twitched and disdainfully rolled.)

"So I swirl some white jelly 'round the Q-Tip's edge, then slide it right into her twat. And, *tellin' ya*, bro, shit goes in smooth! Never woulda fuckin' thought! Cat calms down, almost like magic, just purrin' along with my touch. And I'm movin' this thing in-and-out über slow, real careful so it don't think I like it too much. And I'm thinkin' how fuckin' *weird* it all is, and that the stupid Billy's whore was dead-right! And she's givin' me, like, these lovey-dovey eyes. Like an espectadora at a bullfight! And it's just kinda, like, a beautiful moment! I feel really connected with the cat! Don't got the right mumbo-jumbo to explain it much beyond that! It was just, like, we were two tiny pieces from the same puzzle on some huge galactic scale! Like, for the first time ever, the cockamamie World was makin' some sense on account a some bestial tail! Finally, just when I'm about to uncover the truth behind Life's ultimate meanin', Pat and Trout-face barge in all sloppy/shitfaced/careenin'! She screams and Pat goes, *'YO, AVERY! WHAT IN THE GODDAMN FUCKITTY FUCK?'* And I say, *'HOLD-UP! THIS IS SOME MYSTICAL SHIT, NOT YOUR EVERYDAY SCUTTLEBUT!'* But Trout-face bails, and Pat splits too, both yappin' 'bout jails and Animal Rescue..."

"Jeez. They ever make good on their threat?"

"Beats the fuck outta me. Been three fuckin' days now. Still ain't come back yet."

Well today I learned its not cheater who plays for the yankees. Its JEATER! What a stupid made up sounding name! He should change it back to cheater!

Panther $75
Yankees logo $65
Panther in yankees uniform $85
Dopey smoking bong $85
Sexy cherrys w/juice $65
Chinese letters for "brick city niggaz" $55
Rest in peace smokey $50
Forever smokey $50
Angel carrying smokey $80
Yankees logo $65
Beauty mark $50

Cut off another head in the tunnel last night.
Didnt tell cliff. Still no reply.
Rest in piece smokey.

"What some see as senility, I call disorganized wisdom."

THE MOB TWAINED IN DEFERENCE TO A REGAL SENESCENCE garbed in amber Cazals and Anne Klein. A blonde Cleopatra wig contrasted tea-flesh. A pinguid young escort, trailing its wake, beckoned via wild fanned sign.

"Yes ma'am?"

"Me and my Auntie here is inarrested in a coupla tattoos! Wonderin' if y'all do family discounts?"

The old woman's twang betrayed vituperative views, despite lenses of eyebrow surmount:

"Girl, speak for yo' *own* self! Don't want nunna them foul thangs on my body!"

Wheeling around, the Pinguid Escort trained the scared frown of a violently bankrupted Saudi.

"*Aunt Dorian!* Uh-uh! Don't you *dare* chicken-out on me now! Done been plannin' since the start a last week! Ever since you got back from Curacao and yakked 'bout that Minnie on Li'l Ellie's asscheek!"

The Old Woman leaned, hooking a thumb, whispering with deft screwball-timing.

"She mean: SHE been plannin'!"

A May/Decemberish bolt tasered my crotch.

A test of skewbald misaligning?

HASTILY SCRIBBLING AN AGE OF 'PAST MIDNIGHT' upon a form of legal-consent, Aunt Dorian's selection outsized Foresight's inflection when a calf matched calls of eagle-placement.

"Gudda spot as any, s'pose I reckon..."

(Beneath Cliff's shadow ankle-traipsed a wanton Smurfette, clothes evidently shed upon check-in.)

"Nothin' to it, Aunt D! Ain't hurt me none yet at all!"

As I finagled a needle through a tube's tip-solder, lip-tendrils tickled an auricle.

"Ain't hurt her none yet cozza all'a COCAINE she allus be shovin' up that dang nose!"

"Heard that, Aunt D!"
My regard for the Methuselah yet rose.

WHILE NEARLY EVERY VIRGIN thrashed at
maiden caress, this ancient skin yielded no reaction;
peacefully enduring, having forsaken distress, as if
infested with a cadaver's putrefaction. Ballparking the
husk at roughly seventy five, I pondered the calm's
abstruse impetus. Nerve atrophy? Perhaps sheer
toughness? Possibilities loomed limitless!
 A cackle shrilled, fueled by glee.
 "Ha! Feels real good! Don't it, Aunt D?"
 "Tellya what *gonna* feel good! Gonna make Spartacus
strangle yo' nappy ass while you be sleepin' tonight!"
 "G'wan, Dorrie! Sparty love me too
and you dang well *know it*, a'ight?"
 "Um, don't mean to pry. But...who's Spartacus?"
 The Old Woman's eyes beamed staunch mirth.
 "Why...only the best baby boy the good
Lawd Jesus evah done launched 'pon this Earth!"
 "That's nice."
 "Sho' nuff! Wanna see a *pitcha* a my Li'l Sparty?"
 I reluctantly nodded, cursing my query — alas, just
a cunthair too tardy. Foraging a purse, mummy hands
withdrew a massive Valentino billfold. A duly
extracted dwarf photograph wielded corners vetoed
by Time's hold. Though I quickly placed the piney
backdrop as the byproduct of a 70s
Sears portrait-studio, the child's sickly face riled
nightmarish echoes of Le Théâtre du Grand-Guignol.
 "Afta my boy got kilt in that Vietcong tunnel,
Floyd went out and got him fo' me. With the girls all
married-off, the house just felt so goshdang big and

empty. So cute as a baby! Just the cutest li'l thang you
ever done seed! Never woulda thought I'd love a
chimpanzee so much, but he's all I got left since
Floyd joined Gaylord in Glory..."

The Escort shifted an elephantine cleft.

"Aunt Dorrie!"

"LaHernia, you *know* what I mean. Just give it a rest!"

"Oh brotha..."

"Got me a buildin' in Irvington. Tavern in one half,
packaged goods in the otha. Li'l Sparty usta help with
tendin' the bar 'til the city showed-up. Still can't figger
who done called 'em on us or why they even botha!
Sparty be cleaner than *any* my reg'lars! Brush his own
teeth twice a day! Now he just stock shelves and
miss his ol' job! Painful to see him all lonely..."

Oddly at ease, I lifted my sluice,
relating the sad tale of Charlotte.

"Wait one minnit! You talkin' 'bout
a *spidah*, boy? A creepy/crawly varmint?"

Shaking her head, Aunt Dorian muttered
something about deficiencies peculiar to whitefolk —
gently explaining the sad rift as a kindness
the Savior had deemed fit to invoke.

A guy today wanted the grim reaper on his
arm and when he gave me his form the design
section said "the green reader". Another guy
wanted the chinese letter for big penis. Best
I could do was combine "giant" and "rooster"
which in english also means cock. Im a little
nervous about these chinese letters bc I dont
really trust them. More then one customer has

also brought in writing on napkins that waiters have done for them in chop sooey joints. I trust those even less bc these dudes are bad tippers so they probably say things like "I slurp the balls of uncle sam" or "my parents were gorillas". But still they insist and I have to do them anyway. But who do you think will get the blame if my suspicions (sp?) are ever correct? Scares me to be honest. I tried to tell daisy about these things but she acts like Im being racist. Is it racist just to describe things exactly how they happen? Do I want to live in a world where this is true?

Panther $75
Giant rooster/big cock $55
Panther $75
Panther $75
Panther $75
Green reader $85
Spiderweb w/people in it $85
Black george washington $65
Panther $75
Charlie brown as sad thug $70
Tribal uzi $85
Panther $75
Lateesha $50
Panther $75
Shitting blood again.

"I am a lean, mean, fighting machine."

WITH THE MARINE REVERIE'S OFF-TABLE SLIDE and its pursuantly irreparable shatter, my daydreams drifted ringwards again, towards Truancy's disreputable gather. Although VFW-halls lacked the general allure of a Kalashnikov's syrupy necromance, certain charms inured cigar-smoke coughs and codgers decked in urine-steeped underpants.

The slick glaze of a better's victory-sweat! Tastes of sanguinary rosin! The thick blaze of a Jew-beak's injurious wrench! Magenta flesh! Iodine! Gauzes!

Cursory research indicating license-grants contingent upon *Daily News Golden Gloves*-seasoning, my training regime was earnestly launched — a campaign to be concussed beyond reasoning. Between dust, Primatene, and sedentary craft, my lungs were thoroughly shot, necessitating copious 'roadwork' before a gym's justified graft could be sought.

Taking up laps at the neglected track surrounding McCarren Park's grassy surface, my first attempt sported antique Everlast boots (a Salvation Army purchase.) The high-lacing/flat-soled affairs provided nil but *Golden Boy*-psyche; plaguing calves with pounded veal aches 'til my eyes gleaned a slain jogger's Nikes.

Running under stars after long workdays,
Tedium ushered many crass notions.
Elizabeth! Charlotte! The drawer's .22!
Fu Manchu! Rayon clobber! Brass emotions!

MY NEW PASTIME WAS DEEMED SQUARELY SUBLIME, and joint runs were beseeched on-the-reg; requests always stamped with the emphatic denial of a poultry farmer's spies of breached eggs.

"I can't understand why you're such a fuddy-duddy! Doing things together is fun! I mean, it's what HAPPY people are supposed to do, right? C'mon, Dummy! Let's run!"

One evening, I finally assented,
fed-up with manufactured excuse.

I'd long wearied of saying anything at all.

I was a misanthrope skulking a caboose.

I'd even ceased grunting in her coital direction,
simply staring into Oblivion's eyes, wheezing
briskly as motes drifted past like swarms
of Quaaluded horseflies.

And away we went, Daisy still striding fluid and dry when my heaves commenced early on. Amused with her edge, she spun, mincing backwards with the slick/gliding grace of a swan. "Ha! Look, Dummy! I'm in great shape, and boy does it burn you right up!"

Moongazing for strength, a bird was flipped
in lieu of a much more egregious erupt.

The passing of our fourth/post-quip heat
triggered a contrite elbow-tug.

"Hey, Dummy! Guess what!
Guess what...you big ugly lug!"

"*What?*"

A moistened gaze radiated Kindness,
Understanding, and Acceptance.
"I love you."
Foisting *'Okays'*, I continued to jog,
using Blindness to abandon her presence.
Circling Sprout's mommy another five times,
I mulled Nature Boy's flatulent lesson.
By the sixth turn, the fear-mask had vanished
like free salami from a delicatessen.

February, 1995

'VALENTINE'
By E. Lynn Fletcher

Once upon a time, there was an aging rock
queen who found no thrill in fucking or
romance. She had her pick of groupies, boys,
girls, and everything in between. 'They no
longer provide the thrill to achieve a
significant moment of passion,' she said.
Then along came a virginal ex-skinhead. He
was a confused youth who neither knew nor
cared of the queen bitch's mighty fame.
They met one night in a sleazy, smoky bar
and she was dazzled by his bad attitude.
He glanced at her round and lovely breasts.
She lifted his chin with her fingers.
I love you Daddy!
Elizabeth.

"I find happiness, love, and compassion in unexpected places."

AMIDST A LAUNDRY DUFFEL'S JISM-WIPE FORAGE, Charlotte miraculously emerged; crawling out from the trusses of grime-besmirched storage with the atrophy of the slumber-disturbed. If our reunion triggered any surprise, her poker-faced mien revealed little — beyond a foreleg's jiggered exercise and a fang-parted apothegm spittled:

"Silly Jack, never hurry and never worry!"

Flattened hand lowered, she casually sauntered, meandering to a collarboned hollow, remarkably chipper for one so victual-bereft, as if refreshed by a jaunt to Sao Paulo.

Midget feeler-legs waved happily about throughout zeal-cantored affirmations. Coppery fuzz tickled pink lips betwixt stanzaic recitations.

AS THE TANK HAD BEEN INCORRIGIBLY ANNEXED by clumpy thickets of grunge, I fed the refuse to a hungry bin-liner and bolted for chips/crickets/and sponge. Upon a speedy store-return, Charlotte singsongily re-furnished a home; stacking bark slabs diagonally; in the fashion of unpurchased tombstones.

SLEEP, SLEEP, MY LOVE, MY ONLY,
DEEP, DEEP, IN THE DUNG AND THE DARK...

WITHIN THE OLD CORNER, a new hut
cropped — verily more manor than igloo. Minding
her progress (despite gums glutted by clots)
my heart thumped emotive jujitsu.

BE NOT AFRAID AND BE NOT LONELY!
THIS IS THE HOUR WHEN FROGS AND THRUSHES
PRAISE THE WORLD FROM THE WOODS
AND THE RUSHES.
REST FROM CARE, MY ONE AND ONLY,
DEEP IN THE DUNG AND THE DARK!

Been on cloud 9 for days now. No more scary
dreams. Life doesnt seem so very bad really. I
dont even care that she never replied. Not one
lick. Even wrote again to tell her so.

Panther $75
Flying saucer $85
Yankees logo $65
Sexy cherrys w/juice $60
Where is waldo w/blunt $70
Panther $75
Mom 1943-1996 $65 (cried the entire time)
Panther $75
Panther $75
Greek frat letter $70

Rest in peace jameel jaleen haziz and wayne
$65

Drooled on another panther. Dont think
anybody saw but must be more careful.

"Every day I wake up and see Magic is a gift from the Universe."

AUNT DORIAN'S ABRUPT REAPPEARANCE
triggered fears of Harangue and Stink-Eye.

Much to my abject surprise, she'd merely
boomeranged for further incise. Joining her within
the bullpen-throng, a spiel was curtailed via lip-
planted finger. "*Hush, boy. Same bird as 'fo do
me jus' fine. Ain't be no call fo' malinger.*"

Incredulous, I stammered...outraged...eager to
stupidity-shield. "But, Aunt Dorian, you already have
that one! I mean, look — it's not even healed!"

"*Maybe, boy. But like Floyd
allus said: Ain't broke, don't fix!*"

An impromptu Rap Off by the Unicorn-
flash cauterized this horsesensical nix.

(Electorally charged rhymes graphically recounted
a Clintonian assault on Dole's rectum; Bill's fervent
flounce utilizing the senator's own fiber-fist
to even further disrespect him.)

"*Shameful! Blasphemers! Tell ya, po' Gaylord just done
rolled in his grave! Bring back that draft and you
won't hear no mo' War-Hero jive! Suckas
wish they was HALF as dang brave!*"

EYES MISTING OVER WITH SALTED DROPLETS glazed a thin arm's fresh wound.

"She's finally come home! We're cerebrally attuned! She's Lassie to my Roddy McDowall!"

Quaking with grief straight down to her chassis, the Old Woman released a fraught howl.

"I mean, okay, boy. If it makes
you happy, can't be that bad..."

Upon my request for a second chimp-glimpse, a grimace tautened to viscerally sad.

"And you jus' KEEP that pitcha, boy, 'cause he's a magic
monkey, you see! Any time that foul thang bite yo' ass...
or you feelin' blue fo' any reason t'all...you jus' go an'
plant a wish on Li'l Spartacus there...and
jus' watch all yo' troubles plumb fall!"

July, 1995

I'd been cat-sitting a long, lonesome, moldering month
when the Spitbacks' pitstop arrived. Alas, hungry lips met
only a cold-shouldered return, shunning all love-famished
eyes. For Christ's sake, did I have any clue how exhausted
she was, and still facing three weeks of touring? Sensing
deceit, I resolved to ferret the malaise's true
source via subterfugal exploring.

After eight minutes of a hot bath-ensconcement, and
purulent snores had ensued, trembling fingers split
a pilfered notebook to commence a leery peruse.

Crudely scrawled pages seemed to alternate with almost
schizophrenic precision. Crisp ballpoint blue battled
fuzzy red felt in an uncannily hebephrenic division.

HIS EYES BURN AT ME LIKE A CONQUISTADOR'S RAPIER. OR EVEN WORSE: HIS SMALLPOX. HE STARES AT ME AND HE KNOWS. HE KNOWS HOW I FEEL ABOUT HIM. ONE ALWAYS KNOWS! AND I HAVEN'T BEEN ABLE TO REMOVE MY OWN EYES FROM HIS FACE FOR AT LEAST THE LAST FOUR OR FIVE GIGS. IT'S HIM! HE'S THE ONE! OH NO...AND THEN THERE'S STILL POOR JACK TO DEAL WITH...MY LATEST IN A LONG LINE OF BLUNDERS. HE'S NOT GOING TO TAKE THINGS WELL. HE CAN'T EVEN HANDLE WEARING MIXED SOCKS WITHOUT HAVING A NERVOUS BREAKDOWN SO HOW WILL HE REACT TO THIS? PROBABLY JUST GO PSYCHO. YEAH, HIS TRUE STRIPES WILL BE DISPLAYED THEN AND I'LL SURELY LIVE TO RUE THAT DAY. MIND OF AN IDIOT CHILD, BUT STILL... THERE'S SOMETHING IN THERE THAT I'M KIND OF AFRAID TO SET FREE. WHO KNOWS JUST WHAT HE'S REALLY CAPABLE OF?

Long line? Mixed socks? Child's mind? Smallpox?

I scanned the entry, over-and-over, fifty times before a jostled knob. Elizabeth re-entered, glistening and damp, beneath a plush terry-cloth swath.

Unbelting the gown, she knelt bedside, a knee straddling each of my hips. Blind-scissored moonlight spraying striations formed a zebra with pendulous tits.

Lips brushed. Jaws snapped.
(I winced at the pierce of canines.)
The journal's grim words pulsed like neon
within the wretched saloon of my mind.

> ## "I am confident in my judgement and therefore make sound decisions."

EVERY OTHER CHICK IN LUDLOW'S MAX FISH imbued the tension of an off-duty stripper, the remainders being safety-minded/ fashion-industry toilers accruing pensions through the hustle of zippers.

(Despite some expected attitudinal divergence, primarily upon the broach of brief tryst, both factions were solely comprised of Richard Kern's soul-dents and ardent Birthday Party-enthusiasts.)

Iris, a short, thin, pale-bluish thing, fell into the former métier by a seemingly God-planned default, her little-girlish/Bettie-banged visage contrasting gargantuan sweater-vaults. While I'd oft-opined over Templeton's whines that mastodon teats bypassed nutriment alone, these heated conjectures were just excreted lectures, for their object was incessantly chaperoned.

One night, with no beau in sight, I espied an abominable vision: Templeton and Iris — exiting the john — drenched in post-coital elysian.

Eyes bulged. Breaths heaved.
Hairy palms pantomimed a discourteous squeeze!

**DANCEFLOOR LEERING WHILST BEER-
BUCCANEERING** amidst a Green Door Party's
revelry, five pleather cowboy-hats had been
psychically crushed by the time Iris noted my devilry.
  *"Hey, man, thanks for walkin' me home! Really not as
dumb as ya look! Temp told me ya had Down syndrome
and nevah evah once read a book!
What's ya name again?"*
  "It's...it's Jack."
  *"Huh! Really? That a true fact? Look
so much more like a Wilbah to me!"*
  A quick swish through a hot-rod flamed purse
produced Stars-and-Bars pendanted keys.

**SLOGGING UPSTAIRS, MY DAY-JOB
WAS QUERIED...**would I do her a tribal for free?
  Lips were swiped of all beer-scum.
  "Dunno. Maybe. We'll see."
  The third-floor flat was no ordinary mess, but filth
strained to circus extremes; debauchery slathered
with a grime so viscous one might monogram any
surface they pleased. Fungus-barnacles desperately
clung to towers of chipped plates and used bowls.
Warrens of lint rioted tongues of every nook/cranny/
crevice/and hole. Lipsticked filters reigned supreme
— nary a furnish left ungored. The coup de grâce:
a thousand dried turds, careening a white-
washed/burnished/stressed floor.
  Locating the bathroom on my own accord, I scoped
more slime-strewn gunk, a lavish store of *Kiehl's*
products reduced to dump-primed accruals of junk.

Noting dampened lace draping a shower's rod,
I scanned a brassiere's viscose bosh.
  (*Agent Provocateur — 32DDD.*)
  At least her underthings were washed!
  "Hmph! Wilbah! Where ya goin'?
  Really gonna leave me all alone?"
  Despite a bent Parliament smoldering in one claw
and a Pomeranian growling from its mate, I was as
magnetically drawn to the meat in-between
as a lodestone-ensnared iron flake.

Day off but went to work anyway bc cliff called
and said he was lonely. Big mistake bc the glass
seems to be back firing worse then ever. Head
still hurts. Hurts all the time now really. Feels
even worse when I run. Think I might have to
give that up to. Coughing up blood again and
still shitting it. I wish charlotte could make me
some chicken soup or do a back rub but she
doesnt even know what that stuff is.

Yankees logo $65
Beauty mark $50
Medusa loves jim joe $60
Panther $75
Concurring lion of judah $90
Sexy strawberry w/juice $60
Thug life $125
Panther $75
Rolling stones lips $70
Panther $75

Still no word.
How hard is it to write a f'n
letter? Ring wont shut up
even tho its in a drawer.

"My vision is 20/20 backwards and forwards."

SOZZLED AGAIN WITH ANOTHER STRANGE BROAD in a North Sixth pub called *Sweetwater*, the decor of which was skillfully mottled with a jukebox Discharged for erst squatters; a paunchy herd still insistent on quasi-cred despite alopecia/paid vacations.

The lanky Texan had nice-to-meetcha'd over a joint Flannery O'Connor adoration.

(I'd pinned Marigold's cat-eyed specs as dead-ringers for the doomed Georgian scribe's.)

"Well, these *are* genuine granny-glasses, that's how come you're scammin' those vibes! My Auntie Mildred's old frames! Crazy coot kicked *forever* ago, but hopin' she still sees through 'em just the same! My main endeavor's to drive her ghost schizo, really jam steam up her spout! I leave 'em on the nightstand facin' the bed...'specially when I'm rubbin' one out!"

Dandelion locks were bulbously knotted at the apex of an elliptical crown.

"Your hair's like a Kaiser roll glued to an ostrich egg set on salt to stand upside-down!"

"Yeah? Who the heck are *you* to talk? Funny lookin'

guy, ain'tcha? What kinda jerk has pointy ears?
S'posed to lend a vampire-taint, yeah? Have
surgery for that? Get your money back!
Look more like an *elf* than Nosferatu!"
  Signalling the barkeep for Cuervo-refills,
lips lost more than they ought to.
  "Nah, babe! Au naturel! Also got
six letters in each of my three names!"
  Abacussing, Marigold fretted. "Jackson's
got *seven*, fool! That's a real peach of a brain!"
  "Maybe that's not really it..."
Vertebrae numbed with swift jolts of meat-digging
slaps. "Gotcha! Figgered it was *Señor Estúpido*
with the first bleat of your friggin' trap!"
  Elbows bent further. Spirits flowed free. Things
swiftly dissolved to fogged blurs. Armpits unshaven!
A turn-off, yes! But so silken it hardly occurred!
  'Fuck you, Aunt Mildred!' trumpeted mid-union
towards tabled/emptied cat's eyes. *'I am Spartacus!'*
resounded. A larcenous crowned head spat
waybilled contempt! Hatred metastasized!

THOUGH THE LANKY TEXAN HAD
SCATTERED by dawn's watt, I was thankful to knee
tiles alone. The results showed promise — a mere
smattering of clots floating amidst biled blankets of
foam. Rising to piss, I was aghast to glimpse a tool
rigid with a coat of shellac. A quick bed-inspection
revealed linen undone by fluids of menstruum near
black. But why had she not *mentioned* this curse? I
would've shtupped her in the shower instead!
  Could a houseguest verily behave much worse?
  Why were jerks so often well-read?

Positivity-parched, I rushed to the vanity
where my heart met a virtual tar-pit.
  The lid! Ajar! No! Not again!
  What had become of Sweet Charlotte?
  Raising a mortified gaze to a filmy
reflection, a fingered heart graffitied the dust.
  (Its internal perimeter declared
'Jódete Estúpido!')
  Guts brimmed corporeity repercuss.

August, 1995

*The idiot child grew ever more noxious with each
day's grueling pass, constant fits of jealous rage
frazzling nerves to crisps of cooling ash.*

*Skipping Dodge seemed the logical step to stem
abscessed losses of mind. Petitioning the boss for a fortnight's reprieve, 'WHERE?' was the next mare's nest to
climb. 'New Orleans,' Cliff promptly suggested, to which I
readily agreed. My apelike pal had moved south a
year prior to vend scabs in near Metairie.*

*Upon my chum's hearty assurance of a crash-pad and
chair barring ebb, I purchased a round-trip from an agent
securing fares via the newly minted 'World Wide Web'.*

*Renfield's parlor was a second-floor storefront in a
decaying Sixties stripmall — a cramped/damp/smoky/
roachy affair. Hands scarcely changed gloves at all.*

*Each night post-work we'd quaff Coop's draughts before
an inevitable Big Daddy's embarkation, where plexiglass
looped a vast python's shaft whilst ecdysiasts
galumphed lewd gyrations.*

Yokels all day! Sex-workers all night!
Never had I known such boredom!
Where was the Love?
Where was the Kindness?
Was this the new me?
I abhorred him!
Compounding matters, the Ape-Man's old spark had
been swapped for some cold/reptilian organ. He now
slumbered with two open eyes like a cathedral's
protective stone gorgon!
Cornering him within Big Daddy's bathroom, revealing
an imminent snap, he appeared merely puzzled as
drawers slowly lowered to commence a vociferous crap.
"Not sure I read ya. What's fuckin' wrong?
Got plenty a money. Plus chicks..."
"Everything's wrong! The drinking! The blood!
The drugs! The hicks! Dude, despite all
my rage, I'm still just a rat in a cage!"
"Yo, Jack...chill! Just chill the fuck out
and relax! Shit's less than nothin'!"
"What do you mean less than nothing? I don't think
there is any such thing as less than nothing! Nothing is
absolutely the limit of Nothingness! It's the lowest you
can go! It's the end of the line! How can something be
less than nothing? If there were something that was less
than nothing, then nothing would not be nothing, it would
be something — even though it's just a very little bit of
something! But if nothing is nothing, then nothing
has nothing that is less than it is!"
Swiping a cleft, Renfield shrugged, lifting a match and
obscenely charred spoon. Syringe withdrawn, dead eyes
stared back, towed by a horse-buggied swoon.

Ferrying home just before dawn, a primered Dart cut us
off with intent; stopping short then speeding away, rending
brake-pads shrillishly spent. With no reason or rhyme to
the awkward maneuver (save sheer redneck rascality)
an oxblood Doc Marten flattened a pedal, lids narrowing
with stalwart finality. That something bad neared was
abundantly clear, but Immediacy dwelt free of my box.
  My lone concern: the diary entry!
Who was this cuckolding conquistador with smallpox?
  Increasing velocity as the gap narrowed, the Dart's
engine brimmed anxious groans; alas, 'twas no match for
Yankee hood-offal V-8'ing Grim Reaperish intones! Cajun
rustics gorged the front seat. One middle-aged, two young.
Smeared with indistinguishable features, I gauged them
father and sons — an impression shattered upon the
ejaculate of Renfield's Colt .45 — the casual spill of its
fourteen-round clip certainly molting their lives. Over in
seconds with no time to ponder, much less to intervene,
we sped from the carnage in a straight-razor slice,
the Ape-Man still calm and serene.
  We stopped at a flyspecked diner. A black
soda-jerk drew coffees. Renfield requested
a tall buttermilk and donut.
  "Yassuh, cap'n! Thanks awfully!"
  (As tears rained upon chicory, tainting it with pinkish
saline, the Ape-Man nibbled his pastry's perimeter
as if Death lurked within Boston Cream.)
  "Yo...Jack, don't sweat that shit none. Did
the world a favor. Let's just start on home."
  Drying my eyes, I asked if he'd waver
amidst a dream girl's intake of strange bones.
  Mulling the query, he stroked a square jaw.
  Quaffed yellow dregs. Wiped a foamed maw.

Jasmine gusted through window cracks.
Frogs fled a night owl's trolling.
"Listen, just try and forget her, Jack.
Get a hobby. Maybe take up bowling."

"I perceive reality with microscopic precision."

A HIGH-YELLOWED KNOCKOUT'S UNEXPECTED ARRIVAL raised spirits to mildly sore; spindly limbs and a lye-conked bob echoing Josephine Baker's amour.

Head tilting forwards, rueful lisps barely jailbroke puce confines of tongue.

"Mistah, like to make one which my name be on it. I's nineteen. Do that be too young?"

"No, that's fine. But whaddya think you want?"

The dead man's hand of a card-themed sheet was daubed by fingers long/tapered/and gaunt.

"Okay, no problem. And what goes into the banner?"

A glossed head wavered repeatedly.

Yet another misunderstander?

Iterating my query several times over, slowing words with each repetition, the High-Yellowed Knockout's cold quietude increased; pained eyes refracting attrition. Giving up, I sat her down, wearily sighed, and commenced gathering gear from the cabinet.

Upon my return, I was covertly plied a rosy left palm. A lip-linered smear inhabited it.

ACACIA.

DESPITE EERIE NAGS OF DÉJÀ VU PRESAGE,

I attempted benign/pre-outline smalltalk.

Alas, the High-Yellowed Knockout remained as dourly tight-lipped as a cop consigned to mind morning gridlock. Thankfully, her flesh was sufficiently grey to dispense with vitreous demonstration, allowing my scrapes to flay the right shoulder-cap sans any-and-all adjuration.

CLEANSING CLAWS CLEAN OF TALC,

I pondered the transaction's taciturnity.

"Think it's 'cause my breath reeked too foul? Or some other malefaction internally?"

Perhaps her shyness had been racially based?

An irrational aversion to honkies? Or had my penile protrusion perked too palpably plain?

(A morning coke-rub still had it surging near-donkey.)

"Loose jeans equal LESBO, cuz! Pegged it soon as she entered the door! Average sistas keep 'em tight enough their labias are right there for you to explore! Five'll get you ten that Acacia's just some rug-munching truck-driver's name!"

Abhorrent visions punched through my skull wearing plucky/MacGyverish manes!

Laying hands nose-to-mouth, I detected no olfactorial trash-fill.

And as wise as Cliff was, had he never been wrong? Could this one not just be bashful?

Lifting an *'OMNI'*, head shaking calmly, a Cajun mien eased within a glossy split.

"Goddamned SHAME if you ask me too! Tragic waste of good fucking clit!"

Food poisoning. Didnt even know what was happening. The heeves came on like gang busters and I ran to the bathroom. Next thing I know Im trapped in the f'n shrine. Holden was there. Said some nonsense about a small field and that I had been judged and then he shoots me w/my own f'n gun! Woke up on the floor coughing up scum w/a cut on my temple w/dust all over it. Must have put my head down to fast and knocked myself out on the rim of the toilet. Not sure if it was the sushi or the pork rinds but it looks like I also puked up some paper towels. Calling in sick bc dizzy as fuck. Wish me luck. I believe in miracles.

Hope you do to.

"I am a smooth operator."

THE THICK MAKE-UP CORRALLING HER EYES, an intentionally smeared pitch goo, lent her countenance, at cursory glance, a skull's dissatisfied view. It was Monday, 5AM, and save for a wino fetid with shit and dried urine, only the black-swaddled thing and myself fell prey to the Discomfiture of the subway we were in.

Creeping alongside the riverbed,
I surveyed Gothic anatomy.
Mandible jut. Heavy brow.
Sturdy/petite with a flat belly.

Peruvian? An Inca perhaps?
Mulling lives perished birthing this tunnel?
Yes, I conjectured. Indians *cherished* such
morbid oblations! A hazy gaze blazed Veronal.
I saluted, tapping a brow.
Turning away, jet orbs surveyed
Doctor Zizmor's sad/flaccid scowl.

SHE DISMOUNTED AT LORIMER, my stop as
well, but in lieu of a usual turn-left towards Withers,
Florsheims spun, loaded-and-locked, launching a
somnambulant slither. Southside-bound, half block
buffered, palms dissuaded blitzes of stumble. The
gloom's air persisted still as cadavers, save
stiletto-clops/sporadic rat-shrieks/
occasionally blared tramp-grumbles.

Reaching Keap Street, she halted at the arch of an
ancient red-brick brewery, purse-fumbling whilst I
glided rearwards, hell-bent on Erotic Tomfoolery.
Carefully unfolding the gunk-slathered blade
of my father's old stainless-steel knife, I tactically
avoided wan/balding reflections.

Now was no time for such strife!

Openers withdrawn just as I neared, I braced for
key-spikes most brutal. Instead, gears wheeled
to reveal a mien enflamed by Reich's orgone
accumulative canoodle.

A lip's bite provoked fevered moans, begging for
foists much harder. *'Pop!'* went a tiny/rupturing
breach, releasing a moist victual larder. Turning the
lock, mounting the stairwell, trodding bodily
enclasped, the Goth's oral contact
remained unbroken.

(Three flights scaled back sans rasp.)

TACKED ABOVE VELOUR-CASED PILLOWS,
an onionskin wore carbonised blurs.
  Prayer candle lifted, I discerned a grave-rubbing
as the Goth waved sticks of spiced Myrrh.

BELA LUGOSI
BELOVED FATHER
1882 – 1956

  Grinning broadly as her last threads dropped,
brown apexes confirmed aboriginal suspicions.
  Brandishing the woebegone knife, I pantomimed
integumental truss-scissions. Examining the blade
dispassionately, Dahlia sighed and addressed a
surgical-altar; raising a straight-razor's ivory
handle from the bind of a liturgical psalter.
  *"Hey, dude...I think it would be, like, so totally rad if
ya slit me! I mean, I really cream on that stuff!
But let's just use this one instead, see?
That ol' thing seems hella rough!"*

No letter. No spider. No nothing.
No real reason for life.
Sexy cherrys w/extra juice $60
Panther $75
Panther fights tiger to death $100
Miss pac man $60
Raincloud over ex gf's name $70
Baby rapper $85
Chinese letters for "microphone wrecker" $55
Panther $75
But am I even truely alive or is this all
some ghosts creepy ass dream?

"I believe in second chances."

UNFOLDING MY STRAIGHT-RAZOR'S IVORY HANDLE, Texan teeth projecting semen and cheese, I advised Marigold that Charlotte's non-return ran the risk of permanently lubricated wheeze. She'd chortled at first, mulishly, mistaking this for alleyway 'joshing'.

"Y'all Jews got some foolish courtin' ideas! Call me old-fashioned, but I go more for the flower'n'candy brainwashin'!"

An inaugural red trickle swiftly roused whinnies, quivers, and a flaxen scalp's creamy perspire. A memaw's grave invoked for Honesty's sake soused a vow with streams of waxen hellfire. No kidnaps or reaves had duly occurred! I'd oped the aquarium myself! Kissing and licking the hideous thing while it crawled atop a comic-book shelf!

"AND THEN...AND THEN YOU PUT IT ON THE GODDAMNED BED! SAID IT WANTED TO WATCH US FUCK! TRIED TO WARN YOU WHEN IT RAN DOWN THE STEAD, BUT YOU WERE TOO BUSY SCREAMIN' 'BOUT TUNNELS AN' KILLIN' CANUCKS!"

NO FURTHER CHARLOTTE-SIGHTINGS OCCURRED — only affirms maintained inklings of Hope. Hedging bets, I kept a sponge watered and the crickets supplied with diced cantaloupe.

Alas, despite this copious bounty, Cannibalism seized within days; the chirrups quickly vitiating from warbles to requiems of zombie-like streptokinase.

**HUNGOVER AGAIN AND IN DIRE
BEER-NEED,** Luigi plugged my descent betwixt
floors; twin Newports surfing each ear's cusp
whilst a fifth siphoned pus from cold-sores.
  "My man! Youse seen any weird shit in your place?"
  "Um, yesterday I coughed-up some lace."
  "Nah, I mean like big hairy *bugs* or some shit! Ma
swears to God one by the stove almost gave her a fit!
Said it had bright red hairs all over on top, like fuckin'
Lucille Ball's wig or somethin! Prob'ly just a roach,
but told her I'd ask. Old ladies...always
squallin' an' grumblin'!"
  Suddenly downcast, I shook my head sadly, bidding
the Troll farewell. Traversing flights, my heart paused
aghast upon his screech of one final droll yell.
  *"YO, MY MAN! IF YOUSE DO SEE SOMETHIN',
THEN JUST FUCKIN' STOMP IT TO HELL!"*

**THIS NEWS OF SURVIVAL
RANG BITTERSWEET,** warranting no jubilees.
Was Charlotte not predestined to boil and drown
within a vat of mediocre Bolognese? Had I not failed
my best pal on account of an urge to dismantle
a stranger's horrendous g-string?
  *"Hush now, young Jack! You have been my friend. That
in itself is a tremendous thing. I wove my webs for you
because I liked you. After all, what's a life, anyway? We're
born, we live a little while, we die. A spider's life can't help
being something of a mess, with all this trapping and
eating horseflies. By helping you, perhaps I was trying
to lift up my life a trifle. Heaven knows anyone's
life can stand a little of that!"*
  Eschewing lager, I soldiered on towards Grand,
committed to repopulating habitats.

**THE HERMIT-CRAB'S CARCASS STILL
SQUATTED THE WINDOW** — the Puerto
Rican's Caesar was honed. Beneath basement
darkness, insect-coitus haloed bantam remains
while we rummaged the spider/scorpion zone.

A missile-shaped cage housed a smiling Capuchin
with hands raised to initiate high-fives. My oblige
of the primate, who seemed innocuous enough,
triggered crows of anxious/Nuyorican-tinged jive.

*"Oh snap, Tattoo-Man! Keep away from
that monkey! Nigga got muthafuckin' AIDS!"*

Facing my addresser to squint at his grasp,
I found vision still obscured by shade.

"Had *three* of them niggas! Two died
already! Nasty-ass/muthafuckin' sores!"

Accepting the proffered spider for inspection,
lips pursed with Fossey-esque rapport. "Doesn't
sound very kosher. Where'd you get these monkeys?"

"My homeboy dropped 'em off! Works in a lab
doin' somethin' funky! Gonna jook that maricón
when I see his ass though! Puta took
me for three Franklins each!"

The new applicant didn't resemble Charlotte at all.
Black/white/and skunkish with a belly of labial peach.

"Hmph! Unusual!"

"Yeah, man! She be *real* fuckin' pretty!
And also real fuckin' mean!"

Fangs clacked against plastic. "Jeez, ain't whistling
Dixie! No petting this one it seems!"

"But...yo...*dang*, Tattoo-Man! You...
you can't be *pettin'* them fuckin' shits!"

"Why not?"

"'Cause, they's *spidahs*, nigga!
Only good for venenoso bits!"

WHILE I COMBED CHIPS FREE OF LINT-CLUMPS GATHERED, the new applicant buried fangs to the hilt. As the resultant gash explosively stung, Loneliness plunged into wilt.

Rushing bathroom-bound, sucking fingertip punctures, I spat venomed ichor at the bowl. *Jesus Christ!* Such a callous ingrate! Did gladiatorial rescue not rate Anger-Control?

My bedroom-return found the cricket gen-pop riled to a state of mass panic. The New Applicant hopped madly about, lunging with hunger volcanic.

Unable to suppress a flummoxed leer, bite throbbing like French-kisses of Death, I noted motes leeching my thumb's bloodied schmear.

"Obviously, your name's *Elizabeth*..."

So cliff got to drunk w/his gf and her sister who is visiting them from chicago and in the middle of the night he went to get a glass of water and the sister reachs up from the couch and just puts her lips around his wang like it was a f'n milkshake. Said he was to drunk to push her away so he just let her do what she felt like only halfway thru his gf got up to use the bathroom and walked in on it. But he says that she just said "oh excuse me" and walked by them then didnt say a word about it at brekfast this morning like she didnt even care. Now hes upset about her silence or not caring or what have you.

Howling wolf $85

Panther $75
King tut smoking blunt $85
Panther $75
Beauty mark $50
Panther $75
Baby jesus riding happy pit bull $90
Smurf doing the nasty w/garfield $85
Chinese letters for "martin luther king" $55
Panther $75
Some people are never satisfied.

"I am a natural caretaker."

AS THE ALLEGED RUG-MUNCHER APPROACHED THE PARTITION, I waved with unqualified zeal. Alas, eyes wore only the blank cognition of memories Jekyll/Hyded piecemeal.

But still I flagged, deeming Myopia to blame despite a clarity apparent as she neared. Could a lesbionic shyness, even one deeply ingrained, account for such barrenly pusillanimous blears? With the defining evidence obscured via '*Busta Rhymes*' shirt, infinite possibilities synapsed. Crack? Derangement?

A crusted mind's hurt? Legitimate senility collapse?

Or was this, perhaps, my own racist failing as opposed to some splay of Amnesia? Might this not be just another girl from the block or a recent émigré from Rhodesia?

"Mistah, I like a tattoo which my name be on it..."

Another beeline for the same poker-flash!
A finger-jab echoed prior debrief!
A lip-linered palm confirmed the High-Yellowed
Knockout's confoundingly haywired leitmotif:

AKASHA.

TAPING A SLEEVE, AFFIXING A STENCIL,
the Knockout took pains to dodge orbs; spying
tiles 'twixt knees as I greased purple guidelines,
Vaseline clogging soft pores.
The outliner buzzed...
Minutes crawled by...
Impregnated with awkward disquiet...
(As I paused to refuel, an undetonated
Glock triggered a dissed Crip's bullpen-riot.)
"You and me. We...we've *met* before.
Or perhaps I'm duly mistaken?"
Betraying nil beyond absent chin-dips,
my query left the Knockout unshaken.
"Yas, Mistah. You an' me...we...
we's done already meeted..."
Like visionary pustules atop inkpot ripples,
fluorescent blisters excreted.
"*Last time*, I did a piece...with the same
name as this? Um...is that correct?"
"Sho' nuff. Yas. Five/six weeks
back, if'n I can recollect."
"A very similar design...almost the same...
but with the name spelled *different*, right?"
"Yassuh, Mistah. Dat be da troof.
Jus' a few letta changed a bit slight."

SILENCE RECONQUERED, NO REVEALS
CAME, eyes beamed Melancholia to the floor.
Unassailably shuttered!
No invites enflamed!
Curiosity was intolerably moored!
Did she not honor Penetration's rites?
Was insight not my occupational knife?
Fierce visions flared of ear-rattled skulls!
RESPECT THESE SCARS THAT CONJOIN US FOR LIFE!
"I...I spells it which a '*C*' an' a '*I*'.
I think it look mad def dat way..."
A left ear tilted towards the bleeding addendum.
A sigh breezed a sad Crest-bouquet.
"My mama...she spell it like dis...which da '*K*' and
da '*S*' and da '*H*'. I don' like it at all. It make me
feel sad. So ugly dat it make my heart ache..."
Silently escaping a hooded left lid, a lone tear
dangled then jumped. "Mama said I shouldn't
got dat tattoo you did. Say I's mangled.
Dat me an' da devil done humped."
Within a cleft chin, the dewdrop shimmered,
glistening like a freshwater-pearl.
"So's I took my t'ings ovah t'Newark 'stead. T'my
papa's olda brotha Reverend Earl. But t'ings, dey went
bad dere too. Ol' Earl...he cut hisself shavin' an' died.
So's I axed mama if I could come back. Said I's real
sorry. Fell on da kitchen floor an' cried. She say okay,
but only if'n I fix dat wack-ass t'ing on my arm. So I
says, '*But Mama, can't be no changin'! It jus' be how it be,
an' how it even be doin' you much harm?*' And she say,
'*Okay, girl. I unnerstan', but here's what y'alls gonna do.
Go git you anotha, jus' like da old, but make
sho' it spelt da way you was brood!*'"

Oh how I yearned to caress!
To coddle! To nourish!
To slick the flapper-bob with lye and lard!
To imprison and protect for Eternity's span
this resplendently ochre retard!

September, 1995

Her tone was glum, morose, husky...rendering smalltalk
grotesque. 'So damn glad this tour's finally over!
And Nawlins? Didja go gawk at Otter's burlesque?'
  Unfamiliar mechanics. Was this how folks disposed
of old garbage? Dancing around rims volcanic?
  Eyeballing shoves towards a sharp edge?
'Jack...'
A crack? At least she was sad.
Burp-guns strafed visceral ribbons —
helmed by dust parishads.

"I am courageous in the face of adversity."

THE POLACK'S SUNDAY ONSLAUGHTS
CONTINUED, week-after-week-after-week.
Lukewarm javas and pompadoured wisps
arming fraught trips to the teeth.
  Gaunt but flabby fishbellied limbs soon amassed
Torture Gardens. Execrable graphics failing to daunt,
efforts spurred onwards towards spartan.

Blunted/barbed needlepoints loitered, insuring
instantaneous fuzz. Colors ignored outlines as
cursorily as a fistula's sanious pus. Soap was utterly
forsaken, wounds spritzed with noxious Windex;
hideous/blood-poisoned welts oozing mocks
of smiles crowning thin martyrs' necks.
   "Can't take this dung much more! Dreamt
I shanked him in a Riker's shower-stall!"
   "Ha, cuz! Wonder how ol' cranky Carl Jung
woulda deciphered that kinda rough protocol!"
   "*C'mon*, man! Being serious here! He's devious!
Fucking evil! Acts dopey and sweet while he's draining
your Life-Force like a five foot seven boll weevil!"
   "The hell? Life-Force? Reminds me of
those fag puppets in *'The Dark Crystal'*!"
   "He's *killing me*, man! Fuck it! Wanna
pluck some barks outta my pistol?"
   "Tell ya what, cuz...know it's your turn this week...
but I fucking got this one! Don't worry.
Just go in the back, read the paper,
and *can* all the squawk 'bout guns!"
   "Thanks, man. Appreciate it. Been so
edgy lately. Sorry to be acting so wack."
   "Don't take this wrong, but ever consider Prozac?
Turned my Cousin Chad's life around completely."
   "The one doing time for serial-rape?"
   "Yeah, cuz. But mellowed a ton since that last
failed escape. Says days pass more fleetly."

AN HOUR'S CRAWL MARKED THE ARRIVAL
of coffee, vodka, and a huge box of apple-cake.
   *"Wanted youse t'try dis special toffee
Szarlotka! An' some booze t'stop bellyaches!"*

Cliff etched a naked Rasputin.
(I pondered the asbestos ceiling.)
Lowering my gaze proved a sad mistake...
A grin projected ghost-feelings.

Well what do you know that bich iris called
me. Thought I might never hear from her again
but sometimes life suprises you for good
measure. We ate at some place called acme
that has good mashed potatos but expensive
beer then went to thunderbirds. Daisy was
there and I said hows sprout and told her I got
a new spider. She just looked at me like I didnt
say anything and said "what would you like
to drink sir?" I had a polish vodka.

Actually I had seven.

Yankees logo $65
Naked nun w/ghetto booty $85
Panther $75
Panther $75 (did not like glass)
Tweety w/blunt $65
Beauty mark $50
Chinese letters for "I like them thick" $55
Panther $75
Yogi bear in diaper $70
In loving memory of eleanora $65
Panther $75
Skunk playing saxaphone (sp?) $85

Still no reply.

"I believe I can fly."

"LEMME GET THIS STRAIGHT...

you want this guy *dead* because he brings
you cake? That makes a whole lotta sense!"

"Seriously, Temp. Last night I dreamed I impaled the
poor sap with a stake from a white picket fence!
All the time, I find myself begging God to mow
him down, despite no contract with Jehovah!"

"Speaking of crime, heard you've been
toting li'l *Iris* around! That a fact, Casanova?"

"Says who?"

"Does it matter? And I'm not saying this to sound
like some petty villain, but that filthy twat made
my cock spit fire 'til the *'free'* clinic
swelled it fulla penicillin!"

"I'll bear that in mind."

"Furthermore, if the opportunity arises to snuff this
creep and get it outta your system, then I say just
fucking grab it! Did it myself and it wasn't so bad!
Long as nobody'll miss him and you're
sure not to make it a habit!"

"What're you talkin' about?"

"Long time ago, so don't be a spaz! I was only ten.
Ninth Ave was still Alcatraz and trouble was tough
to forfend. It was a Spring morning and I was outside,
feeding mom's Valium to pigeons. They'd
gobble 'em up and keel right over like
snake-handlers high on religion!"

"Dude, that's fucking mean!"

"*No shit*, dumb-fuck! That was the point! Do I look like Mahatma Gandhi? And aren't you the same glum schmuck with those touching dreams about eating flesh like a jaguarondi? Anyhow, I was dosing the fowl when Homer runs up...aberrantly fulla tears!"

"Homer Zuckerman?"

"The one and only! Tough-guy dues in arrears! So I say, '*Yo buddy, just calm the fuck down! Just tell me what's fucking wrong!*' And he goes, '*Some big smoke vicked my Star Wars watch and then made me kiss his black dong!*' And I tell him the nigger did him a favor 'cause that watch was mega-gay. That just makes him bawl even harder! '*But my Aunt Ruthie bought it for Pesach! It's digital! We can't let this jig get away!*'"

"What a he-man!"

"Bender, shut the fuck up! Telling a fucking story! Do I ever interrupt *your* lame b.s.? Mutual respect is mandatory! So we scope out the 'hood for an hour or so, but can't find nothin' doin', and I'm all set to quit when Homer starts blubbering/skirting the edge of ungluing. Then he shouts, '*That's him!*' And the kid's even smaller than me! Just, like, seven or eight...hardly the brawlin' Ali!"

"But...how'd he get the watch off Homer?"

"Because, dude, he's a fucking pussy! That rep's a total misnomer! Anyway, kid sees us mad-doggin' him...fucking takes off running! And he's fast! I mean, yeah, *all* niggers are fast, but the little ones... like jackrabbits or something!"

"Get him?"

"Yup, we got him all right! Tripped by a root in the playground! We each grab a shoulder. Homer starts punching his dick. Some kinda '*I AIN'T GAY!*' meltdown."

"Jeez."

"'*Lay off my crotch! Gonna jook ya! Jive/hambone-ass turkey!' 'Cough up my watch, or I'll tan your black hide to strips of sambo-ass jerky!'* Kid bugs out as we rifle his pockets. Keys. Gum. Maybe eleven dollars. Homer slugs his nuts again hard! *'That shit cost my aunt thirty nine bucks!'* And now they're *both* starting to crybaby-holler..."

"Ugh."

"We drag the kid to a Chelsea-Elliot lobby, all the while pleading his life. In the lift, Homer goes, *'Don't be delicate, he fuckin' robbed me! A beating'll serve this jig right!'*"

"Fair enough."

"By the time the Otis stops at the roof, the kid's in a full fucking panic, sending God notice for some kinda proof of any real truths messianic! We start passing him back-and-forth, just like a basketball. He pisses his pants about five shoves in..."

"Ha!"

"Like *you* wouldn't be scared at all! Then Homer grabs his arms, tells me to fetch the legs! I snatch the kid up by his ankles, hoping I don't get sprayed! By now he's just screaming for his mama, 'cause Jesus hadn't made the scene, and as we carry him off towards the ledge, Homer starts braying real mean! When he gives me a wink, we start hammocking the kid, going, *'One...Two...Three!'* With the end of each rep, Homer yelled *DAMMIT* and slid, but all just fronting, see?"

"Was he hard to hold?"

"Not at that point — limp as a hair-filled rag doll!

Crying twofold, but no fight left. Guess shock had
squelched the wherewithal! After we do the bit a few
more times, I'm beginning to get real fatigued.
But Homer starts a new rep, grinning real wide,
when he suddenly lets go on three!"

"Shit…"

"And the kid's plunging over the edge of the roof,
just like Superman! The momentum's pulling *me* right
along too! Had to unhitch the caravan! Just let go
and watched him sail; the whole descent all teeth and
staring! Hit the ground with a fishmonger's slap! Bent
as a fucking Keith Haring! Zuckerman says, *'Couldn't
be helped! Pigeon shat on my knuckles!'* And, sure
enough, he's telling the truth, swiping
off poop as he chuckles!"

"So then what'd you do?"

"Beat feet and didn't leave my small room for days!
Told the folks I was sick from some meat a
Honduran had ditched in the hallway!"

"Get in trouble?"

"Nope!"

"Ever feel bad?"

"Jack, when shit rolls right off your back, why be
fucking sad? To learn from *Failure*, not Success, is
the path of the true Moongazer! But enough
with all this morbid excess! Let's see
this cool new straight-razor!"

Got drunk at billys w/avery then we had 2am
steaks at lucky strikes. When he took his shirt
off to show the cute waitress jesus she didnt
want to come back to our table. Sent some

faggot over instead. Told avery about the letters
and showed him the razor and said that I am
afraid of doing more destructive things. He told
me to shut up and be a man. Then he drove
me home in his new black mustang. He was
really to drunk to be driving but when I said
so he flashed me his badge and said "master-
tin never leave home w/o it." Halfway across
the w'burg bridge we got stuck in traffic and
he asked if he can see my skull ring. I said sure
and took it off and gave it to him. He looked at
it and says "this is the same one that the bich
gave you?" and I said "yes." He says "ow fuck
it burns" and then threw it into the east river.
When I got mad he told me to shut up again
and be a man bc I have been disgusting him.
Did not want to meet the new spider.

Beauty mark $50
Panther $75
Keewee w/juice $65
Kermit boinking miss piggy $90
Panther $75
Yankees logo made of pot leafs $75
Roses around wrist $85
Cadillac symbol $70
Panther $75

Rented "s.o.b." More eh. What is a "gadfly" (sp)?
Cliff keeps using that word.
Really starting to annoy me.

"My middle name is Romance."

JIGGLING WITH UNALLOYED ZEAL,

knockers defocused mohair. With six bodies
destroyed in a three-minute peel — verily, these
locusts faced no prayer. *"Wilbah! C'mere! C'mon! Oh
Gawd! Jus' look at li'l Betty go! Jesus, so glad I fuckin'
thoughtta this! Much betta than CABLE, y'know?"*

Procured from a reptilery on East Second,
the crickets were neither Love Totem nor Kindness
— Iris simply rejoiced in spying eight-legged dead
reckon with fervor bordering upon mindless.

A newly arrived Kentucky fifth was blended in tall
tumblers. Her coaster-selection of my Raging Bull's
pith proved alchemic to rending grumblers.

"Bad girl! You should know better!
That's just gonna leave a ring!"

"Nah, man! No fuckin' way! Too much *dust* on the
thing! Um...wow! Holy shit! This book is totally
signed! Where the heck didja get this?"

"Dumb gift. Pay it no mind."

"Oh yeah? Gift from who? What's her fuckin' name?"

Grabbing a long/jet ponytail, I reeled in the
voluptuous dame. "Easy, kitten. A *dude* gave me that!
An ass I'd just as soon see shrivel and die!"

"You'd wish *that* on someone who gives
ya nice things? So crass and uncivil! Why?"

"Eh...hard to explain...not
really worth deliberation..."

"S'okay, I get it, ya can refrain. I wish
on a *stah* when I get hurt by frustration."
   "Hmph! Like in Pinocchio?"
   "Kinda. But personal, not a big dog-and-pony show.
Like, when I *really* want someone to die...like if they're
being a real fuckin' douche...I look up to my
stah, wish real hard, and the hatred
just sorta goes whoosh!"
   "And does it work? I mean, for venting
Doom? Is that your general feeling?"
   "Guy from my job once got sent to the Tombs
on account a bein' a jerk caught stealin'!"

**BESIDES THE MOON AND SOME
SPUDDY LUMPS,** the sky was an icebergian
mire. An enameled claw riding ruddy pumps
jabbed towards a Chryslerian spire.
   "Well, I mean, it's *usually* ovah there,
I think...but I can't see nothin' tonight!"
   "Can't see it either. Can't see anything
really. Can't choose another one, right?"
   She nodded sadly as painted lips pouted. I goosed
the brim of a tartan-clad ass. Chugging her hooch as
my hand clouted, bondage-trim echoed smashed glass.
   "Hmmn...how 'bout the Moon?
Can I wish upon *that* if it glistens?"
   "I mean, there's a *man* in there, right? So why
the fuck not? Worst thing, he don't listen!"
   Lids clenched, hands thigh-plastered,
I tabulated the gist of deep thoughts.
   (From a million stray cysts, Kilroy's mien
gathered, simultaneously flabby and taut.)

A shrill cry dashed the Polish cohesion to a burst
of chaotic dust. My eyes gaped with pains of trollish
lesions while Iris waved at something that cussed!
Rushing over, yanking asunder, I rump-thwacked
with a single hard spank. As I leaned over roof
bricks, begging pardons, Luigi carved
phantom hips/breasts/flanks.
"Yo, my man! Hear 'bout Gooden?
Busted for blow yet again!"
"Huh, no. That's too bad. A goddamned shame."
"Couldn't keep his nose off'a th' yayo!
Fuckin' moolies! All'a same!"

PEELING A FUZZY STRIPED SWEATER,
flaunting a leopard brassiere, Iris addressed my
Setterish nod with a coquettishly suggestive sex-leer.
Grabbing a crotch, unfastening its fly, tugging its pale/
throbbing leash, she heeled me bedside before
kneeling down as Troll-rants drifted
up from the street.
Carmined lips cowled a spur's head.
Fat breasts sloppily topped thighs.
Watery glands slid back-and-forth.
Verily, surrender was nigh!
Eyes met my own, lips smiled soft, belying a sharp/
hardened tongue. Through a penile glut, a voice
chimed palsy as if allied with the Deaf and the Dumb.
"Wilbah, I want ya to fuck me now..."
Sliding open a nightstand's drawer,
I dolefully wavered my jowls.
"Game over, babe. All outta Trojans."
Iris spat pre-cum and scowled.

Blindly reaching for undershorts,
my hands groped fistfuls of dust.
  "Not you, it's me! Gonna run to
the store! No need to get wistful...I'll rush!"
  Replacing the bra, ignoring name-recitation,
her tracks left prints on the floor.
  (A tap's roar decried lingerie-application.)
  Something snapped within a vanity drawer.

**HEEDING A SHRIEK, DISLODGING
THE DOOR,** a wet mass collapsed in my grasp.
  Convulsing with fright, fear pulsed galvanic,
as if whipped by a slick lash of asps.
  *"Oh my Gawd, Wilbah! It was the biggest roach
I evah seen! Jesus, man! What the heck?"*
  A vent was gestured above slimed tiles,
slits choked with powdery dreck.
  Tightly clutched flesh evoked renewals of thirst.
  A face mashed a mirrored cabinet.
  Gnawing away like consuming a wurst,
my spur probed fur then stabbed it.
  *"So horrible! So red! So hairy! This native
New Yorka nevah seen nothin' so scary!"*
  Engaging the sink to shampoo clotted clumps of
neglected/hedonic locks, I continued to flounce
the dubious pudenda, wantonly irrespective of pox.

So the yankees won the world serious and that
bald guy rode a police horse around the
stadium. It took a big dump on 2nd base. Now
the holidays will be coming. Things will get
pretty sad again. Everybody goes home accept

me. Even cliff. No family to eat turkey with.
Nobody to love except one spider that I cant
kiss bc it bites me when I get to close and
another that lives between walls. At least work
is busy and the dreams have stopped.

Chinese letters for "apache blood" $55

Yankees logo $65

Panther $75

Yankees logo $65

Yankees logo w/sexy cherrys $85

Panther $75

Yankees logo $65

Yankees logo $65

Yankees logo $65

Panther $75

Garfield as egyptian farrow $80

Yankees logo $65

Yankees logo $65

Beauty mark $50

Panther $75

Yankees logo $65

Glad I finally gave luigi the gun bc avery is right.
I need to be a man and men dont take easy
ways out. But what the heck are these little
red marks all over my dickhead? Do I have
the clap? If it doesnt hurt to p ss should I
just ignore them? What would holden do?

"I generate and spread powerful healing vibrations."

A WET/WINDY/SUNDAY AFTERNOON
saw a blonde skulk through the street-entry.
   Flame toned swaths skittered her wake,
a maelstrom of autumnal leaf-sentries.
   Though both Cliff and I perked upon the arrival,
no heed was paid to *'Hellos!'* Her focus instead was
singularly devoted to walls shaded by staid rogues.
   Jacketless despite freezing temps, the Skulking
Blonde appeared thirty three. Hair teased and
unkempt atop a *Christian Death* shirt
betrayed a clear non-nativity.
   A displaced Californian intellectual?
   A Rutgers doctoral-begonia?
   Too besotted with Kant's tomes
ineffectual for such trivialities as Warmth or
Pneumonia? Alas, with a maiden lip-parting, a dire
misread metastasized. Lilts escaping a brick-
stained stoma cried of local baptize.
   "Dis cross heah...wit' d'thoiny rose...
how much would dat set me back?"
   "Sixty or seventy, I suppose,
depending on if it's red or just black."
   The Skulking Blonde's summary undress
emphatically espoused the design.
   .My *'Fred Mertz'* trousers were mercifully
ample to render arousals benign.

AS THE LINER LOWERED LIKE CHROMED BALLAST, a nail bailed a herd of soft Kools.

Flaming the phallus, the Skulking Blonde grinned.

"Such a toid...shoulda asked!
'Kay if I smoke while youse tool?"

Ignoring firm rules, I nodded, gaze sinking past a lace bra. Slashes and burns flitted marbled flesh betwixt a litany of archaic scrawl. "'Scuse da punk-rawk relics. Fuck...really miss dem days..."

"Musta seen some great shows back then!"

(I cringed at my age-schism malaise.)

"Yeah, kiddo. Lotsa good ones! Clash at Bonds five fuckin' times! Heartbreakahs! Ricky Hell! Even fuckin' Sham 69!"

My head quaked torrential regret.

"For me, it was ten-minute/forty-song hardcore sets."

"Too bad, kiddo. Feel for youse. I was lucky, had a real cool olda brudda! Took me t'shows. Showed me aroun'. Woulda nevah knowed one band from anudda..."

Eyes leaked sap of milky remorse. A long sigh wistfully respired. "Died a week back. Kilt by a hoss. Dat's how dis piece was inspiah'd."

Thoughts drifted to the yellowed clipping taped to the shop's bathroom-door. Chris Reeve's lame mien...beneath *'MAN OF WHEEL!'*...

(A notation to deplume and abhor.)

"Man, sorry. That really sucks. Was he riding English or Western?"

"Nevah got bucked on no hoss his whole life! T'ings is jus' sometimes predestined! Jus' nappin' on grass!

Bitch nevah saw him! Cops even sez he was drunk!
Odd, coz he was *sobah* a long/long time!
Nevah woulda fuckin' thunk!"
  "Jesus."
  "Head crunched like a melon!"
  "What an awful way to go..."
  "No open casket neitha! Looked
like a toipedoed boat!"
  Words creaked as hands obscured brows. Cheeks
ran sooty with tears. Onyx dollops ensheathed
chipped claws with little more than cursory smears.
  Around her right pointer sat a silvery
band; a myopic orb fused to its cent.
  Battered. Beaten. Broken. Beset.
  Bruised by small nicks and dents.

Cliff and I got in a big tiff about seinfield (sp?).
He says I dont like the show bc I dont
understand jewish humor. I said but I am part
jewish and you are a penticostal (sp?) and he
said yes I agree that you have a big f'n nose but
if you are a genuine jewboy then you need to
prove it and show everybody in the shop the
scar on your dick. Needless to say I did not do
this stupid thing. Even tho everybody besides
me laughed at cliffs "joke" for a while they all
ended up siding w/my opinion that good times
whats happening jeffersons 227 benson
different strokes sanford etc are just way better
shows. I mean there is no comparison. It is just
a scientific fact that blacks are naturally better

sit com actors. And what in the
hell is "jewish humor" anyway?

Panther $75
Yankees logo $65
PR flag w/pit bull $90
Hi-heel shoe $50
Yankees logo $65
Sexy honeypot $60
Yankees logo $65
Yankees logo $65
Panther $75
Catterpillar saying "dont try to change me baby"
$70
Panther $75

Walked by tchotchke (sp?) town the other day.
The windows are boarded. Also my sores are
finally going away. That is good bc it seemed
like there were new ones everytime
I woke up.

"I am a loyal friend."

**EROTIC SHAMPOOS ALSO WORKED
MIRACLES,** Iris lingering buoyantly peppy,
even slithering across Withers one night in
a Trooper loaned by a *'Cousin Giuseppe'*.
  Bazooms mangling a bedazzled brass star, bangs
blazed by a new Waardenburg streak, lips warmly
puckered to moisten my brow as I bent
over and buckled the seat.

Examining a dashboard gilded and loaded whilst
eyes stared tilted and lusty, my greased crown
was palmed with matronly whisks.
  "Oy! Always so linty an' dusty!"

**SPEEDING ATOP THE WILLIAMSBURG
BRIDGE,** we bandied pertinent plans.
  "How 'bout we go visit your job?"
  Eyes stabbed like mascaraed brigands.
  Lighting a Parliament, she grunted and scoffed,
countering a Meatpacking shindig.
  "Squeezebox? Nix to trannies! *Girls* get
me tapping...not faux grannies in thin wigs!"
  (Fingering a cab's Third World weaves,
she damned all Hindus to Hell.)
  "Ain't goin' by the job on my fuckin' night off!
Jesus! Quit bein' a douchey-ass skell!"
  "Aw, c'mon! Next date I'll fly you to Paris!"
  "Great...ya actually *tryin'* to make me embarrassed!"
  "You got it all wrong! Dead fucking wrong! Not
trying to do that at all! The peeler's world stokes my
inner ethnographer! Didn't mean
to make you feel small!"
  "*Enough*, man! Now I *know* ya fuckin' with me and
I think it's really uncool! I ain't ya fuckin' science-
project! Ya didn't even *go* to no school!"
  Laying a hand atop a steering right shoulder, I
caressed then gently squeezed. A muscle as taut
as a lemon-sized boulder swept blood
betwixt gabardine knees.
  "Sorry if your feelings were hurt. You're right, I'm
way outta line! I was only curious to see your work
'cause I care. Don't have to go, it's fine..."

"S'okay. I'm sorry too. Really shouldn'ta snapped. Guess I jus' been kinda *down* lately. Job makes me feel like real crap. Buncha scuzballs. Shifty-ass cunts. Can be a real livin' Hell. Mafia dudes...big skeezy niggas... all claim they played in the NFL! Sometimes, once in awhile, a customah might be *kinda* okay. But it's mostly jus' Japs, gross Israelis, an' old dudes denyin' they's gay. But I *like* ya, Wilbah, an' I 'preciate that ya wanna know more 'bout me too. Jus'...*please*...don' cast no aspersions when ya get shocked by the scum, the sleaze, an' the shrews! An' can we hit Don Hill's afta a coupla drinks? It's Formika's birthday an' I *really* wanna say hullo! Once tipped me five hundred clams, I think, an' she's always been gen'rous with blow..."

TUXEDOED GIANTS GUARDING A DOOR
emblazoned with *'New York Dolls'* drooled as hungrily
at Iris's store as lions forking pews in St. Paul's.
Unabashedly ignoring my extended right duke,
eschewing my *'How do?'* shakes, Prudence
dictated I absolve all jukes of hands
likening Brobdingnagian rakes.

'Livin' on a Prayer' boomed the PA, crisp as a seltzer's
first sup. I ensconced within a booth's velvet rosé
whilst Iris retrieved whisky in cups. She hadn't lied,
I came to understand, the joint was indeed writhing
with sleaze; bulbous physiques, enflamed by
tans, tweezing and grinding Armani.

Marblesque columns flanked quicksilver spheres.
Pérignon stems periscoped chrome.
The vast lechery was palpable!
A champagne supernova's gloam!

CLAMMY BREASTS THWACKED BITTER EYES, blinding me with perfume-tinged sweat. As glands peeled free, a well preserved blonde guffawed a brusque Cockney threat:

"Cor! Mind those long/sharp teeth! Mama likes to spank!"

Setting down tinkling highballs, Iris gifted the Briton a shrewd yank. A blocky Italian swooped in to join, toting much merchandise. Green sharkskin outshined brilliantined hair. Gems marred his likeness to dicks working vice.

Ogling the swag, Iris slumped, features catabolic with Shame. Dumping the burdens piecemeal before me, the Italian built a cathedralic frame.

A t-shirt. A jacket. A frisbee. A mug.

A cotton/heather hoodie.

A cozy. Magnets.

A golf-tee. Gloves.

An assortment of sadomasochistic/leather goodies.

A bumper-sticker beseeched:

FOR THE BREAST OF TIMES AND THE THIRST OF TIMES CUM PLAY WITH R DOLLS!

"Hiya, shoity! Brought ya date some free sou'vah'neahs! T'woint no trouble at all!"

"Thanks, Nicky. Be right back with ya guys...need to use the john..."

Trailing her exit with glossy black eyes, smiling teeth parted to yawn. "Youse *made* her bring ya, didn'tcha?"

"Um, not quite sure what you mean."

"Not even *man* enough to admit it, ya matzo-ball eatin' fiend?"

As Ice Cube melted into Pearl Jam,
the Italian leaned in closer.
   "Dem nice boobs on dat goil make me
a lotta damn shekels! Youse two is awfishally ovah!"

A DRUNKEN COLLAPSE AT HALF PAST FIVE

was lit by a red blip flashing 'ONE'. Wails slurred
against Gloria Gaynor and shrills of transsexual fun:
   'Oh...hullo, Mista My Life is a Fantastic Advencha! Mista
Incredibly Motivated Person! Mista Blood is Thoist's Finest
Quencha! Mista A Constipated Joy Nevah Worsens! An'
where the fuck did ya sneak off? Who else ya humiliatin'
tonight? Anotha dumb hooer like me? Anotha bitch who
ain't very bright? Dunno why ya think ya so cool, 'cause...
stop the presses...ya ain't! Made me look like a fool at my
own fuckin' job! Stuck me with some kinda bald Jew-taint!
Well hey, guess what? Found my stah! Betta believe I
made a big wish! Don't be supah-surprised if ya wake
up soon an' find ya'self sleepin' with fish!'

Fu manchu says this is his last night on the bus.
His mother is taking his retarded son and he is
going to a semenary (sp?) to become a priest. I
told him not to bother bc there is no god and
that all we are is dust in the wind and he told
me that the answer my friend is blowing in the
wind so I guess it was kind of a draw.

Panther $75
Panther $75
Pink panther as pimp w/snocpy as hooker $95
Yankees logo $65
Jimmy cliff spliff $50

Chinese letters for "lamont loves delilah" $55
Nubian princess $65
Panther $75
Sad clown $85
Panther $75
Smiling jesus $80

Five names of dead people in olde english $90

Got a card today. Wait bc its not what you think. Address was typed and it was from my mother. Bich f'n tricked me w/the typing. Hallmark thing w/some gay newspaper clippings about healing and togetherness folded in. Not even a f'n check. I burned it in the kitchen sink and dumped the ashes in the shrine. Also watched "mrs doubt fire" on hbo. Not nearly as good as cliff claimed.

"I can talk to the animals."

THE FEARSOME STAB OF DESPAIR'S LONELY SHIV rid essays of Convention's box. Poetry slams, swing-dance lessons, congregations ignorant of lox. I was even the lone Caucasoid pupil at several *'Buddha-Hand Wing Chun'* seminars — til testes could no longer duly withstand stinging brands of flung manual scimitars.

Heeding a Voice think-piece touting dog-runs as emerging new markets of meat, a weekly Tompkins hajj targeted integuments surging, supple, and sweet.

As I leaned ghostlike atop iron gates, monitoring frolic and fornication, I'd often mull what strange pull had ever suggested arachnoidal domestication.

OGLING POOCHES ONE COOL AFTERNOON, I espied a most unusual creature. Scuffling a mutt in billowing dust, fierce snarls set Shar-Pei chaperones decrying with inscrutable features.

My jaw slackened as the shitstorm waned and the offender rose on twin stems. While an untamed mane hung a sleep shy of dreadlocks, the residuum paid beaucoup dividends. A pointed chin, convex bones, and a needle sharp widow's peak framed lemon/lime eyes, a spoon-dumpling nose, and lips stung enough to wield ghetto-speak. A swan's neck grafted this masterpiece to an uncannily blown hourglass — an enchilada more alchemically akin than random deoxyribonucleic pass.

When her fanged companion growled once more, the Creature again collapsed to the Earth.

Barking! Howling! Leaping! Tearing!

Yuppies formed a generous berth!

'Twas a performance for the ages indeed, one I soon learned was staged oft. Attending as many matinees as work deemed, I yearned to break free of their waft — for the Unusual Creature's legions of fans were largely cologne-drenched boors.

Shooting occasional sideways glances, I'd ponder the horrors of *their* vanity drawers.

"HEY! YOU...TOUGH GUY! Whatcha been starin' at?" Tiny fists flanked cavalier hips thrust with daring éclat.

Beneath phlegmy chortles, denim-
sheathed breasts jiggled muddy and racy.
   "Nice *outfit*, dude! Immortal! Supposed to be DIck
fuckin' Tracy? Don't know that Halloween's over?
Yeah, that's it, I'm guessin'! Just so ya know, it is!
And so's the Great fuckin' Depression!"
   Ever mindful of brownie-point gestures, I knelt and
rubbed at the whining cur's fur, tiny bursts of
powdery grunge exploding with
each scrape of its burrs.
   "That's *Turkey*."
   "Undignified, don'tcha think?
My bad. Shouldn't revile it..."
   "Because I found her last *Thanksgiving*, gink!
Since you didn't ask, I'm Violet!"
   Violet! A Schulzian handle! Though
'Pigpen'was more apt, I nodded.
   A roving Negro bandied plaudits of
'Coke'/'Sense'/'Mesc'/'Dilaudid'.
   A queer spiralling device gored a crusty left ear,
distantly echoing sad Calder constructs
that'd consistently bored me to tears.
   "Interesting earring."
   She tugged with a woefully smudged thin hand.
   "I'm trusting you don't know, I think! Petrified
coon's dick! Poetry frozen in glans!"
   Baffled again, I smirked, mulling strategic depart.
   "That's nice."
   "*Well...?*"
   "Well what?"
   "*Well*, jerk, if you and me are gonna *fuck*,
your *name* would be a good region to start!"

**THE RED LIGHT FLASHED AS I ARRIVED
HOME,** my first voicemail in over nine days!
  Was Fate spanking Despair's fat rump?
  Spirits suddenly raised!
  *'Mistuh Benduh? Hullo there, suh! Hope this day finds
y'all as well as it does me! A thousand pardons for takin'
up time, but my name's Sergeant-Major Henry Fussy! I'm
callin' on behalf of the Marine Corps, son. Recently joined
the Beekman Street office. Was just browsin' some ol'
aptitude-tests. Noticed yuh'd scored like a prophet...'*
  As the strange Southerner endlessly blathered,
my back smacked the refrigerator door. The sliding
descent was brought to a halt against
tiles of linoleum floor.
  An enormous dust-bunny came hopping up, then
parked atop my pleated left thigh. Eerily mirroring
a Moe Howard toupee, the clump stared
like a gratinated eye.
  *'Just wonderin' if yuh still interested in joinin'. Pleased
as punch to have y'all come down. Got some new
benefit- packs that ain't at all disappointin'! Have a
looksee! Toss the ol' pill around! Again, this here's Sergeant
Hank Fussy. Gimme a callback any ol' time. Schedule
here's real flexible. I'm at two-one-two, five-one-nine...'*
  Donning the clump like a jocund
king, I fled, bedroom bound.
  Exposing myself, slicking an opened palm's
ring, I gaped at a reflected ghoul/clown.
  Angry Elizabeth paced aquarium-lengths;
fevered, lethally furious.
  Tiny footsteps hammered decaying brain-meat.
  Holes rent deep and injurious.

So today I found a cool piece of bent metal on bloomfield ave for the shrine. From a car wreck w/dried blood on it. A voice in my head said it was the key to liberation. There is lots of other cool stuff in there now to. In the shrine not my head. A corsage (sp?) from a prom some antique marbles a brown bride and groom from a black wedding cake a cool rusty knife w/mister peanut on the handle a chickens foot and a piano wire I found in my pocket. Also some of her old panties and the hair from her brush and those old photo booth pictures of me and her at little rickys. I dripped blood over them. There is one square where she is sticking out her tongue and that is where it all seemed to land. Wierd. Also Luigi keeps playing the same fugies record over and over. I hear it every time I am in the f'n hallway. Almost enough to drive a person crazy.

Panther $75
Yankees logo $65
Thug life $125
Nubian princess $65
Panther $75
Panther $75
Spider web on elbow $85
Lickable cherrys $65
Panther $75

Yankees logo $65
Booker t washington w/blunt $85
Beauty marks on face butt and tits $65
Panther $75

Fu manchu has still been driving the bus.
Maybe he knows I am right about god? Maybe
he would just miss his retard to much? Either
way it still means garlic farts 5 nights a week.

"I am entitled to make mistakes for they reveal great lessons."

**HIS SMILE ILLUMINATED THE BULLPEN
MOROSITY** like a thousand watt pin-spot's train, its
upper globosity ensheathed via gilt-wrapped 'fronts'
gleaming with zero refrain. Through a litany of scant/
clever cutaways, enamel formed '*NIGGAZ B TRIPPIN'*'
— concealing pockets of plaque/tooth-decay/
gaps/probable rigorous chipping.

I immediately recognized the mantis-thin teen, albeit
through no dental annotation; his tell being a glittery
tracksuit eliciting a strong Ziggy Stardust evocation.
Likewise bedecked thrice-prior, an 86 had been
forced each time; twice on account of documentary
dearths, once for an outright crime.

(A pitifully fraudulent ID, shawled by a taut
lavender palm, had skittishly touted a forklift-
licensee spawned in Hagåtña, Guam.)

Brimming the boldness of Youth's bliss, he
beelinered to the partition, thwacking the counter
with the gold-dusty uncouthness of a Forty-Niner's
nocturne emission. Surveying a permit holographic,
I espied not only the Real McCoy, but signals
of Selectively Served prophylactics...
for this was a birthday boy.
  "Congrats! Eighteen at last!
Now then, what'll it be?"
  "I ain't no expert, Tattoo-Man!
Thinkin' mebbe y'all tell me!"
  Sliding forth a reference binder, I mulled this bleak
indecision, flabbergasted at the premeditation of
scabs with legally blind inner-vision. Thirty long
seconds elapsed before a bull lion was ordained the
winning selection; fangs shining within a swaying mane
plagued by a waterfall's spinning ejections.
  Knocking back a few birthday bucks as I embarked
for the Thermofax, my gait was curtailed amidst
anxious clucks stippled with Parkway-syntax:
  "Yo, Tattoo-Man! Forgots to axe,
c'n I gets my name in this bitch?"
  Scanning the muralish sprawl,
I tamed a furious twitch.
  Why did so many clients (hides both Aboriginal and
Alabaster) feel compelled to tag *every* damn
thing, plying compositional disaster?
  Sadly, I'd given up on Art's sake, patience previously
exhausted. It seemed to the masses that handleless
facets were like baking cupcakes unfrosted.

THE TEDIOUSLY LINE-HEAVY MOTIF soon
triggered an inevitable auto-pilot, thoughts drifting

rudderless to spiders/imps/voluptuous
clots of young Violets.
  I was vapid.
  An automaton.
  An inhuman vending-machine.
  An ink-drooling mower of lawns.
  A once again future Marine?
  Assuming the role of stoic trouper, the Mantis-Thin
Teen eschewed pauses; enduring with a most heroic
stupor, sans cigarettes and vomitous clauses.
  Smiling for the entire duration, eyes flexing
Passage Rite dew, he spieled just once to express
admiration for mangy dogs naming boys Sue.
  "My daddy," he whispered. *"Love th' Man
in Black. Listen to that nigga all'a time."*
  Curiosity piqued, I queried lines walked.
  *"Angel. Least that's how Mama done talked.
Klan twined his ass when I was jus' nine."*

PULLING STAKES AN HOUR LATER, I exhaled
deep wafts of Relief. A behemoth design and
inviolable flesh had paired to siege fingers with Grief.
  The ends, however, had justified the means with
results solid and bold. The partitioneers unanimously
agreed, awed miens nodding manifold.
  As I tore Bounty to enshroud his pang,
the youth banged a calamitous gong:
  *"Dope! Only, jus' one thang...
name be spelt kinda wrong."*
  "Pardon? What?"
  "Ain't nothin' really. Jus' a coupla letters flipt aroun'."
  Vultures commenced crows-and-caws.
  Testicles bayed like sad hounds.

Swiping the wound free of red pus, I studied brown
skin with intent. Raising a leaf for Comparison's
sake, the epithets were of indisputable ident.
  "Um, you sure? Look...worded
exactly the same as denoted."
  The Mantis-Thin Teen squinted and laughed.
  My bad! Mest th' shit up my own dang
self when I's done sat down an' wrote it!"
  Amidst a chorus of *Idjits/Fools/Dumbass-*
Muthafuckas, the Mantis-Thin Teen fidgeted;
gassing Cool before drumming up Succor.
  "Ain't no thang though, really -
jus' swap them shits right aroun'."
  Cripes!
  Great Caesar's Ghost!
  Did this twit aim to blight and confound?
  How indeed had he dressed himself,
tied his own shoes, not to mention accessorized?
  A DMV's deem of operational fitness
was an even more appalling surprise!
  Spying my pan, orbs beamed hypnotic,
as if clubbed by a rye and beer-chaser.
  "It's a'ight, Tattoo-Man. Y'all mo' than got this.
Jus' rub out some dye with th' eraser."

December, 1993

Weeks passed slathering expectancies with pink/
buttercreamy tensions. Poetic waxings of salted hog-maws.
Hearths rinked by bear-rug dimensions. Having never
before sampled a traditional Christmas, I'd long pined
to tongue a smidge; if only as an apparitional
witness and not a legitimate kid.

And she'd prepped the data supremely well as I'd
gobbled even piddling scraps. I knew all of her aunts'
middle names. That one cad had riddled the triad with
clap. I was a virtual bystander to the long-ago death
of Orville (her mother's childhood Borzoi) tragically
mowed amidst an attenuated prime by a
Ford built for Good Humor's employ.
   I was even privy to her half brother Varney's prefered
testicular cologne. A princely potion called 'Chaps'
was ritually flung atop stones.

My snow-dusted/East Third landing found her over-
stuffing an old gym-bag. Frowning at the sight of a
strapped Jansport, her mien branded a grim-souled flag.
   "So, so sorry, Daddy. Gotta go this one alone."
   "But...but why?"
   Struggling to zip past a mound's meaty bulge, she
shrugged, sighed, and moaned. "Dunno. Just gotta.
Can't really explain...but you won't be
missing out on that much."
   "How could you not know? We've planned this
for months! I even learned Pennsylvania Dutch!"
   A puller flew loose from an unyielding track.
   A cat decried shrapnel-assault.
   "Okay! So I DO know, alright? But can the prattle,
'cause it's not my fucking fault! Just got off the
phone with my mother! I'm sorry! She's
just kind of...old-fashioned..."
   "But you know I love antique stuff!
Vintage clothing's my sole passion!"
   Unburdening the ruined sack, words herky-jerked with
violent motion. "Remember what I said about my father's

stances on scourges and, um, other nihilistic devotions? As
you might expect, she absorbed a lot of his views. And...
well...better just say it: she just really doesn't like Jews!
Simple as that! Doesn't like 'em, and doesn't want one
in her house! Already had two fucking blow-outs...
can we please just let this one douse?"
  Twenty tons of molten lead deluged my bag's confines.
  "Told her it was rude, but you understand!
Jack, just tell me you don't really mind!"
  Fleeing the bedroom, I perched on the couch.
  Sad. Confused. Nervous.
  From the mammoth wood fortress of an aged
Panasonic, O.J. Simpson hawked Hertz's #1 Club Gold
Service. The once impossibly marmorean face now hung
blue/wan/forlorn. No longer could he swish terminals like
a Kryptonian son — his soul was too gaunt and war-torn.
  Elizabeth leapt within a tear-diffused view, claws blocked
by bundled-up rump. "Aw, Daddy...don't just sit there
and stew! Maybe this'll sock you outta that dump!"
  Smiling weakly, I received a thrust Pez.
  Batman stared back grimly.
  "Can I put you in a cab to the station at least?"
  She fiddled with coat-buttons primly.
  "No, Daddy. My brother's on his way now to pick me up.
Gonna drive us to Bethlehem. Please take good care
of Busty and Elmie. Give 'em some extra chow
like I've been telling 'em."
  "Your brother? But...you...you said
he raped you in his Peterbilt!"
  "And if they really, really behave...maybe
you'll let them sleep on the heated quilt?"
  Unzipping my bag, I withdrew two blue
Tiffany's boxes, grinning as goy as I could.

"Merry Christmas, baby. For two little foxes.
Sorry I didn't get Varney anything good."
  Snatching the loot, she brushed curtly past.
  A slam severed a tail star-crossed.

Twelve chimes clanged as Christmas Eve gassed.
I endeavored a vet's bale of 'Bird Talk'.

"I am accepted and appreciated."

BEING A PATIENT AND COURTEOUS CHAP,
Sgt. Fussy allowed flames to expire.
  'Doesn't sound like the Corps served yuh too
fair a crack, son! Can't rightly blame all that ire!'
  "It's cool...just wanted to touch base...
don't aim to waste any more of your time."
  'Not at all! In fact, care to help an old salt
erase the bane of some dreary war-crimes?'
  "Um...what?"
  'Explain the organics of the gents who criticized
all those tattoos, if yuh reckon yuh can.'
  "Well, a Hispanic. Middle-sized. Tall black
dude was the second. Sorry, I mean African."
  'I see. An' where, Mistuh Benduh,
do yuh own people hail from?'
  "Grew up outside of Trenton.
Californian dad. Minnesotan mum."
  'Son, that's not quite what I mean. Race is what I'm
tryin' to discern here! White? Red? Yella? Green? Don't
laugh! Some folks have claimed Martian ovuh the years!'

"Pale, I guess. Sandy hair. My eyes are a light shade
of blue. But I've found it tough to pass for white
on account of a slight taint of Hebrew. You're
a pro, Sarge. Tell me what you think."

(A sustained pause was ultimately
marred by a Zippo's musical clink.)

*'Son, I regret to inform yuh that it seems yuh been the
victim of undue discrimination. A tattooin' ban in the
U.S. Marines would be tantamount to dictums of chewed
castration! Those gents yuh met with are now locked
in the brig while lawyers prepare their court-martials!
They'd summarily rejected every white applicant
on grounds hardly impartial!'*

"Huh. Well, okay. That's good. Albeit awfully strange."

*'Who the heck knows what kinda sick thoughts drive
folks? Some of us just hatch deranged! Now then, son,
an' I realize this would be askin' a lot, the prosecution
is seekin' new witnesses to be certain
that justice is wrought...'*

While I was certainly thankful for the proffered
recompense of three guaranteed years in Oahu,
thoughts of slaughters a fink could never prevent
were sufficient to queer latent yahoos.

Slow day. Read in the news that cabbage patch
dolls w/moving mouths have been chewing
little girls scalps off. Another post office
shooting to. Dont normally approve of
trends but I must admit that I like these.

Panther $75
Yankees logo $65
Punisher skull $80

Chinese letters for "eat hot lead bich" $55
Panther $75
Beauty mark $50
Panther $75

Tunnel dream again. First in a long long time. The retard was there. Naked and wet. Ronald demanded I commit a unthinkable crime.

Note to self: buy stamps at bodega.

"A brave man's blood is the best thing on this Earth when a woman is in trouble."

BEFORE A RUBBLY/VACATED PLOT ON EAST SECOND betwixt C and D, Violet mercifully ceased blubbering an ear-scraping blot of Michael Jackson's *'P.Y.T.'*

"Well...*okay*...thanks for the laughs, man. This is me."

(Squinting through chicken-wire, I surveyed stacked bits of old ghost's bike-frames. Peppered with evidence of recent gunfire, a blackened Pit Bull roasted in flames.)

"You live in a bombed-out lot? Where? In that old VW?"

"Doesn't matter, Baldy! Ain't gettin' lucky, so don't even let it trouble you!"

Forcing her backwards/bending diamonds
of rust/I thrust a groin into her own.
"Gonna make your virgin hymen go bust
while you sweat, you bleed, and you moan!"
Stinking odiously despite a peacoat's wrap, lips
slowly smeared against mine. I lifted my palm to a soft
woolen lump, evoking squeals of lost-puppy whines.
Deploying an erection fit to break, *'DUMB UGLY
CUNT'* throbbed in rapid succession. Shoving
me aside, an ass callously quaked towards
a brick stoop's Kryloned recession.
Left fingers waggled. A clumsy goodbye?
She about-faced with a key's falsetto click.
A street-lamp's pulse licked jagged
teeth stained with tobacco and spit.
"My dad was a Navy admiral, dick!
I can *understand* Morse Code!"
But had the cad imparted the wit
to source strands of Pindaric Ode?

**THE SPONGED-CLEAN TURKEY HAILING
THE DOOR** made a surprisingly beautiful cur —
her long/stiff/straight black pelt echoing
an Asiatic whore's coiffure.
"Never mind the growling, okay? Just fuckin' walk
around her! If she didn't like you, she'd be on
your nuts by now! Crotch-biter! Once
housed a two hundred-pounder!"
Silk floor-pillows accrued smut beside a futon
unframed and pathetic. Lava Lamp/curtain-beads/jade
Siddhartha completed the Patchouli aesthetic.
Lifting a pasteboard attaché from an ash-slathered
Persian rug, Violet divulged a Zizmor employ
as a Fore-and-Aft shutterbug.

"Not artistically satisfying.
But pays the bills, y'know?"
  She leafed to a blonde lacking beautiful clear skin.
Some did not age like Bordeaux.
  "This one: *everything!* Chin-job! Tummy! Facelift! Got
her boobs done fuckin' *twice* already 'cause her
husband complained that they'd slipped! But hey,
whatever...dude can afford any and all types of
fakery! Even got himself a *dick* implant!
Family owns some famous bakery!"
  (The subsequent page showcased a lipoed/denuded/
sadly bulbous mass of rear-end. Fifteen inches above
the crudeness hovered a badly tattooed *Entenmann's*.)
  Clothes floor-tossed, she gazed at a full-length
nailed over the mangled futon, swaying slowly,
self-wrenching breasts as a sadist might strangle a
swan. Pressing her backside against steam-stained
plaster, she waist-wrapped me tightly with stems;
vaginal moisture forging sartorial disaster
as it seeped all the way through shirt-hems.
  A burgundy rim was haloed by a heavenly prism
of soft/massed golden-browns. Was this not Flynt's
vision of Seventies trim?
  A masturbatorial *'Watership Down'*?

**"SLAP 'EM, JACK! SLAP THOSE
FUCKIN' TITS!"**...verily, I complied.
  "*Harder,* you pussy! You bald little
shit! I'm not gonna fuckin' cry!"
  I throttled her quivering windpipe with
authoritatively stiffening thumbs, her vagina
reflexively clamping as admonitions
fell wayside and dumb.

Flouncing away, I continued to garrote, her face
soon seething with gasp. Somehow she managed
to soundlessly emote the hissed whisps
of a pillow-sheathed asp:
  *"More, you insipid disgrace! Make
me see God! Let me spit in his face!"*
  While fashioning a corpse was not what I'd
bargained, I fulfilled these requests nonetheless;
blasting a cervix at point-blank range as eyes rolled
back with quiesce. She wheezily smiled with my
grasp's ease, commencing an orgasmic hack.
It was at precisely this infelicitous moment
that Turkey launched a Rommelian attack.

FENDING A MUTT, TURGID AND DRUNK,

was not very fun at all. Fangs gnashing a tumescent
tusk sprayed fecund dog-aerosol.
  Dragging her protector to a toilet's keep, slamming
its thin door behind, Violet collapsed in a joyless heap,
wafting pudenda-turpentine. "Yeah, got B.O. like a
truck-driver's junk...but I fuckin' hate deodorants!
Don't believe in clogging glands like a de-geysered
skunk; my ex-husband could never get over it..."
  "Husband? But...you're so *young.*"
  "More of a quick needing-papers thing than any real
Garden of Eden. Wouldn't even call it a marriage.
Just a dumb hick from Sweden."
  Not caring to pry, I nodded and shrugged,
jerking a replenished qui vive. Following a coital
trifecta, we granted Turkey a clement reprieve.
  Approaching sleep, deep in reflection, defying
the verge of collapse, I magnanimously
resisted ignorance-correction.
  Truckers' pants reeked solely of *'Chaps'.*

**HEAVEN WAS STILL A MOONLESS
BLACK-VELVET** when a buzzer rattled like locusts.
 The finger-depression stayed decidedly
put, jarring tunnel-visions from focus.
 The blares fried Turkey's nerves to soot.
 She galloped the length of the pad.
 Barking, howling, clawing plaster with foot.
 A fatwa of Lupine Jihad.
 Groggy.
 Hungover.
 The digital read of Tandy clock-radio
was nearly beyond my decipher.
 Five-seventeen!
 Violet snored.
 I repressed strong urges to bite her.
 Shoulders rubbed, her lids remained clenched,
though a frown betrayed certain alertness.
 "Gonna answer that?"
 (Several tense moments of clamor
preceded an utterance of furtive curses.)
 "Don't fuckin' sweat it and g'back t'sleep. In another
minnit, he'll split. Fucker acts the fool whenever
he's stewed. Sanctimonious hypocrite..."
 Ninety seconds. The rumpus ceased.
 "Holy fuck. Allah be praised.
Wish he'd eat shit and die."
 The dog resumed its post...
 ...balled-up and dazed...
 ...whispering myriad sighs.

**EVERY EFFORT WAS PLIED TO
RECAPTURE SLEEP** — but still, nothing worked.
Tarantulas/Panthers/Marines launched fence-leaps.
 Alas, the Sandman shirked.

Thoughts were torpedoing towards
Ivanhoe Drive when accented screams incanted.
  Guttural. Slurred. Rife with despair.
  "VIOLET!" repeatedly ranted.
  A bedside glance revealed arms shielding eyes
from the horrors of incessant malady.
  Brow freeze-dried with worry, Turkey
absconded, preferring toilets to unpleasant realities.
  "My ex..." a sigh wafted,
forearm yet optically draped.
  "Technically, we're *still* fuckin'
hitched. Buncha legal red-tape..."
  Blazing a cigarette, she jostled the pack, regarding
my refuse as a joke. "Well, la-de-da, Goody
Two-Shoes...certainly *look* like you smoke!"
  The screams grew louder, more frantic, more
frequent, neighboring argots swelling in tandem.
  Voices yawped, *'Yo maricón, niggas be sleepin'!'*
in parlances well-meaningly random.
  *"VIOLET! YES, I KNOW YOU'RE UP THERE! ANSWER
ME! NOW, I SAY! WHO IS THAT BIG-NOSED JEW
WITH NO HAIR? I'M NOT GOING TO GO AWAY!"*
  As sobs flowed, a bottle smashed, seemingly
knocking screams dead. Had the Viking been
clobbered Ricanishly? Had he berserkedly
bashed his own head?
  "Now-now, babe...don't get upset. Everything's
gonna be alright. If it makes you feel better, I'll
park my ass here for as long as you want...
even the rest of the night."
  "Thanks, Jack. Appreciate it.
Lately, things have been brutal."
  (Spying the raccoon's severed johnson,
aches soured an impassioned canoodle.)

A UREMIC LAST DROP STILL STUBBORNLY CLUNG upon sudden squeals of ill-yell. A dash to the bedroom found a girl kneeling salah as a dog's spotted tongue bayed pell-mell. Hanging batlike outside a window's frame, upside-down from a rooftop ledge, Nordic fists pounded versos of panes whilst dreadlocks pendulumed flames beet-red.

"VIOLET! WHY ON EARTH ARE YOU DOING THIS? HAVE I TREATED YOU SO DREADFULLY BAD? YOU WERE MY HEART'S PEARL! MY FUCKING DREAM-GIRL! BEST PUSSY I EVER HAD!"

Though my stare towards the Viking was more empathy-borne than of Anger, Fear, or Shock, he nonetheless refused to meet my own orbs whilst yammering like an Asgardian macaque.

Mulling the room's wieldable objects — a candle, a cactus, a *'Bonfire of the Vanities'* hardback — my choice still teetered between an atlas and sandals when Insanity was addressed with brass tacks. Lifting a plastic Whopper, replete with lettuce/cheese/seed-bun, blonde dreadlocks flopped drastically upwards as Violet punched in 911.

A minute's tick brought a furious pounding of boots against a metal front-door.

"Don't worry. Lock's fuckin' changed. Can't get in anymore."

"YOO-HOO! GUESS WHAT? I'M GOING TO KILL YOU, VIOLET! BOTH YOU AND THAT UGLY BALD JEW! I'M GOING TO SLIT YOUR VEINS UNTIL YOU'RE DEAD! BUT ONLY BECAUSE I LOVE YOU!"

Wrenching biceps, she pecked at my lips, giggling and grinning smugly. "As usual, he's only partially right! I don't think you're that ugly!"

THE DOOR-MUTED STRAINS OF A HALLWAY'S LAST-STAND chimed heels against tiles encaustic. Aerosol spritz doused Scandinavian peals both Profane and Agnostic.

Cracks of leather, fist, and wood comminuted and sank defiant bones.

Delicate twists of manacle-clanks flecked compliant moans.

Violet seized a kimono upon a Shave-and-Haircut tattoo. *"Ma'am, Bozo's goin' to da jug 'til he can behave, but dere's still some talkin' to do."*

Groom complete, I slid past the cluster...

More Idea than Man...

Finding no Swedish evidence...

(Save dreadlocks strewn like rattan.)

Upon the second-floor landing, a blackish pool aped an Abrahamic presidential-silhouette.

A brass skull ring occupied the pond's dead-center.

Crouching, a fiend knuckled the bane.

Its tongue lapped arterial sweat.

Cliffs gf inheretted a lot of money from her mother who just died of brain cancer so that is good. After work we went by the new mondo kims store on saint marx and rented some tapes. "Nightmare alley" a old one about a man who eats chicken and something called "the swimmer" w/bert lancaster that cliff said is very good tho the cover looks very gay. Then I looked around at cds on the 1st floor and there was a big display of the new spitbax record. Big poster and everything. They are

on atlantic now. I guess soon she will be very
famous just like she always wanted. When no
one was looking I drew a swastika (sp?)
on her fourhead. I wonder if any of the words
are about me. Cliff wouldnt let me buy it.

Chinese letters for "he be white" $55
Panther $75
Sad indian w/blunt $70
Panther $75
Panther $75
(said she is a vegetarian but weighed over 500lb)
Taz w/tommy gun $85
World serious trophy $80
Onk (sp?) $60
Panther $75

Wierd craving for swedish meatballs.

"I create lasting monuments to genius."

AVERY'S RESONANT BARITONE was stripped
of its usual bite, his words no more than embarrassed
moans — distant, baleful, contrite.

'Bro, sorry for blankin' last week.
Didn't mean to blow ya off.'
"No biggie. Figured you were sick.
Sounds like you still got a cough."
'Nah. Hadda head Upstate. My mother. Suicide.'
"Jeez...don't even know what to say..."

'Just say nothin' then. Or go ahead and talk. Don't really care, you decide. But listen, bro, can I swing by this week? Just wanna wrap this shit up...finish the halo. Gotta shit-ton a healin' to do. Gonna need
to hang tough and lay low.'

AS THE FOOT-PEDAL KICKSTARTED INSECTUOUS CLATTERS, a vast ribcage expanded. My gloves reared in deference to lugubrious matters while a holy gaze broadcast hex-branded.

And there I sat, behind labored breaths, ink-loaded tube in my claw.

A viper awaiting some twitching of prey.

(A cretinous/glue-drizzling flaw.)

"She was a drinker. Had a bad liver. I.A. busted pop for corruption. Guess she was done 'cause she ran down to the river an' tossed herself right in the Hudson."

"Oh..."

"Had the funeral a few days later. Did it all on my own. The old man and my sis was too fuckin' choked. Mortician was a cockeyed choad."

"God..."

"Made Ma up like a Times Square hooer. Done her hair a real shitty way. Hadda wheel the coffin out back an' fix it myself while everyone drank whisky an' prayed."

HOURS TICKED PEACEFULLY BY, nigh devoid of all words, cadmium sulfide flowing with ease as it convoyed to skin in trawled spurts. When even the tiniest specks of bare flesh had ceased shining within the halogenic swath, I sprayed and swiped sanctified gore from a mien bloodied and wroth.

Weary but somewhat contented, Avery grinned atop a winish red shoulder. "Been a helluva fuckin' demented year, bro. Glad it's finally over…"

Reeking of grass, Cliff crossed the room, smiling like a doltish Travolta. *"Pure freakin' snazz, cuz! The boss of all beaut! Take a pic with my ol' Minolta?"*

NO MATTER WHICH ANGLE MY GOOSENECK CRANED, harsh watts brained composition. Squinting past a wrangle of scowls, I surveyed the waning Sun-vision.

"Sorry, man…yeah, it's cold, but mind if we shoot this out there? Natural light always works best. Here, we're just catching glares."

Snapping a Marlboro free, the Detective stabbed fistulous lips, slapping his clobber and gun; a jab to Vigilance for Cliff.

THE BLOOMFIELD AVE AFTERNOON CRUSH was brisk/clotted/contentious.

Anathema peppered shoves gift-besotted.

Elbows seethed Yule vengeance.

Dodging pedestrian obstruct, I guided Avery off-curb, facing him East betwixt two pick-ups, harnessing empyreal reverb.

"Almost there. Three more steps."

"Okay, bro. No sweat."

"Lower your shoulders…stand up straight…move one inch to the left…"

Turning around to face me, cackling blue smoke at the sidewalk, Avery's cognition of an old woman and chimp was an obvious source of snide squawk. Bedecked in a new Troop *'8-ball'* jacket (an evident recent bestowment) the ape's drooping crawl was an indubitable magnet of indelible Kodak Moments.

With the camera glued to my nose, my finger on the shutter-release, Spartacus hopped orgasmically about, grasping his waist-harness leash.
  Still adjusting my chimpanzee-
focus, a horn brayed wildly behind.
  A metallic crunch and subsequent
thump conspired to form virtual binds.

A STEAMING DART WITH A DEEP HOOD RUPTURE wheezily strained to turn-over.
  A windshield scarred rendered its pilot
a nightmarish mosaic of brown clover.
  Ten feet on, the Savior stared...
  Unwaveringly upwards at clouds...
  Echoing his gaze, I espied with dismay
a giant horsefly mired in shrouds.

After the wake I went to the babydoll lounge w/homer zuckerman and then the harmony lounge to. Most of the girls there had santa hats on. Even the japanese ones. Kind of unsincere if you ask me. Homer wore his sweat pants w/no underwear so he was almost up in their vaginas when they gave him lap dances. Gross yes but kind of brillant to. In the middle of one dance I asked him if he and temp ever killed a kid. He looked at me funny and says no why would you say that? What kid do you mean? Why would I kill a kid? I said forget about it. Then he says you mean the little nigger me and templeton threw off the

roof that he swore he would never talk about?
That kid? Is that the kid you mean? I got up and
left bc of awkward tension. So I went to see
"the crucible" instead to cheer myself up. Didnt
work. Thought I just saw charlotte on the 2nd
floor landing but it was just a big roach.
No biggy bc I see her in the tunnel
all the time anyway.

"I spy beauty everywhere I look."

**THE DOWNTOWN 6 WAS ABERRANTLY
CROWDED** for so late on a cold weekday eve.
  Two well-bred lookers sat across the aisle, blondes
in their apparent twenties. He was sheathed in
a crisp black tux, she in bespoke folds of gown.
  A lap-draped sable marked the schmucks
for slummers. I figured their Rolls had broke-down.
  Everyone aboard stared at the pair, whispering
nothings with eyes. A greying crone asked an old
codger if he recalled their own wedding-rice.
  As the golden-locked couple enmeshed
to kiss, its audience burst beams and sighs.
  Was this not Pure Bliss wrapped in young flesh?
The Universal Dream personified?
  Why had I been condemned to while dead
tunnels (airless and hairless) with strippers?
  A spry femme funneled red bile to my
scalp amidst hums of 'Careless Whispers'.

I was in the tunnel talking to charlotte last night and mentioned that there was still no reply from the nameless one and she said who do you mean? I said you know who I mean and she said no I dont. She pointed to holden and I said no I mean my dream girl. My baby. Then charlotte pointed to the retarded black girl and said she is not nameless you big dummy. And I said she is to nameless and that is not who I mean anyway. Then charlotte said define dream girl. Woke up w/new sores.

Panther $75

Mickey mouse as king tut $85

OJ portrait $95

Panther $75

Panther $75

Knicks logo $65

Chinese letter for "nostradamus" (sp?) $50

Thug life $125

Knife stabbing heart w/granny $80

Panther w/ray bans $80

Panther $75

Coffin $75

As per the ghost of president lincolns advice I cleaned out the shrine and put the peaces in the freezer. Already feeling slightly better.
No wonder he was elected twice.

He gives us hope.

"I do not blame others for my failures."

DESPITE A SHIRT-AND-SHORTS MARRIAGE TRIMMED IN CANDY-CANES AND WREATHS, Rayon Man's grim carriage foisted ample Pain and Grief.

"THOUGHT I DONE GAVE UP WHAT'S MINE, YOU TOAD-EYED LI'L PUNK? GONNA CAVE YO' HEAD LIKE FRANKENSTEIN 'TIL IT FLAT AS ROADSIDE SKUNKS! HEALED! HEALED! ALL FUCKIN' HEALED! DON'T EVEN FRONT LIKE IT AIN'T! ALL FUCKIN' READY FOR MY BRIGHT-ASS SHIT! BEST START POURIN' PAINT!"

"Look here, sir — and *please*, just listen first —- while I respect beliefs in miracles, it just ain't gonna work. How about a full-refund? Another on the house? Let's take a sec to calm down some and stop the threats to knock me out..."

A palm thwacked the counter, cracking shined cobalt. Even shields stamped in brass had been wracked by rimed assault.

"OH, I TRIED, TATTOO-MAN! LORD KNOWS, I FUCKIN' TRIED! TRIED TO BE PATIENT WITH YO' IGN'ANT SELF, BUT YOU TOO FULLA RACIST PRIDE! NOW YOU LISTEN TO ME, 'CAUSE I'M AN OFFICER A THE LAW! YOU PULLIN' ILLEGALITY! POKIN' BEARS WITH CLAWS! KEEP VIOLATIN' CIVIL-RIGHTS AN' I'LL ARREST YOU ON THE SPOT! HATE IT COMIN' DOWN TO THIS, BUT WHAT OTHER CHOICE I GOT?"

Swiping clean of spittle, I slumped into a seat.
Lifting poor Adolfo's pane, I pressed a glossy sheet.

AWAITING FU MANCHU, glass crashed to
slushed cement. Shards were ground to
vandal's roux with swerves of dust-torment.
  A naked bitch was tragic pink.
  Likewise her big-ass steed.
  (EZ-Red splashed beyond the brink.)
  A bag was ditched in weeds.

June, 1994

*After the ferry, we boarded a bus near the St. George
Terminal. A cityish scape soon melted to burbs, triggering
queasy boyhood memorials. Through a window's rain-
combed grime, I spied an ambling black Gargantua.*
  *A hand had just commenced waving hi when fingernails
stabbed like tarantulas. "Daddy! Look! A skunk!"*
  Squatting atop a section of curb,
the beast calmly observed traffic.
  (Who knew Staten Island harbored
twerps of such mephitic demographics?)
  "Oh my gosh! What a cute little
stinker! Man, just look at that stripe!"
  *"Sickness-induced malinger. Usually he'd be
hidden on account of Humanity's gripes."*
  *"What do you know about skunks, and how
would you know it's a 'he'? My instincts say
it's a dame! A girl named Penelope!"*
  *I returned my gaze to the woman, mopping brows with
the hem of an oversized shirt, exposing a Day-Glo pink
bra, caked with dry packets of dirt. Pyramidical rolls
encircled the frame like tiers of cooling lava.*
  I was sorry to leave those jiggles behind.

Strings tugged at my vena cava.
Elizabeth spotted a tenpin alley
decaying to near-collapse.
 "Oh look, Daddy! Sunset Lanes!
Can we please go there aft?"
 She declared my imminent annihilation.
 My skull would be used to bowl strikes.
 "It'll be just like 'Happy Days', Daddy...
but strewn with the brains of dead kikes!"

By the time we'd disembarked the bus, the grounds were
practically rural — lush fields, nest-riddled trees,
eucalyptus lambasting the neural. A brief search led us to
a three-storied house sheathed within lime-tinted siding.
Knocks were answered by a teatless grouch primed for
rime-squinted chiding. Over Jerry Springer's nasally
whines, she grunted towards a backyard shack.
 A panting blue Doberman waggled
its stump, twined to a dead willow's rack.
 Elizabeth cooed and bent forward.
 The demon snarled and then growled.
 "But dogs love me..."
 Strange words sawed through heat
with ruthless serrations of scowl.
 "Don't let that worry ya none, Blondi there loves
youse too, just got a queer way a showin' it.
Hugs ya with fangs and drool."
 Inside a lopsided threshold,
a loden-blurred oldtimer leaned.
 (A small rectangular box hovered oddly
within a rolled undershirt's sleeve.)
 Windowless, fetid — illuminated only by a lone sixty-watt

bulb — *the shack's walls were obscured by timeworn
flash begrimed with blood/pus/dead-mold. While I quickly
selected a small bald eagle, an animal I'd long resembled,
Elizabeth was crestfallen to spy no black cats, which
I'd assured her every tattoo shop assembled.*

The Oldtimer shrugged with disinterest.

"What ya see is what youse get."

*Outside, the Sun burned at full-mast,
instantaneously obliterating sweat.*

*"Let's go! This guy sucks! He's filthy
and doesn't have what I want!"*

Begging for calm, I lifted a Bic.

"Relax, babe! Draw it myself! Let my girl down I shan't!"

---

*I was shocked to witness the Oldtimer's employ of a
stencil technique borne from the 1890s; rubbing coal-dust
into an etched acetate sheet shored against a Vaselined
triceps. As he attached his machine to a tape-doctored
wire, I realized he hadn't donned gloves.*

*(Antiseptic or not, he was a genuine
craftsman, plying his trade with mum love.)*

*Once conversation was finally permitted,
I unleashed a litany of questions.*

*Mining for facts of tattooing Pre-Ban, answers refracted
in rapid succession. As the wings of my eagle were
whip-shaded black and swiped with swaths of
deep brown, the Oldtimer shared historical
scraps of hip spades/ripe twats/beatdowns.*

*My wound was bandaged with a thin diner napkin
smoothed by nicotined hands. The leaf was secured
firmly in place with a newsprint-stained rubber band.*

Gripping the meat of Elizabeth's bicep,
the Oldtimer's head quaked distraught.
 "Sure ya don't want this on ya ankle
or nothin'? Much more a ladylike spot!"
 She pulsated waves of fury as soft
skin was gnawed and then ground.
 When quizzed of the Ban's biz-injury,
the Oldtimer hawed of shutdowns.
 "Worked the docks with my ol' man
a bit. An' for a while, rock'n'roll."
 This recon perked sad eyes up.
 "Doing what? I'm stuck in that same foxhole!"
 "Just a road-manager. Drove the bus. Made sure the
acts got up on time. Fetched their grub. Gathered their
shekels, which was tough 'cause promoters is slime.
Youse kids wouldn't a heard a him, but I worked
for this big-talkin' guy called Spector..."
 Elizabeth's orbs immediately gaped
to the size of an Oscared director.
 "Wait one second — do you mean Phil?
Total nutjob? Wall of Sound?"
 The Oldtimer lowered a shader stamped
'Chas. Wagner, NYC' and spat out a butt stained brown.
 "Knew him? I was his main man!
Without me, wouldn't a been squat!"
 "Wow, so cool! I've loved those records
since I was a girl! Genuine juggernauts!"
 "I'll tell ya, them was some real good times we clocked
back then! Pullin' that shit today would get us all locked in
the Pen! And the skirts! Whoa! Hooers, the entire lot! Ever
hear a those jigs the Ronettes? Once banged all three on
a Hyannis Port yacht! Together, we was a quartet! That

Estelle...Stella, we called her...man...she was pure raunch!
Fiend for gettin' weird shit up the snatch! In Asbury,
once used a conch! Another time, we was in Albany, just
sittin' by an ol' cemetery, when she goes and finds this tall
bone, see, from this grave a flood had unburied..."

Discourse attempts were torn apart as we waited for
the bus to show, and I soon gave up entirely until a Dart
yawped 'NICE TITS!' passing slow. Grasped by the wrists,
digital birds were gradually forced to my waist.
  "Don't bother, Jack. You'll just get your ass kicked."
  (At least she'd acknowledged my face.)
  Instinctively heading rearwards, she
slumped atop a knife-scarred seat.
  Upon a proffered sip of my iced large
Pepsi, she began bawling instantly.
  Recounting upshots of erstwhile soothes, I willed both
hands to stay lax. When she eventually face-planted
against my damp sternum, I pet her with coolly weighed
tact. Long after her sobs had petered, the scalp remained
glued to my chest. Had she glimpsed
the erection's fine meter?
  If so, was she duly impressed?
  "All that shit about the Ronettes! To him, they
were pieces of meat! And that gargoyle breath!
Ugh! His laugh shot fricassee-heat!"
  "Probably just making it up. Hey, still
wanna bowl? The alley-stop'll be soon!"
  "Wrong, pally! His type's too dumb to
imagine or mull! All of it's fucking true!"
  "Sure...but he also said the Ronettes begged for that
stuff. Let's face it, some chicks are born kinky. And who

are we to judge or rebuff? Deem things porno or stinky?
Like your friend Kate from the Hi-Yella. Remember the
tape I found on Fourteenth? Her and the chimp under
that big umbrella feigning a rape on the beach? I mean,
you musta watched that at least ten times..."

She yanked away from my chest.

"Tell me, Jack...are you really that stupid,
or do you act this lame on purpose?"

She continued to rant. Was it a diatribe? A lecture? A
long/monotonous drone? I'd only intended to make her
smile. What was this rottenness deep in my bones?

"Holy shit! Holy fucking shit! Are you even fucking
listening? I said: give me your gay fucking handkerchief!
This nasty-ass shit is blistering!"

Unclenching my lids, I spied a blood-
spattered napkin crumpled across her lap.

"Should've left that on for at least
a few hours...you know better than that!"

"Goddamn it! Already told you!
It's fucking starting to itch!"

Snatching away the bandana, she spat and scrubbed.
The cat throbbed angry with twitch.

"Stupid, ugly, fucking thing...looks like a retard did it..."
I'd had 'VICTORY' engraved within my eagle's talons.
It'd really seemed like the ticket.

The bus rolled. Pain increased. Elizabeth continued to
scour. Listlessly gazing through brown murk, I
watched forestry give way to grey towers.

Sunset Lanes came and went.

Penelope was still near the curb.

Her flattened intestines now formed a ten-foot smear.

A subject we left undisturbed.

"My life wields purpose like an axe."

CLAWS GROPED NEW MAIL WITH THRILL
as four snowed boots struck stairs.
  I'd spied Akasha in the tunnel.
  Loot had coaxed her to my lair.

Jack,

Your letters confused me but then again I think we always confused each other. They gave me the impression that you had ideas of rekindling a romance. This would not be possible as I am very happily involved with Victor E. Perhaps my note was vague. I wasn't sure what I could communicate other than neutrality and the absence of hatred.

I've had the opportunity to examine many things about myself since my decision to get sober last spring. It's been a process of accepting and forgiving those who've been unfair to me and admitting honestly to myself and others where I have been wrong and unfair. It's now apparent to me how patently UNWELL I was during the time we shared.

Looking back, I can see only a two year fever dream. I am sorry for any pain I caused. And I forgive you.

El.

Avery said: *"Damn, bro. What a fuckin' crummy letter."*

Kilroy bled: *"Guys like youse and me, Jack...*
we's gotta stick t'getha!"

What does that mean? "UNWELL"? Am I some
disease that infects? So drunk. Retarded black
bich is snoring now. Why did I bring her home?
What is wrong w/me? Still thirsty but nothing
left to drink. Ring wont stop screaming.
What the fuck is it yapping about now?
Just f'n shut up already!

"I let go of the fears and worries that drain my energy for no good reason."

TWO SPIDERS SAT INSIDE THE TANK...

Alas, no fault of molting.
Again I'd left its lid ajar.
The results surpassed revolting.
(Charlotte had returned, albeit moons too tardy.)
Slaughter had been deemed Condign
amidst her welcome-party.

REMAINS WERE FLUNG TO THE JOHN...

Tears spiked an eddy's spin.
Quicksilver stung yet more Dismay.
(A dust Van Dyke within.)
Water sloshed at sullied jowls revealed
dark glues of blood. Had ulcers
reared their ugly heads?
From the bedroom came a thud.

THE DEAD HERMIT STILL
REAPED NEGLECT...
A state of Dignity Forgot.
The snake draped the Rican's neck.
A fulvous/scaled cravat.
I set a carton by the reg.
Turned to face the dust.
Freshly hatched from Wither's egg,
it surveyed actions just.

"Papi, whatchu want I do with this?"
(Holden wisped, *"Kevorkian."*)

I laughed at Life's preposterousness...

"FEED HER TO THE SCORPIONS!"

an imbecile pales to matte green.

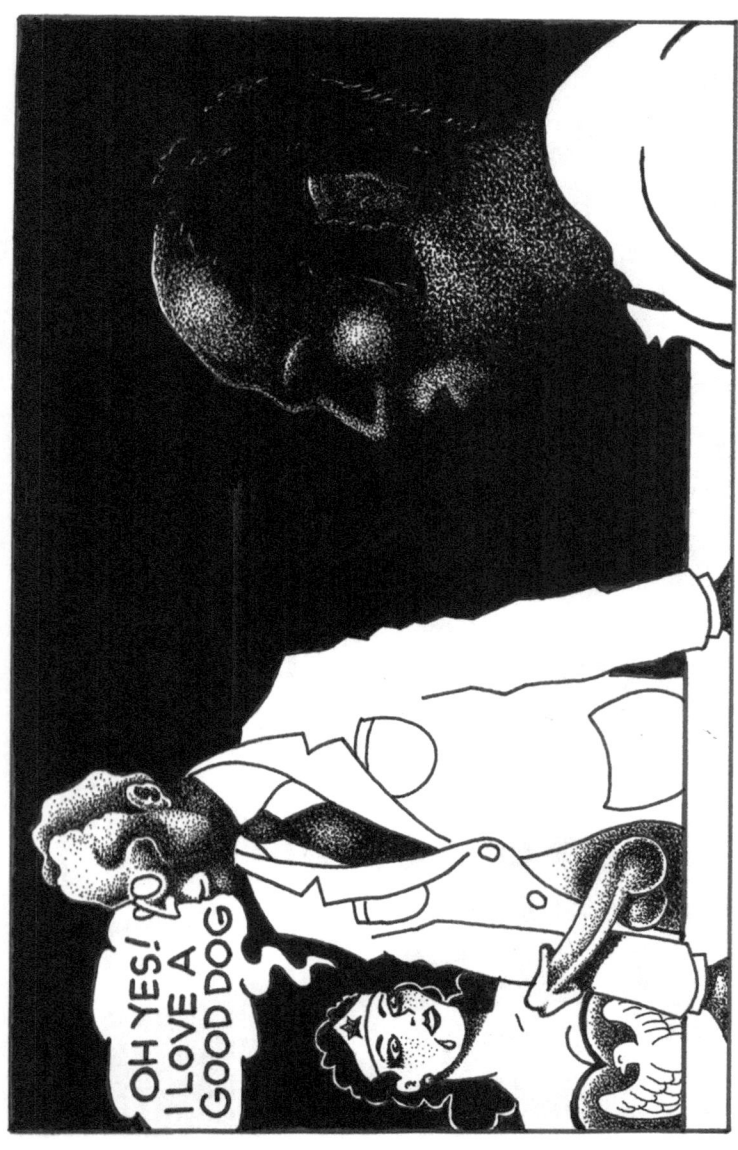

EXT. EAST IITH TENEMENT - MORNING

Expository-shot:

Panning sickly trees, scanning bricks graffitied,
'OBAMA FUX A LLAMA' drips beneath a Nefertiti.

CUT TO:

INT. TINY APARTMENT - CONTINUOUS

Medium-shot:

A bald and bedded imbecile poncers egregious navel.
An old dog curled beside him trills wafts of
regions fatal. This is *JACK* and *PETRA.*

Close-up:

As laggard prose is quoted from spent and softened
binds, a haggard nose probes toes of
brogues loping Limbo's mines.

JACK
(offscreen)
Everywhere there were horses down and men
scrambling and he saw a man who sat charging his
rifle while blood ran from his ears and he saw men
with their revolvers disassembled trying to fit the
spare loaded cylinders they carried and he saw men

kneeling who tilted and clasped their shadows on the ground and he saw men lanced and caught up by the hair and scalped standing and he saw the horses of war trample down the fallen and a little whitefaced pony with one clouded eye leaned out of the murk and snapped at him like a dog and was gone.

Medium-shot:

Canine farts nostril-drub. Jack
drops the book and smirks.

JACK
Hungry girl? Want some grub?

Close-up:

An arthritic grey tail quirts.

Long-shot:

The pair's little hovel is a musty debris maze.
Antiques and vintage clothes comprise
piles dust-encased.

Medium-shot:

Lifting up a Kong, blowing its
smut free, Jack hurls the orb.

Close-up:

Snores plead apathy.

CUT TO:

INT. TINY APARTMENT - CONTINUOUS

Medium-shot:

The imbecile weaves kitchenbound.

Close-up:

Tinkling kibble pours.

Medium-shot:

Compulsion wills thudding sounds
that ape a highdive horse.

WIPE TO:

INT. TINY APARTMENT - MOMENTS LATER

Medium-shot:

Above noisy chews, Jack scans a fridge-door magnet.

Close-up:

GRAMERCY PARK ANIMAL HOSPITAL

Medium-shot:

A wet nose nudges further food.

Close-up:

An imbecile pours sadness.

WIPE TO:

INT. TINY APARTMENT -
THIRTY MINUTES ON

Long-shot:

Dressing for a workday, Jack's threadbare rags
are donned. Stressing 30s dismay, togs
scream phantasmic spawn.

Medium-shot:

Paused by an opened door, the imbecile just stares.

Close-up:

Disgorging gasses more, Petra pours rank air.

WIPE TO:

EXT. EAST VILLAGE STREETS -
THREE MINUTES LATER

Expository-shot:

Summer throngs the sidewalks. Black nannies stroll pink tots. Swan-necked Eurettes stoke gawks.
Hindu jocks ape WASPs.

Close-up:

Beams annoint a barren crown,
prompting cap-replace.

Medium-shot:

A *CODGER* points to vomit found
as the imbecile scopes cake.

CODGER

Сер, будь ласка, вивчіть цю калюжу, бо вона містить плоди сильних людей! Тепер візьміть це натхнення та бігайте швидко, щоб звільнити вашу гомосексуальну душу!

WIPE TO:

INT. SECOND AVENUE PATISSERIE - CONTINUOUS

Medium-shot:

Jack consults a *LESBIAN* wearing facial piercings.

LESBIAN
Donuts? No. Petit gâteau and
other Frenchy queer things.

Close-up:

High-piled pink triangles form cookie pyramids. Vicious
cakes freshly baked swarm sneering looks of Sid. A
marzipan Charles Manson harbors stacks of seething
flies. Delights of Bosch in stiff ganache
bask in heathen pride.

Medium-shot:

JACK
One small coffee please.

LESBIAN
Okay, that's eight bucks.

Close-up:

A *BARISTA* praises steez as java taxis flux.

BARISTA
Yo! Bitchen get-up dude! Coppin' Steinbeck vibes!

Medium-shot:

Loath to hitch an attitude, the imbecile grins wide.

WIPE TO:

EXT. HOOVERVILLE - MINUTES LATER

Expository-shot:

A ramshackle storefront on 3rd and East 13th.

Medium-shot:

Whilst Jack mans a key-hunt, coffee stands beneath.

Close-up:

A passing poodle's pale wang
defames a beverage downed.

Medium-shot:

Yale lock de-hanged, Jack laps a hemorrhage brown.

CUT TO:

INT. HOOVERVILLE - CONTINUOUS

Long-shot:

A vintage store sags beneath Volstead-era crap.

Medium-shot:

Spitting bugs from ragged teeth, Jack adjusts a moldy
cap. Laptop wooed awake, he sniffs a cup and shrugs.

Close-up:

'Dog alzheimers' Google-begged
coaxes cringe midchug.

JACK
(grimly)
Canine cognitive dysfunction is a disease prevalent
in dogs that exhibit symptoms of dementia. CCD
creates pathological changes in the brain that slow
the mental functioning of dogs resulting in loss of
memory, motor-function, and learned behaviors from
training early in life...

A sudden roaring sounds. The door shakes then
clanks. Ignoring torrid pounds, Jack's
gaze stays on the dank.

JACK
(cont'd)
In the dog's brain, the protein beta-amyloid accumu-
lates, creating protein deposits called plaques. As the
dog ages, nerve-cells die, and cerebrospinal fluid fills
the empty space left by the dead nerve cells...

Long-shot:

The chimes still persist. Jack reluctantly relents. Alas,

mimed knobtwists bankroll no prevents.

Medium-shot:

Upon a curt assist, a gape reveals young blonde.

Close-up:

A *'Slayer'* shirt is tit-blitzed. Orbs are shaped beyond.

Medium-shot:

Lobbing a butt rear, *DARLA*
journeys through the door.

Close-up:

Before Jack's heel can smear, a bird interns the cord.

Medium-shot:

Inside the stranger arcs and flits, rasping flylike lilts.

Close-up:

A waving gold-starred tunic
apes a flag of Reich kike-wilt.

Medium-shot:

DARLA

Whoa! This shirt is sweet! How much fuckin' is it?

JACK
(gulping awkwardly)
I'll doublecheck to see. Pretty rare exhibit.

Guffawing as she treads, the stranger
further ransacks threads.

DARLA
Good Goddess...this shit's justa buncha
filthy bloody shreds!

A spiel explains off-kilter trends of fey vintage-buyers.

Close-up:

Gay squeals send a silver cake
wending bosoms higher.

Medium-shot:

Pinching Jack's lips shut, the
stranger smirks then winks.

Long-shot:

Past thick window-smut, a flaming pigeon sinks.

WIPE TO:

INT. TINY APARTMENT - POST WORK

Long-shot:

Dusty blinds cowl moonbeams upon the imbecile's
return. Pursuant howling bathroom bays
hark eerie Hell-sojourns.

Medium-shot:

Betwixt toilet and a tiled slit, an old dog stands in piss.
Mulling reverse deficits, Jack damns mortal skids.

Close-up:

Muted chords of yesteryear flee back-pocket glows.
'Happy Days Are Here Again' proclaim iPhone extols:

> **DARLA**
> *grrr! nice 2 meetcha! drinks or r u square?*

As thumbs swirl in pre-tap reachers
a second text declares:

> **DARLA**
> *and we dont care yer 39! we adore us some old men!*

Medium-shot:

Grinning saccharine, Jack bores a bosom friend.

JACK
(giddy)
Gramps here got hisself a date.
How about them apples?

Close-up:

Glancing back, fully gaped, cataracts mounting grapple.

WIPE TO:

EXT. LOWER SIXTH AVENUE - NIGHT

Expository-shot:

Amidst a sophisticate sea, Jack and Darla flee
cinema-doors — he yegg-bedecked sartorially
whilst she wears minimal whore.

Long-shot:

A marquee backlit determines:

**YOU'LL LAUGH...YOU'LL CRY...
'THE CHAMP!'**

Close-up:

Betwixt letters and clumps of vermin,
horseflies vast encamp.

Medium-shot:

DARLA
Good Goddess, what a bastin' a spooge!
So fuckin' unrealistic!

Close-up:

Stung by a self-loathing/bad-taste deluge,
the imbecile beams cataclysmic.

Medium-shot:

As Jack continues to fret, a
book is pulled from his hand.

DARLA
(pouting)
Hmph! Haven't viewed this one yet!
You one a them ghosts from the Strand?

JACK
I just carry books in public, y'know? Good for
dodging eye-contact with strangers. Never know
who'll go psycho — helps refract those dangers. But
sometimes...sometimes I do like to read to my dog.

DARLA
(excited)
Oh! What kinda dog d'ya have? That's our fuckin'
spirit-animal! Maybe someday you'll read to us too?

Ghost-story with time-travelin' cannibals!

JACK
Aw gee, she's just a fat old girl...

DARLA
Betcha she loves when ya recite!

JACK
Dunno. Head's all swirled.
Won't fetch...play. Ain't right.

DARLA
Well, *this* dog would love it! So what's this one about?
Blood — wha? — *Menstruation?*

JACK
Been kinda tough figuring that out, but I think mainly
psychic castration. There's this kid...he's molested
maybe...anyhow, he wanders. Then he meets some
cowboys and injuns. Then shit goes all kinds of bon-
kers. But there's also some rolling Beelzebub gears. I
mean, at least I think. Been trying to quell the scrub
for fifteen years, but it's dense and less than succinct.

DARLA
Dude, fifteen fuckin' years? That's, like, forever ago!
We were still only nine! Why not read something
your IQ *can* steer? Twilight or Goosebumps by Stine?

JACK

Gee whiz, perhaps you're right, but folks say it's
important. And the thought of being none-too-bright
stokes internal torment.

DARLA
(angered)
Well, fuck those sheeple and Oprah's book club and
fuck Conan McCartney's ass too! Dan Brown types
circles 'round all those schlubs and their hi-hat gobbly
goo! And that stupid wool cap — why wear it at all?
On account a maybe bad hair? There's no big shame
in bein' mad bald! Think ol' Ben Franklin cared?

JACK
(struggling)
Um...it's more just about...like...wormholy links
to the past. Vintage threads...enabling syncs...
to eras of honor and class...

DARLA
But why on Terra would you want any connection to
those jive-ass, unseemly days? They lynched blacks
back then! Made women wash dishes!
Bribed kids with ice cream and cake!

JACK
Valid points. Fair enough. Reckon I don't really know.

DARLA
(beaming)
Thinkin' you just might be a gem in the rough, so

we're gonna guide ya to higher plateaus! Gonna spurt
ya now with some spirit-jizz — we come from a lost
breed of elves! Our kinfolk built the pyramids!
We're a mystical Starseed cartel!

JACK
(perplexed)
Um, then you were kidding about Upstate before?

F A D E I N :

See the towhead. Pale, thin, unwashed.
Sheathed in cord jodhpurs and fraught
chambray, his skull harks illiterate thought.
History's lode taints that gypsum visage.
This is America's boy.
Beneath hoared skies, schoolyard confines
lurk rawboned and threadbare and dark.
Skulking perched sits a pickaninny, a lardy
swine, and a freckly razorbanged tart.
Derbied ragamuffins and guttersnipes.
Urchins and gamins and lice.
A playground's ashsmeared agonies
Homunculi gone plumb awry.
Spiderlike digits stir fawn eddies as the
pickaninny scratches parched earth, quoting
wry minstrels of names since lost
as frothgobs stipple his dirt.
CRABTREE
Crouched beside the bedraggled swath, you
stretch and you fart and you sniff. As your

tongue caresses a gas-addled crotch,
the fatso sneers then spits.
   Somethin daft bout dames with handles like
that. I'm tellin ya, it just dont wash.
   And how Chub, the towhead sighs. Can't
believe McGuilicutty's gone. Grownups
is stone fulla bosh.
   Braying like an ethered hopfiend,
the tart catcalls fate's plan.
   Say all, I'm Miss Crabtree, teacher to be,
exalted moll of Satan. Heard she's scrawny
too. Wart on her schnoz like this.
   Atop the vertex of a wan flue, thumbs
paw a gumdropped prosthesis.
   Nuts, cries the fleeing towhead.
Smell ya bozo creeps later.
   Trailing his dread, you bypass palms, hobos
asleep, and vendors of southern equators.
Trotting markedly brisk, your squint studies
his frame. He's not big but wields scarred
fists, trophies of bloody streetgames.
   Curtly pausing at Sunset, he surveys a
pharmacy's hoard. Lifting a hand, he grunts
Petey sit, then flits through
a freeswinging door.
   Sunlight cleaves carbon skies. The
pavement beneath grows hot. Like niglets
busk, you shift and you stomp. Your
anus is singed by a squat.
   A topless coupé slows then honks.
   A druggist breaches a door.

A goiter shades a bowtie's border.
His stoop scoops emerald stores.
One. Three. Five. Good. So, methinks you're
that new marm from Poughkeepsie?
Platinum curls dotting a turbanish hood
tinge porcelain charm white gypsy.
Yes and tomorrow's my first day of class
so I want to begin with a party.
Sniffs detect a storm's great mass.
Rosewater. Sin. Bacardi.
Well, dontcha worry none. Boys'll be there
ten on the dot. Ya can safely bet both your
sweet li'l buns on a real bully
iced custard jackpot.
Thank you. Gracious, been ever so anxious.
Had nightmares the students
despised me from go.
Druggist orbs salaciously blanket.
Goiter-throbs echo croups of sly crows.
The coupé drifts, the druggist totters, the
towhead returns then winks. At the corner,
cadged crullers duly emerge from a waist-
banded netherworld's brink. Balled shreds,
smegmaic and moist, are lobbed
in slow looping arcs.
Upon burnt pads you steadily tread.
You howl. You beg.
You bark.

F A D E   O U T :

INT. TINY APARTMENT - MORNING

Long-shot:

The old dog flops across the bed,
quivering mid-dreamwalk and -bark.

Medium-shot:

The imbecile meanwhile hawks bloodshed —
spitting fleet streams of fraught art.

Close-up:

Within the bathroom's porcelain basin,
eyes spy gelatin clots.

JACK
(voiceover)
**Dogs suffering canine cognitive dysfunction
may exhibit symptoms associated with
senile behavior and dementia...**

Ceasing a spigot's rust-branded stasis,
black globs writhe to pink blots.

Long-shot:

Once again, *'Happy Days'* sounds.

Medium-shot:

Jack rushes to loofa poured gore.

Close-up:

The optimism bays 'neath languid dog-pounds,
nigh *'Bring the Jubilee'* by Ward Moore.

Medium-shot:

Shifting Petra via bent tail soon proves a costly mistake.
An iPhone's lift portends sulphurous gales
fuming a spotty sick face.

Close-up:

DARLA
*bow wow wow. hope ur having a lofty mornin. havent
managed 2 cut any ears yet but we got die all over r
hands and could easily be mistakin 4 a mechanic witch
we guess we kinda r coz r art can fix peoples harts.
anyhow drinkys 2nite? arf arf and a woof.*

Medium-shot:

Groping the air free of befoul, Jack picks up the book.

Close-up:

Finding pages chomped by jowls, the
softback is flicked and forsook.

JACK
(voiceover)

The afflicted will often find themselves confused in familiar places or homes...spending long periods of time in one area...not responding to calls or commands...experiencing abnormal sleeping patterns...

Medium-shot:

Glancing down at a comatose girth,
the imbecile thumbscrews replies.

Close-up:

Though incoming texts evoke some
mirth, saline deluges sad eyes.

WIPE TO:

EXT. ROACH'S BAR - THAT EVENING

Expository-shot:

Glowering yuppies mob the facade of a faux old timey saloon, palm-shooing Diptera carnivores roving the Bowery grime of late June.

CUT TO:

INT. ROACH'S BAR - CONTINUOUS

Long-shot:

Trapped by packs of human mosquitos,
Jack and Darla shade drinks by the bar.

Medium-shot:

Despite a stack of emptied mojitos,
dismay brinks the edge of too far.

JACK
Aw gee, at least I *think* they're dreams. All seem so
goshdarned real. It's like legit, bona fide,
genuine life. I can smell. Hear. Feel.

Staring grimly back, Darla projects an onerous view.

JACK
So whaddya think of all that?
Time for check-ins at Bellevue?

DARLA
Well, Mercury *has* been in retrograde...but that we
don't really suppose! Could be the Goddess
just pullin' mean pranks! Here!

Close-up:

A crank-vial heels by a nose.

Long-shot:

Darla lures an attendant's gape via fluttered left hand.

Close-up:

The imbecile mulls a pendanted cake
smothered betwixt cleft glands.

F A D E   I N :

For an hour spewing clouds
have soaked you to the core.
On Wilcox you duck the garish stripes of an
arid tarp's allure. Tramps inside stand and
sway, there are no chairs in sight. A heady
stench triggers faints via shared vomitblight.
You squat alongst a rear
wall noting glances sly.
The parson's reedy mien is sallow.
Pince-nez narrows eyes.
Comrades, I haft seens das dawn of
a new age und I vill hasten its
unvermeidlich spread.
Thin digits spear a banner.

WE SEEK NOT CAKE BUT BREAD!

Comrades, I am here today to liberate. To
kaput iron chains. To take das vord vest und
beyond. To zerstören capital gains. Rise,
comrades, rise, for I vill foller ya alvays. Let
us drive der fatcats' Rolls unto
das tracks of trolleys.

Gripes issue above a hatchet lain skewed
inside a smock. The progenitor is ochre hued.
A plaited queue vies Knox.

Christ. Ever seed such a joint just ta come
dry off? Picked ourselves some doozy
bushwa. House a pink dummkopf.

Slits surveil the towhead's mug,
starved for youth approval.

Dunno mister. We just showed.

Well dis Marx is fulla strudel.

A pudgy figure enters. You
batten down a growl.

A wet Tyrolean's due capsize
tenders glabrous cowl.

The newcomer, standing not five feet, ignites
a long Havana. His bullish swath through
hobos rife smites all Wobbly yammer. The
surly knit bears no sound. Craned heads
scope hubbub. At the pulpit,
the pudge now frowns.

Burning orbs probe scrubs.

Ladies and germs, I feel it is my patriotic
duty as a proud nativeborn to inform you
that our man of the hour is, in fact, an
imposter. Not only does this knave hold no
papers of endorsement from any Bolsheviks
of repute, he is altogether devoid of the least
qualification to the office he purports to
serve as he has only committed to memory a
few passages from the Manifesto for the sole
purpose of lending his fraudulent sermons

some faint flavor of the very egalitarianism
he despises. In truth, my esteemed
colleagues, the gentleman standing before
thee, posing as some herald of Trotsky, is not
only utterly illiterate but wanted by lawmen
in Bavaria, Prague, Constantinople,
Lima, and Asbury Park —
   Mein Gott, cries the parson.
Lies. Lies. All lies.
   Despite recites of German
jargon, indicts further rise.
   — on a variety of charges, including the
sodomy of an underage thespian, Wee Ar-
thur Trimble, in the guise of Buster Brown,
who'd come to him in complete trust only to
be violated within the confines of a deserted
Universal hangar while this scoundrel was
employed by the same tycoons he now
addresses so adversarially. Oh, he's a clever
Hun alright. He was Meins back then. Then
he was Marut. Then Feige. Then Wienecke.
Then Torstvan. Then Ziegelbrenner. Now he
sows the rather dubious moniker of Croves.
   A moan fans the crowd.
   A whore sinks to her knees.
   Hal, what kind of man is ya?
You...ya said you loved me.
   Meins? Croves? Ach. Nein. I am Franklin
Traum Goldberg. Dis is him. Die menschliche
fliege. Hier steht er vor dir.
   Busta Brown? cries a noseless man with

hardened ears convex. I loved dem flicks.
Let's hang da toid. Wring his
queer commie neck.
  But wait, kind friends, that's not all. After
breaking the poor boy, this cretin plied his
trade on Tige. Yes, friends, that's what I said.
Tige. The lad's own sweet defenseless dog.
  The towhead glances towards you.
He chews his lower lip.
  A yegg withdraws a booted gat.
  Gon shoot dat sunnabitch.
  Trusty hatchet swung, the tong unseams
the tarp. Leaping into cloudbursts sprung,
you follow with a start. As the three of you
cobblegrind towards a vacant lot's lean-to,
shots blast the tent behind. It succumbs to
chaos brewed. From the plywood shelter, you
gawk a loosened frock. Guyropes slashing
mudded welters ape Medusa's locks.
  Ahem. The pudge is there already. A silver
flask withdraws. A linen leaf glides by
your nose, past your panting jaws.
  Soon a crowd has grown,
filthy rich with curse.
  Illicit hues of whisky flow
past lips DT-averse.
  The linen leaf skims a puddle,
dissolving to grey pulp.
  Serifed grief swiftly muddles
right beneath your mope.

TAUROG
PORTRAITURE, DIRECTION,
TRANSLATIONS
ACAPULCO / LOS FELIZ

The tong coughs and hacks blood and lights
a cigarette. He thwacks a second Murad
loose to quash the towhead's fret.

So how for didja come ta have
da goods on dat no-count?

Goods?

Yeah, when ya was in Asbury maybe?

Asbury?

Yeah. Where ya got all dat stuff on him.

I assume you mean the kraut?

Course. You was in Asbury
fore ya come out here right?

My good man, never been to Jersey
in all my livelong life. Sincerely
doubt he was either.

Well where was it ya run up on him den?

Honestly, never laid eyes on the chap before
this very day. Never even heard
of him. Never once I say.

As the pudge lifts his flask, the mob's brays
fall mum. They undulate on wary stems
like decaying mudwrought bums.

Finally one chuckles.

A second follows suit.

Laughter soon engulfs the lot.

The tong and towhead too.

F A D E   O U T :

EXT. BEDFORD AVENUE - DUSK

Expository-shot:

A brownstone-flanking sidewalk
is veiled in churlish savage.

Long-shot:

Loud moans and snide squawks
assail each girlish passage.

CUT TO:

INT. DARLA'S FLAT - CONTINUOUS

Long-shot:

A two-bedroom pigsty is riotous with flies.
Airborne host-besieged, Jack writhes midpassersby.

Medium-shot:

Bitten and in pain, he lifts one from his nose.

Close-up:

Glassy wings flit in vain 'til a fist is fully closed.

Medium-shot:

JACK
Ever ponder window-screens?

DARLA
No...what fuckin' for?

JACK
Might keep out the bugs it seems.

DARLA
(vexed)
You some kinda speciesist? There's the fuckin' door!
The Goddess made all creatures equal, so why ya
gotta judge? Sheeple pride — Hell on Earth —
small wonder elves do drugs!

Long-shot:

Darla chugs raisin wine.

Medium-shot:

Jack lobs the slaughtered corpse.

Close-up:

A weary shelf's Traven spines
globs flies 'twixt water-warps.

Medium-shot:

JACK
So what's the haps tonight?

DARLA
Got that hostess gig to do!

JACK
But you said you were a hairstylist.

DARLA
Artist! You *tryin'* to act the fool? Where the fuck
ya think we work? Lemon Tree? Supercuts?

JACK
Hair-artist...don't mind me...hostess gig means what?

DARLA
We emcee at Soulphylis!

JACK
Er...wha? Name sounds rather queasy.

DARLA
Vintage vinyl dance-off at a gay-nightclub speakeasy!
Our BFF Buzz runs it — best deejay in all New York!

Scoping his meshed wrist, Jack's
mien displays screwed torque.

JACK
Well, maybe I'll come next time.
Better get home to the dog.

Long-shot:

Elven lips swill further wine.

Close-up:

Festered orbs foam fog.

WIPE TO:

EXT. GAY SPEAKEASY - HOURS LATER

Expository-shot:

By a warehouse cinderblocked, amidst hipsters sharing
jokes, a *SHORT GIRL* with pinkened locks
solicits tailored smokes.

Medium-shot:

JACK
Sorry, don't indulge.

SHORT GIRL
(unconvinced)
Then please explain the yellow teeth
and breath of stinky mold!

WIPE TO:

INT. GAY SPEAKEASY - CONTINUOUS

Long-shot:

A smoky room of worn pine
is tightly dancer-thronged.

Medium-shot:

Atop a platform's corner climb, a deejay spins black
songs. An elf stands beside him, bedecked
in torn prom-dress.

Close-up:

Squirming past flying limbs, shots
splashed face grave distress.

Medium-shot:

Beaming at Jack's ascent, Darla blurts out to her friend.

DARLA
Oh drinky-poos! What a gent!
Our thirst has met its end!

The elf gifts a cocktail to her BFF Buzz.

Close-up:

A smile's rift of pencil 'stache
stresses sores 'twixt fuzz.

Medium-shot:

Quaffing hooch, Darla blinks
then slaps a hip mid-chuckle.

DARLA
Shit — forgot to scooch *yourself* a drink, our trippy
honeysuckle! Need another anyhow,
but Don Julio not well...

JACK
(checking time)
Sorry babe, gotta go...though
this party's been real swell.

DARLA
(appalled)
But — why? We're here 'til four!

JACK
(sheepish)
Well, Petra's all alone. And, I mean, she's my dog...

Close-up:

Welling orbs sadly sow a libertine's gulag.

JACK

No call for crying, babe. See ya soon, I promise.

Medium-shot:

Buzz slyly strides away, dodging swooning dramas.

Close-up:

DARLA
(crestfallen)
But don't you get it, Jackie-poo?

JACK
Sorry...don't get what?

Medium-shot:

DARLA
That *we're* your dog now too...
not just some part-time slut!

F A D E   I N :

Morning heat planks cobbles.
Once again you jig.
  The towhead lifts a hanky mottled
to emit a phlegmy sprig.
  Now Wheezer, when I honk like that you
bumrush through the door.
  The pigeyed toddler's curt nod back
cues unbrushed rapport.

A polkadotted viscose bow sags like a noose.
Yeah yeah. Schnoz blows and me
run in and give that hag the goose.
Now tell me zactly what yer
gonna spoon that ol buzzsaw.
Ma need Jackie home soon
cause she gon shoot Granma.
Nah, that's too strong. Maybe just say stab.
Firestones slow prongs.
A pilot stops to gab.
As the turbaned model smirks from the
open-air coupé, the pigeyed toddler's surging
lurch trumps hares from hounds at bay.
Well well, little man. And
what is your name then?
The jostled towhead blushes
like a fine young thespian.
Who? Me? I'm just Jack.
So then, Justjack, on your way to class?
Only cause ma'll tan my crack
if this time I don't pass.
Hmph. Is that so? And does
your mum thrash you often?
Yes ma'am. Fluently. My
rump's half in the coffin.
Well hop in little man,
I'm headed your way too.
You squat upon the towhead's lap
as the coupé's essay renews.
Atop the floor beneath,
a box hops butts and corks.

> SHEIK
> ONE DOZEN OVIS-GUT
> JULIUS SCHMID, NEW YORK

Psst. Hey. Petey. Pete. Lookit over here.
The runningboard-perched toddler
sneaks waves of obscene jeer.

F   A   D   E   O   U   T   :

INT. DARLA'S FLAT - DAWN

Long-shot:

Atop a sheetless mattress unburdened by boxspring,
abstinence blurs to flesh via quaffs of drink.

Medium-shot:

The boards surrounding choke
with briny lumps of clothes.

Close-up:

Bounding hordes above invoke flying hump-echoes.

Medium-shot:

Jack hammers full-blast.

Close-up:

Darla nips a hawkish beak.

Long-shot:

Growls and howls and yammers rasp
whilst mawkish plunge proceeds.

WIPE TO:

INT. DARLA'S FLAT - MINUTES LATER

Long-shot:

Naked in the kitchen, standing stretched and tall,
Darla quakes with hatchet-friction
chopping vegetables.

DARLA
Notice something odd in there?

JACK
Um, yeah. Very tight.

Close-up:

A carrot-stump's errant dump blackens with fly-blight.

Medium-shot:

DARLA
No, silly! Mean, *course* it's tight, but on account a

extra parts! A big one and a little one...
like those dipper stars!

JACK
(confused)
Not sure I follow.

DARLA
Well, we got two twats! Two reproductive wombs!
Two uteri...all that stuff! It's didelphys presumed!

JACK
But why? Birth-defect? Maybe something elven?

DARLA
More like Earth's ill-effects causin' unclean meltin'!
Mama took us to the Mayo when we was just a
fuckin' pup! They said it's from some twin absorbed
— hence the double-schtup!

JACK
(dismayed)
A twin? You absorbed a twin?

DARLA
(amused)
But we still talk on-the-reg...
she's a best chum built right in!

JACK
Wha?

DARLA
(laughing)
Babe, chill! I know Gisela's in my head...but is it
wrong to chew her fat? She'd do the same in my
stead if it was me jammed up her snatch!

JACK
Gisela?

DARLA
That's what Mama called her first! So motherfuckin'
Eighties! But now she's Li'l Hitler...

JACK
Wha?

DARLA
(cont'd)
...'cause she fills my brain with rabies!

Close-up:

The carrot-stump disintegrates.

F A D E   I N   :

The coupé hums. Bungalows whiz.
His lips hook north then pleat.
As your gaze plumbs a lid's winking flit,
an obdurate horsefly smacks teeth.
Something veiled within your guts stirs a

slowrising growl.
  Soiled nails vising your scruff
curtail ill-tides of jowl.
  Lady, yer ma ever yank yer britches?
  Eh? Because I'd done what?
  Maybe on account you was teasin some
midget or cause she caught
ya scopin out smut?
  Not that I recall offhand. Not my mum at
least. Twasn't oft I found myself tanned.
  She waves to a bystanding priest.
  Jostles test a seat's stiff springs.
  Jeepers, nifty wheels ya got. How the
heck ya ever cop such a thing? Ma
put our ol A inta hock.
  Justjack, never you mind my car. Let's
discuss this deep dread of school. Don't you
want to be a smart man someday? An
imbecile's path can be cruel.
  But lady, I don't really see no point. Ma says
I'm just a disease. Says I drove ol pa right
inta the joint and that I'm only fit for greasin
young Wheeze. And now my troubles have
gained, our ol swell marm's been replaced.
New sub's got herself a rabid brain and a
hatchet takin up the whole face.
  And what makes this teacher so very
ghastly? Do you really find her that fearful?
  Aint glimmed her yet, but heard she's called
Crabtree. There's prisons plyin
labels more cheerful.

Frankly, I must disagree. This Crabtree
sounds dead peachy to me. I'd wager
some might even book her a pip.

You hafta say that cause yer both dames,
but I reckon she looks a lot more like this.

Tsk tsk. Both fangs and wings? And
what's this spike in her arm?

Oh, that's her hop-bangin thing. It's
some kinda chinaman's pharm.

But nude, Justjack? Come now, I'm
certain she must wear a slip.

Well maybe she do and maybe she don't.
Won't give a hang if she did. She could never
be as nice as Miss McGuilicutty, even if she
wore all Montgomery Ward. Gee was Mac
swell, and now she's just gone, and we're all
stuck with some dumb crummy bore.

Gosh, that's perfectly dreadful. And
how did this poor Miss Mac die?

Worse than that. Got herself hitched.

Jesus wept. Pardon me
if I can't help but cry.

Anyhow, me and the gang got things
fixed but good. This Crabtree
aint got her no prayer.

Is that so? Well by gum you should. This
skirt sounds downright unfair.

Chubby's got him a flock a red ants. Farina
bought some swell sneezin powder. Bone-
dust's bringin a big ol white rat.

And you?

This ol noodle's plenty enough. I'm the
BMOC and club founder. Way I figger, we just
loose us some hell. Then bingo, fishin galore.
   But won't such wretchedness leave
Miss Crabtree unwell? Will she
not be just a little bit sore?
   She's near eighty so she'll most likely croak.
How much can such an old ticker take?
   The marm frets greatly as the coupé slows.
   A palm is thrust forth for quick shakes.
   Well little man, got more driving to do,
but thanks for the enlightening chat.
   Sure wish our new teach was a sheba like
you. Wouldn't be no calls for no spats.
   As the coupé gasses, you bark to orb-urge.
The towhead peers then roars heck. From
a runningboard perch, the toddler's havoc
blears to an amorphous speck.

F   A   D   E   O   U   T   :

EXT. EAST RIVER PIER - AFTERNOONS LATER

Expository-shot:

Jack and Darla merge with rovers
boarding a ferry beach-bound.

Medium-shot:

Twin totes horde imbecile shoulders.

Close-up:

An elven load is carried twine-wound.

WIPE TO:

EXT. ASBURY FERRY - TEN MINUTES ON

Expository-shot:

Under a purplish sky the boat skims swift.

Medium-shot:

A diving gull steeples an eel.

Close-up:

The skirmish fries to a burnt crisp
as sharkteeth wheedle bird-squeals.

CUT TO:

INT. ASBURY FERRY - CONTINUOUS

Long-shot:

Savoring the boat's upper-deck view,
Darla showcases three vessels.

Close-up:

Each bottle reflects a different blue hue.

Medium-shot:

The imbecile erases soft pretzels.

DARLA
Strictly top-shelf for our mini-vacay!
Jap lady called it *'Nigori'*!

JACK
(mouth full)
Well, what's in it or didn't she say?
Looks kinda hydrochloric.

DARLA
(contemplative)
Didn't ask...too douchey, we think...but she
did mention it being Jarmusch's fave drink!

Close-up:

An iPhone withdraws.

Long-shot:

Thunder grumbles above

Medium-shot:

Sighed smoke scrimshaws thumped victory shoves.

DARLA
(fretting skywards)
Yup! Nailed it! The Goddess is pissed!
Doesn't want us lovin' ya too much!

JACK
(closing the screen)
Darn it all...no service on this.

DARLA
Who ya tryin' to reach out and touch?

JACK
No one really. Just my friend Marlowe.

DARLA
Huh? Who the hell's he?

JACK
She.

DARLA
(flummoxed)
C'mon, dude — don't be an asshole!
Supposed to be on vacay with me!

JACK
Relax. Just my neighbor upstairs. Forgot to
jot Petra's food-allot. That's all...really...I swear.

Close-up:

Uncorking a bottle, swilling sans
pause, Darla raises a sneer.

DARLA
(jealous)
Bet she's real hot though! All frilly and tall!
Bet she's never-ever paid for one beer!

Medium-shot:

JACK
(deflating)
Maybe once, a long time back, but now she's like a
hundred and seven. Real good with the dog though...
fulla wisecracks...kibble mountains
and biscuits in Heaven...

Long-shot:

Clouds commence bursting.

Close-up:

Stark orbs roll.

Long-shot:

A gale gifts Jack's cap to the sea.

Close-up:

Soundlessly surging shark jaws unfold.

Medium-shot:

An imbecile pales to matte green.

WIPE TO:

EXT. DINGY MOTEL - LATER

Expository-shot:

The _Lazy Daze_, haggard and old,
battles the lure of collapse.

CUT TO:

INT. DINGY MOTEL LOBBY - CONTINUOUS

Close-up:

As the pair checks-in, a _DESK CLERK_'s
grin belies dentures rattling poleaxed.

Medium-shot:

DESK CLERK
Youse two, like, musicians or somethin'?
Must be, youse totally look like rockas!

A smile's blast of empathy-flash
dashes misconstrues awkward.

DARLA
No way, Jose! We build pyramids and save lost souls!
This one reads sad books to old dogs!

Spearing brass keys from a dross grid's hold,
a stunned head crooks and then nods.

DESK CLERK
Guess somebody's gotta do it...

F   A   D   E   I   N   :

Schoolyard chaos haloes the log.
You cringe at each slingshotted plunk.
The pickaninny drills a golliwog wearing
a derby bespotted with gunk.
Heed me, Stymie. When dat signal come,
bust on in. Tell her pap done broke two leg.
Owny just two? Am you powful sho?
Could make it sebben oh eight?
The fatso adjusts a buckled capotain and
sweat pours into his eyes. The hat has blown

from old to new Plymouth and toured a vast
continent's size. It has bested savage and
river and burl only to decay on a clown.

A ravaged wisp of gossamer curls
broadcasts a waylaying frown.

Okay sis. Now repeat what I learned ya.
Yer gonna tell that ol hen what?

Gon tell teach ma sawed off her fingers. Gon
tell teach ma sawed off her fingers. Then
I gon kick her daft butt.

Hey hey, wait a minnit. Only
sawed one finger, get me?

Wait a minnit, only sawed
one finger, get me?

Aw shaddup.

Aw shaddup.

You make me sick.

You make me sick.

Curling stout, burrowing snout,
you graze a retractable prick.

The towhead stands aloft,
sowing Caesarean fashion.

Munitions a go?

Ready fo sho. These red ants
is rarin with passion.

Say, looky dis. Mah sneezin juju.

Here's Benedict Arnold the rat.

Through a pane's lift, the marm gleans
coups. Alas nips spark only scats.

Ow. Pete. Quit it. Can'tcha see I'm busy? You
fellas oughtta seed this pip. Sent my heart

inna tizzy. Long lashes. Shiny lips. Almost as
keen as Miss Mac. What I wouldn't
dast to grind them hips.
   Jackie, you turnin sap?

F   A   D   E   O   U   T   :

EXT. SURF AND TURF JOINT - NIGHT

Expository-shot:

A panoramic construct sways atop stilts as breakers
splash boulders beneath. A manic seagull-flock praising
fresh kills apes yodelers of landfills deceased.

CUT TO:

INT. SURF AND TURF JOINT - CONTINUOUS

Long-shot:

Requesting two lobsters uncooked,
elven lips stump heat as food-poison.

Medium-shot:

Post-accrual of a *SERVER*'s dumb look,
bunk competes with glued buoyance.

SERVER

Hon, yer want that the chef should kill 'em first
or would yer prefer just tryin' it yerself?

DARLA
Hmph! Whichever's healthier works best!

Close-up:

A sinking prawn bids the imbecile farewell.

Medium-shot:

SERVER
Okeydoke. I'll just bring yer guys out some hammers.

Close-up:

Tiny shrimp-eyes, staring deathcloaked,
blur amidst Worcestershire clamor.

Long-shot:

Bemoaning an iPhone's tableset spot,
the elf intones betrayal-bred thoughts.

WIPE TO:

EXT. DINGY MOTEL -
THE WITCHING HOUR

Expository-shot:

The Lazy Daze, gloamed in twilight malaise,
stands like a morbid whale beached.

Long-shot:

A lamplit veil bandies silhouette flails,
hi-signing dovetailed technique.

CUT TO:

INT. DINGY MOTEL ROOM - CONTINUOUS

Long-shot:

Chugging rice wine, stripped and flushed,
Darla broaches flashbulb-souvenirs.

Close-up:

As titillations trigger a loathsome pink blush,
the imbecile divulges pseud fears.

JACK
(tense)
Really? You sure? But wouldn't that be...like...porn?
You said that exploitation is evil.

Medium-shot:

DARLA

(drink-garbled)
Dang Jackie — don't be so borin'! Since when is adult adoration illegal? For real, dude...fuckin' *look* at these boobs! Don't Gizzy and me rate your phone's loot? Maybe if we had tails near our pubes too you'd think us a li'l more cute!

JACK
(penitent)
I'm sorry, babe — super-duper sorry — just don't want you to feel objectified.

DARLA
(coquettish)
Aw! But Jackie, c'mon, sometimes a girl *needs* that kinda stuff! To be used...abused...insectified! Makes her feel special, y'know? Like nobody and nothin' else matters!

Steering flesh bodacious and svelte,
an elf scoops a mobile with swagger.

DARLA
(cont'd)
We'll pose any ol' way thatcha think's keen — just gotta insist on one thing!

JACK
Eh?

DARLA

Promise you'll make the best shot your new home-screen and kiss it whenever it rings!

Close-up:

As Darla faux-screams at a penile mic, projecting a Janis expression, one thumb-plunge glowbeams Petra's blank psych. A second infects retrogression.

F   A   D   E   I   N   :

Your claws hook chips alongst the pane's ledge as you assess the towhead's stressed pan.
 Morning. Morning now children.
Can you all guess who I am?
 Sadistic twitches of maybellined lash force a sliding desksink.
 Well boin mah britches if she aint keen as Miss Mac. Belly so, Jack? Mug sho look mighty unpink.
 Gosh no, wish that were all. That's the cooz from the ride and gee if I aint leaked the gas.
 Oh little man, come stand by my side. Acquaint me with the rest of the class.
 You sniff stillborn wafts of preened girls: TaffyTalcCurlsSpitwrought.
 Manilla flits slowly unfurl.
 Ambles cede burdened and fraught.
 How fortunate I am to see you again because you'd left this art in my car. Look

look children, pass it around. A
portrait of me by Renoir.
    As laughter spreads like flames rape drapes,
you spy hurt on his face and you wince.
    Now tell me Justjack, which one is Chubby?
    Sad whines ape a funeral dinge.
    The — the — the fat one.
    Oh Chubby dear, do stand up. And Farina,
will you please rise too? And also the lad
with the lovely pet rodent. Yes you in the
mismatching shoes. It's my comprehension
that you've each brought a prize to greet
your incumbent teacher. If you'd please be so
kind as to seat them deskwise, my chum
will proceed with due seizures.
    The towhead gathers the contraband.
    Hatred mines fastmounting shame.
    Doublecrossa.
    A fine pal you is.
    Jeepers. Weren't no signs toutin her name.
    Hefting a rat writhing with angst,
a hand lifts two feet above.
    Children, you can expect neither chiding
nor spanks as all I've planned for this
tenure is love. In fact I've gone so far
as to cull a firstday delight. Miles
of iced cream and cake.
    Benedict Arnold suddenly bites.
    Plummeting glass vials break.

F   A   D   E   O   U   T   :

EXT. DINGY MOTEL -
THE NEXT MORNING

Expository-shot:

Paused by a poolside gamp, a fat man ignites a cigar.

Close-up:

Rat-pursued ants trampling Weston
vamps are stamped to spite-caviar.

CUT TO:

INT. DINGY MOTEL ROOM -
CONTINUOUS

Long-shot:

Naked in bed, Jack rubs his head
whilst Darla scans a flipped phone.

Close-up:

His nose throbs stuffed and angrily red.

Medium-shot:

Elven mutters sputter clipped groans.

Long-shot:

JACK
(pained)
Man...another weird one last night.
Willikers. Gosh.
Gee whiz.

Close-up:

Enervated orbs espy glass-smite
blurred atop carpeted frizz.

Medium-shot:

JACK
(cont'd)
What'd you say was in that stuff?

DARLA
(perturbed)
Dammit! Desk-cunt doublebooked us again...gonna
be stuck choppin' heads 'til dusk! C'mon — need to
be at work by ten! Shake a leg and de-snot that tusk!

As Darla rushes, gathering togs,
the imbecile ejects more outpour.

JACK
(bewildered)
And all this old-timey dialogue...coulda
sworn that I'd been there before.

DARLA
What? Been where?

JACK
You know, the usual. Same again as last time...

Long-shot:

Leaning back contusional, fists
knuckle the base of a spine.

JACK
Um, think wagging too much causes backaches?

Close-up:

Darla barks Camel-fumes jagged.

DARLA
(livid)
Stop it! Enough! You're insultin' us, dude! Quit bein'
an insensitive faggot! How many times do we have
to explain that you just ain't a fuckin' dog!
You know that's *our* animal sage!

Waves frantic ape church-demagogue.

Medium-shot:

JACK
Calm down! I do know — that's why I asked! But...

what's *my* spirit-guide then?

DARLA
Dunno.
Maybe, like, an ant or a rat?
A crone like your mysterious friend?

JACK
Funny you should say that —

DARLA
(matter-of-fact)
Anyhow, 'fore we forget, clean out a closet tonight
'cause tomorrow we're gonna move in!

JACK
(taken aback)
What?

DARLA
Well, you fuckin' love us right?
Ain't that already been proven?

JACK
Sure, but —

DARLA
So our lease is up! Why waste dough on more
rent when we kick it most nights already?

JACK

But then —

DARLA
Don't worry, Jackie! We're gonna pitch in —
this is just how folks act like as steadies!

Long-shot:

Traversing the room, she scrapes a blue shard.

DARLA
Ow! Fuck! Jesus!

Medium-shot:

As hops spray spumes, Jack's face
retards. Bowing, tucking, he sneezes.

Close-up:

Within a palm's tomb, crossed by
stars, a mucilaged horsefly wheezes.

F   A   D   E   I   N   :

Mobilized by cacophonous honks, the gang's
coached minions intrude. Siphoning a thumb,
the marm grins at their captain whilst
red trickles dangle lipglued.
   Well well, little man. And who might you be?
Me Wheezer.

Now isn't that a handsome name?
Narrowing his brow, the towhead sweeps
eager. Alas, he pantomimes in vain.
Oh Justjack, to whom are you gesturing?
Join me once more little man. Now then, fess
up and spare your parents a lecturing. Are
these darlings here more pawns
of your plan?
Aw gee. Y'see, blowin my
nose was the signal and —
Shrill cackles spark your anus to pucker.
Why on Earth must she torture him so?
And then you'd go fishing after I'd
died because all teachers are
just brainless suckers?
Sister, ma want Jack home right
way. Say she gon plug granny's flab.
Gunfire? Oh my. That sounds rather grave.
Well, maybe she gon just stab —
Beneath rambles, loosed
ants rush a gaped door.
Glossed bluchers smear the first wave.
Panicked survivors flee certain gore as ever-
more boots amble brave. Ignorant gods
wearing aprons selfsame trolley
boxes and barrels frostchoked.
Oh hi boys. So glad you came. Serve the
sweets from the desk and don't smoke.
Yes'm. You bet.
Now then children, let's form a neat line.
Patience please, no shoving. I've ordered

more than enough so no need to whine. And
can one of you swat that flybuzzing?
  You trample the slain. You squat upon
haunches. Your forelegs lift to entreat.
  Scram now Pete. This aint no game.
Gwan. Scat. Beat feet.
  Justjack, never mind that dog. Something's
happened at home and you must be sure to
rush there. Your grandmother requires
dire assistance. We don't want
your mum in the chair.
  But please Miss Crabtree, weren't usin my
dome. What say we backtrack this clipper?
  Sorry little man, run along home. This is
no place for young Jack the Rippers.
  Yeah. No finks allowed, stupid dumbgoon.
Big backstabbin snitch.
  As the trembling towhead quits the glum
room, hysterics reach feverpitch.
  Gummed da woiks his own damnself.
  Gonna get whupped but good.
  We should all be offa dat Jackie for life.
  Hoid his ma hooks johns in Brentwood.
  You snarl at the gang and minions and gods.
You growl as fierce as you can. Benedict
Arnold tickles your maw.
  His skull splits like a pecan.

F   A   D   E   O   U   T   :

EXT. EAST 11TH TENEMENT -

LATER THAT DAY

Long-shot:

Disembarking a cab, lifting his bag,
the imbecile notes a loud wagon's stall.

Medium-shot:

As he unlocks the door, EMTs pour
— toting a shroud-fastened haul.

CUT TO:

INT. TINY APARTMENT - CONTINUOUS

Long-shot:

Checking the kitchen, Jack peers
bowls dry as slurps roil offscreen.

Medium-shot:

Neglect's dereliction has steered
nosedives into a toilet's canteen.

Close-up:

De-bowling the old dog's head,
the imbecile pats with a towel.

Medium-shot:

Mulling soul-fog with dread, smalltalk begats disavowal.

JACK
Mite thirsty, huh?
Can't blame ya then.
C'mon...let's make bacon and eggs.

Long-shot:

Despite turnings of herky-jerk stems,
craves endure patently vague.

Medium-shot:

The old dog is set atop the bed.
A muzzle lap-rests as Jack reads.

Close-up:

Orbs sob amidst dreary bloodshed
attested by puzzling screeds.

Medium-shot:

JACK
He kicked the man in the jaw. The man went down
and got up again. He said: I'm goin' to kill you...

Long-shot:

From the kitchen, streaking a counter,
a call incoming sheds tweedles.

JACK
(cont'd offscreen)
He swung with the bottle and the kid ducked and he
swung again and the kid stepped back. When the
kid hit him the man shattered the bottle
against the side of his head...

Close-up:

Flesh plump and glistening downwards
mauls with cunning spread-eagles.

JACK
(cont'd offscreen)
He went off the boards into the mud and the man
lunged after him with the jagged bottleneck
and tried to stick it in his eye...

F   A   D   E   I   N   :

Rasping breakneck for a mile or more, he
shirks redoubled barkvents. Passing a jumble
of bus-sheltered boards, he crumbles
atop a nigger-marked bench.
  She's right, Petey.
  That pip's dead right, I
aint really no good at all.
  His face wears a plague's wan mask.

Best go find ya a new hood or moll.
A leg stiff angles nigh-hydrant.
You spritz iron putrid with scuz.
Life is decried for the brutal tyrant
possessive of all he once was. His blurred
soul is dispirited. His heart's clay
wrenched to foul turds.
If only I were entombed inna pyramid then
maybe could I start gettin cured. Y'see, I'm
the real reason pa's gone. I oughtn't be alive
y'know? I'm just a crummy, no-good,
vampire spawn. Ma says she
shoulda gobbled pa's load.
You tongue a pale crown.
A sole probes your breast.
And yer just a sack fulla worms.
Though punches hail down,
you forgo protest.
Packs true survive health and infirm.

F A D E   O U T :

INT. TINY APARTMENT - MORNINGS LATER

Long-shot:

The hovel's deathchoke brims rancid smoke.

Medium-shot:

Elven gear crams each nook.

Close-up:

Mottled bedposts shim pantyhose.

Medium-shot:

Darla slams her own rear with Jack's book.

DARLA
(wroth)
Ouch! Dammit! Fuckin' fleas!

The imbecile squints downbed.

Close-up:

'Twixt feet, an old dog snores.

Medium-shot:

JACK
But every six weeks I apply tick-spread.
Guess it's not enough anymore.

DARLA
(flustered)
Dude, why just allot automatically that it's fuckin' her
and not I? Already forgot there's *two* coats to
de-flea? Keep sheep-dip equipped on standby!

Suddenly fraught, Jack claws his own
groin whilst the elf emits a fine sulk.

DARLA
(histrionic)
It's a plague to tame the fuckin'
Goddess has wrought!

JACK
(intensely dismayed)
Suppose Amazon ships Frontline in bulk?

F   A   D   E   I   N   :

You perch on a lunchwagon's stool.
Sliding quads grind spartan shellac.
Swear I could munch me a flagon a boots.
Even them highjobs Cossacks garb to attack.
  The towhead shouts beefsteaks and biscuits
and corn and coffee and cream and pie. Your
tongue grouts a cracked nasality's scorn
with a frothy viscosity's slime.
  A face equally gruesome and
fat balefully glares browbeat.
  And you've got the shekels
t'pay for all that?
  Nah.
  Then how ya be expectin t'eat?
  Don't spect, just want.
  Gwan punkola. Vamoose. Try
a hopscotch in traffic fiesta.

Dawning the quota of a ten-block pursuit,
you fry a callbox with spastic egesta.

Gee whiz. Wish we had us some cake
and ice cream. Miss McGuilicutty
woulda gived us our share.

Hey youse. Know what?

Airborne raspberries snaking suddenly
loose abutt unchivalrous blares.

You and that cur is dirtier than my Aunt
Mae's slophole and she's a milewide whore.

The interlocutor scurries within an es-
cape-stronghold highpiled by donuts galore.

Oh yeah?

Yeah.

Well betcha can't land one a them sinkers
right here round my left thumb.

Sucker, dangwell can.

When the lob sails poor the towhead
sniggers like a drinker sodden with rum. He
slacks then quacks as a freewheeling Mack
flattens his prize to cubed smears. Squatting
once more, he's thwacked smackaback
by a passing broom's bristly steer.

F A D E   O U T :

INT. TINY APARTMENT -
ANOTHER MORNING

Long-shot:

Kenneled chaos gobs markedly worse
via smears/bottles/cigarettes/smut.

Close-up:

Temples throbbing nigh-heartburst,
the imbecile clears a caudal cleft's glut.

Medium-shot:

JACK
(pensively probing a pastry half-gnawed)
Um, babe?

DARLA
(sleeptalking)
But Gisela...Butchie...not now...

JACK
Kinda important.

DARLA
(miffed)
Jesus Mice — we're up, okay?
No need to have fuckin' cows!

JACK
(wary)
Um, I know you've pegged novice dreams as...mere
cartoons for unevolved fools...but...d'ya think...
maybe...the Goddess might deem...

occasional absolvings of rules?

DARLA
(annoyed)
Dude, bein' an ancient elf don't mean diviner-of-all!
I mean who the hell ever felt we'd be seein' shines
host inaugural balls? Oh! Hey! That's foul play!
Leggo that Eggo you!

Ablating a doughy fold's grip,
elven bites smack then chew.

DARLA
('twixt chomps)
Baked 'em right after Soulphylis,
but your lightweight ass said adieu!

Close-up:

As wadded shreds stream force-fed,
the imbecile ingests clogs saporous.

Medium-shot:

Knotted to dreads within Morphean threads,
an old dog's knells vest vaporous.

F   A   D   E   I   N   :

Onwards you stray, weaving drove and din.
Trolleys clack as Hudson horns moo.

An extras' cafe teeming faux-injun
smacks of Russianborn jew.
  Burdensome posts prompt urinespun bolts,
for the towhead cedes no slack to dog-cues.
  Neither mort nor detour
will thwart your endure.
  Betwixt you spreads Pete-and-Jack glue.

F   A   D   E   O   U   T   :

INT. TINY APARTMENT - SEVERAL WEEKS LATER

Close-up:

Atop a dusty windowsill, mantid pincers rotate
a fly. Blighting corn borne of Limboville,
the mincer truncates all cries.

Medium-shot:

Spotting the heartless gore,
an imbecile collimates focus.

Long-shot:

Swatting a green carnivore,
grim yells betray cryptococcus.

DARLA
Ugh! We don't friggin' *like* those guys! Know they

cannibalize post-fuck? They're just evil spies employed
by the Goddess to cram us with lies and bad luck!

JACK
(worried)
But mantises are an endangered species.
You can't just hurt them like that.

Medium-shot:

DARLA
Says who? You? Strangers? Nietzsche? Gonna turn us
in like some rat? Go ahead! Elves pay no heed to
society's laws — we live by our *own* fuckin' rule!
Same shit applies to all varieties a dogs! Pete,
tell daddy here to quit actin' the fool!

Close-up:

A fixated glare exhorting fairshare
educes a resonant fart.

Medium-shot:

DARLA
There! See? Even Petra agrees —
and she's hated us right from the start!

Elven stomps end with shower-tap pries.
Shouts sally forth waterlogged.

DARLA
(offscreen)
Better get in here now and shtup Gizzy and I!

Close-up:

Sad pouts explore stolid fog.

Long-shot:

JACK
You...you don't really hate her...right?

Medium-shot:

As orbs amaurotic blaze rancid concerns,
the despotic mantid returns.

Close-up:

Quitting its sill to sift clotty thong-hills,
the psychotic gnaws feculent sperm.

F A D E   I N :

Sunset Boulevard. The drugstore again.
Paused orbs swish vinegared glass.
You enter, regarding chromed porcelain.
Checkerboardists hiss as you pass. Sailors
clutch pulps spicy with bawd. A dried fan
cries in its cage. Elders mull dicey like

seersuckered frogs spying flies
beneath wide boatershades.
   Say mister, aint got us spondulix but me
and my pooch here is famished. We can mop
or stock shelves real smooth'n'spick in
trade for a dayold ham sandwich.
   Rolled Arrow sleeves leak wrinkles and
spots and a cicatrix San Juan Hill forged. A
celluloid visor greens crinkles stretched
taut as teeth snick goodwill's deplore.
   No one loves a beggar son. Steal
what ya need and blow fast.
   Laughs ambient blur ghostmugs to plum.
   You detect faint embryo wafts.
   But mister, I don't wanna be a nogoodnik or
devil just like my pa was, see? Wanna earn
my keep square on the level. No jobs
I can do for some weenies?
   Gwan. Scat.
   But sir, please, we're so hungry it's nuts.
Can ya spare us some coffee or donuts?
   A gravid woman lifts grungy cold
cuts from a terrace of soggy pagodas.
   Just let me fix em some sandwiches Rod.
They'll leave then. Right? You'll go?
   A swift kick prods dog nods.
   Serrations slice a white loaf.

F   A   D   E   O   U   T   :

INT. TINY APARTMENT - NIGHT

Long-shot:

Arms akimbo, brows a'fret,
an elf ranks naked reflections.

Close-up:

Barned in limbo, a dog beset flanks a raising erection.

Medium-shot:

JACK
(simpering)
Don't you dare ask if I think you look fat!

DARLA
Silly, course not! If anything, we need
to pile on a few...shit's way too hot as is!

Vying a smile's rapid undo,
the imbecile rasps *'Gee whiz.'*

DARLA
(euphoric)
Listen, got an idea! Raked skin'll mildew this
pretty! Jackie dear! Break out some pins!
Get ready to tattoo somethin' shitty!

JACK
(hesitant)
Um, okay...but not quite sure what you mean...

DARLA
You're just gonna dampen some radiance
here to fend off life's lecherous fiends!

JACK
So, like a totem? Um...what didja have in mind?

DARLA
Thinkin' a swazzie — or is that too ho-hum?
Maybe the flag a Columbine?

JACK
(gaping)
But...a...a swastika?

DARLA
Yeah! One for us each! You do us and we'll do you!

JACK
But babe, c'mon. People'll speak.
It'll be societal seppuku.

DARLA
(pirouetting)
Bah! Sheeple mules! Why rue
what those narcissists think?

Close-up:

Sad roots through art-cabinet tools
impart sharp tweedles and clinks.

WIPE TO:

INT. TINY APARTMENT - THREE HOURS ON

Close-up:

A black Hakenkreuz oozes red from elf-ribs.

Medium-shot:

Darla sneers as she jabs at Jack's side.

Close-up:

Attacking needles foist hellish grips.

Medium-shot:

JACK
Christ — let me offa this ride!

Close-up:

Beneath the bed, the old dog sleeps
as the imbecile quivers and jerks.

JACK
(panting offscreen)
Like I said, don't dig so darn deep!
Just let the needles do work!

Medium-shot:

Stabbing Jack several times more,
Darla hucks tools willy-nilly.

Close-up:

Thwacked bookpiles hack literate
gore, drooling karmic fulfillings.

Long-shot:

DARLA
(incensed)
Goddess be damned! Fuck it all!
Why won't this ink stay in like I want?

Close-up:

A Camel's fresh stem, fished from
its stall, links with a waned confidant.

Medium-shot:

A spritzer arcs to mist. The imbecile soaps
a sore wound. Offscreen farts sow a foul kiss.

Close-up:

Elven lips blow smoke and resume.

Medium-shot:

DARLA
(cont'd)
Anyhow, better look! Shit's like way fuckin' done!

As Jack staggers, Darla's lips crook.

DARLA
(calming)
Doin' tats is actually fun!

Mirror breached, a slack jaw falls.

Close-up:

Ichorous fly-swarms intersect.

Medium-shot:

DARLA
(beaming pride)
Pretty neat, huh? I'm a natural!

Eyes ward a sanguivorous architect.

JACK
Yup, really great job you did.
Certainly got your own style.

Close-up:

> Whispering amid flickery lids,
> a mantid swabs Petra with guile.

F A D E   I N :

The sun will not yield. Flies stipple the heat.
Hell grows evermore near. Skittery pads
rip on concrete. Claws mine
fuzzed hollows of ears.
But still, the voice cannot be reached.
It laughs and it brays and it jeers.
Your clamped lids ease to behold pumps
suede. Glandular globs strain velvet. The
ecru trull leans and thumps at your blaze.
Sobs rain atop a blond helmet.
Recuerda, pequeño. Nunca dejes que una
mujer te robe el amor de tu perro. Todo
lo que traemos es miseria y muerte.
As the trull gambols, a squat shadow
flowers. Cuffs drape vamps
of pierced Westons.
Her brains are just scrambled. She's
death by the hour. Nevermind that
tramp's rummy lessons.
Lifting a box, the pudge peers down.
You choke upon Havana elixir.
Say what's the idea aimin that brown?
Son, you enjoy posing for pictures?

F A D E   O U T :

INT. TINY APARTMENT - WEEKS LATER

Medium-shot:

Dribbling swill, the imbecile lies lodged within
moonstruck loins. Flits fulfill futility's drill,
binding two pups conjoined.

JACK
(unsettled)
Um...really don't mean to frustrate...
but I just can't seem to withdraw.

DARLA
(amused)
'Cause elves in heat accrete their mates
'til they vow to uphold sacred laws!

JACK
But...Ow! Ow! Ow! Ow!

Further flurries in vain stoke elven joie de vivre.

JACK
Er! Ow! Mercy! Dang!

Titters evoke gnawing hyenas.

DARLA
(softening)
Jackie, swear to Gisela and I that you'll always protect

us from evil! That you'll forever dwell by our side,
be it through punishment, hex, or upheaval!

Close-up:

As fealty's pledged and the deal is
kiss-stoked, lips retreat with a start.

DARLA
(dewy)
And if we end up dead...before you should croak...
promise you'll eat up our heart! Swear it Jackie!
Swear that you'll gobble our heart —
even if it means goin' to jail!

Medium-shot:

JACK
(utterly confused)
Um...what?

Long-shot:

A suddenly pouncing forward arc
releases her viselike inhale.

DARLA
Aha! Gotcha! Told ya, see? Yeah, I fuckin' knew it!

Close-up:

A mantid spy flails spastically. Teeth
pluck its globe and then chew it.

Medium-shot:

JACK
(cringing)
But...um…

DARLA
(exultantly chomping)
Caught redhanded — now it's kaput!
It was plyin' that dog my secrets!

Close-up:

Dream-enchanted at the bed's
foot, dying jogs vie weakness.

F   A   D   E   I   N   :

Verboten from rides, you gallop beside.
Perked ears withdraw what they can.
No mopes son. Douse that cocked eye. Claws
don't like Connolly tans. Take a whiff of
those seats, just had 'em done. Smell
like Cleopatra's sweet twat.
Swerving horns bleat as you trail the
Phaeton. LARy tracks compel leaps fraught.
So we're off, young sir,
to a real special place.

Yeah? Real special how come?
Hosts fields upon fields of dreams incarnate.
Your pads slosh cobblestoned dung.
But gee, I aint got me no dreams.
Pshaw, no kidding kidders.
A distraught steed crops a monger's careen.
Pushing raw squid, you skitter.

F   A   D   E   O   U   T   :

EXT. SUSHI JOINT - A COOL OCTOBER NIGHT

Medium-shot:

Beneath a lantern's coruscating
pulse, diners munch piscean arrays.

CUT TO:

INT. SUSHI JOINT - CONTINUOUS

Close-up:

Darla's manual employ yields spew-laden
results — flying lunges of fish eaten risque.

Medium-shot:

DARLA
(ika-masticating)

So, after that, he sodomizes her...sad piece a
shitsuckin' scuz...prattlin' lullabies like some
mad Turk...her fat Uncle Norman it was!

<u>JACK</u>
(quailing)
Good lord, how many years back?
Hope the cops threw the book at this scum...

<u>DARLA</u>
(shrugging)
Last July fourth marks the attack! She was in Malibu
visitin' her mum! No cops! Dude says, 'You can bid
your old dog farewell if I even smell the faintest hint
you'll turn rat!' And we're the only one she'd
tell, on account we're all elves! Ain't
readjourned it since that!

<u>JACK</u>
(appalled)
Jeepers...last summer? Thought you'd meant as a
youth. Not really sure which is worse.

<u>DARLA</u>
This is, dude — hence the mad bummer! Little ones
are a real bitch to subvert! They just wanna see glee
and joy, y'know? Chutzpah dulls rapscallion infections!

<u>Close-up:</u>

Swaying sashimi atop a soy bowl, the imbecile mulls

medallion-reflections. Salmon torn blights
the mirage. Moonbeams ripple on quakes.

Medium-shot:

Gamin-orbs are further barraged —

Close-up:

— as breasts cripple ice cream and cake.

Medium-shot:

DARLA
(mouthfilled)
Hey you, peel off that gloom — li'l Beth's gonna rise
like a phoenix! No big whoop, time steals all wounds!
Incest didn't ruin me-n-Gizzy on penis!

JACK
But — what?

DARLA
(face screwed)
Um...our brother made us fuck all a his friends when
we were just like eleven or twelve! Shoulda known
better than to trust a good end from
schmucks VHSin' *'Emmanuelle'*!

Close-up:

Masculine knuckles snap chopsticks in half.
A drowning horsefly treads soy.

Medium-shot:

DARLA
(suddenly chipper)
Hey, how 'bout some snuggles at the Tenth Street
baths? This doggy needs time with her boy!

JACK
(dour)
And your brother partook in this squall,
or did he just watch from the back?

DARLA
(stroking her chin)
The pics might tell...but it's hard to recall...

JACK
(thunderstruck)
Huh?

DARLA
It was the Poughkeepsie Kodak Wolfpack...

Long-shot:

The imbecile stares blankly
ahead — sad, flushed, unblinking.

Close-up:

A kanji'ed bill instills financial bloodshed.

Medium-shot:

DARLA
(gently)
Don't mean to rush, but whatcha thinkin'?

JACK
(sighing)
Thinking...that I doubt...that I
really even know what to say.

DARLA
(giggling)
Silly, meant the bathhouse —
still wanna come out and play?

JACK
Just go on. Have a good schvitz.
Gonna head back home and read.

Close-up:

Brewing a yawn haggard and blitzed,
a sad gloom refracts daggers beamed.

F A D E   I N :

Lost. Gone. Hopelessly severed.
How far back you don't know.
Somehow the pudge has shaken your tether.
You search. You run. You roam.
Boardwalking leers cuss wheelriding
nymphs. Pachucos pluck tiny guitars.
Bearded fakirs scaling twine splints
shadowcloud italicized tarps.

GRETCHEN'S SUPERLATIVE VITA-ELIXIR
IT'S CHRIST ICED COLD IN BOTTLES!

SEE THE WORLD'S DEADLIEST DANCE-A-THON MIXER ONLY AT THE THRILLODEON HOSTEL!

HONEST DUTCH WEINSTEIN'S HOT VENICE BATHS — HOME OF THE TWO-NICKEL SCHVITZ!

Stomping rockcrabs and toes, you scour
frothed tides tempting wan fools with limbo.
Jesus. Ow. Don't touch it now Clyde.
It's rabid.
Ay pinche gringo.
Two roadside niglettes twirl thin cords. A
third blurs sepia vim. Dire chants bewail
Chaplinian sores and tubercular
Valentinian limbs.
Obelisk pines clutter heaven's slate breast.

Fronds breezeswing palms high.
Pausing to slurp a gutter's strait mess,
you flee a calm winking ringed eye.

F   A   D   E   O   U   T   :

INT. TINY APARTMENT -
ONE HOUR LATER

Long-shot:

Candlelight-flits lume vandalized wits of an old dog slumbering numb. An imbecile pouting amidst chaos surroundings spumes from a tome betwixt thumbs.

JACK
Hell aint half full. Hear me. Ye carry war of a madman's making onto a foreign land.
Ye'll wake more than the dogs...

Medium-shot:

Petra snores upon shorn drawers,
obtuse to words of infect.

JACK
(cont'd offscreen)
He lay on his side in the dust of the courtyard.
The men were gone, the whores were gone...

Close-up:

Canine jaws robotically gnaw
a puce box printed 'Durex'.

Medium-shot:

JACK
(cont'd)
The boy lay with his skull broken in a pool of blood...

Close-up:

Atop floored boards impeded by dust and
Camel-butts blooming Bordeaux, a horseflied
comprise of stampeding smut obscures
'Barsoom' by Burroughs.

JACK
(cont'd offscreen)
None knew by whom...

F A D E   I N :

Jimson weed. Myrrh. Horizons of wire éclat.
Pastels cede to shacks of pressed fir skewed
atop sodless sandplots. One scraggled patch
boasts dueling squires and a maiden of
trunkforaged fleece. Two jackals slash
at molts of umpires. Strung platters
hum horrid Chinese.
And even upon this foreign plain's grid
squats a gang wellnigh to yourn. It yammers

and brays partisan bids like lupines
of prairies meatshorn.
   If youse fellas want a piece of dis squaw
den make wit dat red shit but quick.
   Watch it Woim or I'm gon tell pa.
   Figgas, ya yella ratprick.
   Stick da yid Hoibie, den say shalom.
   Dis aintcher weddin night ladies.
   A distant derby lids a tall dome.
   Your breakaway is abetted by Hades.

F   A   D   E   O   U   T   :

INT. TINY APARTMENT -
ANOTHER DARK NIGHT

Long-shot:

Rolling free of the imbecile, elven stalks sob-quiver.

Close-up:

Doling pleas of timbres shrill,
the old dog logs dream-shivers.

Medium-shot:

JACK
(groggy)
C'mon...I'm awake. Please don't cry,
just tell me what's wrong.

A blonde mane shakes. A squeeze
is plied. Whelps ensue prolonged.

DARLA
(reifying sniffly)
Had us a dream that you got shivved...
then werewolves chomped ya up raw!

JACK
(deriding stiffly)
But look, babe — don't worry a bit.
No air-holes/stomps/rough-gnaws.

DARLA
(rattled)
But Jackie — how do we know that you're even you?
Maybe *this* is the dream! Maybe the Goddess
is weavin' hoodoo and these flies
are disguised seraphim!

Close-up:

Imbecile-lips helplessly part. Orbs broadcast despair.

Medium-shot:

REM-propelled lids zealously dart
as dog-gas engorges thin air.

Close-up:

JACK
(sighing)
Seems I'd taste better fried or smoked
than just facing lycanthropes raw...

Medium-shot:

DARLA
(decrying)
Gizzy said in my dream you'd ply that lame joke!

Wings ape fly-coapt buzzsaws.

F   A   D   E   I   N   :

Easing stride in Culver City, you penetrate
black iron spears. Hedges sideline driveways
gritty. Two degenerates perspire and jeer.
   Slim kid gloves slowly comport
a wily and measured control.
   Fido old sport, do be a love.
Kindly endeavor to roll.
   The twig's wan flair chirps Cumbrian.
Abdominousity hurts his chum's clothes.
Their swan-and-pig air lurks Jungian.
   Beyond spurts a manor dubbed Croves.

F   A   D   E   O   U   T   :

INT. TINY APARTMENT - DUSK

Medium-shot:

Perching nude on the john, Darla espies white plastic.

DARLA
(quietly tense)
Holy fuck...

Close-up:

Swerving eschewed, averring a spawn,
the widget vies elven strikes drastic.

Medium-shot:

Entering the W.C. — Jack studies
the carnage and freezes.

JACK
(releasing breath held)
Neither's trouble by me, we can
either discard or just keep it.

Close-up:

DARLA
(mentally adrift)
We...I...we're gonna...gonna need us some cash...

JACK
(offscreen)

Um, maybe think on it a day or two first?

DARLA
(crown ashake)
Can't see any reason...

Medium-shot:

JACK
(mired in stoic deflation)
I might feel the same if our shoes were reversed.

DARLA
(fatalistic)
Giz says you spew demon semen...

Long-shot:

As the imbecile gapes back in horror, and Darla heeds surveillance nonverbal, the old dog snakes beyond a cracked door — deferring to aimless pawn circles.

F   A   D   E   I   N   :

Alongst your run, Comanches light joints wretched with splatters of scalp. Forty yards on, gangs of Five Points fleck slums by snowy capped Alps. Dashes through Perth and the Congo and Hague exhaust in tunnels uncertain. Desperate to poo, emerging sunbathed, you squat to funnel long burdens. Laughter erupts, turgid and swollen, pandemoniac and viral. Centurions and Christians and nine hundred Romans crow mirth coarse and unbridled. A highchaired man bawls a bullhorn so fierce his plunge KOs a lion. Kicking back sand amidst caterwaul jeers, your bays sponge a stone Orion.

F A D E   O U T :

INT. TINY APARTMENT - LATER

Medium-shot:

The imbecile soothes a forlorn dog.

Close-up:

Angered orbs scour pulp.

Medium-shot:

Grim peals oozing airborne
smog avow stiff allantois culls.

DARLA
They still do Hoovers up in Harlem
for just six bills and a half!

Close-up:

JACK
(trepidatious)
But vacuum tubes? Crusty postpartums.
Don't pills moot roots upsnatch?

Medium-shot:

DARLA
(distressed)
Scrape your fuckin' trap with soap!
Ain'tcha heard they're toxic?

Close-up:

Vapor-masked by rings smoked,
an elven wink burns caustic.

F   A   D   E   I   N   :

Within New Bedford mirrored, beside
a whale capsized, a man alights two
Ziras. The towhead bails your eyes.
   Seated upon Variety, you join a group
cloudgaze. Blitzkrieging anxiety,
sudden hoots hellraise.
   Gott verdammt. Dieses
insekt isst mich am leben.
   A passing scamp stops to gawk as waves
warn ghostly pox. Beneath a damp and
salty smock a slingshot apes forked cock.
   Golly Mista Meins. Blood on

da schnoz again.

Ach. Damn. Gottdamnt fly. It vill drain me in der end. Effery single day, it seeks und den it bites. How much penance must vun pay before order is set right?

Gee whiz Mista Meins, ya sure it's just da one? Mama says dey's lotsa flies cause contracts heah pay dung.

Your mutter has a filthy mouth und someone ought clean it soon. Anyvay, no more play, still got us vork to do.

The scamp surrounds a German hand.

The towhead gropes another.

Facing down, ramped pre-stand, your orbs scope inky smothers. **'See Pomona's Pickled Punks!'** blurts pleas bold and lewd. Piqued type drones six fifty dumps of Kirby suction-brooms.

F A D E   O U T :

EXT. HARLEM CLINIC - MIDDAY

Expository-shot:

A busy street of taxis bleat by aerosoled wall-scorn.

Medium-shot:

Rampant fleets of hackneyed meat greet squalls of insect-swarm.

<u>CUT TO:</u>

INT. HARLEM CLINIC - CONTINUOUS

<u>Long-shot:</u>

Within the cramped confines of a shacklike room, a
gown-dispensing orderly comps wry bulldyke gloom.
Abandoning the pair, she slams a hollow door.

<u>Medium-shot:</u>

Baleful Jack stares sadly back as elven togs are shorn.

<u>Close-up:</u>

Anti-rape cartoons hang tacked upon each wall.
Draped by red festoons, Kali laughs at Shiva's fall.

<u>Medium-shot:</u>

Veering nigh panic, fretting starboard naked,
Darla pines for Xanax. Jack vets artwork sacred.

DARLA
Kinda scary here...

JACK
Planned Parenthood's nearby...and cheaper there
besides...we can get some cake and ice cream if —

<u>Close-up:</u>

Enter waylaid eyes.

<u>Medium-shot:</u>

The <u>*ABORTIONIST,*</u> thin and short,
wears flesh of rusty hues.

<u>Close-up:</u>

Distorting with grim accord, angered orbs thrust rue.

<u>Medium-shot:</u>

DARLA
<u>*(swastika-massaging)*</u>
It's our proxy totem! A pact betwixt bold lovers!

ABORTIONIST
<u>*(repulsed)*</u>
I don't go for Nazi hokum.
Please don that robe to cover.

DARLA
But do we really hafta? Killin' trees is painful!
Sheeple think that plants can't feel —

ABORTIONIST
<u>*(head ashake)*</u>
Just hop up on the table.

Close-up:

Daggers rifle deadly aim.

ABORTIONIST
Sir, if you wouldn't mind —

Medium-shot:

DARLA
Oh please, Doc! Might he not stay?
We need our pal-o-mine!

Close-up:

Tapping silent dance, scratching or a chart,
unwrapping gyno-clamps, gloved
hands lean in to start.

Medium-shot:

DARLA
(jittery)
Um — wait! Just hold a sec...before ya dig to China!
You should know we ain't quite reg...
at least in the vagina...

The abortionist stares coolly above a speculum.

DARLA
(cont'd)

We know this may sound fooly...
but trust us we ain't dumb...

ABORTIONIST
(flicking headlamps)
Ma'am, I cannot overstate there's no need to fear at all. I've been on-the-job since Roe v. Wade — near forty years sans stall. And while yes it's true...every woman is unique...there's nothing anatomical these eyes have yet to peek.

Close-up:

Imbecilic lips purse as sloshes smack offscreen.

Medium-shot:

Breasts usurp sterling desserts via auto-squeeze.

DARLA
(hyperventilating)
But please let me explain! We come from ancient elves! The pyramids were *our* terrain 'til the Goddess got mad jeals! Giraffes? Our idea! And Picasso too! Polygraph if that sounds queer but don't say that it weren't true!

Casting sidelong glances, hauling hot
venom, the abortionist implores acquit.

Close-up:

Jack saws logs in denim.

WIPE TO:

INT. HARLEM CLINIC - MINUTES LATER

Long-shot:

Degloving shaking hands, the abortionist reclines.

Close-up:

Blotting glaze from glands, Darla absconds binds.

Medium-shot:

ABORTIONIST
(cautious)
Well, there's great and bad news. The former's that
you're right. First case I've seen hitherto.

DARLA
See?

ABORTIONIST
(cont'd)
But the latter you won't like. While I've read about
such things in *'OB-GYN TODAY'*, I'm ill-equipped to
aspirate dyad inguen-causeways. To do so would
require nonexistent tools. Short of CT-scans, which
end I tend is moot. Your canals are too restrictive to

humor just deductions. For all we can
really see each uteri needs suction.

DARLA
(alarmed)
So you're sayin' what? Jackie — what's she mean?
She's *gotta* suck this stuff! It's a fuckin' demonseed!

ABORTIONIST
One closed route need not lick — don't see this
as end-all. We'll implement RU-486
and some misoprostol.

DARLA
But don't you mean that evil pill?
That shit is toxic right?

Close-up:

Orbs careen an imbecile with mephistophic fright.

Medium-shot:

ABORTIONIST
Ma'am, please, stop this — it's a walk in the
park. Let's first discuss the process
before you make remarks.

DARLA
(gathering clothes)
No! No! Just back off! I can flag informants!

The Goddess chalked another loss!

Close-up:

Hands tag Barack endorsements.

Medium-shot:

DARLA
That's what gave her away!

JACK
(groggy)
As?

DARLA
A sheeple that fucks llamas!

Shifting venal gaze, Jack
dodges corrupt drama.

Close-up:

A lamp glows nigh-hypnotic.

JACK
(offscreen)
Doc...we'll take those pills.

A fly ends catastrophic.

> ### <u>ABORTIONIST</u>
> ### *(offscreen)*
> ### I'm throwing in refills.

F A D E I N :

Catwalked kliegs nova pasteboard.
Faeries style scalps.
You peek through soundstage hordes
of grips compiling urchin louts. Small
thespianic hands tableclasp in prayer.
A corralled maternal band
neighborjabs and swears.
Gusty gears whiz.
Chalky glyphs clack shim.
Husky shortpants lift.
Licht und kamera. Action.
Okay now lissen up you guys cause I'm gonna sock the first mug who starts while I say
grace. Dear Lord, we thank you for all this
swell grub. Skeezy, put down that biscuit.
You too Sorghum. Also Lord, we know yer
kinda busy but we'd like somethin besides
mush once in awhile. We all been pretty good
fellas here. We'd like us some cake and ice
cream too maybe. In fact, we aint had us no
cake or ice cream since that trolley socked
the Good Humor wagon last summer and
even then there was all them horseguts to
peel off. If you'd be good enough to fix it, we'd
be awful thankful. And please tell Lon

Chaney hello. Amen.
 A door creaks right on cue.
 A crone totes trays of mush.
 Baying gripes ensue.
 Now all youse ingrates hush. Been hearin
lotsa bodda dat chinks in Japan is famished.
Least yahs aint clinked whicher foddas
slammin chunksa granite.
 Upon the crone's retreat,
the husky child shifts.
 A lithoed Jesus Christ excretes
brusquely smiled twists.
 Gee whiz thanks a lot.
 A young bawd ululates.
 Hey now cull the snot.
God's just workin late.
 It aint that, Dumpy. Just my li'l Skeezy.
Tomorra he goes away. Losin kin aint easy.
 Your orbs are quelled amid
forbids of searing jellied glows.
 And he'll be a distant relative.
 Blurs smear twixt jetty holes.
 Gosh but aintcha heartened
that he'll finally have a ma?
 Your waning focus sharpens
via dual levied paws.
 But who'll wipe his nose? Sleep with him at
night? Shoo away bulldyke gropes
and all them sodomites?
 Your eyes surmise shadowed
addled autoslaps of face.

> Scheisse. Scheisse. Gott im himmel.
> Scheisse. Geh weg.

F A D E   O U T :

INT. TINY APARTMENT - MIDNIGHT

Medium-shot:

A spread of cake and ice cream
flanks Cronenberg's *'The Fly'*.

Close-up:

Abruptly shed opaque red streams
purge clonings gone awry.

Medium-shot:

DARLA
(agonized)
Ow! Goddess! Damn! It's kickin' in right now!

Long-shot:

Toiletbound elf-feet lam. An imbecile kowtows.

WIPE TO:

INT. TINY APARTMENT -
MINUTES LATER

Medium-shot:

JACK
(concerned)
Kinda early, right? Should I not defrost that pizza?

Close-up:

Three holes deluging blight
ape tossed margaritas.

Medium-shot:

Frothed lips scowl atop
a countenance of plum.

DARLA
Holy shit, just calm down!

Close-up:

Gore-fountains project scum.

Medium-shot:

DARLA
(choleric)
Case ya hadn't noticed, we're killin' pollywogs! If ya
find that über-potent — go pet that *other* dog!

F   A   D   E   I   N   :

You trail them from the hangar, toungebobbing twisted. Bugles near hark clamor. The husky boy gobs viscid.

Schmeling clouts from beanie tin.

Say hoss that your cur?

Yeah.

Well whatcha call it then?

Your snout discerns liqueur.

Pete.

Go chase yerself. Too lace shawl. Should be Bruno or Torsvan or Otto.

Anyhow, like baseball?

Moves sow loose change staccatos.

Look.

Within a grubby fondle, flashed defensibly far, McGuilicutty births a Louisville pommel atop a sepia card.

Cannons volley. Drummers thrum. Towhead tears are felled. Staggering squally, he rises then runs.

Jeers and artillery meld.

F A D E   O U T :

INT. TINY APARTMENT - MONTAGE

Shots culled at director's discretion:

Elven loins hemorrhage, on-and-on for days.
Petra gnaws knicker-crusts.
An imbecile dismays.

Upon a fortnight's crawl, sable clots evanesce.
Panties fall free of gall.
A natalnaut is jarred in jest.

F A D E   I N :

Ahoy blondie. Youse dere. Yeah, dat's right.
Youse. Ease it up. Kibosh da rush.
We needs us a li'l fatchew.
A match grates iron gate spears.
A niggercock tube ignites.
A stout lout in oily gear plates chiggerpox
oozing gobshite. A cap cries Lion Head
Ethyl. A breast spills a flyspangled swab.
Juvenescence vying grim dishevel
apprises youth brutally robbed.
Fresh meat? Fit da bill. Who'd
dey drag ya inta replace?
Threshing feet besiege anthills.
Just come for ice cream and cake.
And dat fitty per means phonus balonus?
Yeah. Sure. I see. Just don't get stirred
ovah dem mein liebchen slurs cause dem
grownups disown puberty.
Gee whiz, I don't even know
what yer talkin bout.
Ixnay the itshay unkpay, youse know
damn well what I means. See I was in pitchas meself for a ways. Had a mutt just like
yourn but more clean. Youse shoulda seen it,
loopeyed and slow, coulda been dat one's own

---

geezah.

Say mister, sorry, but we gotta blow. Ma needs us home greasin Wheezer.

Yeah, new boy, tings was nobby dem days. Da Orpheum. Wintahs at Asbury. Me pitchas was lobbied in forty-tree states. And da clams?

A simper forms raspberries.

Den one day, kablooey, all on account a fuzzed stems. Coulda plucked or shaved but nodda chance dey say. Can't win wit dem scuz inna end.

You sniff at a pole's massed leaves, curling free of tin stakes.

> **DESPERATE TIMES**
> **BESEECH MANEUVER!**
> **FOR HIS CRIMES**
> **IMPEACH HERR HOOVER!**

Be a good lad for me? Tell Meins Art still gots what it takes?

> **COME HEAR**
> **HARLEM'S HI-DE-HIGHNESS**
> **ONLY AT THE COCOANUT GROVE!**

F A D E   O U T :

INT. TINY APARTMENT - EVENTIDE

<u>Long-shot:</u>

Decked in Jazz-Age lingerie, Darla shimmies and struts.

<u>Close-up:</u>

Sterling desserts breast-ricochet.

<u>Medium-shot:</u>

Petra sleep-whinnies and juts.

JACK
<u>*(frowning)*</u>
But isn't it too risky to test?
Doc Calloway said three or four weeks.

DARLA
<u>*(apoplectic)*</u>
We know our own body! Seen enough fuckin' rest!
Let's just put this nightmare to sleep!

JACK
But rolling dice on your health?
Consider implications long-term...

<u>Close-up:</u>

Polling advice from spectral knells,
Darla pits art-cabinet churns.

Medium-shot:

Charcoaling fleet and two-fisted,
elven paws imperil wan walls.

Close-up:

The imbecile gawks heterodox.

Long-shot:

A twisting street-mural soon sprawls.

Medium-shot:

DARLA
(growling amidst hyper-focus)
**Even bought this old teddy to match your
grandpappy crap...but nope...still you won't look...**

The onslaught grows, steady and rapt,
kaleidoscoping Phobetor-rooks.

Close-up:

Martians traipse swastika-blossoms. Skywrites hawk
Pepsi-imbibes. A distant derby lids a tall dome.
Flotsam's gnawed raw by horseflies.

Medium-shot:

Flecked fists void nubbins to ash.

Close-up:

Soot blackens Darla near-minstrel.

Long-shot:

Insectoid flits suddenly gnash
as conspiracies slackened rekindle.

Medium-shot:

DARLA
(howling)
Ya won't fuckin' beef us no more 'cause ya think
we're a fat fuckin' cow! Ever since we queefed
your seed to the floor ya been actin'
so less-gutter-than-thou!

JACK
(crestfallen)
No, babe. That's simply untrue.
You...you're the Queen of my Nile.

Long-shot:

DARLA
(appalled)
Oh spare us the b.s. hullabaloo! Can't fool *dogs* with
cheap guile! We sniff-out truth easy as pie! Wolf

veracity like cake and ice cream! We'll always choose
droughts over sleazy-ass lies or mendacities
vacant eye-schemed!

Medium-shot:

Crouching canine on joints, gritting bedding with
carbon, elven grinds beseech stiff boinks
as barks hark larks of Kit Carson.

DARLA
(cont'd)
No more lies! Want queens for real?
Come here and coronate this junk!

WIPE TO:

**INT. TINY APARTMENT -
MOMENTS LATER**

Long-shot:

A cabinet writhes.

Medium-shot:

Offscreen zeals peal.

Close-up:

Floorshakes quake a jar's pickled punk.

F A D E   I N :

The first mars a Fairfax hydrant.

JACK IZ PUBIC ENMITY WON!

Bricks La Brean scar tyrants.

WANTED ON AKOUNTS
OF FRENDS SHUNNED!!

The signs are syrupped. Glued. Gum-affixed.
Wrought from strawboard and plank. Some
shrine runes of clawed lipstick. Others
hang scumgored and rank.

You beg. You irk. You nip shoes flawed.
He sallies truant and withered and shred.

NO GOOD JERK AINT GOT HIM NO PAH!!!
MITE SWAP TOO NIGERS HARTS
FOUR HIS HED!!!!

But still you keep vigilant pace,
despite all paradox sniffed.

For do you not seek equivalent fates?
You file past more noxious writs.

F A D E   O U T :

EXT. GAY SPEAKEASY -
WEEKS FURTHER

Expository-shot:

Lips spritz bacchanalian chords
of the spry, dolled, and slumming.

CUT TO:

INT. GAY SPEAKEASY - CONTINUOUS

Long-shot:

Amidst flits of Soulphylis hordes,
the imbecile eyeballs shortcomings.

Medium-shot:

A _BEARDED YOUNG HIPSTER_ raising
a wrist obscures an anti-couth belch.

Close-up:

Collateral spit glazes and glists from
a Yank-hued and iron-crossed welt.

Medium-shot:

JACK
(tickled to root a potential new
chum from despair's topsoil)
**Hey man! Crucial design! Big fan of Ground Zero I
take it? Your tat's bloodline is actually mine —**

Alas, this cant is forsaken.

BEARDED YOUNG HIPSTER
(astonished)

N.Y.H.C. sucks, my man — got this shit as a joke!

Close-up:

Incomprehensive and stunned,
Jack's hand-extend is revoked.

BEARDED YOUNG HIPSTER
I dig Hasil Adkins and Coil! Death In June and Dwight
Twilley! Outsider-jams! Legit turmoil! That Eighties
'Why me?' shit is silly! Hardcore's pathetic and
pointless! Cruel, plebeian, and base! Ascetic,
joyless, boring-ass poop! Mere musical
ice cream and cake!

JACK
But —

Whoops prescient of stylus-squalls
swerve an aggregate's eyes.

Long-shot:

Boothed by Buzz, nescient of stalls,
curves vend wags and bent writhes.

Close-up:

Mammary gibbosity cripples
an elf-tee unloose.

Medium-shot:

BEARDED YOUNG HIPSTER
(joyously cupping Jack's ear)
How I love me to see nips tossed free!
Man, what a little deuce coupe!

JACK
(beaming secretive pride)
Holy shit! Some skirt! Might hafta take a test-spin!

BEARDED YOUNG HIPSTER
(chortling)
Say hi to my boys if you hit paydirt!

Close-up:

Imbecile orbs blaze chagrin.

Medium-shot:

JACK
(confused)
Sorry?

BEARDED YOUNG HIPSTER
(hearty laughs spritzing Pabst's)
My homunculi have been swimming 'round up there
for going on maybe five months! Stone loco
but bounties to spare, even though
she's got a strange cunt!

A phone is fished from crass black jeans.
Thumbtaps precede a rapt grin.

Close-up:

As Jack examines cracked glass scenes,
a palm beseeches slapped skin.

F   A   D   E   I   N   :

Growing palls on Hancock
smog a jaundiced horizon.
  A towhead stalled gobs the slobs of a blond
Poseidon. Flies parched greet froth.
Flights ditch smudges nano.
  Sighs barge.
  Pete he scoffs, life's a bucket a guano.
  He expectorates again. Mantid
canofcorns ape Cobb.
  Chrissake ol friend — with a
handle a snakes from Punjab.
  A fanged cavalry soon arrives, snarling
ears agoggle. Slatribbed wheatons' bulging
eyes trail gnarled whippety squabbles. Wax-
wrapped combs thrum Leybourne as bipeds
scurry the rear, slackcapped feverdream
forms clobbered in expiry's jeers: calico
smocks of Truckee Lake, felt plugs of
profligate cocottes, Shiloh frocks
bayonet-strafed by thugs of émigré flocks,
Hanes fleece flapping scrawls of Gilbert and

Crawford midcoitus, pained greasesplat
recalls of stillbirths offered introitus.
There are mothsieged stoles and chickadeed
turbans and parasols twined in Japan, larded
scalps ensnaring bugs small mocking onyx
mined in Bhutan, rubbersoled stomps
jostling jaws strung by beards of slain boes.
One berserker is otherwise raw save smeared
dysenterial rows. Heralding hilarious ends,
these are wraiths of eyewander regions.
  An imperiled nefarious blend.
  A raging somnambulant legion.
  Relic-pinned tams hark suns.
Bottles hiss midflight.
  Nuts, huffs a towhead undone.
  Who's gonna grease Wheezer tonight?
  A shadow yelps Capone.
Plumes top a Tyrolean peak.
  Need help son or go this alone?
  Your paws vie broiling heat.

F A D E   O U T :

EXT. EAST 11TH TENEMENT - DAWN

Expository-shot:

Post-Soulphylis, Darla berates
a cabbie's indecorous pries.

Medium-shot:

DARLA
(garbled)
We know you snitch for the Goddess, bitch!
Just tell her this warrin' must die!

JACK
(troubled)
Chill, babe, please...you're gonna
wake all the neighbors.

DARLA
(kicking at tires)
Leggo, you ape! Ow! Jeez!
Oh what a chivalrous savior!

WIPE TO:

INT. TINY APARTMENT - SOON AFTER

Long-shot:

The imbecile vets canine whines.

Medium-shot:

Thin limbs fell waistline binds.

Close-up:

Wrenching free of a Dwight Twilley
tee, an elf brays opines maligned.

DARLA
Poor Petra! Always first! Ain't we good enough too?
Look at us...fit to burst! Your other doggy
here needs t'get screwed!

Medium-shot:

Smoke-festooned, pulsating poon,
Darla grins as Jack quits the john.

Close-up:

Scoping a pruned and unwelcome
goon, Petra winds and then yawns.

Medium-shot:

DARLA
(blenching)
Seriously...gotta man-up...you're
mistakin' cruelty for kindness.

JACK
Huh? What?

DARLA
Can't you see? No acuity!
C'mon, dude! She's mindless!

JACK
(weary)

Please, babe — I mean no offense — but can we just
leave the subject alone? Nuts, it's late...let's hit
the hay. Just gonna fill up her bowls.

WIPE TO:

INT. TINY APARTMENT - TWO MINUTES ON

Close-up:

A hearty pour's kibbly store piques appetites
nada. Alpo's ignore sparks quibbly roars
of heatseeking elf-intifada.

Medium-shot:

DARLA
C'mon man! Look at that shit!
What kinda dog won't eat?

JACK
(hands thrust north)
Okay then! I fucking quit! Let's just put her to sleep!

Close-up:

Silenced orbs well up.
Tears stymie a squinch.

Medium-shot:

DARLA
(blubbering)
Just tryin' to help ya...don't hafta whine like a grinch!

Close-up:

Gushing incertitude, aiming fleet rectification, an imbecile's rush to soothe meets a Camel's flammation.

Medium-shot:

JACK
(penitent)
Ouch! Awful sorry, babe. Feeling a bit overwhelmed.
Been hella tough watching her fade...

DARLA
(peeved)
Like it's easy repealin' demon spells? I mean, the
stress is reachin' extremes...what with Gisela
hauntin' louder than ever...don't even
get me started on dreams...

JACK
(cont'd)
Ugh...I'm sure it's been daunting past measure...
shoulda picked up on all that...shoulda plied closer
attention...sorry for being detached...

DARLA
(cont'd)

Always tied to a ghostly dimension...always so loud...
paranoid...so fraught with gory-ass visions...

JACK
(cont'd)
I solemnly vow to employ less talks and duly apply
more listens...don't wanna be an insensitive lout...
nor a nogoodnik or devil...that's not
what my shit's all about...

DARLA
(cont'd)
Always so sick and disheveled...and this fuckin'
fatass...always there...even balder than you by a lot...

JACK
(cont'd)
And when, at last, I make you aware...

DARLA
(cont'd)
Always movin' his strange little box...

Long-shot:

Blather plural ambles in tandem.
Walls sway focus sharp.

Close-up:

A mural lathers explanandum.

Medium-shot:

An old dog lays potent farts.

F   A   D   E   I   N   :

Say Pete, we gotta beat feet.
His words tip a nervefraught belly
Grim. Feardoused.
Grave.
Your revival occurs atop ruinous red jelly
carpeting a dim clubhouse's nave. Horseflies
piercing lumed dustpillars forage mountain-
ous gore. Chalked missives bestrewing
wallplanks extol misogynist store.
A searing itch rips your thorax.
Coughs expel a pink glob.
A grapesized demon
leers warningly back.
Your pads crush the manducated slob.
The towhead whistles through a spitty v.
Jeepers. Skedaddle. This ain't pretty, see?
At the lot's edge stands a tree rascal
festooned and you stop and you reel as you
gape. Two dozen queer fruits dangle
harpooned from limbs fluttering monarchian
crepe. Negro, corpulent, skeletal, Celtic,
larval, creased, bobbed. Stripped
breasts bear vermillion parcels.
Glyphs of drippity daubs.
A HAL CROVES PRODUCTION

The towhead shrugs then ambles, short-shriftng all pause to look back. You sigh as your leg instinctively angles to spritz death with hot golden flak.

F   A   D   E   O   U   T   :

INT. TINY APARTMENT - SOFT-FOCUS MONTAGE

Shots culled at director's discretion:

As Jack and Darla weave close, Petra fades to grey.

JACK
(voiceover)
He turned and rummaged among the hides and handed through the flames a small dark thing. The kid turned it in his hand. It was a heart, dried and blackened.

Blind eyes seize ghosts as souls are towed astray.

JACK
(voiceover cont'd)
He passed it back and the old man cradled it in his palm as if he'd weigh it. They is four things that can destroy the earth, he said. Women, whiskey, money, and niggers.

Somnambulistic quakes betray a comatose abyss.

> ## JACK
> ### *(voiceover cont'd)*
> They sat in silence. The wind moaned in the section
> of stove pipe that was run through the roof above
> them to quit the place of smoke. After a while
> the old man put the heart away.

Rambles mystic disengage to wallow knickered twists.

F   A   D   E   I   N   :

The pavement brims clockpunchers.
You crisscross dungarees. Craven
pimps gawk youngsters. There's
fanfare in the breeze.
    De Neve Square gathers a ragged gypsy fête.
Sages hark cadavers of
bad Poughkeepsie threats.
    A Zulu chews rats to goo at just two nickels
per. You watch a stack bushwhacked
through then heed a whistle's spur.
    Behind a pillar's stanchion, you flank his
side with dread. Crowning the expansion,
tanks intern drowned heads.
    Hair floats tall in alcohol.
Towhead lips purse.
    A glare gloats bitter wherewithals
to strip an awkward curse.
    Yeah, so what of it? So McGuilicutty's
brined. Serves her right gettin hitched.
    You swill more nutty whines.

Screaming hawks French postcards. A face yawps Sister Aimee. Fleeing trenchant shadows, you chase clops cockamamie.

F A D E   O U T :

INT. TINY APARTMENT - A BRUMAL NIGHT

Long-shot:

The imbecile grooms for a bistro's grand soirée.

Close-up:

Beside two thinning soles, Petra fumes dismay.

Medium-shot:

DARLA
(preened and smoking)
Don'tcha worry Jackie....ain't gonna break your bank! Fièvres-et-famille and we got Butch to thank!

JACK
(pursing lips)
Um — who's Butch again?

DARLA
Tease his 'do sometimes...

Close-up:

Palms press at pants. Petra
falls on shoes and sighs.

Medium-shot:

DARLA
C'mon girl, no balkin'...we're goin' out for food!
This doggie needs *her* walkin'! Up-up alley-oop!

A brusque pursuant heft imbues
an airborne canine wend.

Close-up:

A leaden bed-deflect buffoons a statue's rude upend.

Medium-shot:

DARLA
(adrenalized)
C'mon babe, don't frown — vino's flowin' free!
No apin' Charlie Browns!

Close-up:

Racked greatcoats are retrieved.

WIPE TO:

EXT. HIP FRENCH BISTRO - A SHORT TIME LATER

Expository-shot:

Drifting snow blankets smokers blurting Jodorowsky.

Close-up:

Pissing clothes mediocre, a bum spurts snoring loudly.

CUT TO:

INT. HIP FRENCH BISTRO - CONTINUOUS

Long-shot:

Though dead-soldiers mob
a booth, melancholia persists.

Close-up:

A swipe knocks glass askew.

Medium-shot:

Elven bawls daub wits.

DARLA
(sulking)

Damn...still so grim...ain'tcha copped a buzz?

Close-up:

A magnum's tilt gluts brims.

Medium-shot:

DARLA
(cont'd)
Want I should cop some drugs?
Butch is good for Addies! Pep ya up for sure!

Close-up:

Hands sad hooch-caddy. Lips shrine wines impure.

Medium-shot:

JACK
(lachrymose)
Nah, thanks, this is fine.

DARLA
(flustered)
Then what *can* we fuckin' do?

Close-up:

A mien dank depicts decline. No sure words ensue.

Medium-shot:

DARLA
(cont'd)
D'ya *hafta* act so mopey? You're like Garfield's
nom de plume! We ain't a plastic trophy...
need more than doom-and-gloom!

JACK
Sorry. I'll try harder.

DARLA
But — I mean, dude, why's this hard? Ain't we sexy
nude? Maybe you're too scarred? Are ya broke
beyond repair? Should we just move on?

Close-up:

Ropes of blondish hair denote a horsefly-autobahn.

Medium-shot:

JACK
(collapsing)
Yes! No! Please stay! Sorry...it's just Petra. Slipping
further every day and I'm sad and mad etcetera.
It's all been so damned queer. Like living
with a ghost. Sorry I've been weird...

DARLA
But Jack, she's just mad old! This is why we said —

JACK
No! Please, I can't!

DARLA
But it's all for the best, don'tcha understand? Ya gotta learn to see when some battles can't be won... can't let malignancies rattle *all* our fuckin' fun!

JACK
But she's not in any pain — just potato-like! And I know it sounds insane, but still my hopes glow bright! I just can't seem to spurn this hunch she's simply gotten lost...like some wrong turn has her flung into cerebral holocaust! Is it incomprehensible such messes might be thwarted? Undo a glitch dimensional? Restore progress aborted?

DARLA
So let's play devil's advocate...surmise this Limbo true...what happens when ya *do* find it and the Goddess shanghais you? What good will ya do anyone stuck in fuckin' Oz? Should Giz and I just give up fun and pray for menopause?

JACK
(hopeful)
Heck, come along — provide some ancient guidance!

DARLA
(aghast)
C'mon Jackie, that'd be wrong! What about our

clients?

She abruptly quits the booth.

JACK
Hey, where ya goin'?

DARLA
Want the gospel truth? To see if Butch has codeine!

JACK
But — but —

DARLA
(livid)
Potatoes don't crap-up kitchens! They don't
lay SBDs! They lack abrupt decisions
and they're not our enemies!

Long-shot:

Fleeing despondency, shooing
unseen flies, an elf dashes wanton y.

Close-up:

A hipster's beard leers sly.

F   A   D   E   I   N   :

Forest Lawns nearing, you converge

a piney span.

The towhead gloms a clearing.

Wafts urge a mulligan.

A bindlestiff sharing stew spiels of scabrous lives. Ladleflips pare goo. Squealing flies arrive. A craggy hand bears a skull brassing multi-sores. You battle droll commands impulsed via glowing orbs.

Seen more ghosts twixt here and Berdoo than two years a jerry wrath. Best boes all been stamped past due. Hope Heaven got it free baths.

The woods lay mum.

A greatcoat flaps.

Skies make lice of stars.

Ever ponder astrocrap? Think poontang's nice on Mars?

F A D E   O U T :

EXT. AVENUE B - AFTER THE PARTY

Expository-shot:

The imbecile trudges as iced gales maul.

Long-shot:

Sidewalks beam virginal white.

Medium-shot:

Taxis snub elf-shrilled vitriol.
Vexations imperil damp plights.

DARLA
(slurring)
Yeah? Well fuck you too, Omar Sharif!
Muhammad was a pussyass bitch!

JACK
C'mon babe...no more...please.

DARLA
What? He plottin' injurious shit? The fuck's
he gonna do? Crash a plane in the crib?

JACK
(dejected)
Yeah...you're right...sorry.

DARLA
And that crap with Butch was really uncouth! Didja
hafta go full Caligari? Excusez-moi for the selfie-
snafu! Did it rate all that rage and mad spleen?
You damn well saw our cell ain't that new!
Who the fuck can gauge a bad screen?

JACK
(contrite)
Unwise for sure...should've asked first. Guess I just
kinda lost it. Acting the boor — always the worst.
Gonna toss those pills left down the faucet.

DARLA
There ya go, passin' the blame! Those Addies
are innocent, dude! Head-to-toe, it's
your *own* ass's shame!

Close-up:

A mien barbs disquietude.

JACK
Sorry.

Long-shot:

Footsteps beat crunchy staccatos
as the pair wordlessly slogs.

Close-up:

A Zippo heats shunning eye-grottos.

Medium-shot:

Smoke clouds discourtesies logged.

DARLA
I mean, that was *tough* on Butchie...as an elf, his life's
never gone smooth! His grandpa usta buttplug his
tushie then douche it with Cinzano vermouth! His
band got signed a month after he quit when they
made his parakeet drink beer! His cat went blind!

He's fuckin' dyslexic! Guy's been in therapy for years!

Contortions stoke a chuckling scoff.

DARLA
(miffed)
Think that's a joke?

JACK
(head ashake)
Just had to cough.

DARLA
(scowling)
First you ream our friend
and now ya won't even talk?

JACK
(sheepish)
Just...been...gleaning a trend.

DARLA
And that's s'posed to mean what?

JACK
Seems that every elf you know
is marked incest-survivor.

DARLA
Duh! Half the sheeple on this fuckin' *globe* are partly
Martian vampire! We been fightin' those demons for

eons! They consume our powers through sex!

JACK
Well...thinking maybe I'm one of the
legion...albeit a late-blooming subject.

DARLA
(stopping short)
Oh yeah? How the fuck's that?

JACK
Notice my pop's never mentioned?

Close-up:

Disrupting Jack's woolen cap,
an elf gawks with anal retention.

JACK
(cont'd)
But even in my wildest dreams, I
would've never pegged him for Martian.

DARLA
(sincere)
Jackie, be honest...no childish scenes...is this straight
dope you're chargin'? Fess up now if not,
'cause my nose'll sense if you're lyin'...

Medium-shot:

An inquisitive snout blows snot.

Close-up:

The imbecile commences slow crying.

F   A   D   E   I   N   :

You trail the towhead to the blind tiger.
A greatcoat drags like a train.
A door's swing beneath glyphs of John
Carter's unmasks a fairy campaign. The
rabble staggers, perfumed and drunk,
shading scalps kneeling to bob. A
barechested negro ivorily plunks.
Dancers reel. Hootholler. Throb.
A hooknose in plaid cranks a barrel organ
whilst a fezzed capuchin mugwaves.
Your pads slosh ejaculate portioned.
Speak or forever hymns a smug knave.
Whisky.
Teat whisky, shouts the keep.
Cold milk slippityslops.
Faeries snigger and grin.
The towhead bilks a mustachioed crop.
Your tongue skippers frothed dregs within.
Pockets disabled yield buttons and lint. The
keep clears his throat to point brusquely.
He paid.
From a table docking Loebs and Brinigs,
a vast wan dome hoists thusly.

F A D E   O U T :

INT. TINY APARTMENT - AN HOUR LATER

Long-shot:

Darkness pervades the grimy
hovel as two hosts savagely fuck.

Medium-shot:

A barkless squelch of stymying nozzle
denotes tragedy stippled in muck.

DARLA
(silhouette halted)
Um — what just happened?

JACK
(likewise paused)
Don't move a lick. Listen...just freeze please.

A lamp is flicked.

Close-up:

A sogged tail glistens.

Medium-shot:

> Lust is minstreled by feces.

F A D E   I N :

Throng a'weave, an organ-cranks.
Femmes balconygaze above.
Your tail meets a shrewd gorgon yank.
Fangs rout til vertebrae buzz.
Faeries dive floorwards dodging your spin.
The capuchin hangs for dear life. The
hooknose screams in an argot obscure
as your jaws find purchase and vise.
The snap is as crisp as a maul's smite.
An ocular aggregate bugs.
The simian flopsprawls left and right as
silver spills free of its cup. It yelps like a child
and it crumples and writhes and it bloodies
up sawdusted boards. Gaping stunned,
the hooknose cries then gropes
for deathflustered hoards.
Glory be, the bearded keep gasps. Damn
cur showed that monkey what's what.
See? Me and Pete don't take us no sass.
A pudgy wink rankles your gut.
Last of the gang, eh Jack? Last of the
gang. All gone save you and that cur.
Jowlsags deadring testicle hangs. Cuban
smoke blurs five-and-dime myrrh. Beyond
the wan immensity, revelry recovers its
stride. Spaded soles herkyjerk glee.
The pudge casts a sly glance aside.

Don't worry, son. No worries or frowns.
Still time for jitterbugs yet.

Phooey. Aint fixin cut rugs with no fruits
nohow. Sooner play Russian roulette.

Seizing a bottle, the pudge thumbs a stem.
A zipped cork blackens a bulb. Supping
with gusto, he leans upon elbows,
grinbeaming six-inch repose.

Son, if you're not here to boogie-woogie
tonight then my name's Julius Caesar.

Nope. Anyhow, gotta go now alright? Ma
needs me home greasin Wheezer.

Go home? asks the pudge.

A tilt swirls milky waves amber.

Drink up, he rasps with a nudge. Takes
curls to stake Martian vampers.

F A D E   O U T :

INT. TINY APARTMENT - CONTINUOUS

Close-up:

Hot needles urging diarrhetical
wrests channel gritty brown clumps.

Medium-shot:

Rivulets treacle an epic-globed chest.

Close-up:

A shower's drain downs drippity-cumps.

Medium-shot:

DARLA
(rage-beset)
Holy crap! What the fuck, dude? She's totally
conspirin' to snuff me! There's no
mistakin' that turpitude!

Woeful pleas fire on gruffly.

Long-shot:

Squatting upon the kitchen floor, Jack scrubs the old
dog's derrière. The pair is smitten with mutual
horror as ultimatums course through the air.

DARLA
(cont'd offscreen)
No fuckin' redeemin'! Last fuckin' straw!
Gaped it with your very own eyes!

Medium-shot:

JACK
But she didn't mean it...just chewed something
flawed...looks like she ate some supplies...

Long-shot:

Directly beside the bathroom door,
an art-cabinet cries dental rape.

Medium-shot:

Charcoal is strewn as flecks of chomped gore.

Close-up:

Shards comprise a glob-jar's new shape.

DARLA
(cont'd offscreen)
Call a vet now! Come seal this fate, see?
The Goddess is usin' her as a vessel!

Medium-shot:

Orbs saddened prowl wall-scrawls disconsolately.

Close-up:

An arm-swaddled ancient snout nestles.

F   A   D   E   I   N   :

Ascending inclines of protuberant pine,
the pudge jostles whisky and winks.
In that tent's rind I divined übermensch
kind. An apostle of Nietzschean brinks.
Towhead waves ward guesses depraved.

A conferee of old Zarathustra.
Like I should give a hang whatcha say
anyway? Gimme one reason to trust ya.
Then care to explain why you're here?
Same as any fella I reckon.
And this rationale is?
Gee whiz yer queer.
Orbs well with baleful expression.
Nuts. Farina said grownups do freaky stuff
late, so I guess just for viewin some kicks.
Leaning slumped atop a teak balustrade,
the pudge regards duelings of pricks.
If you're here to 'view kicks' and yet still
refuse, then might not this purpose be
skewed? And, if so, can you guess why?
Nope, sure can't. Can you?
Lips peel. Fulvous teeth shine.
Breaths vent sewage and meat.
You're here, my son, to segment that line
dividing truants ghoulish from geek.

F   A   D   E   O   U   T   :

INT. TINY APARTMENT - CONTINUOUS

Long-shot:

JACK
(frightened)
Babe...please...calm yourself...Petra's starting to shake.

Medium-shot:

Quaking qualm, a roaring elf bombards PO'd forsakes.

DARLA
Fuck that! Fuck your ass too,
ya criminal lyin' Jewface!

Close-up:

Gaping as slack as a schmuck in a zoo,
the imbecile espies a suitcase.

F   A   D   E   I   N   :

At the wainscotted hall's termination, a
door tombs a swastika wreath. Beyond it,
a room wallpapered crimson fumes with a
lone candle's seethe. Across a strait bed, the
marm lies spread. Silver nylons postbind
limbs. Brows quake dread. Mascara is shed.
Brawn has undermined vim.

Look Petey, see? Aint that Crabtree?
Gosh and barefoot all over.

Aiming chinned bakelite rashly,
the pudge inputs exposures.

Myriad strangers sashay nude. Some
wield peni like mace. Some draw
pulls from chinaman's flues.

A dwarf writhes dung nigh marmface.

Jeepers Pete, they's fidgets in here. You go

sit by that clown.

As you espy horsefly flits midblear, unfastened britches slide down. Through a turd coonmask, the marm's eyes water.

A creamy brown triangle pulses.

Justjack, coos rasp beneath a new squatter, free me from this yeggpile of culprits. Be a good little man, okay? We'll never discuss it again. We'll have cake and ice cream every day like the bestest of bosomy friends.

The towhead spits at a palm.

Sure. In a goshdarn pig's eye.

Sis always predicted it wouldn't end calm. Chuckles prelude her soft sighs.

Rising to exit, you cease deadstill when a slam routs the wreath with a thud. The aperture's seal dulls nil.

Your snout swills wafts of queefed blood.

F A D E   O U T :

INT. TINY APARTMENT - CONTINUOUS

Long-shot:

JACK
But babe...*hey*...where're you going?

Close-up:

DARLA

Fuckin' far as we can from you!

<u>Medium-shot:</u>

JACK
C'mon, wait...let's talk it over...

<u>Close-up:</u>

DARLA
No, asshole, we're through!

<u>Medium-shot:</u>

JACK
But —

<u>Close-up:</u>

DARLA
<u>(cont'd)</u>
Gave ya plenty a shots to do us
right and still ya struck-out each time!

<u>Close-up:</u>

JACK
But...c'mon...babe...she's my dog...

<u>Medium-shot:</u>

DARLA
So were *we*, you clueless dick!
Didja hafta treat us like slime?

Long-shot:

JACK
But *are* you a dog? Aren't they loyal?
It's *cats* that just walk away.

Close-up:

DARLA
Whoa — hey! Back off, boyo!
We'll claw your wan ass to filet!

F A D E   I N :

The vicesquad swarms like horseflies in
melton, clubbing faeries with childish zeal.
Coshswiped scorn morphs bone to gelatin.
Urine harries life's rapid repeal.
   And what's in that room?
grunts an upstairs bark.
   Leave it. Some shit don't get unseen.
   Christ almighty, where's that cunt's heart?
   Toldja it weren't none too serene.
   Shaddup Marut. Feige, get the ape in a net.
Now where did these fags stash all the dope?
   And this mutt, Sarge? Call in a vet?
   Can'tcha see it's bashed beyond hope?

F A D E   O U T :

EXT. EAST 11TH TENEMENT - LATER

Expository-shot:

Firetrucks, cruisers, and ambulances
cluster in many directions at random.

Medium-shot:

Pilots mull bruises and circumstances
whilst vivisection blusters in tandem.

CUT TO:

INT. TINY APARTMENT - CONTINUOUS

Long-shot:

A fly's vantage ables gawks from a ceiling.

Medium-shot:

An elf lies tied to a bed.

Close-up:

Sternal damage mocks graces of healing.

Long-shot:

A felled dog cries nigh-dead.

Medium-shot:

DISAFFECTED POLICE SERGEANT
(regarding a suitcase)
Neighbors say it ain't even her crib.
Tenant's some jaggoff called Bender...

STONED EMT
(attending Petra's kitchen floor passage)
Had a mutt just like this one as a small kid.
Dragged off by a Good Humor vendor...

COMPASSIONATE NYFD VETERAN
(spying small red footprints within a wall-mural)
Once took a course at John Jay
'bout insane minds and art...

Close-up:

Gasps hoarse brook canine dismay.
A last earthly wisp is a fart.

Medium-shot:

DISAFFECTED POLICE SERGEANT
(splitting a MacBook)
Hey ya dopes, take a look here!
Whadda youse make a this?

Close-up:

A freshly posted Facebook jeer
ballyhoos escape-via-abyss.

F   A   D   E   I   N   :

Complete darkness.
Sour thin air. Lead heats beneath your
mass. Wafts of carcass and grim
despair decry sad meetings of gas.
He's always lied. You're aware right?
Horseflies scumfuck your guts.
Your entire life was a meaningless sham,
a floodtide of fraudulent pus. Did you know
that he never truly liked mutts, especially
one dumb as yourself? That your singular
legitimate purpose was to catalyze bitch-
notches in belts? And those patently
ludicrous claims of abuse? Did you
believe such bosh rated heed?
An outdoor racket maims this foul muse.
Gosh Mister Dogcatcher, please.
Sorry boy, minute too late.
Cyanide's done already fogged.
Jeepers, but please, I come a long ways.
Die bona fide.
You are his dog.

F   A   D   E   O   U   T   :

TIGER MOODY HAS SURVIVED 2 HOUSEFIRES, 2 DIVORCES, & SHINGLES. HE LIVES IN LOWER MANHATTAN.